Praise for Ray Keating and his Pastor Stephen Grant Thrillers & Mysteries...

"Exciting, tightly written action scenes comprise the final act, but there's humor sprinkled throughout the narrative, as well... A short but kinetic tale featuring a consistently entertaining hero."

- Kirkus Reviews on *The Traitor*

"In this 11th installment of a thriller series, a combat-trained pastor helps protect a Chinese golfer and his cleric father... when the action does hit, it's exhilarating, and Stephen proves once again he's as capable in fights as he is in quieter times of prayer and worship. A fast-paced, exuberant outing for the virtuoso clergyman and his numerous comrades."

- Kirkus Reviews on *Deep Rough*

"Keating has accumulated an impressive assortment of characters in his series, and he gives each of them ample opportunity to shine... As in the preceding novels, the author skillfully blends Grant's sermonizing with intermittent bouts of violence. It creates a rousing moral quandary for readers to ponder without either side overwhelming the storyline. Tight action scenes complement the suspense (uncertainty over when the next possible attack will be) ... The villains, meanwhile, are just as rich and engrossing as the good guys and gals. The familiar protagonist, along with sensational new and recurring characters, drives an energetic political tale."

- Kirkus Reviews on *Reagan Country*

"Grant is a selfless and fascinating protagonist. Keating pulls back the walls of the pastor's psyche and lets readers root around, providing a sense of intimacy and closeness with the central character from very early on in the novel.

Warrior Monk is full of intentional, thoughtful writing that hits hard and carries the story to the end. After devouring this opening salvo, new fans will dive in eagerly to the future adventures of Pastor Stephen Grant."

- *Self-Publishing Review*, ★★★★½, on *Warrior Monk*

"Author Ray Keating delivers a timely, high-octane, and well-penned thriller with his latest novel, *The Traitor*. The inimitable Pastor Stephen Grant must unexpectedly navigate the shadowy waters of international espionage to keep his country safe and strong. With a gripping plot that feels torn from last week's headlines, Keating knows how to capture his readers immediately and never let go. Pastor Grant continues to surprise as a character and the dialogue hums with authenticity, making the newest Pastor Stephen Grant Novel another hit in this ever-growing series."

- *Self-Publishing Review*, ★★★★½, on *The Traitor*

"It was my great privilege that Ronald Reagan and I were good friends and political allies. This exciting political thriller may be a novel but it truly captures President Reagan's optimism and principles."

- Ambassador Fred J. Eckert on *Reagan Country*

"First-rate supporting characters complement the sprightly pastor, who remains impeccable in this thriller."

- *Kirkus Reviews* on *Lionhearts*

"A first-rate mystery makes this a series standout..."

- *Kirkus Reviews* on *Wine Into Water*

Murderer's Row was named KFUO's BookTalk "Book of the Year" in 2015.

"Ray Keating has created a fascinating and unique character in Pastor Grant. The way Keating intertwines politics, national security and faith into a compelling thriller is sheer delight."

"The author packs a lot into this frantically paced novel... a raft of action sequences and baseball games are thrown into the mix. The multiple villains and twists raise the stakes... Stephen remains an engaging and multifaceted character: he may still use, when necessary, the violence associated with his former professions, but he at least acknowledges his shortcomings – and prays about it. Action fans will find plenty to love here, from gunfights and murder sprees to moral dilemmas."

"It's kind of a cool book. If you like Tom Clancy, if you like action, if you like some nail-biting stuff, this is it."

The River was a 2014 finalist for KFUO's BookTalk "Book of the Year."

"Ray Keating is a great novelist."

"A gritty, action-stuffed, well-considered thriller with a gun-toting clergyman."

"I miss Tom Clancy. Keating fills that void for me."

- *Lutheran Book Review* on *Murderer's Row*

"President Ronald Reagan's legacy will live on in the U.S., around the world and in the pages of history. And now, thanks to Ray Keating's *Reagan Country*, it will live on in the world of fiction. *Reagan Country* ranks as a page-turning thriller that pays homage to the greatest president of the twentieth century."

- Tom Edmonds, producer of
the official documentary on President Reagan,
Ronald Reagan: An American President

"Mr. Keating's storytelling is so lifelike that I almost thought I had worked with him when I was at Langley. Like the fictitious pastor, I actually spent 20 years working for the U.S. intelligence community, and once I started reading *The River*, I had to keep reading because it was so well-crafted and easy to follow and because it depicted a personal struggle that I knew all too well. I simply could not put it down."

- The Rev. Kenneth V. Blanchard
The Washington Times review of *The River*

Marvin Olasky, editor-in-chief of WORLD magazine, lists Ray Keating among his top 10 Christian novelists.

"Keating's creativity and storytelling ability remain on point, for a fun and different take on Pastor Grant, and one that's just as satisfying as longer books in the series."

- *Self-Publishing Review* on *Heroes and Villains*

"Pastor Grant continues to be one of the most entertaining heroes in the political thrillers and suspense genre. With occasional pop-ins from fan-favorite recurring characters, *Deep Rough* fits in perfectly with the rest of the series – quirky, tightly woven, and difficult to put down. Keating manages to keep his writing fresh and surprising with every new Pastor Grant book. This series satisfies yet again, finding unique ways to entertain and enlighten along the way."

- Self-Publishing Review on *Deep Rough*

"Must read for any Reaganite."

- Craig Shirley,
Reagan biographer and presidential historian,
on *Reagan Country*

"Ray Keating has a knack for writing on topics that could be pulled from tomorrow's headlines."

- Lutheran Book Review
on *An Advent for Religious Liberty*

"*Root of All Evil?* is an extraordinarily good read. Only Ray Keating could come up with a character like Pastor Stephen Grant."

- Paul L. Maier, author of *A Skeleton in God's Closet, More Than A Skeleton,* and *The Constantine Codex*

"*The Traitor* is a game-changer for the *Warrior Monk* series starring Pastor Stephen Grant. It is in many ways a return to the worldbuilding Ray Keating did with *Warrior Monk*, and is an excellent jumping on point for new readers. (Read the Second Edition of *Warrior Monk* first!)"

- Lutheran Book Review on *The Traitor*

"Good summer reading."

"Thriller and mystery writers have concocted all manner of main characters, from fly fishing lawyers to orchid aficionados and former ballplayers, but none has come up with anyone like Stephen Grant, the former Navy Seal and CIA assassin, and current Lutheran pastor. Grant mixes battling America's enemies and sparring with enemies of traditional Christian values, while ministering to his Long Island flock. The amazing thing is that the character works. The Stephen Grant novels are great reads beginning with *Warrior Monk*, which aptly describes Ray Keating's engaging hero."

"*Warrior Monk* by Ray Keating has all of the adventure, intrigue, and believable improbability of mainstream political thrillers, but with a lead character, Pastor Stephen Grant, that resists temptation."

"This is a fantastic novel... If you are a comic book fan who is fed up with the political correctness that's going on, you have got to pick up *Heroes and Villains*... I highly recommend this book... I'm definitely going to be paying more attention to Ray Keating, and getting more of his novels."

VATICAN
SHADOWS

A Pastor
Stephen Grant Novel

RAY KEATING

For more information:
Keating Reports, LLC
raykeating@keatingreports.com

ISBN-13: 9798654255006

Cover design by Tyrel Bramwell.

Important Points:

Chapter 1 in this book also was the Epilogue from the second edition (2019) of *Warrior Monk: A Pastor Stephen Grant Novel*.

Chapter 20 in this book also was the Epilogue from *The Traitor: A Pastor Stephen Grant Novel*.

While *Vatican Shadows: A Pastor Stephen Grant Novel* stands alone as a story, for more background on some happenings mentioned in this book, such as Pope Augustine and his "Public Mission of Mere Christianity," or what occurred at the Monastere de Saint Paul, please read *Warrior Monk* and *The Traitor*, respectively.

For
Beth,
Jonathan
and
Mikayla & David

Previous Books by Ray Keating

Root of All Evil? A Pastor Stephen Grant Novel
(Second Edition, 2020)

The Traitor: A Pastor Stephen Grant Novel (2019)

Deep Rough: A Pastor Stephen Grant Novel (2019)

Warrior Monk: A Pastor Stephen Grant Novel
(Second Edition, 2019)

Shifting Sands: A Pastor Stephen Grant Short Story (2018)

Heroes & Villains: A Pastor Stephen Grant Short Story (2018)

Reagan Country: A Pastor Stephen Grant Novel (2018)

Lionhearts: A Pastor Stephen Grant Novel (2017)

Wine Into Water: A Pastor Stephen Grant Novel (2016)

Murderer's Row: A Pastor Stephen Grant Novel (2015)

The River: A Pastor Stephen Grant Novel (2014)

An Advent for Religious Liberty:
A Pastor Stephen Grant Novel (2012)

Root of All Evil? A Pastor Stephen Grant Novel (2012)

Warrior Monk: A Pastor Stephen Grant Novel (2010)

In the nonfiction arena...

Behind Enemy Lines:
Conservative Communiques from Left-Wing New York (2020)

The Disney Planner 2020: The TO DO List Solution (2019)

The Lutheran Planner 2020: The TO DO List Solution (2019)

The Pastor Stephen Grant Novels Planner 2020:
The TO DO List Solution (2019)

Free Trade Rocks! 10 Points on International Trade Everyone
Should Know (2019)

A Discussion Guide for Ray Keating's Warrior Monk
(Second Edition, 2019)

The Realistic Optimist TO DO List & Calendar 2019 (2018)

Unleashing Small Business Through IP:
The Role of Intellectual Property in Driving Entrepreneurship,
Innovation and Investment (Revised and Updated Edition, 2016)

Unleashing Small Business Through IP:
Protecting Intellectual Property, Driving Entrepreneurship
(2013)

Discussion Guide for Warrior Monk:
A Pastor Stephen Grant Novel (2011)

"Chuck" vs. the Business World: Business Tips on TV (2011)

U.S. by the Numbers:
What's Left, Right, and Wrong with America State by State
(2000)

New York by the Numbers:
State and City in Perpetual Crisis (1997)

D.C. by the Numbers: A State of Failure (1995)

"The truth is like a lion; you don't have to defend it. Let it loose; it will defend itself."

— St. Augustine

"I hope, by God's grace, that I am truly a Christian, not deviating from the faith, and that I would rather suffer the penalty of a terrible death than wish to affirm anything outside of the faith or transgress the commandments of our Lord Jesus Christ."

— Jan Hus

"May a merciful God preserve me from a Christian Church in which everyone is a saint! I want to be and remain in the church and little flock of the fainthearted, the feeble and the ailing, who feel and recognize the wretchedness of their sins, who sigh and cry to God incessantly for comfort and help, who believe in the forgiveness of sins."

— Martin Luther

Brief Dossiers on Recurring Characters

Pastor Stephen Grant. After college, Grant joined the Navy, became a SEAL, and went on to work at the CIA. He subsequently became a Lutheran pastor, serving at St. Mary's Lutheran Church on the eastern end of Long Island. Grant grew up in Ohio, just outside of Cincinnati. He possesses a deep knowledge of theology, history, and weapons. His other interests include archery, golf, movies, the beach, poker and baseball, while also knowing his wines, champagnes and brews. Stephen Grant is married to Jennifer Grant.

Jennifer Grant. Jennifer is a respected, sought-after economist and author. Along with Yvonne Hudson and Joe McPhee, she is a partner in the consulting firm Coast-to-Coast Economics. Her first marriage to then-Congressman Ted Brees ended when the congressman had an affair with his chief of staff. Jennifer loves baseball (a Cardinals fan while her husband, Stephen, cheers on the Reds) and literature, and has an extensive sword and dagger collection. Jennifer grew up in the Las Vegas area, with her father being a casino owner.

Paige Caldwell. For part of Stephen Grant's time at the CIA, Paige Caldwell was his partner in the field and in the bedroom. After Stephen left the Agency, Paige continued with the CIA until she eventually was forced out. However, she went on to start her own firm, CDM International Strategies and Security, with two partners – Charlie Driessen and Sean McEnany.

Charlie Driessen. Charlie was a longtime CIA veteran, who had worked with both Stephen Grant and Paige Caldwell. Driessen left the Agency to work with Paige at CDM. Prior to the CIA, he spent a short time with the Pittsburgh police department.

Sean McEnany. After leaving the Army Rangers, Sean McEnany joined the security firm CorpSecQuest, which was part legitimate business and part CIA front. He later signed up with Caldwell and Driessen at CDM. He maintains close contact with the CIA, and has a secret, high-security office in the basement of his suburban Long Island home, along with a mobile unit disguised as a rather typical van parked in the driveway. McEnany's ability to obtain information across the globe has an almost mystical reputation in national security circles. For good measure, Sean, his wife, Rachel, and their children attend St. Mary's Lutheran Church, where Stephen Grant is pastor.

Rachel McEnany. While a preschool teacher now, Rachel McEnany met Sean while she worked for the Defense Intelligence Agency. In addition to being a mom and a teacher, she helps Stephen Grant and others with an initiative known as the Lutheran Response to Christian Persecution.

Father Tom Stone. A priest and rector at St. Bartholomew's Anglican Church on Long Island, Tom is one of Grant's closest friends, and served as Stephen's best man. He enjoyed surfing while growing up in southern California, and is known for an easygoing manner and robust sense of humor. Along with Stephen, Tom and two other friends regularly meet for morning devotions and conversation at a local diner, and often play golf together. Tom is married to Maggie Stone, who runs her own public relations business. They are the parents to six children.

Father Ron McDermott. Father McDermott is a priest at St. Luke's Roman Catholic Church and School. McDermott is part of the morning devotions group of friends at the diner. He is a strong and caring leader of the St. Luke's school.

Pastor Zackary Charmichael. Zack also is a pastor at St. Mary's Lutheran Church, and the most recent addition to the breakfast clergy club. He grew up in the state of Washington, is a comic-book and gaming nerd, and a big fan of Seattle's Mariners and Seahawks as well as Vancouver's Canucks. Zack also is Tom Stone's son-in-law, married to Tom's oldest daughter, Cara, who is a nurse.

Chase Axelrod. Chase worked with Sean McEnany at CorpSecQuest, and then became an employee of CDM. He grew up in Detroit, became a star tight end with a 4.0 grade point average in college, and then earned a master's degree in foreign languages from N.C. State. He has mastered six foreign languages – Mandarin, German, French, Russian, Spanish and Japanese.

Phil Lucena. Charlie Driessen brought Phil from the CIA to work at CDM. Lucena is well known for his courteousness, as well as expertise in close combat.

Jessica West. Paige Caldwell wooed Jessica away from the FBI to join CDM. West thinks fast and acts accordingly. She has suffered major losses, with her father and brother, both Marines, dying in Afghanistan and Iraq, respectively, and her fiancé, a fellow FBI agent, perishing in a terrorist attack in New York City. She came to work at CDM in part to dispense a kind of harsh justice that would not have been possible with the FBI.

Rich Noack. Supervisory Special Agent Rich Noack has long worked at the Federal Bureau of Investigation (FBI). His job often pulls him into the orbit of Stephen Grant, as well as the undertakings of Paige Caldwell. Noack works primarily out of the FBI's J. Edgar Hoover Building in Washington, D.C.

Edward "Tank" Hoard. Tank Hoard has risen through the ranks of the CIA. He worked with Stephen Grant while Grant was at the Agency. Hoard is a bodybuilder, who also happens to be well-educated and adept at managing people and politics at the CIA.

President Adam Links. Links graduated West Point at the top of his class, and was awarded the Bronze Star while serving in the first Gulf War. He left the military when his wife was diagnosed with pancreatic cancer. After her death, Links joined and buried himself in the CIA, where he had a secret relationship with Paige Caldwell. Post-CIA, he came out of nowhere to win a U.S. Senate seat from Louisiana, and later was picked to be the vice-presidential running mate for Elizabeth Sanderski. He subsequently won his own full term as president.

Prologue

Stephen Grant came around the bend of the building still holding the gun in his right hand. It hung at his side, blood dripping down the weapon. He halted his movement when seeing Caldwell, Driessen and Hoard on their knees, hands clasped behind their heads, and three men pointing AK-47s at the backs of their skulls.

Shit.

He didn't pause. Grant knew he had only one chance, and it was now a longshot given his injuries.

At least their backs are to me. Lord, one more time?

He looked at the terrorist to the right – the one with the rifle pointed at Paige's head – and suppressed the urge to spring forward.

Forty-five minutes earlier...

Their two firm bodies were covered in sweat, as were the sheets crumpled underneath them.

Paige Caldwell rolled onto her left side, and Stephen Grant wrapped his arms around her from behind. He brushed aside her long black hair with his chin, and kissed the back of her shoulder. Paige closed her steel blue eyes, and smiled in response.

As a stillness now replaced their vigorous activities, Paige asked, "Hey, are you okay?"

"It would be hard not to be okay after that."

"Yeah, I know, but that's not what I was referring to, lover."

"What did you mean?"

"Since you returned from that Chenko assignment, you've been kind of different. I hope killing that fat Russian double agent didn't bother you."

Vladimir Chenko's duplicity had resulted in the deaths of as many as 12 people, including a man who had been Stephen's mentor at the CIA, not to mention his friend. Grant had been given the off-the-books assignment of dispensing justice on Chenko.

Ah, she's noticed. "How different?"

"I don't know. Just different. You tell me."

Is this the right time? "I definitely don't regret taking down Chenko. He got exactly what he deserved. But I've been thinking."

"Uh-oh. I have to make sure that the next guy I have regular sex with doesn't think so much."

"You want high performance but not so bright?"

"Hmmm, sounds pretty good."

Stephen tickled her most vulnerable spot, and Paige jerked her body while laughing. She rolled over and their noses touched. She observed, "You're alright. I like the black hair and green eyes."

"Well, thanks."

"And you're in pretty good shape."

"Continue."

"But there's always room for improvement." Stephen kissed the tip of her nose, and Paige continued, "Seriously, what is that brain working on?"

Before he could broach the subject, there was a loud knock at the bedroom door. Charlie Driessen, part of the four-person CIA team in this Rome safehouse, didn't wait for any response. He opened the door and said, "Get your clothes on. We've got movement, and it ain't good. These shits are heading to the Colosseum."

Paige declared, "What the hell?"

Driessen merely replied, "Move, now!"

Within three minutes, Grant and Caldwell were dressed, armed and jumping in the back seat of a gray Range Rover.

Edward "Tank" Hoard, at the steering wheel, and Charlie Driessen, in the front passenger seat, were an odd couple. Hoard was a massive body builder, with close-cut, light brown hair, while Driessen's entire appearance was unkempt, from his sparse hair to an unruly mustache to wrinkled clothing.

As Tank Hoard hit the accelerator, Grant demanded, "Details."

Hoard said, "We'll be there in three minutes." He didn't have to deal with notoriously bad Italian drivers at nearly 2:30 in the morning, and the safehouse was just a few streets away from the Colosseum, a structure that had been standing in Rome since opening in 80 A.D. He slowed up a bit, made a hard left onto Via Labacana, and reaccelerated.

While checking his gun, Driessen said, "We wanted more information on who's giving orders to this cell? Well, my man in the group finally got the name of a guy in Iraq. But it doesn't matter right now because they received orders to do as much damage to the Colosseum tonight as they could. Unfortunately, they have two young zealots ready to go to heaven, and a fair amount of C4."

Caldwell asked, "What about your man?"

"He managed to bail," replied Driessen.

"How many total?" asked Grant.

"Supposedly seven. Two strapped suicide bombers, and the other five assigned to stop anyone from interfering. The police and the AISE know. But we're ahead of everybody else – except the fucking terrorists."

As the Range Rover approached the Colosseum, the four CIA operatives spotted the bodies of two security guards lying next to a small blue and white hatchback. Hoard bore right at a fork in the road, and moved along the north side of the Colosseum. They passed two more guards who had been shot, and approached a couple of sedans parked on the cobblestones. Four terrorists were set up to use the vehicles as cover, with the other three moving around the building behind them.

Hoard pulled the steering wheel to the left, and announced rather calmly, "Hold tight."

As bullets started hitting the Range Rover, Hoard never let off the gas, and pointed the vehicle at the few feet between the two parked sedans.

Driessen declared, "Shit," as their SUV split the two cars, sending them spinning outward. Two of the terrorists were able to leap clear, another was sent tumbling, with the fourth taking a direct hit to the head, ending his life.

Unfortunately, after the impact, Hoard couldn't regain control of the Range Rover. It turned sharply, tipped on its right side, and slid into one of the high wrought iron fences used to keep people out of the Colosseum. One side of the heavy fencing tore away from the stone column.

Grant was sitting behind Hoard, but now was on top of Paige. She took the crash harder than Grant.

Grant noted that she was moaning and moving, so he maneuvered himself to push open the door of the vehicle, which was now above him. Hoard had been cushioned by an air bag, and was doing the same thing in the front seat.

Hoard popped his door open first, climbed partially out of the vehicle, and began exchanging gunfire with approaching terrorists. Grant followed suit.

But once Charlie started demanding they make space, Grant glanced over his shoulder at the partially torn down fence. He said, "Charlie, get up here. I'm going inside after the bombers."

Grant didn't wait for a response, nor was one given to him. Hoard provided cover fire as best he could. Grant climbed out, onto the SUV, and then jumped through the fence opening into the Colosseum.

Behind Grant, still in the back seat of the Range Rover, Caldwell began to stir. She felt around and found her gun.

Grant had his Glock 17 in hand, and moved quickly but quietly along the stone floor. He halted his progress when he heard a small explosion around the bend in front of him.

Took them longer to blow the door and get in than it took me.

He quickened his pace in the direction from which the explosion came. Grant spotted three figures emerging from a dissipating cloud of smoke, and before they saw him, he fired off three shots.

A projectile found a target. One of the bombers took the hit in a leg, and fell against the wall.

The attacker not wearing a C4 vest unleashed a torrent of shots at Grant from an AK-47.

There was no real cover for anyone. Grant merely stayed as close to the cold stone wall as he could.

One projectile ricocheted off the rock, and scraped along Grant's head, just above his right ear. He instinctively reached up, but quickly refocused and returned shots. He emptied the magazine, and the AK-47 terrorist fell to the ground.

The two bombers started moving away from Grant – one now limping and the other moving more quickly.

As Grant ran forward, he ejected the used magazine, and slipped another into the gun.

Moving past the fallen attacker, Grant was caught off guard by the lunge from the man. The attacker had a knife, and he caught Grant's right arm, just above the wrist.

The gun fell out of Grant's hand. But he reached around with his left and grabbed the attacker's knife hand. Grant moved his body, so that he could press down with his weight while also working to turn the knife. His opponent was weakening thanks to two gunshot wounds. Grant fully turned the knife, and plunged it into the man's neck.

No time.

Grant pulled the knife out, jumped to his feet and ran in the direction where the two bombers were heading.

The limping terrorist probably didn't hear Grant over his own grunting. As the man began to look back, Grant was on him.

Please, Lord, not a dead-man switch.

Grant drove the knife into the base of the man's skull, and shoved it in with all of his strength. The bomber hit the ground hard.

I'm still here.

He grabbed the dead man's gun that had slid a few feet away, and he continued his pursuit of the last bomber. As he moved, Grant failed to notice that the distant sounds of gunfire being exchanged between his colleagues and the other terrorists fell silent.

Blood from his head wound was finding its way into his right eye, but the gash in his right arm presented even more serious problems. While Grant practiced shooting both righthanded and lefthanded, he was a natural righty. He had closed the distance with the other bomber, but only because the terrorist had stopped. The man spread his arms out and looked skyward.

Grant raised the gun. *Lord, please.* He squeezed the trigger.

The projectile exploded into the back of the bomber's head, and the trigger for the C4 vest fell harmlessly away as the man's body toppled forward to the stone floor.

The distant silence now registered with Grant. He turned and ran back in the direction from which he had come. He moved the gun to his right hand in order to pull a couple of pieces of debris aside allowing him to exit the Colosseum through the door that the terrorists had blown open.

By now, he couldn't see out of the right eye, and his right arm was just about completely useless.

Stephen Grant came around the bend of the building still holding the gun in his right hand. It hung at his side, blood dripping down the weapon. He halted his movement when seeing Caldwell, Driessen and Hoard on their knees, hands clasped behind their heads, and three men pointing AK-47s at the backs of their skulls.

Shit.

He didn't pause. Grant knew he had only one chance, and it was now a longshot given his injuries.

At least their backs are to me. Lord, one more time?

He looked at the terrorist to the right – the one with the rifle pointed at Paige's head – and suppressed the urge to spring forward.

Instead, Grant reached over with his left hand, grasped the gun, raised it, and took a deep breath. He steadied his arm – in fact, his entire body – and focused with his left eye.

He squeezed the trigger three times in quick succession.

The first terrorist standing behind Caldwell was hit in the shoulder, and dropped his AK-47.

The second, perched behind Hoard, jumped slightly in surprise before he was knocked off balance and down onto one knee by Grant's second shot, which had penetrated his left leg.

Rather than firing into Driessen's head, the third terrorist started to turn to see who was shooting at them. Grant's third shot missed. But by this time, Caldwell had picked up the AK-47. She spun, fell onto her back, and pointed the rifle, which was set to automatic. She pulled the trigger and sprayed death on the last three of the terrorists.

The third man wound up falling onto Driessen, and they both crashed onto the cobblestone.

Grant ran forward, and asked, "Everybody okay?"

Caldwell moved to him, and offered support, which Grant gladly took. "We are now," she said. "I assume the three inside are done?"

Grant nodded.

Hoard said, "Nice work, Stephen. You, too, Paige."

After pushing the dead man off, Driessen remained on the ground, looking up. "Yeah, great." He looked at Grant. "But I noticed you shot the other two before you got to the guy holding an AK-47 on me, and then you missed."

Grant smiled, and said, "Priorities, Charlie."

Driessen laughed. "Yeah, I get it."

Four days later...

Charlie Driessen turned on his barstool and looked at Stephen Grant. "Shit, Grant, I don't know what to say. You actually haven't told Paige that you're seriously considering this?"

Grant took a gulp of beer, and replied, "No, not yet. I was going to just before everything hit the fan in Rome."

Driessen laughed and took a swig from his glass of bourbon. "That's not going to work out well for you."

"The right moment hasn't presented itself again, and I've been thinking more deeply – wrestling with it – since the Colosseum incident."

Driessen shook his head. "Grant, you just saved all of our asses, and you're thinking about walking away?"

"I'm thinking about it. This isn't easy."

Driessen finished his drink, and put the glass down on the bar. "Listen, I'm honored, and a bit perplexed, that you chose me to talk to about this."

"Well, other than me, you know Paige best."

"Maybe. But this isn't about Paige. It's about you making a decision about your life."

Grant knew that Charlie was right, but also understood that personal decisions most certainly affected others. He drained the last of the beer.

Driessen continued, "Do you know Scott Sheridan?"

"No, should I?"

"Yeah, you definitely should. He's an Agency old-timer. I mean back to OSS days."

"Wow. How old is he?"

Driessen shrugged. "I guess he's about 80."

"Still active?"

"Well, kind of. Anyway, I spoke with him a few years ago about a big decision he had to make very early in his career."

Grant was both bewildered and curious. "And?"

"This is right up his alley. He's a guy that can give you real insights on this thing you're wrestling with. Let's just say, he's been where you are right now."

"Really? What does that mean?"

Charlie ignored the question. "He's local. Lives out a bit in Virginia. Nice farmhouse with some land and horses. I'm going to call him in the morning, and I'll set something up for you two to meet and talk."

Grant hesitated, "Well, okay, I guess."

Driessen said, "Trust me, and it's your turn to pay." He slapped Grant on the back, turned, and left the bar.

Late the next afternoon, Grant arrived in Haymarket, Virginia. He turned his Ford Explorer onto a gravel lane that ran between two large fenced fields where thoroughbred horses roamed. At the end of the lane, the driveway ended in a circle in front of a large stone home with expansive windows.

As Grant got out of the SUV, the front door of the home opened, and a tall, thin man wearing light blue jeans and a white, blue-striped, button-down shirt stepped out. Grant noted that the gray hair and wrinkled face pointed to the man's age, while his erect posture and ease of movement made clear that the aging process had treated him well.

The man said, "Hello. Stephen Grant, I presume?"

The two shook hands.

Grant replied, "Yes. Mr. Sheridan?"

"Please, it's Scott. Welcome. Come in, and we'll talk."

Grant followed Sheridan into the home, which was decorated meticulously in a combination of colonial American and horse-related themes throughout. Grant also noted that assorted Christian symbols – a cross here, a crucifix there and an occasional statue or wood carving – were present as well.

"You have a beautiful home."

"Thanks. Most of the credit goes to my wife. She's away on a trip to Ireland."

Grant nodded, and merely said, "Ah, I see."

"Come on, we'll go to my inner sanctum."

Sheridan led Grant toward the back corner of the sprawling home. He opened a door to reveal a big room with large windows looking out on more green fields and a barn. Grant saw that this was a combination home office and personal retreat. The themes that ran throughout much of the rest of the home continued here, but Sheridan's interests were on clear display, namely, books, assorted items related to the Chicago White Sox, pictures of horses, some historic firearms. But what truly grabbed Grant's attention was a kneeler, facing a Holy Trinity icon hanging on the wall.

Sheridan said, "Please grab a seat." He pointed to a large, leather armchair.

Grant said, "Thanks," and sat down.

"How about a drink? I have water with lemon, and iced tea, or I can grab you a cup of coffee?"

"Iced tea would be perfect."

Sheridan poured two glasses, handed one to Grant, and sat down on a couch that matched the design of the armchair. "Now, I understand you're pondering some big life decisions, thinking about leaving the Agency to become a pastor."

Grant took a sip of the tea, and said, "Well, yes. But I'm at a disadvantage."

Sheridan smiled. "Right. Charlie set up our meeting, and told you that I might be able to help. But that was it. He left things vague."

"'Vague' would be generous."

Sheridan chuckled, and then leaned forward and placed his drink down on the glass-top coffee table. "Why don't I explain?"

"Please, thanks."

Sheridan sat back and started to sum up parts of his story for Grant. "At the start of World War II, I was a young Lutheran pastor serving a small congregation in Oklahoma."

Grant shifted in his chair, and said, "Really?"

"Yes." Sheridan went on to explain how he wound up serving in the Office of Strategic Services, the World War II predecessor to the Central Intelligence Agency. He then zeroed in on the decision eventually confronting him, that is, to go back to his work as a pastor or to continue with his work in the OSS. He paused, and took a sip of tea.

"And you chose to stay with the Agency?"

"I did. It was the hardest decision of my life, and that includes an assortment of life-and-death situations I've faced over the years. The Agency, as you know, trains you –

well, as best it can – for such scenarios, but no one ever prepared me in any way for deciding whether or not to continue as a pastor. I never thought about the possibility, until the possibility presented itself."

Grant said, "How much did Charlie tell you about what I am considering?"

"Charlie gave me what he thought necessary. Basically, he said that you were thinking about leaving the Agency to become a pastor."

"Right."

"And a Lutheran, nonetheless." Sheridan smiled, and said, "The Lord makes life interesting, and often ironic, doesn't He?"

"Apparently. How did you go about it, I mean, making such a decision?"

"The same way, I'm guessing, you are right now. Prayer. Reflection. Talking to assorted people. Figuring out who is providing worthwhile advice and who isn't. And trying to figure out how your decision will affect others in your life."

Grant nodded. "I'm not sure which part is more difficult – how this is going to affect me or others?"

Sheridan smiled. "Yes, I understand that. All I can say is that some people will never understand or agree with you, but others will accept it, or come to accept it, and perhaps even appreciate it. In the end, be honest – with God, with others and with yourself – make what you deem to be the best decision, and you can't do much about anything else. Well, you can do a lot – pray, provide compassion and help, and so on – but you know what I mean."

Grant drank more deeply from the glass, and then asked, "Was there some particular deciding factor for you?"

"In the end, for me, the best place where I could make the most difference for Christ and His Church actually was to continue in my national security vocation."

"Ever regret it?"

"I've wondered what might have been. But regret? No. I've been able to be a witness for Christ in very unique situations, and along the way, I was able to serve as a kind of unofficial chaplain at times. I feel – well, I hope and pray – that I was able to make a difference." He paused, and then added, "I also came to realize that I was far better at Agency work than I was as a pastor, and a key reason for that was that I enjoyed the work more. That was a weird realization, and it felt like being selfish at first. But I realized that it wasn't selfishness, it was about where I could serve best. That played a real part in my final decision."

Stephen nodded, once more, and said, "That helps."

They spoke for nearly two more hours, discovering along the way that they shared assorted views on both theology and national security. Grant also talked about Paige and their relationship, with Sheridan discussing his wife and their family.

After they shook hands outside the house, Grant climbed into his SUV. He lowered the window, looked at Sheridan, and asked, "Did your wife play a part in your decision?"

Sheridan chuckled. "Of course, she did. That's another story that we can share the next time we get together. But it's not like I was a priest. Marriage was an option for me as a pastor." He added, "Stephen, I'm a very lucky man. I have no doubt that we would have gotten married whether I chose the life of a pastor or a spy."

"Thanks, Scott. I really appreciate you giving me this time and your insights."

"Any time, my friend. And may God bless you no matter which path you take."

"And God bless you, too, Scott."

As he drove away from Scott Sheridan and the stone house, and by the horses, Grant made his decision.

Six weeks later...

"So, no one during any exit interview was surprised by what you're doing?" asked Charlie Driessen.

"Well, they at least didn't indicate any surprise – certainly not as much as you might expect. It was mentioned that my choice wasn't completely unprecedented," replied Stephen Grant.

It was nearly two in the morning, and everyone else had left the gathering. This was Grant's last day at the CIA, and he had received a relatively quiet "Thanks for Your Service" party. The send-off was held in a downstairs room of a Georgetown restaurant that had quietly hosted such events before. In fact, it had done so for several years. Grant had been at a few, and he couldn't decide if the Agency had a hand in running the place, or perhaps the owner simply possessed some kind of link to or admiration for the CIA. After all, the place actually was called The Hale Tavern, after Nathan Hale, one of America's first spies.

"No shit?" Driessen shrugged his shoulders, and took a swig of beer.

The two men sat at a long, wide, cherry-wood table that dominated the room, with the walls a mix of brick and shelving holding bottles of wine and books. The restaurant's staff had cleared away all vestiges of the party attended by three dozen Agency employees who had worked with Grant on a wide range of endeavors. The gathering turned into part roast, and part somewhat sad farewell. Grant was particularly touched by the jokes, the bear hug and the trace of a tear served up by Tank Hoard. The rest of the evening involved a good deal of casual chitchat that revealed nothing of substance regarding what people were doing at work.

For the past hour, a waiter occasionally came down the stairs to see if the pitcher of beer needed to be refilled.

Driessen asked, "Are you surprised that she didn't show?"

"Paige?"

Driessen grunted. "Of course, Paige. Who the hell else would I be talking about?"

"She's pissed."

"Kind of figured."

Grant decided to say a bit more. "Paige doesn't understand my decision at all."

Driessen interrupted, "Who does?"

Grant shot him an exasperated look.

Driessen said, "Sorry."

"Anyway, she thinks this decision means that she and I are done."

"Doesn't it?"

Grant was a bit surprised by Driessen's response. "It doesn't have to be," he replied defensively.

"Maybe with some people, but not Paige."

It wasn't like Grant hadn't thought about the point Driessen was making, but he had fought against it.

Driessen continued, "Quite frankly, I can't imagine Paige as someone who would compromise even in a relationship. Her first love, if you want to call it that, is the CIA. Plain and simple. If you think otherwise, you're just bullshitting yourself."

Hearing someone else say what Grant had been considering in his own mind over the past several weeks confirmed things for him, but also served as something of an annoyance. This wasn't what Grant *wanted* to hear. He was going to make the argument that Paige could certainly stay in the CIA while he worked as a pastor. But Grant didn't state that part of his case. He knew that Driessen's likely response would be to laugh. So, instead, Grant just took another gulp of beer.

As he finished what was in his glass, Driessen looked over Grant's shoulder to see someone definitely not a waiter standing at the bottom of the stairs. With his back to the stairs, Grant hadn't noticed the new arrival yet.

Driessen looked Grant directly in the eyes, and said, "Grant, I wish you good luck."

Grant straightened up in his chair, and said, "Thanks, Charlie, but I'm confident that this is the right thing for me."

Driessen smiled, and said, "Yeah, well, I wasn't exactly wishing you luck on the pastor thing."

Grant turned to see Paige Caldwell standing at the bottom of the stairs. She was wearing a very short, strapless black dress, with matching high heels. Her black hair flowed down onto her shoulders, and her full lips brandished shiny, pink lipstick.

Driessen got up from his chair, and leaned down toward Grant. "Good luck with this."

Grant managed to pull his stare away from Caldwell. He stood up, and shook Driessen's hand. "Charlie, thanks. It's been an honor working with you."

"Yeah, same here with you, Grant."

Driessen started to walk away when Grant said, "I'll see you around, Charlie."

Driessen paused, looked back at Grant, and said, "You're one of the best, Stephen, and I hope that somehow we do get to work together again."

Charlie Driessen just called me "Stephen." Was that a first? And he gave me a compliment. Another first?

Grant replied, "You're one of the best I've ever worked with as well, Charlie."

Driessen nodded, and then added, "You're also a bit of a pain in the ass, and I feel for the church where you become a pastor."

Grant laughed and shook his head.

Now, that's Charlie.

Driessen smiled at his own joke, turned, and walked toward the staircase. As he moved closer to Caldwell, he smirked. "Nice of you to show up, Paige."

"Fuck you, Charlie," responded Caldwell.

Driessen's smile broadened. He said, "Good luck," and then climbed the stairs.

Caldwell walked over to Stephen, stopped and kissed him on the cheek. She then took Charlie's seat at the table, reached for the pitcher, and poured herself a beer in Charlie's glass. After taking a sip, she asked, "So, how did your little going-away party go?"

Still pissed off.

"It went well. It was nice that so many people showed up."

That comment froze Caldwell briefly, and then she put the glass down. "I wasn't going to come at all."

"Well, I'm glad you did."

"Are you?" Caldwell asked.

"Of course, I am. Paige, I care about you, a great deal."

She smiled somewhat sadly. "But not that much."

"Are we going to talk about what this...?"

"We talked a lot that night. You made it clear that you had a calling..."

"A new calling."

"Right, whatever."

This is not going to go well.

Caldwell picked up the glass, and took a long drink.

Grant said, "Paige, we really need to talk some more about what this could mean for us."

"Stephen, has your decision changed at all from what you told me weeks ago?"

"Well, no, but..."

"You're set on leaving the Agency to become a pastor?"

"Yes, and I'd hope that you would understand, and we could..."

She held her hand up in the air, indicating that Grant should stop talking. Grant could tell that Paige was working to hold it together, and he now struggled to do the same.

Caldwell stood up, looked down at Stephen, and waited.

Grant reluctantly rose to his feet.

She moved close to him, and grabbed hold of the lapels of his sports jacket. Caldwell pulled him closer, and kissed him gently. Grant's hands moved onto her hips. Their lips lingered together while their eyes remained shut.

She finally whispered, "Stephen, I don't know if I'll ever understand this decision. I'm sorry."

Caldwell took a step back, and Grant's hands fell to his side. They stared at each other for several seconds, and then she took a step to the side, and moved past him, heading toward the stairs.

Grant didn't turn to watch her go. But he said, "I'm sorry, too, Paige."

She paused for the briefest of moments. Their backs remained facing each other from across the long room.

Paige Caldwell then ascended the stairs, and Stephen Grant sat back down at the table.

Chapter 1

12 Years Later...

Cardinal Renaldo Bessetti leaned back in a thick leather chair, and took a sip of his Cynar and tonic over ice. "Ah, Pietro, another public appearance by the Holy Father without incident."

Across the desk sat Bessetti's aide. Father Pietro Filoni also was enjoying the same type of drink. "Yes, Your Eminence."

"Thank God that I managed to gain this position after Augustine's death." As cardinal secretary of state, Bessetti served as Pope Paul VII's chief assistant – as the old saying went, he was "the eye, the heart and the arm of the pope." Bessetti continued, "I was worried about Augustine's 'Public Mission of Mere Christianity.'"

"And justly so."

"But then again, the devil you know."

"Yes, but thankfully, the Holy Father is not as sure of himself, not as bold as his predecessor."

"True." Bessetti took another sip of his drink.

"Your Eminence has performed a tremendous service to the Church."

Bessetti nodded. "Thank you, Pietro. Yet, it is tiring, and I don't know how long I will be able to raise questions and doubts about this foolish idea. I am making sure, of course, that it is not just my voice he is hearing, but assorted voices. We seem to have made headway, but, unfortunately, he also is not completely forthcoming."

"If he were to take this step, it would do irreparable harm to the papacy and the Church."

"You are correct. But as we have discussed, that is why I brought you on as my aide."

"I understand."

Bessetti smiled broadly. "Of course, Pietro, you are a multi-talented priest, and will go far."

"Thank you."

"And I pray that your other experiences and skills will never be needed. But if they are..." Cardinal Bessetti shrugged and finished his drink.

Father Filoni replied, "Whatever the calling, I will gladly serve you and the Church."

"Good, good. Another drink to celebrate the New Year, Pietro?"

Chapter 2

Six Years Later...

"Have I mentioned how proud I am of you, Harry?" asked Ruth Fuchs, as she handed her husband a plate with a grilled ham and cheese sandwich, a baked potato and carrots resting on it.

Harold Fuchs, professor of history at Concordia University Chicago, smiled and said, "You have, and thank you." He leaned in and kissed the forehead of his wife of 37 years.

Ruth picked up her own plate, and followed her husband to the table in the breakfast nook. The university sat in the upscale neighborhood of Lake Forest, and the Fuchs' home was a red-brick colonial just a couple of streets from the campus.

Between bites of sandwich and sips of coffee, the two reviewed their travel checklist. Late tonight, their flight would take off with the ultimate destination being Rome.

Eventually, Ruth declared, "I think we have everything covered. I'm so excited about spending two years in Rome."

Harold nodded, as he chewed the last of his sandwich. He swallowed and said, "It could be more than that." After shaking his head, Harold continued, "Even after the conversations with the Vatican and the research I've done over the past eight or so months, it still doesn't feel completely real."

"And the times you spoke directly to Pope Paul VII, don't forget those."

Harold smiled. "How could I? This lifelong Lutheran and professor of Reformation history collaborating with the pope."

"Collaborating? I don't think that's the right word," protested Ruth.

"You know what I mean. Although, as we've discussed, there will be some who will see this in a nefarious light, and yes, call it 'collaborating.'"

The plump, gray-haired, short Ruth Fuchs sat up straighter, and said, "Well, they're idiots."

Harold laughed. "You've always got my back."

"For more than 37 years."

Harold pushed the wire-rimmed glasses up on the bridge of his large nose, and then ran his hand over the top of the almost completely bald scalp, which had been his habit since his hair loss accelerated some 20 years earlier. He rose from his seat, and picked up each of their plates. "I'll do the dishes, and clean up the kitchen. Everything will be ready for when Professor Perry and his family arrive next week."

Ruth called into the kitchen, "And you have someone checking on the house until they arrive?"

"Yes, as I mentioned, Bess, the department secretary, is more than happy to stop by, bring in the garbage can and check on things. And before you ask, again, she has the keys for the Perrys."

"Okay, okay, I'm just being thorough," replied Ruth. "I'll do another run through the house, and make sure everything is in order."

"Ruth, you've done that, I think, four times now. Everything is set. Why don't you go into the living room, put on some music and relax? We have a couple of hours before heading to the airport. I'll be in after I finish up in the kitchen."

Ruth agreed, adding, "You know, over the years, with the kids and when money was tight, I usually wasn't able to go with you on speaking or book-signing trips."

Harold returned to the doorway between the kitchen and breakfast nook. "I know, Ruth, and I've always been sorry about that. You know that, right?"

She waved her hand in the air. "There's nothing to be sorry about. I wouldn't trade our life together for anything. My point was going to be that now I'm going with you on the best work trip ever."

Harold said, "I'm so glad that the invitation included you coming as well." As he rolled up his sleeves, Harold smiled when he heard that Ruth had put on the Electric Light Orchestra. They'd gone to one of their concerts on their first date.

Harold quickly finished washing, drying and putting the dishes and glassware back in the kitchen cabinet. He cleaned up the rest of the kitchen, tied up the garbage bag, and walked out the front door of the house. He dropped the bag in the garbage pail, and rolled it down to the curb.

As he walked back up the driveway, the sound of a car engine caught his attention. He turned, but in the dark, all he could see were headlights, until the vehicle turned into the driveway. It was a midsize, black SUV.

Harold stood just short of the front steps and waited.

The SUV was turned off, the driver's side door opened, and a man with dark hair and coat got out and walked toward Harold. The man extended his right hand, and in a low voice with a distinct Italian accent, said, "Professor Fuchs?"

Harold squinted a bit to get a better look, and as he shook the man's hand, replied, "Yes, and who are you?"

The man's features became clearer in the light by the door, including his narrow eyes, thin face, pointed nose, and the clergy collar around his neck. "I am Father Pietro Filoni. The Holy Father, Pope Paul VII, sent me personally to drive you to the airport, and fly to Rome with both you and Mrs. Fuchs. I have taken the liberty of upgrading your tickets to first class."

"Oh, my goodness, that's very kind, but wasn't necessary at all. We would have been fine. We had a car coming to pick us up, and especially considering that the Vatican is picking up most of our costs, flying coach would have been more than fine."

Father Filoni shrugged, and said, "Ah, I understand, but all has been arranged."

"Well, thank you."

"Have your guests arrived yet, or is it just you and your wife tonight?"

"Professor Perry and his family arrive next week. It's just Ruth and me." Harold then said, "Where are my manners? I'm sorry. Please come in."

Filoni responded, "Thank you, thank you."

Before entering the house, Filoni looked to his left and then right.

Once inside, Filoni stood waiting as Harold closed the front door. The ELO song "Birmingham Blues" was emanating from the living room.

Harold said, "Sorry about the music."

Filoni shook his head, "It is not a problem. Who is that?"

"The Electric Light Orchestra." Harold began to lead Filoni toward the living room. "Have you ever listened to them?"

Filoni merely replied, "No."

They stepped into the living room, and Harold said, "Ruth, we have a special guest."

She actually jumped a little in surprise while still seated in a recliner. Ruth stood up, and said, "Hello."

Harold explained, "This is Father Pietro Filoni." He proceeded to relay to his wife what Filoni had told him outside.

Ruth smiled. "Well, how nice. Thank you, Father Filoni."

The priest replied, "Of course."

Ruth said, "Oh, let me shut off this music."

As she walked across the room and toward the old-style record player, Jeff Lynne continued singing:

Across the world I've seen
People and places

Could be the same
But with a different name.
I'll go and stay awhile and all the folks I meet
They'll say: You won't stay long,
You got them travelling feet
You'll soon be long-gone
'Cos boy, you got the rest of the world blues.

Ruth raised the needle arm, and shut off the player. She asked, "What can I get you, Father, perhaps coffee?"

Filoni said, "No, thank you. That will not be necessary." He then reached inside his dark coat, and rather casually pulled out a handgun with a suppressor attached.

As Filoni pointed the weapon at Harold, the history professor managed to say, "What the...?"

Filoni squeezed the trigger. The projectile plunged into Harold Fuchs' chest, and he fell to the floor.

Just as Ruth Fuchs started to scream, Filoni turned, and squeezed off another shot into her chest.

Filoni took three steps forward, and looked down at his two victims. Both Harold and Ruth's breathing was labored, and their eyes looked up in fear. Filoni kneeled down, and as he made the sign of the cross over each, he said, "May the Lord who frees you from sin save you and raise you up."

Filoni then stood back up, and pointed the gun down at Harold, and shot him in the forehead. He then did the same to Ruth.

Filoni pulled a dark cloth bag out of his pocket, and unfolded it. Over the next 10 minutes, he swept through the home, stuffing an assortment of small valuables, cash, Harold's wallet and Ruth's pocketbook into the bag. He left the house looking ransacked.

Filoni hit the switch to shut off the outside light. He stepped out of the home, moved to the SUV, and drove off into the night. In five minutes, Father Filoni was speeding north, away from Lake Forest and the city of Chicago on I-94.

Chapter 3

18 Months Later...

"Thanks, darling, for doing all of this." Haley Whittacker kissed her husband, Conrad, on the cheek, and then proceeded to slip into the back seat of the Rolls-Royce Phantom.

Before he closed the door, Conrad leaned down and said, "Come now, Haley, you know I would do anything to help your work."

Haley smiled. She had a wide mouth and fairly large, pearly white teeth. Her long blond hair was tied up in a bun, and now that she was seated, her royal blue dress pulled up, showing off more of her long legs.

Conrad closed the door, and as he walked around the back of the car, he proceeded with two habits – adjusting the sleeves of his charcoal-gray, three-piece suit, and tugging down a bit on the vest.

In the back seat, Haley adjusted her dress and sitting position, seeming to struggle to get comfortable. As she did so, her black, rectangle-shaped glasses slid down her nose. When Conrad opened the door opposite her, Haley pushed up her glasses, and finally settled into one spot.

Conrad smoothly moved into his seat, and as was his typical manner, sat perfectly straight. He picked up where their conversation left off, "Besides, you know that Rome is not a problem, what with the apartment, and one of my offices being there. It is another home. It all works out very conveniently."

"It certainly does," agreed Haley.

Though she had been married to Conrad for more than eight years, it was clear to those who knew her well that Haley had not fully adjusted to being married to this wealthy English businessman. While she grew up in a very nice home in a Westchester County, New York, suburb, and went to some of the best schools in America, there had been few pretensions.

Conrad, however, had been born into old British wealth – well, "old" by U.S. standards. The Whittacker fortune came courtesy of coal, but Conrad had set a new course in recent years with electricity-generating windmills, and batteries for electric cars. While being on the edge of popular technologies, Conrad's idiosyncrasies, and most other aspects of his life, were firmly entrenched in much older ways. The media focused on the inherent contradictions. Conrad seemed oblivious to them.

As for Haley, she had earned a doctorate in religious studies, and at a young age had written two influential books – one of the two best biographies of 15th-Century Church reformer Jan Hus, and a much-praised history of the Council of Trent. Fairness and impartiality won Haley praise in Catholic, Protestant and secular circles. Those two works, in a sense, served as bookends on the history of the Reformation period, while also making her an expert on two very different stages and perspectives on that period in church history.

But it wasn't just the work that she had done on those two books that made her an excellent professor and engaging speaker. Haley Whittacker had an infectious joy about her work. That joy seemed restrained, however, when Haley and Conrad were together.

Even at home in the Sewards End estate they were now leaving, there was a difference in day-to-day life. Conrad largely kept his work away from the home – but for necessary calls and email – leaving it for his company's London building, or other offices sprinkled around the world. At the same time, Conrad carried a certain business formality with him always, even at home. Haley would tease him about it good-naturedly during the first few years of their marriage. Conrad had responded with a laugh and kiss, but that reaction eventually evaporated, and so did Haley's teasing.

Meanwhile, outside of her teaching at Cambridge, Haley's research and writing very much was brought home to the estate. But not long after they married, she learned that her work habits required a separate space. So, she and Conrad agreed to upgrade a cottage resting nearly two hundred yards away from the main house. The small building had been a home for one of the estate's caretakers years earlier, and it was largely hidden from view of the main house, with a manicured lawn, rows of hedges and walkways, and a large fountain separating the two buildings. In that cottage, Haley worked in her "natural state," as she called it in conversation with friends and family back in the states. That "natural state" meant either shorts or jeans, some kind of graphic t-shirt, music turned up loud, shelves of books and files spread throughout the cottage's three main rooms, a large crucifix hanging on the wall above the main table at which she wrote, and two laptops. It was clear to anyone who knew her – perhaps except Conrad – that Haley was happiest in that cottage.

Indeed, most people saw a certain oddity in their marriage, including that the 18-year difference in ages – Conrad now in his late fifties and Haley in her early forties – seemed wider given the apparent differences in how they embraced day-to-day life. But what they did share was a strong Roman Catholic faith and a love of its history.

A decade earlier, Conrad had attended a conference in which Haley was a speaker. He introduced himself. They had a cordial chat, but that was it. However, they met again at the next two events where Haley spoke, and Conrad served as a primary funder. He asked her out, and to the bafflement of most who knew them both, they continued to date and eventually were married.

After buckling his seat belt, Conrad asked, "Are you comfortable, my dear? Do you need anything?"

"I'm fine, thank you."

Conrad turned his attention away from his wife's blue eyes, and to the driver sitting at the right-side steering wheel, who wore a patch over his left eye. Conrad said, "I know that I need not ask, Albro, but please bear with me."

Albro Dawson, military veteran and aide to Conrad Whittacker, said, "Of course, sir."

"So, we have everything?"

Dawson effectively reigned over Conrad's daily schedule, as well as much of life on the estate. "Yes, sir. Everything that you and Mrs. Whittacker said would be needed immediately in the apartment, we have in the boot. The other items will arrive some time tomorrow via our delivery service."

"Excellent. Thank you, Albro," said Conrad.

Haley added, "Yes, Albro, thank you."

"Of course, sir and madam. You are quite welcome. Shall we go?"

"Yes, Albro. Please proceed."

"Very good." Dawson pushed his foot down on the accelerator of the Phantom, turned the vehicle around part of the large, stone-covered circle in front of the Sewards End home, and then drove down the long driveway.

Chapter 4

"To be honest, this feels very – I don't know – strange." Father John Kohli sat in the principal's office at St. Michael's High School in Cape Canaveral, Florida, across the desk from Sister Katharine Malone.

"I understand. But it's also an incredible opportunity. I mean, the Holy Father asking you to come to Rome – to research and teach – all because of the book you wrote. What an honor." Sister Katharine smiled, and added, "I'm kind of jealous, Father."

Kohli returned the smile. "Thank you, Sister. But it feels like I'm leaving my home. St. Michael's has meant so much to me – the students, coaching basketball, and my colleagues and friends."

The word "friend" hung in the air for a few seconds. Both Kohli and Malone were in their mid-forties, and had been in their respective positions – Malone as school principal and Kohli as head of the religion department, varsity basketball coach and school chaplain – at St. Michael's for several years. Their relationship had grown beyond the professional, into a friendship. They found common ground in their faith and related callings, and in the fact that both had played basketball in high school and college. Given those basketball histories, both Kohli and Malone were tall – Kohli at 6 feet, five inches, and Malone standing at 6 feet, two inches. Each also was thin, and had brown hair – Kohli's cut close, almost like a crew cut, and Malone's also cut short in rather old-style nun-like fashion. For good measure, they also shared an interest in motorcycles, which, in turn, made them rather cool among the students. Malone had gained her love for the Catholic Church from her mother, and became a combination grease monkey and gym rat from her dad. The story was much the same for Kohli, except motorcycles entered his life thanks to a college roommate.

A few years ago, after having taken several motorcycle rides together, they had cleared the air over lunch one day. The two had a very open discussion explicitly recognizing their friendship, but in effect warning each other not to press it to something that would violate their vows. After talking about it, the two went silent for a few minutes, eating their respective meals, until Malone said, "Well, that was awkward."

Kohli agreed, "It was." And then the two laughed about it, finished eating and got back on their bikes.

They left the topic there, and had not spoken of it since.

Malone replied to Kohli's point on missing St. Michael's and friends by saying, "Yes, I'm going to miss you, too, but this is the life we have chosen."

"It is." Kohli nodded in response.

Malone added, "Besides, I think what you're really going to miss is coaching basketball."

"That is going to be very hard." He paused. "Mr. Belmont, though, loves the game and kids. He's been great taking over the varsity team this year. And though I have not met him, I've been told from my reliable sources inside the Church that you're going to be pleased with Father Just as both chaplain and history teacher."

At the school, Malone, Kohli and the staff always referred to each other by proper titles and last names. In private moments, for these two, it was "Kathy" and "John." And since it was now after-school hours, Malone lowered her voice, and said, "Yeah, but can he ride?" Before Kohli could reply, Malone continued, "John, the fact that your book has been read by Pope Paul VII, and that he liked a work focused on making Martin Luther, in effect, more understandable and even sympathetic from a Catholic perspective speaks volumes about your scholarship and abilities. While I said that I was jealous, as your friend, I'm so proud of you and what you've accomplished."

Kohli looked down for a brief moment, and then up. "Thanks, Kathy. That means a lot to me."

Their stare lingered, and then Malone said, "But what really has me kind of pissed off is you tooling around parts of Europe on a bike without me for a couple of years."

Kohli's face brightened. "Yeah, the fact that the pope is making sure that I have access to a motorcycle is awesome. I promise to send pictures."

"How nice ... for you."

They again laughed.

Kohli then said, "Okay, before I go home and finish packing, what else do we need to cover in terms of my work here at St. Michael's?"

They briefly went over a few more items, and when finished, Malone said, "That's it. Go pack. I'll see you at the send-off dinner tonight with the staff, and then tomorrow, I'll drop you at the airport."

The next morning at Orlando Melbourne International Airport, Sister Malone pulled her Toyota Highlander up at the passenger curbside drop-off. The two got out of the SUV in silence. Malone popped the tailgate, and Father Kohli pulled out his two large suitcases. He set them down on the sidewalk, and turned to see tears forming in Malone's eyes. He said, "Oh, Kathy."

She stepped forward and they hugged each other.

While holding the hug, Kathy whispered, "I'm going to miss you so much, John."

Tears were now forming in Kohli's eyes as well. "Me, too, Kathy, me, too. You have no idea."

They held each other a little tighter. Malone was the first to step back. She wiped her eyes, and said, "Now, go. Teach them in Rome. Teach the pope, if you have to, and enjoy it all. Enjoy the research, and the open roads of Italy and beyond." Her tone wasn't angry; it was a combination of wishing true happiness, and feeling bewildered and sad.

Kohli cleared his voice, as Malone moved to the other side of the vehicle, standing with her hand on the driver's door handle. Kohli said, "Thanks. I will." He paused briefly, breathed in deeply, and said, "Kathy, you know that I..." He stopped.

She replied, "I know, John. Same here." She opened the door, looked back at Kohli, and said, "May the Lord be with you."

Kohli responded, "And with you."

Malone moved to get into the SUV, but again she hesitated. "And send me those damn pictures of you tooling around Europe on the pope's motorcycle."

Kohli responded, "I will."

They smiled at each other. Malone got into the car, and Kohli watched as she drove away. He then turned and entered the terminal.

Chapter 5

The woman actually screamed as the man groaned, and soon her body collapsed down onto his. They kissed, and then she said, "I'm going to miss this, Killian."

"I know. So will I."

The 19-year-old, red-haired student said to her 38-year-old professor, "The boys, well, they are not as experienced as you are."

Killian Dvorak smiled. "Of course not, Ivana. They are boys."

Ivana asked playfully, "Whatever will I do?"

Dvorak answered, "Well, it is only a two-hour flight. We can visit each other."

Ivana smiled, "Do you mean it?"

"Of course, I do."

"You are toying with me. You will not have time. You are going to Rome to work, with the pope even. It has to do with your book about... Who was it about, again?"

Dvorak grunted, and pushed her off him and onto the bed. "How can you not know what I wrote about? You have taken two of my classes, and we are sleeping together."

Ivana said, "No, no, I am sorry. You know when we are in bed I can only think of one thing of yours." She grabbed him.

Dvorak laughed loudly. "Ah! Nonetheless, you should know that I have written one of the foremost biographies on Jan Hus."

"That's right. Hus." She paused, and then repeated, "Hus."

"You don't remember who he is, do you?"

"That is not true. I recall the name."

Dvorak growled his irritation. "He taught at our own university 600 years ago. Hus stood up against assorted abuses by the Church at the time, what he saw as going against Holy Scripture. He taught and preached about such things, and that eventually got him in trouble. Does any of this ring a bell? We covered it in one of your classes with me?"

Ivana said, "Well, yes, of course. He was a follower of Martin Luther."

"Nice try. Hus came 100 years before Luther. But you're right that they were both reformers."

Ivana smiled, "What happened to Hus?"

"He was not as lucky as Luther. Hus accepted an invitation to the Council of Constance to address the issues he raised. While guaranteed safe passage, he was arrested and burned at the stake as a heretic."

"How awful."

"Yes, it was a horrific way to die. Do you know what else is horrific?"

Ivana shook her head.

"It is when my most special student fails to remember anything about Jan Hus, even though my book about Hus is the reason why I have my teaching position and why I have been invited to work with a pope."

Ivana began to kiss his chest, and asked, "Am I forgiven?"

"My dear, you have special talents that your fellow students lack, and that is why you are receiving such special treatment, and forgiveness."

In reality, Professor Killian Dvorak had provided special treatment to several of his students whom he deemed to have special talents over the last few years.

Dvorak moved on top of his partner, and whispered, "Ivana, your talents are always welcome, and that includes in Rome."

Chapter 6

"It is amazing what Martin Luther has done for us," observed Pastor Gerhard Fletcher.

His wife, Ada, replied, "Yes, he helped. But it was the Lord, and your work and perseverance, that brought us here, Gerhard. God be praised."

"And you, my love. If it were not for your sacrifice, none of this would have been possible." Behind oval-shaped glasses, Gerhard's eyes moistened. "You are God's greatest gift to me."

"And I thank him every night for you, our children, and the wonderful people you served over the years as their pastor."

Other than the two being in their late fifties and on the short side, Gerhard and Ada Fletcher presented themselves in strikingly different fashion. Ada was neat, fashionably dressed, and her hair and make-up done to perfection. In contrast, Gerhard's receding gray-and-brown hair was always awry. His glasses were slightly crooked, and his shoes scuffed. If it weren't for Ada, his clothing – clergy attire and otherwise – would have been wrinkled.

Gerhard nodded, adding, "It was you who set me free to finish that." He pointed to four large books stacked on the bed, waiting to be slipped into one of his suitcases. It was his four-volume magnum opus titled *The Lutheran Reformation: From the Foundations to the Fallout*. He had struggled writing it for 25 years. And after their two now-adult children had left, Ada pressed her husband to retire from being a full-time pastor, and finish the work. After resisting, Gerhard succumbed to his wife's argument, which she said over and over, "You will still be serving Him and His Church, but in a different way."

Gerhard found it hard to retire from being a parish pastor. At the same time, he found joy in being unshackled from the larger church bureaucracy in Germany. He finished the book project, and the four volumes were published, not just in German, but in English and Spanish as well.

About the books, *The Wall Street Journal's* reviewer wrote, "There are works of history that seem to include every tidbit of information on the topic, but are downright painful to read. On the other hand, there are breezy, highly readable histories that leave too much out, failing to capture even the essence of the moment. Neither is the case with Fletcher's four-volume *The Lutheran Reformation: From the Foundations to the Fallout.* Fletcher writes in engaging fashion, and seems to leave nothing out."

After publication, invitations came forth to speak and teach. At each public event, Fletcher had to win over students and audiences who were initially surprised by his rumpled state and disorganization. But once he dove into the many people, events and issues explored in his books, Fletcher won nearly everyone over. He went from being viewed as the odd little man with crooked glasses to being the leading Reformation historian and thinker in the room, and far beyond.

As for her "sacrifice," Ada reassured her husband time and time again, that her work was in no way a sacrifice. She once again reminded him, "Gerhard, you must stop calling what I am doing a sacrifice. I am running a successful business, and doing so with our daughter. This has been a true blessing."

Gerhard nodded, "Yes, it has. I will stop calling it a sacrifice. I promise."

Ada smiled, and said, "Good, but I know you will forget."

"Ah, what will I do without you in Rome, Ada?"

"You will do your work – and you will make a contribution to His Church. And you will try to make sure that those Catholics do not make the same mistakes again."

The two shared a laugh at that comment.

Ada then looked around at the half-dozen boxes of books spread around their bedroom. "Are you sure you need to take all of these books? You know, I believe the Vatican has a substantial library."

Gerhard looked at his wife sheepishly. "Well..."

"I am teasing you, Gerhard. I know that to be truly happy, you need your books." She smirked, adding, "At least you are not trying to take all of them."

"That would require a very large truck."

"Yes, I know." She shifted her tone slightly to remind her forgetful husband of what would be happening for the rest of the day. "I will leave you to finish packing up your things. I am going to the office. I will have the delivery service we use come by in the afternoon to pick up the boxes. We can have an early dinner with the children, and then to the airport."

Gerhard said, "Yes."

Ada looked at her husband. "We will manage this. As we discussed, it's a quick flight from Munich to Rome. You know how much I love visiting Rome."

"Yes. I know. While I'm reluctant to be away from home for such a length of time, I also am intrigued." He hugged his wife, and said, "You were right."

Ada stepped back, and replied, "I always appreciate when you recognize when I am correct. What are you talking about in particular?"

"You convinced me to retire to finish writing the books by assuring me that I would still be serving Him and His Church. And you were right."

She smiled. "Yes, I was." Ada turned to leave their bedroom. She called from the hallway, "Gerhard, I only worry about you forgetting things. What did I say to do while you're traveling?"

He called back, "Write everything down."

"Yes. Do that, and all will work smoothly."

Gerhard Fletcher looked around, spotted his pad and pen, and wrote, "Boxes being picked up this afternoon."

Chapter 7

Three Days Later...

After the death of Pope Augustine, his predecessor, it took Pope Paul VII time to find his way. In fact, by his own account, it took years.

After reflection and much prayer, Paul – formerly Cardinal Juan Santos – acknowledged that it took far too long to find the courage, focus and purpose required to hold the office of the Vicar of Christ. Paul told his two closest aides of the regret he felt in terms of the time wasted after the death of Augustine, a man whom he had served as cardinal secretary of state. Paul expressed how disgusted he was with himself for relying upon the Vatican bureaucracy, for being diverted, and for, as he put it, "failing Christ and His Church."

Three years into his papacy, and Paul finally started to move more confidently. He began to make skillful decisions – mainly changes in staffing – that allowed him to stake out increased independence from the Vatican, while working to minimize the creation of new enemies within the Church.

He also started to fully engage his efforts to re-energize his predecessor's work to bring about greater unity among Christians around the world and across denominations during this time often referred to as being "post-Christian." That phrase – "post-Christian" – was something that this pope rejected, even detested.

As part of the effort, Pope Paul VII had invited a few key thinkers and teachers from across parts of broader

Christianity to take the first steps with him. And Paul now looked around the table at four of those individuals, along with his two close aides.

The group had just finished dinner and a comprehensive discussion of how this project would work over the coming year or so. Enthusiasm ran high.

After taking a sip of wine, the pope said with a wry smile, "So, you see that our task is simple: Strengthen and bring some unity to global Christendom by rehabilitating Martin Luther and Jan Hus in the eyes of Catholics, and by doing so, rehabilitating the Catholic Church in the eyes of Protestants. What could go wrong?"

That generated smiles and laughs around the table. A quick familiarity had grown among the group thanks to Paul putting each at ease during several one-on-one telephone conversations, and a few video meetings for the group in recent months. After the initial awkward moments at the start of this dinner, everyone seemed to quickly grow comfortable with each other.

Haley Whittacker said, "I'm excited about this entire effort, and thank you, Holy Father, for including me." She raised her glass, and the pope returned the gesture. That sparked the three remaining guests to address the pope as well.

Killian Dvorak added, "Absolutely, I am honored to be included in this group, given our purpose." He paused, and added, "And a year or two in Rome, and staying at this hotel, is nice, too. Thank you, Your Holiness."

The pope chuckled with the others.

Pastor Gerhard Fletcher tried to straighten his glasses in futility, and commented, "I feel truly blessed to even be considered for this undertaking and to be part of such an august group. It is much appreciated, and I hope that I can make a real contribution."

Father John Kohli said, "How could you not, Gerhard? Your four-volume work on Luther and the Reformation is a masterpiece."

"It is, indeed," added Pope Paul. "As is your work, Father Kohli."

"That's gracious of you, Holy Father. But quite frankly, I have to admit that I'm bewildered as to why I'm here, and a bit..." He paused, looked around the table, and finished his statement, "...well, intimidated."

Each person reacted to that comment with varying degrees of encouragement, noting that Father Kohli most certainly deserved to be in the group.

Whittacker added, "It was wonderful to discover your book, John, because of this project. It's excellent, and I've been telling everyone I know that they should read it."

"Thank you, Haley," replied Kohli.

"Yes, when this project is completed, I am sure that your book, Father Kohli, will see a jump in sales," the pope commented wryly. He shifted gears, and said, "I also want to thank each of you for agreeing to keep this project under wraps. As I've said to each of you privately, I am sorry that we need to work in secrecy like this."

Dvorak said, "I respect your wishes on this, Your Holiness, but I remain unconvinced of its necessity."

"I know that each of you might be harboring doubts about that. Perhaps you think I am being paranoid. I have mentioned several of my reasons, including that there are forces that would work to undermine your efforts, including from inside the Vatican."

Fletcher interjected, "Yes, I am sure that there will be many within Lutheranism who will be displeased with what I am a part of here. But you really think this warrants secrecy?"

The pope glanced at his two aides at the table, and then said, "I do. And as we have arranged, each of you are teaching at the Pontifical Lateran University, and that is what we are letting people know publicly. And I believe that each of you will benefit our students. It is this project that is being done at my personal and private invitation." He looked around the table. "I hope none of you feel like you are being dishonest?"

Whittacker replied, "Of course not. I regularly work on projects that I do not let anyone else know about until it's ready for publication."

Dvorak, Fletcher and Kohli nodded in agreement.

"Good. I am glad to hear that. Then it is time for our little field trip." The pope was met with quizzical looks from his four guests. He continued, "We have arranged for you..." He glanced at Whittacker. "Well, there is a reason that I have arranged for three of you to stay, and all of you to work at this particular hotel. Allow me to show you why."

One of the pope's aides had arranged a long-term contract with the Trevisani Luxury Suites to cover five rooms, or suites, on the hotel's top floor – three serving as personal rooms for Dvorak, Kohli and Fletcher, with Whittacker staying at the Whittacker's Rome apartment; one as a common gathering room; and another as a conference room. The group was enjoying dinner and conversation in the conference room.

As they exited the room, the pope's personal bodyguard, Vincent Mazzoni, was waiting in the hallway. Mazzoni ranked as the inspector general of the Vatican police force's corps. One of Mazzoni's men was in the hallway as well, with another in the staircase, and a fourth who was outside. He drove the pope's private, armored SUV.

The pope smiled and asked, "All is well, Vincent?"

"Yes, Holy Father."

"Well, we're going for that short walk I mentioned."

Mazzoni sighed, and said, "Yes, of course, we are."

The pope chuckled, and announced to the others, "Vincent does not appreciate my insistence on moving about, well, let's just say, not according to a set schedule at times."

While he nodded at the other officer in the hall, Mazzoni replied, "I do not mind at all, Holy Father. Your unpredictability is something of a plus, since if I am unaware of what you might be doing next, anyone seeking to do you harm would be even more clueless."

"That is one of the reasons why I like you, Vincent."

"Thank you, Holy Father." Mazzoni rarely smiled while working, and he didn't in this instance. Indeed, there was an intensity in his dark brown eyes that told a story of deep concentration. But at times, a tonal shift in the voice of this intense cop, standing just under six feet with thick black hair and matching eyebrows, indicated a friendly relationship between pope and bodyguard that went beyond strict professionalism.

Mazzoni received clearance from his officer, and Pope Paul VII and his party were led down the stairs. They passed by the front desk of the hotel without incident. When venturing out on his unscheduled journeys, Pope Paul VII wore distinctly non-pope attire, in effect, the clothing of a humble priest. He was rarely recognized as a result. However, as the group approached the front of the hotel, recognition began to dawn on the face of the doorman. Paul simply smiled and then raised a finger to his lips, indicating that the man should remain silent. The doorman said nothing, though he half-nodded, half-bowed with his head several times as he pulled open the door and the group stepped into the cool night.

They crossed the street, and turned left. The pope was guiding the small assembly toward a church that stood a couple of hundred yards away.

With hands on holstered weapons inside their dark suit jackets, Mazzoni and his men constantly surveyed the area as the group moved forward.

Fletcher commented, "Ah, we are headed to the Chiesa del Gesù. I had assumed that it was a mere coincidence that our hotel was just down the street from the mother church of the Jesuits."

Paul smiled and shook his head. "No. It was no coincidence. Nor is it a coincidence that you can see this church from the windows of your rooms."

They crossed another street, entering the Piazza del Gesù, and approached the church. They stopped, and Pope Paul VII turned and looked at the group. "I do not want what I am about to say to you to be misinterpreted. It is not meant to be a slap at the Jesuits, nor at this beautiful 16th-century church." He glanced directly at Father Kohli. "In fact, I love most of the artwork found here, ultimately created to honor and perhaps bring us closer to the Father, Son and Holy Spirit. I also am not one who agrees with changing or covering up history when we do not like certain things. Yet, those who believe that all in the Church have always acted constructively over the centuries are guilty of their own form of historical distortion. We are the Church, warts and all."

The pope's four guests nodded slightly, and waited.

Pope Paul VII went on, "Now, I've brought you here to simply point out a statue." He looked at Mazzoni, and said, "Shall we, Vincent?"

Mazzoni unlocked a church door, and sent in one of his men. "Please give us a moment, Your Holiness." After it was announced that the building was clear, the group followed the pope inside, and then to the Chapel of St. Ignatius. The saint's remains were contained in a gilded bronze tomb on an altar. The pope led his guests and aides to the large statue on the right.

Paul said, "I understand that you know all or most of this, but please indulge me. It is important that this statue be kept in mind as you proceed with your work. It is called *The Triumph of Faith over Heresy*, created by Pierre Le Gros. And his skill and craftsmanship are evident. However, what exactly are we looking at?" As he proceeded to talk about the large statue, he pointed. "Mary stands with a flame in one hand and a cross in the other. In fact, she is standing on two men who seem to be crying out in fear and even agony. The men also are wrapped by a serpent, with all three apparently falling into hell." He took a deep breath, and turned to look at the group. "The two men, of course, are Martin Luther and Jan Hus."

Dvorak commented, "Subtle."

Paul replied, "Well, you do have to look more closely to read words on the covers of these scrolls and books. There is 'Luther,' and just in case you thought he was forgotten, there is 'Calvin.'"

Fletcher chimed in, "I'm sure our Presbyterian and Reformed friends feel better about not being left out."

Pope Paul VII returned his eyes to the statue. "Yes, and I believe the angel" – he pointed to an angel also at the foot of Mary – "is tearing pages out of a work by Zwingli."

"Subtle *and* comprehensive," added Whittacker.

The pope said, "This is a product of a very different time – highly politicized with government and the Church deeply intertwined, and seemingly all dissent, on occasion even debate, met with accusation of heresy and sometimes the worst kind of suppression. Yet, it also is a celebration of the Counter-Reformation."

The others stood in silence.

The pope looked over at the coffin. "St. Ignatius of Loyola there, or what remains of his body, not only founded the Jesuits, but he did much of the work to get this church built. And there is a statue of him in St. Peter's Basilica with his left foot on Martin Luther, who is wrapped by a serpent with his face contorted in agony."

Dvorak again interjected, "There seems to be a pattern here."

Kohli said, "Yes, well, it is important to understand that the Jesuits were officially formed in 1540, in part, as a response to Protestants, and the society played a central role in the Counter-Reformation and the Council of Trent."

Pope Paul VII declared, "All true. My point for bringing you here is that this is more than distant history for many. Significant segments within Catholicism remain strictly attached to the sentiments expressed in this statue." He paused. "Once your work goes public, there will be many negative reactions, including accusations of heresy."

Fletcher noted, "Yes, and there will be similar charges from certain Lutheran and Protestant circles."

The pope nodded. "Indeed. Hence, beyond what each of you already has accomplished independently, your work together must be thorough, fair and truthful, and make clear why Catholics should put aside notions that Luther and Hus were enemies of the Church, and instead, that these two men can and should be embraced as heroes of the faith – even given our ongoing disagreements, along with the shortcomings of all involved in these earlier disputes, including both Luther and Hus. And as I have made clear to you, the differences that remain must be acknowledged, not glossed over, and you also are not in the business of hagiography." He looked at each of his four guests, and added, "I apologize. Not only do I repeat myself, but I do a disservice to each of you as scholars. I know we are in agreement." The pope once more paused and took a deep breath. "Given the historic and controversial nature of this project, it is crucial to communicate the results and overarching message at the right time. This statue serves as a symbol of why your work is essential, and why it must remain secret until completed and the time is right."

Whittacker commented, "I see your point, Holy Father."

Dvorak smiled, and said, "Okay, you have convinced me."

The other two researchers declared their agreement.

Pope Paul VII asked, "Do you know what I think about at my most enthusiastic moments regarding this undertaking?" The group waited for him to continue. "At the end of your public presentation on your work, I dream of announcing that two works have been commissioned – a statue of Jan Hus and a statue of Martin Luther that will find homes inside St. Peter's Basilica. Perhaps some would see it as a small gesture. I disagree. I think it would send a clear message to brothers and sisters across Christianity." He paused, smiled and added, "Ah, we can dream, correct?"

Kohli commented, "Yes, and we can pray, Holy Father."

Fletcher added, "At least in terms of where the Jesuits are today, I think it's safe to say that you would, ironically, get some strong support from many of them."

Whittacker said, "Yes, well, the Jesuits of today are quite different from the days of St. Ignatius and the Counter-Reformation."

The pope looked at Kohli, and asked, "Being a product of Jesuit education, Father Kohli, would you agree?"

Kohli answered, "Like much of the Church, Your Holiness, the Jesuits possess a wide array of views."

Chapter 8

After leaving the Chiesa del Gesù – or the Church of Jesus – Father Kohli, Pastor Fletcher and Killian Dvorak returned to the hotel. Haley Whittacker started up her car, which had been parked on the street not far from the church, and began the short drive to her apartment.

Pope Paul VII was in the specially designed SUV for the drive to the Papal Apartments in the Apostolic Palace. Vincent Mazzoni was in the front passenger seat, next to the driver, and the other two Gendarme Corps officers sat in a bench-like seat looking out the back of the vehicle. In the middle was a forward-pointing bench, and two separate chairs backed up against the driver and front passenger seats.

Pope Paul VII sat on the middle bench, with his two aides – Cardinal Winston Treadwell and Father Mariano Concepcion – facing him. He said, "I don't recall such a stretch of time in which the two of you said so little."

At 38, Father Mariano Concepcion was the youngest of the three clergy. His short black hair had no traces of gray, unlike Paul and the cardinal. The age difference and the fact that he traveled with a pope and a cardinal set Concepcion's default position at deferential. He shifted his brown eyes to Cardinal Treadwell, who looked back at him in silence. The nasally tone to the priest's voice was almost expected given how thin his nostrils appeared. "I was content to listen for most of the night, Holy Father."

Treadwell nodded in agreement.

Paul said, "Listen? You two knew what I was going to say before the night started."

Treadwell responded, "We were not listening to you, Holy Father..."

Paul interrupted, "Oh, really, Winston?"

The Australian cardinal replied, "What? Oh, no, that's not what I meant, Holy Father. You must know that I would never..."

As Concepcion smiled and shook his head slightly, Paul VII said, "I know, Winston. I was merely joking."

Treadwell, a tall, obese man in his early sixties, shifted a bit in his seat, which generated some redness in the face along with heavy breaths. He held a black cane, with a silver frog on top, in his right hand. "Yes, of course. Mariano and I were listening to the responses from your researchers, as well as watching their body language."

"And what did either of you discover?"

"I am afraid not very much," replied Treadwell.

However, Concepcion added, "It became apparent to me that each is committed to the work and the goal."

Paul VII said, "I agree. I also like each of them. It is a good group."

Concepcion nodded.

Treadwell replied, "Yes, but I am not completely sure about Professor Dvorak."

The pope said, "His scholarship is excellent, but I understand what you are saying. However, you will have time – at least a year-and-a-half – to work on him, Winston. We are all sinners."

Treadwell seemed taken off guard once again, and answered, "Well, yes, naturally." He actually spun the cane.

"You know, it was Professor Fuchs who specifically recommended Professor Dvorak. I miss that little Lutheran. He was so good-natured, and I wanted to meet his wife. He had said that she was terribly excited to be coming with him. That was so horrible. God rest both their souls."

Treadwell said, "Last I heard, no one had yet been arrested for the murders."

The pope said, "No. No action."

Treadwell broke a few seconds of silence. "Other issues remain."

"Yes, they do, as the three of us have discussed, with you" – he looked directly at Treadwell – "my friend, ably playing the role of devil's advocate. I appreciate your not being a mere 'yes man' for what I am trying to do, but at the same time, having faith in my, in our, efforts." He turned his head to Concepcion and said, "And your support, Mariano, and willingness to undertake so many tasks has been a precious gift."

"You are welcome, Holy Father," replied Concepcion.

Treadwell waved the frog atop the cane. "No, Holy Father, thank you for what you are attempting, and for having me play some part."

Paul stared at his top aides, two men who had become trusted friends. "The best decision that I have made in this office was to finally move Cardinal Bessetti into another position, and make you, Winston, my cardinal secretary of state. Bessetti is not exactly subtle in playing politics, and maneuvering the bureaucracy for his own wishes." Paul VII seemed to be speaking out loud to himself at this point. "Why I let that go on for so long, I don't know. He is still too close. It will soon be time to move him again." He stared out the SUV window as the vehicle crossed over the Tiber River. He then seemed to shake off whatever was on his mind. "And the second best decision was to invite you, Mariano, to work with me."

The three fell silent, once more, as the driver guided the SUV along the tight streets of Vatican City. Each head turned to catch a view of Saint Peter's Square as the vehicle crossed over a wide avenue.

Treadwell merely said, "Hus and Luther." He then looked at the pope and laughed. Paul responded with a broad smile.

Concepcion added, "It is a bold undertaking, Holy Father."

Paul VII declared, "As Father Kohli reminded us, we can pray." He then added, "Yes, let us pray."

As the three men blessed themselves, bowed their heads, and the pope started a brief prayer, Vincent Mazzoni glanced over his shoulder and then closed his eyes.

Chapter 9

One Year Later...

"Well, I don't know about the rest of you, but I'm looking forward to the week off," commented Father John Kohli. "I need a break from Hus and Luther. Time to clear my head."

"Where are you headed on that motorcycle?" asked Haley Whittacker.

"Taking the coast all the way down to Marsala. And the weather is supposed to be perfect – sunny and warmer than usual."

"Sounds like a bucket list kind of thing to do, well, for you, John," commented Killian Dvorak. "Something you should be doing with a very good friend, perhaps?"

Pastor Gerhard Fletcher raised an eyebrow, as he scratched a spot on his scalp under messy hair.

Kohli sighed. "Yes, thanks, Killian. Sister Katharine Malone flies in tonight, and we are riding and sightseeing together."

The four were seated at an outdoor café around the corner from the Trevisani hotel where they had been working, and three of them had been living, for the past year. Pope Paul VII's team of researchers had made considerable progress on this still-secret project, while also teaching at the Pontifical Lateran University. Their work eventually was to be assembled into a multi-volume report detailing the key aspects of Hus and Luther's respective writings on Scripture and theology, including the sacraments and the Church, along with evaluations of those views as well as arguments from both supporters and critics during an era covering more than 150 years. Areas of agreement and disagreement between these two reformers and the post-Vatican II Catholic Church were to be examined, and finally, an assessment made of how far an attempted embrace of Martin Luther and Jan Hus might be able to go more than 600 years after the death of Hus and more than 470 years since Luther died.

Dvorak commented, "That is shocking, Father. I trust you and Sister Katharine will be staying in separate rooms during your journey?"

The four authors and scholars had coalesced into a close-knit group of friends, even given their different backgrounds, personalities and idiosyncrasies. A sense of comradery and working together for a larger goal, in service of the Church, hadn't taken long to develop. That wasn't surprising, given what they shared in terms of scholarship, interests and passions – at least when it came to Church history. Each person and the group benefited from encouragement from Pope Paul VII.

Whittacker said, "Oh, Killian, stop it."

Looking at Dvorak, Kohli replied, "Yes, Killian, there will be nothing inappropriate on my end, and what are your plans for the coming week?"

Dvorak laughed, "Very good, John, very good. Let's just say that I will be spending the week showing a special young lady around Rome."

Kohli and Whittacker shook their heads, while Fletcher commented, "Killian, I pray for you every night."

Dvorak's expression turned serious for a moment, and he said, "I know, Gerhard. Thank you."

All four were getting close to finishing their respective lunches. It was typical for them to eat lunch at this café on a Friday, particularly during nice weather. It was convenient; the sandwiches, salads, soups and other dishes ably represented food options of Rome; and the group found that the outdoor setting led to more relaxed conversation, whether pertaining to their project or whatever else might be going on in their lives.

Kohli was eating a prosciutto and crusty ridged roll sandwich. Dvorak worked on devouring *porchetta di ariccia* on a crusty roll. And Fletcher had prosciutto, arugula, and robiola cheese on a thin flatbread, with Whittacker clearly enjoying *mozzarella di bufala* combined with tomato juice, olive oil and basil on a soft, thick roll.

After chewing a bite of her sandwich, Whittacker looked at Kohli, and observed, "But she – I mean, Sister Katharine – is on your mind a good deal, John. It's obvious to each of us." She looked at Fletcher and Dvorak, with each looking down and taking large bites of their sandwiches.

Kohli shifted in his chair, and said, "We're good friends, and share many of the same interests. Yes, that's true. But each of us has chosen to serve the Lord in particular ways." His voice trailed off, and he, too, took a bite of his food.

Dvorak swallowed, and asked, "You're heading home to England, for the week, Haley?"

She nodded, "I am. I miss Sewards End, and my cottage."

Fletcher said, "Your cottage? Are you going home to do more work?"

"I am. I'm enjoying everything that we're doing here – the research, the writing and the lecturing at the university. But there's something about my cottage. It's my happy place. It allows me to rest, recharge and clear the head, and generate some thoughts and ideas."

Dvorak commented, "Well, I look forward to hearing what insights you return with after this short break."

Fletcher asked, "Do you and Conrad have any plans?"

Whittacker's usual enthusiasm seemed to deflate ever so slightly. "No, he is staying in Rome for work."

Kohli inquired, "Is everything okay, Haley?"

She looked at her colleagues and friends around the small table. "To be honest, it's been a trifle odd of late. Conrad has been a bit – well, there's no other word for it – cranky in recent weeks whenever I bring up our work."

Fletcher said, "Hmmm. Why?"

"I'm not sure. He won't talk about it, other than pushing to find out when it will be finished." She took a sip of her sparkling water. "He's never exactly been talkative. But this is different. He won't acknowledge that something is bothering him, but it's clear to me that something is."

Dvorak smiled, "Ugh, the woes of being married." He turned to Kohli, adding, "Something we don't have to worry about, right, John?" When no one laughed, Dvorak defensively added, "Okay, friends, I was just trying to make a joke, you know, to help."

Whittacker smiled, not as brightly as usual, and said, "Thanks for trying, Killian." She added unconvincingly, "I'm sure everything will work out." The sandwiches were finished. After swallowing her last bite, Whittacker said, "Thank God we only do this on Fridays. Otherwise, I'd be putting on a lot of weight. And Conrad and I are having dinner before I fly back to England tonight."

Fletcher said, "At least you're more disciplined than me, Haley. I have added 20 pounds over the past year." He looked around the table, smiled sheepishly, and added, "Ada thinks I look cuter."

Everyone laughed.

Whittacker said, "So, you're heading home, rather than Ada coming here?"

Fletcher smiled, as he usually did at the mention of his wife. "Yes, this time I am actually driving home, rather than flying."

Kohli asked, "Isn't that a long drive?"

Fletcher shrugged. "It's probably ten or eleven hours driving. But like you, John, I enjoy the drive. I take in the countryside. I'll start out in a couple of hours, and tonight I'll stay at a little inn just south of Bologna. Ada and I love it. It's called the Full Bloom Inn." He looked at Whittacker, and added, "You and Conrad should stay there. It's quiet, beautiful, and has wonderful local food and wine." When Haley merely nodded in response, Fletcher continued, "I will then make the rest of the journey tomorrow. Once home, the children will visit." He paused, looked around the table, and asked, "Did I mention to each of you that a grandchild is on the way?"

All three of his colleagues smiled, nodded, and congratulated him for the third time since the news had been delivered earlier in the week.

Fletcher continued, "Ada and I plan to have dinner at a couple of our favorite local restaurants as well. I am looking forward to it."

The group paid their check, and began the short walk back to their hotel workplace. While strolling along, Whittacker moved next to Kohli, and beyond the earshot of Dvorak and Fletcher, whispered, "You know, as Gerhard reminds us, we can choose many different ways to serve God and His Church."

Kohli briefly looked at Whittacker, but said nothing.

Chapter 10

During their early dinner, the conversation between Conrad and Haley Whittacker was little more than perfunctory. It amounted to a comparison of schedules over the coming week or so.

Haley would be flying home to Sewards End, while Conrad remained in Rome to deal with work.

The couple sat in the back seat of the Rolls-Royce Phantom gazing out separate windows in silence, with Albro Dawson behind the wheel.

Conrad turned away from the window, looked over at Haley, and gently placed his hand on hers. Haley actually jumped ever so slightly in apparent surprise. He said, "I'm sorry, Haley."

She looked at her husband, and replied, "Sorry?"

"I have been increasingly distant for months now, and I apologize. It certainly has not been fair to you."

Haley's face actually brightened. "It's been very strange, Conrad. You not only seem distant, but annoyed whenever my work comes up."

Conrad responded, "That has not been your fault." He shifted in the seat slightly, and quickly glanced at Dawson's eyes in the rearview mirror. "I have not been forthright with you in terms of what has been happening with the company."

"Yes?"

He took a deep breath. "We are having cash flow issues. It's a timing matter. We are still investing heavily in various technologies, but have yet to experience the expected revenue growth."

Haley nodded, "How bad is it, Conrad?"

He smiled, and said, "Actually, it appears that we have just secured the additional investments needed to solve the problem."

Haley also smiled. "That's wonderful, Conrad."

He nodded, and said, "It is. Finalizing the details largely will be my focus over the next two or three weeks. But it will make the difference, and things should get back to normal."

Haley leaned over and gave her husband a quick kiss on the cheek. "I can't tell you how happy I am to hear that."

"And no doubt, you also will be pleased to see your cottage, once again."

She nodded.

He added, "And what will your colleagues be up to during their week off?"

"John is riding his motorcycle down the coast to Marsala. Killian is staying in Rome, let's just say entertaining."

"That man needs to grow up, and get responsible."

Haley continued, "And Gerhard actually is driving home to Munich."

"Driving?"

"Yes. He enjoys the drive, and is staying tonight at a place that he recommended to us. It's just south of Bologna, and supposedly is quiet, pretty and there's some great food and wine. He and Ada stay there on occasion."

"Sounds nice. What is it called?"

"Oh, what did he say?" She thought for a moment. "That's right. It's called The Full Bloom Inn."

"Well, since Gerhard and Ada like it, perhaps we should give it a try at some point?"

"I'd love that." She paused, and then added, "I failed to mention it, but Gerhard and Ada's daughter is pregnant. He's very excited about becoming a grandfather."

Conrad glanced out the window, and replied, "Oh, that is very nice." He paused, and turned back, and said, "I'm also sorry about ignoring your work throughout this. Are things coming along well?"

Haley got visibly more excited. "It is, very much. Killian and I are very close to getting our first drafts done on Hus. We're perhaps a month away, and then the plan is for each of us to trade off the work we've done so far in order to review, question, suggest and so on in terms of what the others have done."

"So, you are feeling good about putting forth a publication and plan that the pope will be able to use regarding both Hus and Luther?"

She nodded. "I actually never doubted it. That's part of the reason I took this project on in the first place. But you know that. We discussed it."

"Yes, yes, we did." He smiled. "I'd be more than happy to take a look at what you and Killian have achieved so far, if you need another set of eyes."

"That would be wonderful, Conrad." She pulled her briefcase up from the floor. While opening it and looking inside, she said, "I have it all backed up on a few thumb drives, as does Killian." She pulled out a small, black and red thumb drive, and presented it to her husband. "Here, take this one. I'd love to get your thoughts. Thanks."

He took the thumb drive, dropped it in the inside pocket of his suit jacket, and replied, "You are welcome."

Dawson interrupted, "Sir, madam, we will be arriving at the airport shortly."

They both thanked him.

Chapter 11

Pastor Gerhard Fletcher was seated at a table on a stone patio several yards away from the main backdoor of the Full Bloom Inn. The night sky was clear, and the moonlight luminous.

Fletcher had arrived at the inn 45 minutes earlier. He checked into his room, and immediately made his way back downstairs. Given that it was just after ten, Fletcher clearly was pleased to be able to still order a small antipasto plate, along with a half-bottle of a Dolcetto red wine.

While waiting for the order, he gazed out at the countryside, while talking on his cellphone. "Yes, it is an amazing night, Ada. The moon is so bright that I can actually see the hills rolling away from me."

His wife replied, "You are now guilty of what we complain about others doing while staying there."

"What do you mean?"

"You are talking on a phone, and not fully appreciating everything around you."

"Ah, but I love it more when you are here with me."

Ada said, "I understand. We will be staying there again soon, together. And fortunately, I will see you tomorrow right here at home. So, now is the time for you to savor the moment there."

"You are always so wise."

"Thank you, Gerhard. Please do not forget to check the room fully to make sure that you do not leave anything behind."

Gerhard smiled, and said, "Should I write that down on my list?"

"Of course you should."

As the two laughed, a waiter quietly deposited a tray on the table. Gerhard looked up at the pudgy young man and nodded. The waiter smiled back, and went back inside the inn.

"I love you, Ada," said Gerhard into his phone.

"I love you, too, Gerhard. By the way, are you having a glass of Dolcetto?"

"A half-bottle just arrived. Do you know why I drink this wine?" This was a game the two played.

"I do not know, Gerhard, why?"

"'Dolcetto' means 'little sweet one,' and it reminds me of you."

"You, too, are sweet, Gerhard. And a half-bottle will help you sleep. Good night."

"Good night, Ada, my little sweet one."

Gerhard Fletcher failed to notice that it was now a different man arriving at the table. Dressed like a waiter, he had come through an opening in the hedges rather than from inside the building.

The man was quite different from the waiter who had brought out the wine and food. His face was thin, with narrow eyes and a pointed nose. He asked, "Shall I pour your wine, sir?"

Gerhard smiled, and said, "Yes, thank you."

Since Gerhard's gaze, once again, returned to the hills drenched in moonlight, he failed to notice the small amount of liquid the new waiter deposited into the glass along with the wine. Even if Gerhard had been watching, however, it's unlikely he would have spotted the tiny vial attached to the man's wrist, and the movement of a middle finger that triggered the liquid being shot into the glass.

The man stood waiting after placing the glass in front of Fletcher.

Gerhard took note of the man not moving, and said, "Oh, yes, of course." He picked up the glass, considered the wine's aroma, and took a healthy sip. Gerhard nodded, and said, "Yes. Very good." He placed the glass back down on the table.

After several seconds, he glanced up at the waiter who had not yet moved. Gerhard asked, "Is there something else?"

The man waited, simply staring down at Fletcher.

Suddenly, Gerhard's face contorted in a look of both surprise and fear. He grabbed and began to pull at the shirt covering his chest. He then started to kick his right leg.

The man impersonating a waiter calmly looked down at Gerhard Fletcher. And then he reached out with his right hand, and placed it on Fletcher's forehead. While Fletcher's eyes darted around in fear, Father Pietro Filoni then closed his own eyes, and said, "May the Lord who frees you from sin save you and raise you up."

Filoni opened his eyes to see Gerhard Fletcher's body absent of any movement. Filoni felt for a pulse. There was none. He then ran his hand over Fletcher's eyes, hiding the vacant gaze behind closed lids.

Filoni turned and disappeared between the hedges. He left behind no trace of being there.

Chapter 12

As Father Pietro Filoni emerged from the hedgerow, he removed the white waiter's jacket, rolled it up and shoved it under his left arm. He now was dressed entirely in black, though the moonlight didn't allow him to be fully cloaked in night darkness.

Nonetheless, as Filoni moved by the handful of cars parked in the inn's lot, he didn't run. Instead, he walked with an air of casualness.

A dark sedan was waiting along the side of the road just a few yards beyond the parking lot.

Filoni walked up to the front passenger side door, opened it, lowered himself into the seat, and closed the door. Two men, both in their mid-thirties, were waiting.

Father Lorenzo Conti was behind the wheel. Conti was six feet tall, muscular, and square-jawed, with thick, unruly eyebrows out of sync with tightly cut black hair.

In the back seat was Father Michael Russo, who was notably shorter than Conti, and built like a fireplug. His head was shaved, which accentuated the size of a noteworthy nose.

Filoni took a deep breath, and then turned to his comrades. "It is done."

The two men nodded.

Filoni continued, "Let us give thanks." The three men bowed their heads, and Filoni said, "May God the Father continue to bless these arduous tasks we, the Shadow Servants of the Holy Father, undertake to protect His Church and His servant, the pope."

Conti and Russo replied, "Amen."

Filoni looked up, and said, "This work is hard, but it is what we are called to do."

Conti and Russo nodded, and, again, said, "Amen."

Filoni then pulled on his seat belt, and said, "Let's get out of here."

Conti started up the car, and drove away.

It would be several more minutes before the pudgy waiter discovered the work done that night by the Shadow Servants of the Holy Father. That is, before the lifeless body of Gerhard Fletcher was found.

Chapter 13

The funeral for Pastor Gerhard Fletcher in Munich overflowed with mourners. It wasn't that the church was small. Rather, the attendance reflected the number of lives that Fletcher had touched as a parish pastor, author, friend and father.

During the two-day viewing and after the funeral, Ada Fletcher heard a seemingly endless string of people saying "thank you" and trying to articulate an appreciation for how her husband had made a difference in their lives. Her strength and faith were apparent throughout, as was her deep love for her husband. Over the three days, Father John Kohli watched Ada up close and at a distance.

After prayers and some farewells at the cemetery, Fletcher's three friends, along with two more people, found their way into a small pub. The five individuals sat quietly in a booth at a round table. A waitress distributed their drinks. Pints of beer were deposited in front of Killian Dvorak, Kohli, and Sister Katharine Malone, while glasses of wine went to Haley Whittacker, and her husband, Conrad.

Kohli broke the silence. He raised his glass, and said, "To Gerhard, pastor, scholar, and our dear friend. God rest his soul. And to his wife, Ada, and the rest of his family. May God grant them faith and strength."

The other four raised their glasses, and said, "Amen."

During the next hour-plus, Killian, Haley and John told stories about working and becoming friends with Gerhard. Laughter was mixed with some tears, and quiet reflection.

Throughout, Conrad sat straight, smiled periodically, but largely remained silent. If one got the impression that he was patiently waiting for this gathering to end, it would not have been without reason.

As for Sister Malone, she seemed to more naturally fit in with the group – laughing and showing empathy along the way. The nun's support for her friend, Father Kohli, was unmistakable.

After a pause in the conversation, Killian asked the question that had only been hinted at since news of Gerhard's death. "Well, what are we telling the pope? Are we forging ahead?"

Haley answered, "How can we not? This was the last project that Gerhard was working on, and I know he viewed it as being important to the future of the entire Church."

John was about to add something, but Conrad interjected. "Is it possible to continue without Pastor Fletcher? And given the earlier death of – what was his name? – Professor Fuchs, can the work be completed properly?"

Haley's body language made clear her discomfort with the comments from her husband.

John looked at Haley, and said, "I agree with you, Haley." He then shifted his gaze to her husband, adding, "But you raise a legitimate question, Conrad." He then looked back and forth at Killian and Haley, adding, "How do we make up for the loss of Gerhard, not to mention that Harold Fuchs was supposed to lead this effort?"

Killian looked at his glass, and said to no one in particular, "We've lost our two Lutherans." He took a drink of beer.

Haley asked, "What are you thinking?"

He replied, "It had not occurred to me, but I know a stellar historian who understands this material inside and out. He actually studied with Professor Fuchs as well. He would be perfect to step in, if we can get him interested."

John asked, "Who is it?"

"Richard Leonard. He is a history professor and a pastor in New York City. He heads up the department at the Lutheran University of New York. But he also is in the midst of some rather considerable career and life changes. This project, however, might work for him."

Haley took a deep breath. "We should discuss this at length. But now is not the time. It feels wrong."

John and Killian nodded in agreement.

Some additional thoughts about Gerhard were shared, and finally, it was time for the group to go their separate ways.

For Haley and Killian, the focus turned to Katharine.

Haley and Katharine hugged briefly. The taller Katharine had to lean down slightly. Haley looked up and said, "It was nice to meet you, if only it were under different circumstances. I'm sorry that you missed out on your motorcycle tour of Italy."

Katharine replied, "Thanks, but never mind that. I'm so sorry about the loss of your friend."

Haley nodded, as Conrad said his good-byes. The couple left the pub.

Katharine said, "It was good meeting you, Killian."

Killian Dvorak smiled slightly at John, and then looked at Katharine. "It was nice meeting you as well. I, too, am sorry about your missing out on the riding tour down the coast. However, it was good, I would say, that you were here for John." Both John and Katharine looked down somewhat awkwardly. Killian added, "Ah, but perhaps you two will get another chance for such a memorable motorcycle ride."

With a touch of exasperation in his voice, John said, "Alright, Killian. You take care."

Killian's smile broadened. "Yes, of course. Good-bye."

As he started to head for the door, John said, "Behave yourself, Killian."

Turning, Killian wore a mischievous smile. He said, "You, too, John."

Kohli raised an eyebrow.

Dvorak turned and exited the pub.

John and Katharine were left alone, and sat back down at the table. She said, "That's a good group, John."

"For the most part."

"Ah, Killian?"

He nodded, and drained the last drop of his beer.

Katharine said, "He is the person in the group who likes to tweak the others."

"Most definitely."

"But he also sees something. I'm guessing that so does Haley?"

John merely nodded.

Katharine volunteered, "I've missed you as well."

After a few more moments of silence, John said, "Listen, you're still here for three more days. How about we get back to Rome, and hit the road, at least for a day or so?"

She smiled, and replied, "I'd like that."

He added, "And since people are seeing things, perhaps we need to talk some more about ... our situation?"

Katharine's voice got a bit smaller. "Yes, we should."

Chapter 14

During the short flight from Munich to Rome, Father John Kohli and Sister Katharine Malone excitedly planned out the following day's ride.

They set out at daybreak. Two rooms at an inn on the coast in Acciaroli awaited them at the end of the day. The two planned to leisurely enjoy the ride, the views, and some food on a daylong journey. After staying for a few hours at the small hotel, they would take a straight ride back to Rome early the next day, gather up Katharine's remaining items, and then get her to the airport for her flight home.

Mid-afternoon they made one of their several stops – this time to look down on the Mediterranean Sea in Santa Nicola A Mare. They sat next to each other on a large boulder.

The sun made everything bright, shimmering on the crystal blue waters below. Given the recent focus on Gerhard Fletcher's death, the view had the effect of raising their respective moods. It was clear to anyone who might have been watching throughout the day that the two were enjoying the journey south. Indeed, it might even seem like they were a happy couple, in love and enjoying a vacation.

Katharine stared at the waters, and asked, "Did I ever tell you why I became a nun?"

John looked at her, and replied, "You said that after your parents died, you felt like that was what you were called to do. That you felt lost, and that the Church was there for you, and you wanted to be there in return, and for the children you could help by becoming a teacher."

Katharine smiled. "I guess I did tell you. Sometimes I forget how much I've told you, how much you know about me." She turned and looked at him. Their mutual gaze lingered. She turned back to the water first, and he then did the same. She continued, "It was a bit strange. I know I've never told anyone this, but I never felt comfortable during my postulancy and novitiate."

"Really? Why?"

"I never felt like I completely fit. It was just a nagging in the back of my head."

John nodded his head. "I think we've all had doubts at times along the way."

"Yeah, I suppose."

"Is there more? When did you finally get comfortable?"

Katharine sighed, and turned her head slightly away from John. "It wasn't until I became the principal at St. Michael's."

John said, "It was evident to me when I arrived at St. Michael's. You were in the right spot."

"I had only been the principal for a year at that point. I was still figuring things out."

"Sure. But you definitely figured it out. You grew into the job quickly. I've watched you do great work."

She remained silent for several seconds, and when she turned back, Katharine's eyes were moist. John's eyes widened in surprise.

Katharine said, "I swore to myself that I'd never tell you this."

"What is it?"

"It never felt right until you and I got to know each other, worked together, and became ... friends."

John stared into her eyes for several seconds, and then he turned to look out at the Mediterranean. After several minutes of silence, Katharine asked, "What are you thinking?"

"Can I make a confession?"

"Please, join me."

They both smiled.

"Part of me was jealous or envious of Gerhard." He paused. Katharine said nothing. So, John plowed ahead. "Everything I learned about Gerhard and Ada while working with him, seeing them both together a few times and then watching her at the wake and funeral, they had a deep love. As some people put it, they had the real thing. And they shared in each other's work and interests, and their faith."

Katharine seemed to be fighting off tears and could only manage a nod in response. She looked back at the water.

John slid off the boulder, looked up at Katharine, and smiled. He said, "Let's get back to our ride."

She stared back at him, and finally began to move to get off the boulder. John reached a hand up to her. Katharine paused, looked at the hand and then at John's face. He continued to smile, and then nodded. She took his hand, and jumped down.

As they turned to walk back to the motorcycles, rather than letting her hand go, John kept her hand in his. She didn't pull away, but did just the opposite. They then intertwined their fingers. The couple walked hand-in-hand back to the bikes.

*   *   *

John stirred just before 3:30 AM. He rolled over. Kathy was no longer next to him, but she had left a crease in the pillow.

He pushed himself up onto his elbows, and said, "Kathy?"

There was no light coming from the bathroom.

When they had exited the elevator earlier, she never made it to her room. After the elevator doors closed, the two kissed in the hallway, more or less stumbled into John's room, and then undressed while maneuvering their way into bed. They eventually fell asleep together.

John got out of bed, and slipped on sweatpants and a t-shirt. He grabbed his room key off the desk, and exited into the hallway. He went to the room where Katharine was registered, and knocked. No one answered.

John returned to his room, and spotted the hotel notepad with writing on it resting on the small dresser. He picked up the note and sat down on the edge of the bed.

Dear John,

I am so sorry to do this to you. I'm on my way to the airport, and please don't follow me. I have to think about what's happened, about us, well, about everything.

I'm so torn about the wonderful day and night we just shared. I wouldn't trade away a moment of it for anything, but I also know that we were wrong to do it. I woke up next to you, and that conflict hit me hard.

I'm suddenly unsure about everything in my life, except for two things - my love for the Lord and my love for you. Yes, I left it unsaid, obviously, for so long. And I didn't even say it while with you this night. But I love you, John. I have for some time, and will throughout whatever comes our way.

I promise to talk soon.

No matter what we choose, yours forever,

Kathy

John said out loud, "It's literally a 'Dear John' letter." He chuckled, and laid back on the end of the bed. As he stared up at the ceiling, tears formed in his eyes and began to slide down his cheeks.

He reached for his phone on the nightstand. He texted Katharine: "I'm having the same thoughts. Take some time. Pray. I know I have to as well. I've loved you since shortly after arriving at St. Michael's, torn between hoping that you would come to love me, while also hoping you wouldn't. No matter what, this will be hard, but my love for you will never falter."

Chapter 15

It was nearly three weeks after the death of Pastor Gerhard Fletcher. Professor Killian Dvorak sat across from Pope Paul VII in a relatively small, comfortable room in the Papal Apartments. The two men were alone, and their discussion had been running for more than an hour.

The pope glanced at his watch and said, "Well, Killian, indulge me by summing up the case for Professor Leonard becoming part of this group."

Dvorak smiled, and replied, "Of course. Richard's not only a Lutheran pastor, but he's a brilliant historian. His expertise and scholarship focus on the Reformation, the Church, Islam and the Crusades. He earned the position of chairing the history department at the Lutheran University of New York. Interestingly, Richard managed to gain that spot while still making the right friends and the right opponents, if you will, by defending traditional Christianity and thanks to correcting errors regarding the history of the Christian Church, whether those errors be sins of omission or commission, or simply due to ignorance. His work fits in nicely with our mission. And he is no pushover. His integrity is not in doubt."

The pope nodded, and said, "Impressive for a man so young."

Dvorak continued, "Yes, he's only in his early thirties. He also was the pastor at St. Mark's Lutheran Church, which, in effect, is the home congregation for the university."

"One of the churches targeted in those series of terrorist attacks."

"Correct."

"But now he is involved in this effort to counter Christian persecution?" asked Pope Paul VII.

Dvorak now was nodding in response. "Yes, the fledgling Lutheran Response to Christian Persecution. My understanding is that he just completed his pastoral position at St. Mark's, and is on a kind of long sabbatical from the university, in order to do that work."

"What, again, does 'a kind of sabbatical' mean?"

"From what I've learned, the university is one of the sponsors or supporters of the effort, and Richard with his fiancée, Madison Tanquerey, will be making videos. They will be a mixture of short and longer reports about persecution, about mission work, along with some things tailored for the classes back at the university."

"That sounds impressive."

"Madison is a well-respected investigative journalist, who is now operating independently."

Dvorak paused and looked at the pope, who sat quietly.

Pope Paul rested an elbow on the armrest of the chair, and rubbed his chin with two fingers. "I have seen a few of her reports. She seems quite good. Ms. Tanquerey is a truly independent newsperson?"

Dvorak seemed temporarily bewildered. "As far as I know, yes, that is the case. Again, she has an excellent reputation."

The pope continued, "And you believe that Pastor Leonard's thinking aligns with what we are trying to accomplish with this project?"

"I cannot speak for Richard, obviously, but I believe he would view the Catholic Church recognizing Martin Luther and Jan Hus for their contributions to Christianity as a major step in the right direction. So, yes, in my opinion, Richard Leonard very much would appreciate this effort."

"Good." Pope Paul VII suddenly stood up. Killian Dvorak followed the pope's lead more slowly. The pontiff said, "Well, then, if the three of you" – he meant Dvorak, Haley Whittacker, and John Kohli – "are in agreement on Pastor

Leonard, then please contact him with an offer, pending, of course, a personal visit with me for a final agreement."

They shook hands. While Dvorak was smiling, he replied, "I will."

Pope Paul added, "Killian, and make sure the invitation is extended to Ms. Tanquerey as well. I wish to meet and speak with her."

Dvorak remained silent for a few seconds, as if waiting further explanation. Getting none, he said, "I will do that, Your Holiness."

A few minutes after Dvorak left, his top aides, Cardinal Winston Treadwell and Father Mariano Concepcion, joined the pope.

After going over what was said about Pastor Richard Leonard and that he had given tentative approval, pending a meeting, to Leonard joining the project team, the pope added, "I also requested that Pastor Leonard's fiancée, Madison Tanquerey, come here for the meeting as well."

Treadwell asked, "Why do I know that name?"

Concepcion actually answered, "She is a reporter on television."

Pope Paul VII said, "Yes, she is, and now she is doing her work independently. From what I understand, she is very good."

"I have watched several of her reports, and have always been impressed," added Concepcion.

The pope said, "Good. Let's do some additional checking on her background and work. If it is all in good order, I think we might have work for Ms. Tanquerey."

Concepcion nodded, while Treadwell raised an eyebrow and spun his cane.

The pope got up and walked over to a large window. He parted the curtains slightly so he could look out at St. Peter's Square. While viewing the many people moving around the expansive area, he said, "I know I have no reason to be so, but I am worried about this Luther-Hus project. Two deaths. First, Professor Fuchs and now Pastor Fletcher. I know it makes no sense. One was the result of a robbery and the other a heart attack. There is nothing nefarious at work. But nonetheless, I feel some occasional, vague unease about this now."

Concepcion smiled and said, "I think it is safe to say, Holy Father, that God is not against us."

Treadwell chimed in, "Others might disagree with that assessment, Father."

Pope Paul VII turned, and looked at Treadwell. He sighed, and said, "On that, you are correct, Winston. Hence, we operate in secret."

Chapter 16

"Yes, I'm definitely interested, Killian," declared Pastor Richard Leonard into his cellphone. "There just are numerous moving parts that I have to think about and work out, to say the least. Some things would have to be pushed back, others adjusted, while considering some possibilities."

"What about Madison?"

Leonard actually chuckled. "She's up for every new challenge. Obviously, as I said, we have to discuss this, but if I know my fiancée, she'll be making flight reservations while I'm still pondering things."

"Good!"

"Why so pleased about that?"

"My friend, I have never been married, but I know women and the effects that they have on their men. If Madison is for this, you will, eventually, be as well."

Leonard replied with a touch of annoyance, "Ah, very funny." But he added, "Although, you're probably not far off base."

"I know I am right." Killian laughed. "Talk to Madison. Work this out, and then let me know when you are flying in. I will set up a time for you two to meet with Pope Paul."

"Okay, I'll get back to you as soon as possible."

Killian said, "Let's try to talk tomorrow or the next day, shall we?"

"I'll try."

Killian laughed again. "I know you will. Take care, Richard."

"Yes. You, too."

Dvorak ended the call, and Leonard dropped his phone on the desk and sat back in his chair. He looked around his book-lined office, which sat on the second floor of one of the stone-exterior campus buildings at the Lutheran University of New York. He smiled, and said to himself, "Madison is going to love this."

*   *   *

Five days later, Father Mariano Concepcion showed Pastor Richard Leonard and Madison Tanquerey into a sitting room in the Papal Apartments.

The two made for a striking couple. Leonard stood six feet, three inches in his dark clericals, with blond hair on the long side, a matching robust beard, and blue eyes. As for Tanquerey, she presented herself to near perfection, as one might expect from someone who had worked in front of the television camera. She was a few inches shorter than Leonard, and wore a simple, yet chic dark blue dress. Her long brown hair with blond highlights was pulled up in a bun.

In contrast, the pope wore what is casually called his housedress, that is, a white cassock and matching zucchetto sitting atop his head.

Introductions were made, and the pope welcomed each of his guests. It was mid-morning, so tea and coffee were offered.

As the pope and his two guests went to sit at a round table, Paul VII said to Concepcion, "Thank you, Father."

"You're welcome, Holy Father," came the response, and Concepcion left the three to their conversation.

After some general niceties, including the pope congratulating the couple on their engagement, Paul VII said, "I know that Dr. Dvorak spoke to you about what this project is about, but I would still like to personally tell you about it, in my own way, and then I can answer any questions you might have." He was looking back and forth between Leonard and Tanquerey, and continued to do so as he relayed most everything about the project, including its purpose, reasons and goals. Leonard and Tanquerey largely listened.

When the pope finished his explanation, Leonard said, "I'm honored that you would consider me for this project. Though I understand why, given the unfortunate deaths of Professor Fuchs and Pastor Fletcher. They were both brilliant men. I had the good fortune to study under Dr. Fuchs."

The pope nodded. "I got to know both of them, and they also were faith-filled, gentle souls. I know they were both Lutherans and would probably frown upon it, but I still pray for their souls, as well as for their respective families." He smiled.

Leonard replied, "I'm sure each would understand, and appreciate your praying, especially for their families."

The pope took a sip of tea, and said, "Having studied with Dr. Fuchs stands out as a big plus in my mind, Dr. Leonard, and I have had the chance to read your work. It is impressive – thoughtful and fair. It reflects the work of a serious scholar, and a serious Christian."

Tanquerey smiled at the pope's compliment, as well as her fiancé's sheepish "Thank you" in response.

The pope clearly noted her response, and said, "Ms. Tanquerey, I have seen a few of your reports, including the work you did during the terrorist attacks in the U.S., which, of course, included your interviews with Dr. Leonard. I also had the chance to review a few of your in-depth, investigative specials. I'd call them documentaries."

"Thank you, Your Holiness," responded Tanquerey.

"And you are now doing your own work, correct? Like your own news network?"

She smiled, and said, "Well, yes, I'm an independent now. As for my own network, from your lips..." She hesitated, looked back and forth at Leonard and the pope, and then completed the comment, "... to God's ear."

Everyone chuckled, and Pope Paul said, "I will see what I can do."

Tanquerey added, "Thanks, that would be much appreciated."

The pope looked back and forth at the couple. "Thinking about the two of you working together, I am encouraged for the Church. A unique combination of mission work and communications. You are going out into the world to communicate the truth about real persecution of Christians going on in the world." He waved his hand in the air. "Not the easily-offended, armchair Christians in places where freedom reigns who complain and do nothing. But going where basic freedoms of religion, assembly and speech are denied, and imprisonment and death often stand as the harsh realities for being a Christian. And then you are doing mission work as well" – he looked into the eyes of Richard Leonard – "following the instructions of Jesus, 'Go therefore and make disciples of all nations, baptizing them in the name of the Father and of the Son and of the Holy Spirit, teaching them to observe all that I have commanded you.'"

Leonard and Tanquerey sat silent and still.

The pope continued, "It is my hope that you can delay this work for a relatively short time in order to be involved in our effort to hopefully bring greater allegiance and trust among wider Christianity through what I expect to be an act of reconciliation by the Roman Catholic Church in regard to Martin Luther and Jan Hus. I believe this will strengthen Christianity in the world, and thereby assist, to some degree, your efforts."

Leonard and Tanquerey slightly nodded at each other.

Leonard looked at the pope, "Again, I would be honored to contribute to this project, that is, if you can use whatever contributions I can make."

The pope smiled broadly, and said, "Yes, that would be wonderful. Your participation would be of true value and appreciated greatly."

The conversation continued over an assortment of logistical, theological and historical points. At an appropriate point, the pope asked, "Ms. Tanquerey, I have another issue that I would like to bring to your attention. I think it would appeal to your vocation in the news business."

"Yes?"

"I know this is going to sound like a cross between old news and conspiracy theory, but I have serious concerns about some Vatican finances and, well, I don't know whom I can trust."

"I'm not sure how I could help with that?"

"Well, there is a story here, and I want to know what it is. I also believe that you would investigate things thoroughly, and report on matters honestly, without speculation or compromising bias. So, if you would like a pope as a source, who can open doors and provide complete access for you, and who would place no strings or limitations on you, might that interest you as a reporter?"

Tanquerey's brown eyes were brightening and widening as she listened. She said, "Would it interest me? Of course, it would."

Chapter 17

Cardinal Renaldo Bessetti rubbed his forehead and groaned. "This pope" – he spat the words – "is taxing my patience."

Sitting across the large desk, Father Pietro Filoni didn't reply.

Bessetti stood up, and started pacing around the massive, ornate office. The cardinal normally exuded an extreme calm that usually served him well, though during moments here and there it could make some people feel uncomfortable. Bessetti left others either at ease, or wondering what he might be hiding. But on rare occasions, in private, Bessetti would rant about whomever or whatever happened to be standing in his way. During such moments – with one now developing – Filoni would silently listen.

Bessetti declared, "The man has never understood that I am working harder than anyone else to protect his office and the Church. Yet, he counters me at every turn. As his secretary of state, I helped him avoid the landmines laid by his predecessor. I sought to guide him away from some of his own worst instincts. I kept trouble at bay, truly serving as his eye, heart and arm. Yet, what did he do?"

Filoni didn't answer the rhetorical questions.

"He pushed me away. This pope actually wanted me somewhere else. Such foolishness. I knew, however, that I could still serve him and Christ's Church here. So, dear Lord, I took a demotion to lead the Secretariat for the Economy. Yes, I have been able to accomplish much through the purse strings, while also staying within earshot of the pope himself. Why? Again, I work to help this man."

Bessetti sat down at his desk, once more. He continued, "You, Pietro, have been invaluable in my efforts, a faithful servant of the Church."

Filoni finally spoke, "Thank you, Your Eminence."

Bessetti nodded, and added, "Thank God for you and your Shadow Servants of the Holy Father…"

Filoni actually interrupted Bessetti. "Your Eminence, that is most gracious. However, they are in no way 'my' Shadow Servants. These are men of God who serve only the pope and the Church. I am but one of these humble servants."

The calm returned to Bessetti. "Of course, Pietro, and I meant no other. Perhaps Pope Paul VII will one day gain clarity and be able to thank each of you for your service."

"That will come with your help and guidance, Your Eminence."

"Thank you, Pietro." Bessetti sat back in his chair, and stared up at the high ceiling.

Filoni returned to his silent waiting.

While still looking up, Bessetti said, "Two of the heretics have been eliminated, and rather than putting aside these subversive efforts, the pope persists. He brings in this Lutheran professor from America. For good measure, he invites this woman in who is a television reporter. I know that she is supposed to marry this man, but there is something more at work there. What does the pope want with her? I do not like this at all, someone from the media in the midst of this." Bessetti pulled his gaze down from the ceiling, and looked at Filoni. "It is time to take the direct step that I hoped would not be necessary. But I see no alternative given that this pope continues down the path of undermining his own papacy."

Chapter 18

The last eight years had not gone well for Pastor Rusty Spuel. The bustling Lutheran church that he arrived at in southeastern Michigan was now barely a shadow of itself. But Spuel wasn't shy in telling anyone who would listen, "I'm doing the Lord's work. I can't be responsible for these people who are weak in faith, and decide to leave because they don't like what Scripture says."

While Spuel was in the pulpit, many parishioners over the years had drifted away to other churches in the region, with the exodus accelerating in the last couple of years.

And now Spuel sat at his desk gritting his teeth as a onetime church council president, Jim Press, was explaining why he and his family were leaving as well.

The gray-haired man, sitting in a chair on the other side of Spuel's desk, said, "Pastor, this was one of the hardest decisions that my family ever had to make. I want to be clear why we're leaving this church where I got married and my children were baptized. I've watched too many people leave, but lack the courage to tell you why. I'm laying this out in a last ditch attempt to give you some added perspective."

"How kind," replied Spuel condescendingly.

The parishioner's shoulders sagged. "See, that response, dripping in sarcasm and barely disguised anger. Is that constructive or pastoral?"

"I've tried to be a real pastor to this church, and I've only been attacked, including by you countless times at council meetings."

"Attacked? How so?"

While failing to look Press directly in the eyes, Spuel seethed, "I *have* fixed the many things that went wrong here, getting back to the true faith, and yet, I've only suffered as a result."

"Yes, you were very adamant that things needed to be fixed when you got here. And many of us saw the way you went about it as disrespecting Pastor Lewis, who had served this church so well for nearly 30 years."

"Pastor Lewis got sloppy, and was in error."

"See what I mean?"

"What? What do you mean, Jim?"

Press sighed. "Alright, Pastor, I can see that, as usual, you're not interested in listening or having a conversation. So, I'm just going to lay out for you what I probably should have years ago, and then I'll pray that you at least consider some of it at some point in your career as a pastor. You're arrogant, and that doesn't serve Jesus well. You came in here years ago telling everyone that what we were doing was dead wrong, and that you were changing it all, immediately. It never occurred to you that if there were things that needed to be changed, perhaps the best way to do so would be to teach and bring your flock along. You're good at lecturing people, but you lack empathy and compassion. You also reflexively dismiss anyone who has even a minor disagreement with you as either a heretic or a person who lacks true faith. And you constantly present yourself as a kind of martyr, constantly being persecuted."

"I don't need to hear this. You won't be missed."

Press shook his head, and said, "How many people have you told that to in recent years? But that seems to be okay with you, Pastor. You seem to like the idea of preaching to an ever-smaller group, as long as they agree with you. And never mind showing any interest in spreading the Good News."

Spuel jumped up from his chair, and yelled, "Get out! I don't have to listen to this. I'm the pastor here, and you don't know what the hell you're talking about. You and your family are troublemakers."

After the surprise at Spuel's outburst melted off Press's face, it was replaced by a sadness. "I know I shouldn't say this, but I'm going to anyway. You also have no social skills whatsoever, and no idea how to talk to another person in a reasonable, friendly way. In fact, I'm sad to say that I wonder if you have any real friends. And Rusty, don't fool yourself, the reason that this church now teeters on the edge is because of you. Sure, there were people who left over the years that would have found some reason to move on no matter what. You're right when you say that there are 'cafeteria Christians' out there. But you always take it way too far. You managed to push people out the door who love Lutheranism and who love this particular church. It had been their home, and you took that away from them − including me."

Press rose from his chair, looked sadly at Spuel, and turned toward the door.

"Go ahead. Get out. Leave like the others. Go to the Catholic Church across town, or another so-called Lutheran church. Good riddance. We don't need you, nor does God. You're damning yourself to hell, just like the others who rejected what I've done here. Your faith is weak."

Press stopped and turned to look at Spuel, who was now sweating and breathing heavily.

Spuel continued, "Do you know how many times I almost walked out of this church to never come back? Why? Because people like you were against me. But I knew I was right, and that I had this cross to bear. So, I stayed."

Press actually smiled wryly. "I would have been strangely disappointed if you didn't play the martyr card. Rusty, you're in the wrong line of work, and you need help. Please get some."

As Press walked out of the office, Spuel called out, "Hell, that's where you're going! And you and the others who have wrecked this church deserve it."

After Press left the building, Spuel banged his hand on the top of his desk over and over again. "God, why don't they see what we're doing?"

Spuel sat back, took several deep breaths, and then turned to his computer. He pulled up the word processing software on which he wrote his blog posts.

His fingers moved quickly over the keys as he wrote a piece explaining how "the most faithful pastors usually suffer persecution within their own churches," and how the persecutors, "those faithless individuals," probably "shouldn't be in the Church in the first place." He then went on to explain that while "we might be tempted to walk away altogether, the truly faithful pastors, who are being abused unjustly, must stand firm, since they are the last best hope of the Church."

Spuel continued to write furiously, finishing another section of what was becoming a very long blog post. He attacked the Catholic Church, people leaving his church for Catholicism, as well as pastors who were "Lutheran in name only and in reality were crypto-Catholics."

As he paused, his cellphone rumbled. Spuel looked at the number on the screen, and answered, "Edgar, what's going on?"

Edgar Spuel was Rusty's youngest brother, and he was studying at the Lutheran University of New York. He detested seemingly every moment of it.

The two exchanged no pleasantries.

Edgar replied, "Guess where Professor Leonard is?"

Rusty stopped banging away on the keys, and said, "I could tell you where I wish he was."

The two laughed.

Edgar reported, "The word around here is that he's in Rome."

"What?"

"Yes, Rome. And I hear that he might teach at one of the pope's colleges over there. Is he allowed to do that, you know, as a Lutheran pastor?"

Rusty Spuel had a history with Richard Leonard. They crossed paths at seminary, and wound up at loggerheads on an assortment of things. Classmates had noted that Spuel seemed to hate Leonard, while Leonard basically tolerated Spuel in a kind of bemused fashion.

"No," replied Rusty. "Or, well, it depends on exactly what he's doing or teaching. Well, it shouldn't be allowed. He shouldn't be allowed to teach over there."

"Yeah, I didn't think so," commented Edgar.

"Do you have anything else on this?"

"No, that's it."

"Okay, let me know if you hear anything more. I'll write something up on this."

Edgar kind of snorted his approval. "Great. I'll let you know."

The brothers ended the call, and Spuel returned to striking the computer keys – now harder and faster than earlier. He said out loud, "These people have to be stopped."

Chapter 19

After he finished reading the letter, Father Mariano Concepcion actually blessed himself. He then handed the piece of paper back to Pope Paul VII. With his mouth slightly agape, Concepcion looked back and forth between the pope and Cardinal Winston Treadwell, and asked, "How could this be?"

Treadwell looked at the pope, and said, "Perhaps this is a twisted mind taking advantage of what has occurred." He sat up straighter, seemingly gaining some strength by what he had just said. "Yes, that must be it. It is ridiculous to think otherwise."

Pope Paul raised an eyebrow, and replied, "Perhaps."

Concepcion asked, "Nonetheless, we must act with an abundance of caution." His gaze narrowed on the pope. "Do we not, Holy Father? After all, if this is true, then we cannot keep anyone else in danger."

Pope Paul VII looked down at the letter. His hand shook ever so slightly. "This person is aware of a project that we have worked to keep a secret, not just from the world at large, but from everyone inside the Vatican, from people that the three of us work with nearly every day. He names each person involved. And dear God, he claims..." His voice broke. The pope took a deep breath, and then continued in a low voice, "... claims to be responsible for the deaths of Dr. Fuchs and Pastor Fletcher." He looked up at his two closest aides with a shocked expression, as if the full implications of this anonymous letter, found on Concepcion's desk when the priest had arrived in his office, fully registered in Paul

VII's mind. "And he threatens to kill each person involved if the project is not ended."

Concepcion's voice blended fear with anger. "Yes, yes, and that is why we need to stop what we are doing. We need to send these people home. What else can we possibly do?"

Treadwell said, "Professor Fuchs was killed during a break in at his home in Chicago. Pastor Fletcher died due to a heart attack. God rest their souls. That is the reality. The authorities confirmed Pastor Fletcher's cause of death. So, only one person is dead at the hands of another human being, yet this letter claims both."

The pope replied, "Yes, I realize that."

Treadwell persisted, "That tells us something, does it not? Yes, this is someone who somehow has found out about this project, and that is deeply troubling. However, thinking that two men were murdered by someone or some group looking to stop this effort is absurd."

Concepcion asked Treadwell, "So, we should ignore this, and just continue doing what we are doing?"

"I didn't say that, Mariano."

"Well, what are you saying, Winston?"

Treadwell paused, and then replied, "My initial reaction is to put the project on hold, send each person home, and we implement an investigation to find out who this sick individual is." He turned to the pope. "Let us be clear, this individual likely works inside the Vatican, and that is a real danger."

The pope said, "I am not sure if sending these people home is the right course of action."

Both aides replied in unison, "What?"

Concepcion added, "With all due respect, Holy Father, how can you even think that?"

Treadwell said, "I know that this project will be exposed, and under the resulting criticisms, perhaps come to an end, but I hope that is not what you are thinking about, Holy Father?"

Pope Paul VII shot a withering look at Treadwell. "I know what matters here, Winston."

Treadwell responded, "Yes, of course."

The pope rose from his chair, and went over to the window. He looked out on St. Peter's Square. He observed, "I have no idea who can be trusted, and who cannot." He turned, looked at his two aides, and smiled sadly. "Present company excluded."

Treadwell and Concepcion glanced at each other, but didn't respond.

The pope returned to looking out the window. "Mariano, I was standing in this exact spot the other day, and you assured me that God was not against us on this Hus-Luther project. Do you still think that?"

"I do."

The pope nodded. "You, Winston, warned that others might disagree with Mariano." He sighed. "That unease about something nefarious working against us has only intensified. I pray about it. Yet, our secret has been discovered by someone who is displeased. Perhaps this person, as you indicated, Winston, believes that God *is* against us." After a few minutes of silence, he shook his head and said, "There are two others whom I trust in this situation."

Treadwell said, "Yes?"

The pope walked back to where Treadwell and Concepcion were, but he did not sit back down. He said, "I am going to have Vincent gather the research group in the hotel suites, and stay with them." Over time, the pope had made clear to Treadwell and Concepcion that his personal bodyguard, Vincent Mazzoni, had earned trust without reservation.

His two aides nodded, clearly waiting for more information.

Pope Paul VII continued, "I will reach out to the other person whom I know can be trusted under these circumstances. He also will bring a certain objectivity, or at least, a different point of view, and have insights on how we should proceed."

Treadwell asked, "And who is that, Holy Father?"

"You will know soon enough. For the moment, however, I need the two of you to leave me alone."

The two aides failed to move from their chairs, as they looked at each other and back at the pope.

Pope Paul VII said, "Gentlemen, please, trust me."

The two stated their ascent, rose from their chairs – Treadwell using his cane to help – and reluctantly left the room.

Chapter 20

Pastor Stephen Grant exited a store. He opened the front passenger door of the Renault Scenic, and said, "Well, it's all in the hands of Fedex now."

Father Ron McDermott responded, "Thanks for sending my packages of the monks' chocolate as well. We can straighten out what I owe you on the plane home."

"Sounds good."

The two men were on their way to the Charles de Gaulle Airport, where they were supposed to return the rental car and board a flight for home. After the Hunter Bryant incident at the Monastere de Saint Paul and the funeral of Father Charles Borget, McDermott and Grant left earlier than what was originally planned. Grant also canceled meetings for the Lutheran Response to Christian Persecution that he had scheduled for after their stay in the monastery.

The time at the monastery was supposed to be about reflection and relaxation. It had turned out very different, and Grant now found himself feeling more at ease as Ron drove toward the airport.

Grant leaned his head back and closed his eyes. He said, "Thanks again for driving, Ron."

"More than happy to get behind the wheel."

A mere minute of silence passed when Grant's smartphone rumbled. He picked it up, and looked at the screen.

Blocked number?

He answered, "Hello."

"Pastor Stephen Grant?"

I know this voice?

"Yes, who is this?"

"Stephen, I am so glad I reached you. When we worked together, you knew me as Cardinal Juan Santos."

Grant sat up straighter, and said, "Pope Paul, how are you?"

After the death of Pope Augustine, Cardinal Santos had been elected pope, and became Pope Paul VII.

Ron whipped his head and raised an eyebrow. He silently mouthed, "Pope Paul VII?"

Grant nodded.

Pope Paul replied, "I am not well, Stephen."

"What is it? Can I help?"

"I think you might be the only person who can help. However, I cannot talk to you about this over the phone, nor do I have time right now to fully explain. But I need you to understand that this truly is an emergency, and it not only involves the future of the Church, but..." He paused.

"Yes?"

"One person has died, and I believe that more lives hang in the balance."

"Juan..." – *Juan?* – "...what can I do?"

"I understand you are in France? That is what Pastor Charmichael told me."

"Yes."

"Can I impose upon you to come to Rome?"

"Now?"

"I apologize, Stephen, but yes, can you come immediately?"

The pope of the Roman Catholic Church sounds desperate, and is seeking my help.

"Of course, I happen to be on my way to the airport now. I'll simply change my flight, and head to Rome."

"Thank you, Stephen."

Grant could hear some minor relief in the pope's voice.

Pope Paul VII added, "When you receive my text, just follow the instructions on where to go."

"Yes, of course."

"May the Lord be with you, Stephen. I look forward to seeing you soon."

Before Grant could respond, the pope ended the call.

McDermott looked over at Grant, and asked, "What the heck was that all about? Why is Pope Paul VII calling you?"

"He was grave and cryptic. The pope said that he needed to see me immediately, and that the future of the Church and lives were in the balance."

Ron managed to only say, "Wow." After several seconds of silence, he asked, "What now?"

Grant looked at his friend, and said, "I'm changing flights, and heading to Rome. Care to come along? I'm sure your boss won't mind."

Chapter 21

"There, unfortunately, has been a change of plans," reported Stephen Grant into his cellphone.

On the other end of the call, across the Atlantic Ocean, Jennifer Grant responded with humor. "Oh, and are we stopping to save the world, again?"

Stephen had found a private spot to talk in the Charles De Gaulle Airport. He laughed, and said, "Let's hope that's never the case. But I actually received a call from Pope Paul VII."

"Really?" Jen's tone quickly shifted to one of interest.

"He asked if I could divert to Rome."

"Why?"

"Good question. He was cryptic, but he did say it was an emergency, lives were at risk, and so was the future of the Church."

"So, you are stopping to save the world."

Stephen said, "I'm sorry about this, Jen. I know I've been away from home for too long."

"You have, but I think you better see what the pope wants. Even though you're a Lutheran pastor, I don't think you can ignore a call like this to save lives and the Church."

"Thanks. I love you."

"You're lucky to have such an understanding, and independent, wife."

"I know."

They continued to talk for several more minutes about the house, Jen's projects, and St. Mary's.

Jennifer said, "You should call Zack before getting on the plane to let him know the latest."

"I am, but he already knows something is going on. The pope apparently tracked me down by contacting St. Mary's and Zack first."

Jen laughed, and said, "Zack and the pope – that must have been an interesting call."

"You're right."

Jen instructed, "Alright, talk to Zack, have a safe flight, and let me know once you know what the pope wants."

This better work out better than the last time...

Stephen cut off the thought. "Will do. I love you."

"I love you, too."

After the call with Jen ended, Stephen immediately called Zack.

Zack answered, "Hello, St. Mary's Lutheran Church."

"I understand you spoke to the pope."

"Stephen! What the heck is going on? First, you and Ron get in trouble at a monastery in France, and now I presume you're headed to Rome?"

"We are. It's been quite an adventure, and apparently, it's not over yet. Everything going okay at St. Mary's?"

"Yeah, It's pretty standard stuff." Zack gave a quick rundown on the highlights, and they discussed a couple of those items.

Stephen said, "So, it sounds like you've got things covered, but I owe you big time."

"You do. We'll talk about that when you get home. What exactly did the pope say?"

Stephen gave much the same answer as he had to Jen. "He was cryptic, but made clear that there might be lives in the balance, and he talked about the future of the Church."

"Jeez, you have all of the fun."

Stephen laughed. "I don't know if I would use the word 'fun.'"

Chapter 22

While Stephen was speaking to Zack, Father Ron McDermott was just a few feet away on his own call.

Father Stanley Burns was seated in his living room, and was watching *Seinfeld*. He had the sound off now, as he was talking with McDermott.

McDermott asked, "So, you don't mind?"

"Well, wait a second. The Holy Father has asked for Stephen, and you're basically going along for the ride at this point?" Burns laughed.

McDermott replied, "Thanks for putting it that way, Stan. But, yeah, you're basically right."

"Have you ever met Pope Paul VII?"

"Yes, but before he became pope."

"Ah, yes, of course."

"Why do you ask?"

"Well, I thought with his contacts, Stephen could get you in to meet him."

"Again, funny, Stan. Have you been watching *Seinfeld*, again?"

"I always watch *Seinfeld*, but that has nothing to do with my sense of humor."

"Hmm. I don't remember you being this funny before you retired."

Father Burns had been the senior pastor at St. Luke's Catholic Church and School for many years. Father McDermott was added as an assistant. And after Burns retired, McDermott took over the entire effort. However, since Burns retired locally, he often returned to St. Luke's to pinch hit for McDermott when needed. Burns stepped in when McDermott left for what was to be a retreat in France.

Burns laughed. "Ronald, I've always been quite amusing. And no, I certainly don't mind. Go, see the pope, and try to enjoy Rome. And for goodness sake, stay out of trouble this time."

"Thank you, Father."

"May the Lord watch over you and your travels."

Chapter 23

After arriving at Leonardo da Vinci International Airport, Pastor Stephen Grant, along with Father Ron McDermott, followed the instructions provided in the pope's text. They simply needed to go to a certain spot outside the terminal, and they would be picked up.

A black sedan approached, with only the driver inside. The man parked the car, got out, and walked up to Grant and McDermott. He stopped in front of the two men, glanced at McDermott, and then looked at Grant. He extended his right hand, and said, "Pastor Grant, I am Vincent Mazzoni."

Grant shook his hand, with his face reacting with a slight twinge of pain due to a lingering gunshot wound on the upper part of his arm. Mazzoni raised an eyebrow at the reaction.

Grant replied, "Hello, Mr. Mazzoni."

Before Grant had the chance to introduce McDermott, Mazzoni turned and asked, "And who are you? My assignment was to pick up Pastor Stephen Grant, no one else."

In his dry style, McDermott said, "It's nice to meet you as well. I'm the Lutheran pastor's Catholic priest sidekick."

Mazzoni extended his hand, and said, "In that case, welcome."

After the three men had deposited luggage in the trunk, Grant took the front passenger seat and McDermott got in the back.

While pulling the car into traffic, Mazzoni said, "You received the wound to your arm during the incident at the Monastere de Saint Paul."

"That's right. You've been briefed?"

Mazzoni nodded. "It's a shame what happened to the abbot, but what you did was impressive."

Grant said, "Thank you." He then added, "Can you tell me a little something of what's going on here in terms of why the pope contacted me?"

"No. That is for the Holy Father."

Okay.

Grant said, "You're with the Gendarme Corps?"

"Yes. I am an inspector general."

"You're Pope Paul's main bodyguard?"

Mazzoni glanced over at Grant, and replied, "I serve the Holy Father."

The three drove in silence for several minutes, and then Mazzoni asked, "So, Pastor Grant, have you been back to Rome since you helped stop that attack at the Colosseum?"

"Inspector Mazzoni, you've done your research."

"Yes. Once the Holy Father told me whom I was picking up, I pulled your file. I didn't have very long to review it, however."

As expected.

Grant nodded. "Well, then, anything you'd like to ask me about, or need some clarification?"

Mazzoni answered, "Nothing pressing, at least at this point. I know how you met the Holy Father, and I thank you for all that you did relating to Pope Augustine."

Grant turned and stared out the window. Lights were coming on as the sun was setting on the Eternal City. "I liked him a great deal, and agreed with what he was trying to do. It didn't turn out the way I wanted – the way any of us did."

Mazzoni looked in the rearview mirror, and said, "But I know nothing about you, Father McDermott."

McDermott said, "My background is far less interesting, apparently, than either of you. What would you like to know?"

Mazzoni answered, "The basics."

By the time McDermott gave a quick review of his background and being at St. Luke's, Mazzoni stopped the sedan at a private, nondescript door at the back of the Apostolic Palace. Within ten minutes, Mazzoni offered Father McDermott a chair in a room serving as a reception area during normal business hours, and led Grant through a set of high, ornate doors.

Pope Paul VII was sitting by himself on a couch, with a tablet in his hands. He looked up and smiled. He rose to his feet, and said, "Pastor Stephen Grant, it is good to see you. Thank you for coming, and so quickly."

Grant replied, "Your Holiness, it's good to see you again."

The two men shook hands, and Grant again winced slightly.

"What happened to your arm?" asked Pope Paul VII.

Grant glanced at Mazzoni, who stood off to the side, with his back to a wall. The pope turned in his bodyguard's direction as well.

Mazzoni said, "Yes, Holy Father, I did not have a chance to inform you, given the time constraints, but Pastor Grant played a central role in the incident at the Monastere de Saint Paul – obviously, in a positive way."

The pope nodded, "I see." He turned to Grant, and noted, "Vincent and I have a routine. I tend to ignore certain protocols on the security front, and then he has his way to remind me that I did so."

Grant said, "I see."

The pope continued, "I assume that such behavior would have annoyed you when you were with the CIA, but that you now understand a bit more."

"Well, there's still enough CIA in me that I understand Inspector Mazzoni's ... frustrations."

The pope smiled, and said, "It seems that you have an ally, Vincent."

"Good," replied Mazzoni from a distance, as the pope pointed Grant to an armchair cattycorner to the couch. The pope returned to where he had been sitting, and Grant took the armchair.

Should I?

Grant added, "Please, Your Holiness, keep in mind what happened to Pope Augustine."

Pope Paul VII nodded slowly, and glanced at Mazzoni, who raised an eyebrow in response. The pope cleared his throat, and said, "Obviously, you would like to know why I contacted you?"

Grant simply replied, "Yes."

"Allow me to explain."

Grant nodded.

"Bear with me, as this requires some background. I will be brief, and then you can ask whichever questions you like." Grant waited and then the pope continued. "I know that you, like so many others, supported Pope Augustine's 'Public Mission of Mere Christianity.' No doubt, like many others, you wondered what happened to the effort after Pope Augustine's death and the move into my time in this office. For now, let us just say that during my first years as pope, I failed Augustine, Christ and His Church. There were various reasons for this, and perhaps we can have a private talk on such matters at another time, but as I said, for now, let us simply acknowledge this. However, in recent times, I have tried to move forward on a few fronts. That includes a project that could inject some depth to efforts to bring about greater Christian unity. My hope is that, if this is successful, then the next step would involve furthering what Pope Augustine was attempting."

"That sounds exciting," commented Grant.

The pope nodded slightly. "I have quietly" – he glanced over at Mazzoni – "well, secretly launched an effort led by a group of scholars to explore the possibilities for the Catholic Church to recognize, even honor, the efforts to reform the Church by two major historical figures in Christianity – Jan Hus and Martin Luther."

Wow!

Grant replied, "If that were to happen, some 500-year-old wounds would start to heal. It would be a meaningful foundation upon which to build some greater unity and trust across the Church."

"I believe it would. So, I have brought together this group with complementary expertise to immerse themselves in the matter, and present their conclusions to me, and to the world, on whether or not we can move forward on this front in a meaningful way, along with some suggestions for how to do so."

Under any other circumstances I would be caught up in this, but the pope certainly didn't bring me here for a one-on-one briefing.

Grant interjected, "And what does this have to do with a death and an emergency?"

"Yes." The pope took a deep breath, and then started to reference Professor Harold Fuchs and Pastor Gerhard Fletcher.

Grant interrupted, "I was familiar with each of these men. I had met Dr. Fuchs at a few conferences, and I certainly read Pastor Fletcher's magisterial work."

"Like you, Stephen, these men were faithful Lutherans serving the Church according to their gifts." Pope Paul VII went on to explain what was in the letter, and summed up, "This person claims to be responsible for the deaths of Dr. Fuchs and Pastor Fletcher, and threatens to kill anyone else involved in this project if it continues."

Grant moved fully into his old CIA mindset. "So, Your Holiness, two men are dead, not one."

"Technically, yes. But the authorities have confirmed that Pastor Fletcher's death was of natural causes. He died of a heart attack."

"Perhaps that's what it looked like. A death can appear to be due to one thing, but turn out to have a very different cause. Not knowing that you need to be looking for other possible causes can sometimes mean that the true cause, if cloaked properly, can go unnoticed."

The pope replied, "If that is the case, then the situation is worse than I had feared. I chose to hold off on sending this group of scholars home mainly because I am worried about their safety. I'm not sure that sending them back to their homes, for example, necessarily keeps them safer, if this threat is real. After all, we understand today that people can work together in the same room or across the world via the internet. Why would some person willing to murder suddenly be placated if this team could work together remotely?"

Grant said, "Your instincts were right. We obviously have no idea as to the state of mind of this person, or group."

"Group?" the pope asked.

"We can't assume that this is a person acting alone."

The pope added, "And to be honest, Stephen, other than three people, I must admit that I have no idea who can and cannot be trusted."

"That's unfortunate, to say the least."

"What is your suggestion?"

"I know a group led by three of the best people for work like this. One was a CIA operative who played a key role in helping with the Pope Augustine case. They are the best. Their firm is CDM International Strategies and Security, and it can provide the security needed for your group of scholars, *and* perform an investigation, in the shadows, if necessary. These people are your best chance at solving all of this."

"You trust them?"

"Implicitly."

The pope fell silent for a minute or so. And then he said, "I trust you, Stephen, so I accept your recommendation, with two caveats."

"Yes?"

"First, obviously, we will have to talk to this group of scholars, explain to them what we are thinking, and then let them make their decisions as to what they wish to do."

Grant said, "Of course. At the same time, though, if some or all of them decide to go home, you should still supply security. In addition, there is the issue of protecting their immediate families."

"Dear Lord, I had not thought about that. You are, of course, correct."

Grant asked, "You mentioned a second caveat?"

"Yes. My second requirement is that you remain here and be part of this effort."

Grant was taken aback. "I don't know if that's possible in terms of the amount of time away from my pastoral responsibilities."

"Stephen, I just told you that I feel like there are only three people inside all of the Vatican whom I can trust without reservation. I need another person I know I can trust involved in this effort."

A battle that had become far too familiar began to rage once again in Grant's mind. His current responsibilities as a pastor were being pitted against another endeavor springing from his past as a SEAL and with the CIA.

Pope Paul VII continued, "I understand the problem you face. You do not want to neglect those responsibilities. Perhaps we can find an answer with the Lutheran Response to Christian Persecution."

Is the pope trying to cut me a deal?

Grant asked, "What do you have in mind?"

"Did you know that Pastor Richard Leonard has joined this group of scholars?"

Richard?

"I didn't."

"He just arrived, and is meant to serve – I am not sure how to put this – as Pastor Fletcher's successor."

"I see. He'll make an excellent addition. He's a brilliant guy."

The world is amazingly small at times.

Grant and Richard Leonard had known each other for years, with Stephen serving in the SEALs with Richard's father.

"In addition to the work you and Richard would be doing behind the scenes, why can't the Vatican partner with you in advancing and expanding efforts in taking on persecution? This truly is an issue that has been weighing on me, and I've discussed and cajoled various people and departments, yet little happens that actually makes a difference."

Grant couldn't resist. "Are you complaining to this Lutheran about the infamous Vatican bureaucracy?"

"Stephen, you have no idea."

What does that mean?

Pope Paul VII continued, "I am trying to do what's right for justice, for the victims, for these fine individuals who came to help, and for the Church, in terms of greater unity, fighting persecution and being prepared for what lies ahead. And I believe that we need you to be part of this."

And how do I say "no" to that? Well, if Jen and Zack will tolerate more of this, I guess I'm staying in Rome for a bit.

After Grant told the pope that he would stay on for "a period of time as long as my wife and Pastor Charmichael agree," Pope Paul VII thanked him. They discussed additional details, including that the pope would discuss matters with the project's scholars in the morning. As they rose and shook hands, the pope asked, "Father Ronald McDermott is with you, correct? Waiting outside?"

"Yes."

"Can I trouble you to ask him to come in after you leave the room?"

Grant was slightly surprised, but quickly recovered. "Of course, Your Holiness."

The pope added, "He is a good man and priest in your view?"

"One of the best people I know. I'm blessed to call him a friend."

The pope smiled slightly, and said, "Good. I have another challenge with which I think he might be able to help."

As Grant went to leave, he noticed the pope and Mazzoni exchanging another knowing glance.

Chapter 24

After Father McDermott finished his meeting with Pope Paul VII, Vincent Mazzoni led McDermott and Stephen Grant back to the car in which they had arrived.

Grant said, "If you don't mind me asking, where will we be staying?"

Mazzoni responded, "The Holy Father's scholars have been staying at the Trevisani Suites, except for Dr. Whittacker, since she and her husband have their own apartment here in Rome. We had reserved five suites and expanded it to six the other day – to accommodate Ms. Tanquerey. Given the changing situation, while Father McDermott was meeting with the Holy Father, I arranged for the Vatican to take the entire floor."

McDermott smirked, and asked, "How did the hotel manager feel about that?"

"He appreciated that an entire floor of his establishment would be filled and paid for at full price for an extended period of time. He was, though, less happy about having to move several guests to different rooms. But that was a small, immediate inconvenience in exchange for a longer run benefit."

"Extended period of time" and "longer run"? How long is this going to take? Ugh, I'm amazed at what Jen, not to mention Zack, put up with in terms of my extracurriculars. Lord, thank you.

While McDermott was in his meeting with the pope, Stephen had called both Jennifer and Zack. Each insisted that Stephen stay in Rome and help. It was clear to Stephen that Zack had said it with his typical enthusiasm – getting somewhat excited, once more, about Stephen's mix of the Church and clandestine undertakings. As for Jennifer, she was sincere in telling her husband that he needed to do this. Stephen couldn't tell if there also was a trace of melancholy in her voice, or if he simply imagined it.

Grant asked, "So, Ron, care to share what the pope said?"

McDermott shifted a bit in the back seat, and answered, "No, not right now." His eyes went to the back of Mazzoni's head, and then to the rearview mirror. Mazzoni's eyes never met his, instead remaining forward looking as he drove.

Mazzoni's smartphone buzzed. "Yes." After listening for nearly a minute, he said, "Good work. We're just a few minutes away." He then reported to his two passengers, "The floor has been cleared, and my men have checked and secured it. The entire floor will be at the disposal of you and the CDM people."

Grant replied, "Thank you. Well, that is, if the group decides to stay and go along with the pope's plan."

Mazzoni merely said, "They will."

"What makes you so sure?"

In a matter-of-fact, police-like tone, Mazzoni answered, "I have observed these people for some time now. They are honorable and want to do the right thing, for the most part."

Upon exiting the hotel elevator on the now-fully-reserved floor and moving beyond Mazzoni's two guards, Stephen and Ron were met by Pastor Richard Leonard and Madison Tanquerey. After exchanging general greetings, Grant said, "By the way, Madison, your website is great. I watch and read it religiously."

Tanquerey smiled, and said, "Thank you, I've got a lot of work to do." She turned to McDermott, and said, "Father McDermott, I understand you're willing to work with me on this project?"

"I am, Ms. Tanquerey, though I'm still not sure how I can help exactly. But when the pope asks, you don't exactly say 'no,' especially when you're a priest. So, I'm more than willing to pitch in however I can."

"Trust me, Father, I need your help, and it's much appreciated. How about we talk in the morning?"

McDermott said, "Perfect."

I guess I know what the pope was talking to Ron about. But what are these two working on exactly?

Grant shifted gears. "If you don't mind me asking, do you guys have anything set on the wedding front?"

The two glanced at each other, and Leonard answered, "We need to talk to you about something on that front. Can we try to carve out some time for dinner amidst these unfortunate circumstances?"

Grant was intrigued, and said, "Of course."

Leonard then said to both men, "Come on. I'll introduce you to the group."

Leonard and Tanquerey led Grant and McDermott into the group's common room. Father John Kohli, Professor Haley Whittacker, and Professor Killian Dvorak were waiting.

After introductions and exchanging courtesies, Grant said, "I'm sorry for your loss. I had met Professor Fuchs a few times, and knew of Pastor Fletcher's work." McDermott also offered condolences, and each person responded with appreciation.

Eventually, it was Dvorak who cut to the chase. "I do not mean to be rude, Pastor Grant, but who exactly are you and why are you involved in this?"

Fair question. So, how much do I tell them?

Grant said, "Before I was a pastor, I served as a SEAL in the United States Navy, and subsequently, worked at the Central Intelligence Agency."

Dvorak laughed. "Wait, you are a pastor who used to be with the CIA? That's wonderful."

Haley Whittacker interrupted, "Killian, please."

Dvorak replied, "Haley, do you not find that amusing?" He chuckled some more.

Kohli said to Grant, "That's actually pretty interesting, Pastor Grant."

Grant continued, "I also know the pope from when he was in America with Pope Augustine."

Kohli asked, "You were there when the Holy Father was killed?"

Grant nodded, and quietly answered, "I was."

Kohli responded, "I see."

After a few moments of silence, Dvorak declared, "That still does not exactly explain why you are here."

Grant said, "Yes, I know. The pope will be explaining that when he talks with you early in the morning."

Whittacker now chimed in with a question. "I was wondering why the pope set up a video call?"

I don't think there's a downside to getting them thinking about this. After all, the pope simply wants to make sure the right decision is made ... I hope.

Grant replied, "The pope consulted with me on a letter."

Kohli asked, "Letter?"

"Yes. Now, please hear me out. The pope received a note, and we don't know who sent it. But the author claims to have murdered both Dr. Fuchs and Pastor Fletcher."

The reactions were immediate, with Dvorak's "What?" being loudest.

Grant pressed on, "I know. I know. But ..."

He was interrupted by Whittacker, who said, "This sounds like an ugly, well, for lack of a better word, prank. After all, the reports have been clear that Dr. Fuchs and his wife perished during a robbery, and Gerhard died due to a heart attack."

Kohli interjected, "But there's more to this letter, I assume?" He was looking at Grant.

"There is. The letter also said that this effort that all of you are involved in here, regarding Luther and Hus, must stop. And if not, the author threatened to kill each person involved."

Whittacker, Kohli, Dvorak and Leonard fell silent, as did McDermott and Tanquerey. Eventually, each set of eyes returned to Stephen Grant.

Grant said, "I know that this is shocking, and all kinds of things are running through your heads. But before you let your minds go off in assorted directions, let me say a few things. First, this could turn out to be nothing more than the rantings of a disturbed individual. However, we need to take this seriously until we know for sure who this is and what it's really about in the end. Second, there is additional significance because this person, or group, knows about this secret project, as well as who is involved. Third, whether each of you and the pope decide to go on with this project or not, at this point, that really doesn't matter in terms of how we need to respond."

Whittacker whispered, "What do you mean?"

Grant continued, "We have to assume that this threat will not simply disappear because the pope decides to end this project. And along those lines, the pope and I agree that it would be better, until we end this threat, for all of you to not return home, but instead stay here for security reasons. I'll answer all of your questions, but you should know that if you agree to stay here it will be easier to provide security, that is, to protect each of you. I have recommended to the pope that a group called CDM International Strategies and Security provide that security. They are the very best, and will not only be able to provide protection but also will uncover what this is about and who is behind it." Grant paused and moved his gaze to each person. "For what it's worth, I have entrusted my own life, my wife's, and the lives of others I care about to CDM. I know and trust these people."

Kohli asked, "And you?"

"The pope asked that I stay on as well, and assist however I can. And I've agreed to do so."

Dvorak said, "And if we each decide to say this is enough, and wish to go home?"

"You, of course, are free to do so, and we would arrange to provide protection. But again, the best security situation, in my view, would be for you to stay here. For good measure, we will make sure that security is provided to your immediate family."

Dvorak chimed in, "I don't think that pertains to me or Father Kohli, and I get the feeling that Haley's husband, Conrad, will be just fine."

Haley Whittacker raised an eyebrow, but said nothing.

Dvorak continued, "And well, Madison is here for Richard."

Kohli responded, "Thanks, Killian, for that assessment."

Leonard added, "I know I'm new to the group, but I need to speak up. You know that my church was targeted during the string of terror attacks in the U.S., and so was Madison." Leonard and Tanquerey were sitting next to each other, and joined hands. "Stephen, who served with my father in the SEALs, is a man of God and a man of honor, and he knows what he is doing. You should heed his advice."

The conversation went longer than Grant had expected, and he wound up coming to a similar conclusion that Mazzoni had. He already knew quite well who Richard Leonard was, but during the evening's discussion, Grant came to see that Whittacker, Dvorak and Kohli, while different, were committed to what they were doing, to the pope and to each other. He decided that he would be surprised if they walked away.

Chapter 25

Madison Tanquerey and Father Ron McDermott started their partnership on slightly different notes – at least in terms of breakfast. Tanquerey was not a breakfast person. She simply looked for a beverage with no sugar and a maximum amount of caffeine. Meanwhile, McDermott had become accustomed to eating breakfast to get his day rolling, while often finding himself skipping lunch due to assorted priestly duties.

So, while Tanquerey seemed completely satisfied with some high-octane Italian coffee, McDermott barely hid his disdain for the protein breakfast bar he found in the group's common room. Though he also appreciated the coffee.

Given that Vincent Mazzoni had reserved the entire floor of the Trevisani for the group, no one challenged Tanquerey when she claimed a suite for her pope-requested undertaking. As she handed several sheets of paper across the round table to McDermott, Tanquerey said, "Thanks, again, for doing this."

McDermott replied, "I'm more than happy to help out however I can. To say that I was surprised by this, however, would be understating it."

"That makes two of us."

McDermott observed, "What you've been asked to do, and the Luther-Hus undertaking, make me wonder about the Holy Father."

"What do you mean?"

McDermott took a deep breath, and said, "Given that we'll be working together, it's important to be honest and forthcoming."

"I completely agree."

"I am not one for rumors and speculation, but given his time in the papacy, Paul VII had earned the moniker of the 'Do-Nothing Pope' among many clergy."

"Interesting. I had read some pieces here and there that were less than kind about his papacy, but I had no idea it went beyond the media to the clergy."

McDermott nodded. "In the relatively brief talk I had with him, the Holy Father basically admitted that he had failed early on in his papacy."

"Yes, he seemed to indicate the same to us – to Richard and me."

"But now he's got these two major undertakings happening, or getting under way in our case, and they could shake the Catholic Church at fundamental levels."

Tanquerey leaned back in her chair, and asked, "Are you on board with these, Father?"

"I am. I'm just pointing out that when all of this comes out, it's going to be very interesting to see the reaction. Does Paul VII go from the 'Do-Nothing Pope' to the pope who challenges past mistakes, leads Christianity to greater unity, and takes on corruption in the Vatican bureaucracy? One of those goals, if partially achieved, would be monumental. Yet, here is Paul VII pushing ahead on each of these fronts."

"I hadn't thought of it that way. What do you think the reaction will be when all of this comes out?"

McDermott shook his head. "Unfortunately, for too much of the world, they'll take, at best, passing notice, and then move on to the next shiny object. Many will appreciate what he is doing, and praise him for it. As for others, well, there's a reason why we are in this hotel under tight security."

Tanquerey leaned forward, and said, "Yeah, I get it." She shook her head, and then continued, "Shall we review the notes I've put together on this, and start exploring how we should proceed?"

McDermott responded, "You're the boss, Ms. Tanquerey."

She smiled, and said, "Okay, if we're going to work together, let's drop the 'Ms. Tanquerey.' It's Madison. And we're partners in this. I'm not your boss."

"The informality thing is not my strong suit, but I accept your first name recommendation."

As McDermott hesitated, Tanquerey asked, "And do you prefer 'Father,' 'Ron' or 'Ronald'?" She again smiled at McDermott's continued hesitation, and continued, "How about 'Father'?"

"Yes. If you don't mind. Thanks. Also, you are the boss on this. I'm here to help out, in particular to serve as a priest who can hopefully guide you through and provide insights on the bureaucratic morass that can be the Vatican and the Church. But let me be clear, I will do whatever you need me to do to get at the truth. My experience in helping to run a local church and school has made clear to me the enormous responsibility the Church has to practice good stewardship, to responsibly use the resources provided by parishioners, businesses and other donors, as well as whatever is earned by the Church through its investments. I've long been outraged by what I've heard over the years in terms of waste in the Church hierarchy. So, I am honored that the Holy Father asked to me to help you on this, and I take this very seriously. I know I might sound like a broken record, but I'll do whatever is needed."

"Thanks, Father. I'm glad to hear you say that. And if I'm to be your 'boss,' you need to know that I prefer to be an open-door kind of boss. I want to hear ideas, warnings, feedback – positive and negative – and so on. This is too important to *not* have open communications."

McDermott said, "Sounds good."

Tanquerey shifted to the papers in front of each of them. "Okay, I'd like to review what the pope said to me in terms of what this is about and what he is looking for, and see if that lines up with what he told you. You know, did I miss something, misinterpret anything, etc."

"Makes sense." McDermott looked down at the papers provided by Tanquerey.

Tanquerey began, "So, Pope Paul is in agreement with you. He takes the responsibility of being a good steward very seriously, and is not pleased with large amounts of money lost in black holes that seem to pop up around the Catholic Church."

McDermott nodded in agreement, indicating that this was the message communicated by the pope to him as well.

She went on, "He is counting on us to start an independent investigation of assorted Vatican accounts. And he wants us to delve deep, and report honestly and publicly."

"I was somewhat surprised that the Holy Father had said that, by the way."

"What?"

"I certainly understand the independent investigation. But it took me off guard that he didn't want a heads-up on the findings before it went public."

"I was glad that he didn't request that. As a journalist, it would have made me feel uncomfortable. This way, there's not the possibility of even the appearance of any influence or conflicts of interest."

McDermott responded, "Okay. I get that."

"The pope wants the information public, and then he is going to assemble a plan of action to prosecute any wrongdoing, fire those guilty of incompetence, and bring in a new team to fix, streamline and rationalize budgets and bureaucracies, and to start to steer resources and efforts in the direction of what Pope Paul VII is calling, at least for now 'Missions That Matter.'"

McDermott confirmed that this largely was what the pope had relayed to him.

"And according to the pope, I'm here for my independence and experience with investigative journalism, and you're here given your knowledge of the Catholic Church, and as a priest who can invoke the pope's intentions and authority."

"Well, right, as far as that can go."

Tanquerey also pointed out, "As productive as the two of us might be, we are going to need some assistance, including filling in a big gap in our expertise."

"Meaning?"

"I know that I'm not an expert on the budgets of large organizations. How about you?"

"Budgets for a church and a school? Yes. For something along the lines of the Vatican? No."

Tanquerey smiled. "I've worked with a guy – Roger Neun – who retired from the Government Accountability Office in D.C. He knows his stuff, and he also is like a dog with a bone in pursuing the truth."

"Sounds perfect."

She nodded, and added, "Plus, he's a practicing Catholic. This just might be his dream assignment."

"Even better."

"In addition, Sofia Chavez is a top-notch producer and researcher. We used to work together at my network gig. She left for family reasons. Her husband died, and she needed to be there for their two kids."

McDermott said, "I'm so sorry."

Tanquerey nodded slightly, and continued, "Her parents are able to help out, and we've been working together here and there. I'd like to hire her full time, and this might be the opportunity. But either way, she's professional, does great work, and is a genuinely nice person."

"Good," replied McDermott.

The two went on to talk and start laying out a plan over the following hour and a half.

In the middle of that stretch, Pastor Richard Leonard entered the room, and declared, "We just finished speaking with the pope. Everyone is in agreement to stay here."

After a few questions from Tanquerey and McDermott, Leonard added, "And since we're going to be stuck in terms of limiting our movements, at least for a while, we'll have plenty of time to get more work done on this project."

Chapter 26

"Rather than retreating and playing it safe, Pope Paul VII does the exact opposite," observed Cardinal Renaldo Bessetti. "I am impressed, while also being annoyed. He has changed since gaining the papacy, and even since he pushed me out as secretary. He is not the same man. The pope actually has grown a backbone – unfortunately for us."

Bessetti sat at his desk, speaking with Father Pietro Filoni.

Filoni said, "This Lutheran pastor, Stephen Grant, is formidable."

"Yes, I am aware of that. He has something of a reputation, including his work tied to Pope Augustine." Bessetti pushed back in his chair, and looked up at the high ceiling.

Silence descended upon the room. Filoni closed his eyes, waiting to hear what Bessetti would utter next. After more than five minutes, Bessetti spoke and Filoni opened his eyes.

Bessetti continued to look up and said, "I thought with greater control over the bureaucracy, I could make up for not being at the Holy Father's side. However, I did not anticipate this degree of change in the man."

Bessetti paused, and Filoni closed his eyes once again. The silence returned. After another few minutes, Bessetti declared, "We need someone in the room, Pietro."

"Yes, well, that would be ideal, Your Eminence, but how could we possibly insert someone near the Holy Father at this point?"

"Perhaps we do not need to 'insert' someone, but instead, we merely need to use leverage on someone already in the room."

Filoni now wore an expression of bewilderment. "Who would that possibly be?"

Bessetti replied, "We all have our secrets, Pietro, and some of those secrets are particularly, well, let's say, troubling." Bessetti finally pulled his gaze down from the ceiling and looked at Filoni. "Pietro, what I am going to ask you to do will be hard. Rest assured, however, that it is in the service of Christ, His Church, and the Holy Father and his sacred office."

"As I have said before, Your Eminence, whatever the calling, I will gladly serve you, the Holy Father, and the Church. Please, never doubt that."

Bessetti replied, "I do not, Pietro. May God bless you."

Chapter 27

Paige Caldwell was still asleep when the phone on her nightstand buzzed. Her eyes shot open. Caldwell looked at the screen, and answered, "Stephen, my alarm was about to go off in a half-hour, but here you are waking me up. My, my, it's like old times." She continued to tease, "Is there something I can help you with?"

It was a few minutes after five in the morning in the Old Town neighborhood of Alexandria, Virginia. Paige Caldwell was naked and alone in the master bedroom of her townhouse.

Being used to, as Stephen often put it, "Paige being Paige," Grant didn't rise to the bait. He knew that Paige, Charlie and Sean would agree to take on the task that Pope Paul VII had for CDM, but other questions lurked in his mind.

I'm not sure how playful Paige will be given that this is Rome, where the end started for us.

He allowed himself to discount the possibilities.

Grant, give it a rest. You think way too much of yourself.

"I'm sorry about waking you, Paige, but I've got something important for you ... for CDM."

She persisted, "Oh, it's business. How disappointing. But then again, you being married and a pastor, I guess I couldn't expect much more."

"Right, and there's also the fact that you're engaged."

"Yes, there's that, too. What's up?"

Grant started providing a summary of the situation, with Caldwell sprinkling in questions along the way. While still without clothes and now sitting on the side of the bed, her voice had shifted gears into an all-business tone.

"Well, thanks for suggesting CDM. I'll doublecheck with Charlie and Sean, but I'm confident in saying that you can tell Pope Paul VII that we'll accept the job."

"I thought so."

"Perhaps this is a chance at redemption, given what happened to Pope Augustine."

Paige Caldwell talking "redemption"?

"I'm with you on that, Paige."

"Yeah, I thought you would be." The two proceeded to cover additional details, and then Paige said, "Okay, let me get dressed, and head to the office. There are a few things we'll need to juggle."

I'm still not fully used to CEO Paige.

Caldwell continued, "Again, I'll let you know what Charlie and Sean said. But I want to be in the air to Rome by the end of tomorrow, at the latest."

"Great. Thanks, Paige."

Caldwell hesitated in her response, and said, "It's been a long time since we were in Rome ... together."

There it is.

"Seems like a lifetime ago."

"Yeah, it was," she responded in a low voice. She then shifted back to a more typical tonal combination of being in control and carefree. "Well, enough of that shit. I'll talk to you soon."

Grant merely replied, "Right."

Caldwell ended the call.

Well, all things considered, that went well.

Chapter 28

Noah Lucas had quietly endured for decades. For most of that time, he had done so alone.

But over the past six years, it had been with Melanie, and now with their newborn son, Sebastian. In fact, Melanie made life more than mere endurance. She brought light into his life, and hope.

Lucas told his wife that because of her, and what she had done for him, he thought less and less about what had happened to him those many years ago. He confessed to her that this was a transformation he previously thought to be impossible. His anger was ebbing. She even got him to start reading the Bible with her. Noah told Melanie that he was discovering comfort there that he had never known before.

Of late, the hurt and anger would reappear almost exclusively when he drove into town to get supplies. That inevitably took him past the local Catholic Church. The sign on the front lawn proclaimed, "Catholics Come Home."

Decades earlier, the priest had become a friend of the Lucas family, and regularly came to their home to dinner. He eventually joined them on a few of the family's camping trips on the Spencer Gulf on the coast of South Australia.

It would take decades for Lucas to recognize how the man spoke about the importance of priests. The entire family had accepted quickly the idea that priests were above others in the Church, that they were holy and that everything they did was for the glory of God. His parents, in hopes that Noah would consider the priesthood, echoed the priest's comments about the holiness of priests.

So, when Noah went on a camping trip alone with the priest, it seemed perfectly normal. In fact, it brought joy to his parents. But when the priest came into his tent on that last night, and molested Noah, the young teen was confused and frightened. Feeling unable to tell anyone about what had occurred, confusion gave way to anger. He lashed out at everyone, including his family and himself. The priest had disappeared from their lives. Years of aimlessness and alcohol abuse followed. And even when he managed to jettison the alcohol and build a career in the financial world, the anger persisted.

When Melanie came into his life, though, the anger slowly was crowded out by her love and kindness. They eventually got married, and chose to simplify their life together. They bought a horse farm far out in the country, and Noah did financial planning remotely. He earned less, but he often spoke to Melanie of the peace in his life now.

The pickup was filled with the monthly supplies, and Noah managed to ignore the sign at the Catholic Church.

Night had fallen. That meant he couldn't see the smoke in the distance. But as his truck got closer to the entrance of the horse farm, Noah saw a strange glow in the distance. As he got closer, Noah Lucas could see that the light was flickering randomly.

"Oh, God, please no," he said aloud, as his foot pressed down on the accelerator.

A few minutes later, he turned hard and guided the vehicle through the open front gate. From there, Lucas could see that the fire had completely engulfed his home.

He again pleaded, "Please, no."

An expression of relief came across his face when he saw the silhouettes of people standing in front of the house. He allowed himself the hope that Melanie with Sebastian were among them.

The pickup truck skidded to a halt in front of three men standing perfectly still. Lucas jumped out and started running to the house. He yelled, "Where are they? Is my family safe?" He stopped abruptly when seeing how the three were dressed. They were priests.

One standing in front of the other two asked, "Noah?"

"Yes. What's happening? Please, please, tell me my family is safe."

The priest in front replied, "Let us pray that their souls will eventually know comfort with the Lord."

Tears filled Noah's eyes. "What?" He looked at the inferno, and dropped to his knees. He whispered, "Melanie. Sebastian."

The priest standing in front, signaled that the other two should move to Lucas. They did so.

Noah's head hung down, and now he was weeping. The two priests pulled him to his feet. The lead priest stepped forward and stopped just a yard away from Lucas.

Father Pietro Filoni looked at Lucas, and said, "I am truly sorry for what Father Winston Treadwell did to you years ago. It was evil, and he will pay. I will end your pain, and by doing so, rest assured, Noah, that this will make a difference. Your sacrifice will have meaning."

Lucas continued to look beyond Filoni at the fire that was consuming the bodies of his wife and son.

In the distant barn, horses were neighing and kicking at their stall walls.

Filoni pulled a knife out of a sheath tied to his right leg. He looked back and forth at Fathers Michael Russo and Lorenzo Conti. They tightened their grips on Lucas' upper arms.

As Filoni drove the knife into Noah's chest, he said, "May the Lord who frees you from sin save you and raise you up."

At the knife's plunge, Noah Lucas turned his head to look at the priest who had murdered his family, and now him. He managed to spit in Filoni's face before life drained away.

Filoni wiped away the bits of saliva, and said, "Get the photos, and then toss him in the flames."

Chapter 29

Vincent Mazzoni greeted the team from CDM International Strategies and Security, shaking hands with Paige Caldwell, Charlie Driessen, Jessica West and Phil Lucena.

Caldwell remarked, "Stephen Grant speaks highly of you, Inspector."

Mazzoni replied, "As he does you. Indeed, each of you."

"Where is Stephen? I thought he was going to be in the meeting with Pope Paul VII as well."

"Yes. He is in with His Holiness already."

Mazzoni led them into a sitting room in the Papal Apartments. In addition to Stephen and the pope, Cardinal Winston Treadwell and Father Mariano Concepcion also were present.

With formalities and introductions taken care of, Caldwell and Driessen took seats in the circle of chairs that had been set up, along with the pope, Grant, Treadwell and Concepcion. Mazzoni, West and Lucena chose spots around the room, allowing each to watch the room and its lone door, as well as being able to access the room's two large windows, with the curtains currently drawn on each.

The conversation proceeded basically as an interview. The pope asked wide-ranging questions about CDM, including its past undertakings, as well as about the backgrounds of the staff, including direct inquiries about Caldwell, Driessen, West and Lucena.

Grant, Mazzoni, Treadwell and Concepcion were left to watch and listen.

*The pope was well briefed by, I assume, Mazzoni. And the
pope apparently took in everything from that briefing. He's
asking these questions without any notes. Impressive.*

Grant caught Mazzoni looking his way, as if reading his
thoughts. Stephen gave the slightest of nods, as a signal of
respect as to what was going on in the room. Grant thought
he saw a slight smile on Mazzoni's face.

At one point, Pope Paul VII said, "Ms. Caldwell, Mr.
Driessen, your firm came with the highest recommendation
from Pastor Grant." The pope looked over at Grant, and then
returned his attention to Caldwell and Driessen. "I
appreciate you coming to Rome on short notice, and your
obvious concern for what is occurring. I would like to hire
you to take the lead in protecting our group involved in this
project, and to get to the bottom as to who is behind all of
this." Caldwell started to respond, but was cut off, as the
pope added, "As long as we can come to an agreement on
terms."

*The pope and Paige are going to haggle, and in front of
us? Doesn't he have someone else who does this?*

The pope did, in fact, engage in the question of costs with
everyone else still in the room. "So, how much would this
cost?"

Caldwell quoted a bottom line weekly cost number.

The pope sat back in his chair, and simply responded,
"With all due respect, that seems high."

Stephen wasn't surprised that Paige wasn't intimidated
by negotiating prices with a pope. She smiled and replied,
"Well, Your Holiness, we have the best at CDM, and that's
what you are paying for."

Pope Paul VII returned the smile, and said, "Indeed, I am
impressed, and have no doubt that you are the best at what
you do. But still, there must be something we can do. After
all, we are paying for your rooms at the Trevisani."

Grant was fascinated to watch the give-and-take
negotiations that proceeded for the next 15 minutes. This
was a side of Paige largely unknown to him, at least in terms
of the nitty-gritty business end of CDM. He also was

interested in the ease at which Pope Paul VII handled the negotiations, which no doubt was aided by his time as secretary to Pope Augustine.

It was settled with handshakes all around.

Before the gathering officially came to a close, the pope asked, "Would you mind if I said a quick blessing?"

Caldwell answered, "Of course not, Your Holiness."

Grant was trying to read if Paige's quick agreement reflected her being at ease with a papal blessing, or if it was merely being gracious to a client.

Everyone lowered their heads as the pope raised his right hand in the air. He proclaimed, "Lord, bless these people who are working to aid Your Church. They work to protect lives and seek justice. Please watch over them, guide them, and protect them." As he made the sign of the cross in the air, he continued, "We pray in the name of Your Son, Jesus Christ."

A few minutes later, after Caldwell, Driessen, West and Lucena had left the room, the pope said to Grant, "Thank you, Stephen. The CDM people are exactly as you presented them."

Grant nodded and said, "Thank you." He couldn't resist adding, "And if you don't mind me saying, Your Holiness, I was impressed by your negotiating skills."

Pope Paul VII smiled at that. "Ms. Caldwell is not easily intimidated."

"She most certainly is not."

"I was pleased to see that."

Was that a further test? Hmmm, very crafty, Pope Paul.

Grant said, "Well, if you'll excuse me. I will escort the CDM team over to the Trevisani hotel." He looked over at Mazzoni, and asked, "Are you coming, Inspector?"

Mazzoni said, "I will meet you there."

After stepping out of the sitting room and shutting the door behind him, Grant looked at four people he considered friends, and on some level, still colleagues. He now had the opportunity to greet each individually.

He and Paige exchanged light kisses on the cheek. Grant said, "Your negotiating skills with a pope are impressive."

"That was easy. After all, he's a genuinely nice person, unlike some that I have to deal with."

Grant shook hands with Charlie. "How are you, Charlie?"

"Good, Grant. Rome, again, huh? I assume this time around it's not going to get as bloody."

At that comment, Grant's eyes moved briefly to Paige and then back to Charlie. He replied, "I trust you're going to be right about that."

He then came to West and Lucena. After initial "hellos," Grant asked, "And how are you two doing?"

They glanced at each other, and West answered, "We're doing really well."

"Glad to hear that." He added to Jessica, "And what about the dual career thing?"

"It's all pointed in the right direction. Mel is pleased. My CDM bosses seem to be as well. Phil puts up with it. And I'm loving it all." Jessica West not only worked for CDM, but also recently became a player on a professional beach volleyball tour, partnered with the tour's owner Melissa Ambler.

Grant said, "That's great. You sound like that tennis player in that old 60s television show. He was a tennis pro and a spy. What was that called?" He looked around, and it immediately became clear to Stephen that no one had any idea what he was talking about.

West stepped up to bail him out. "The Santa Cruz location is ideal, and seems to be working for everyone as well." After a recent mission, CDM took over a special, secret operation in Santa Cruz, California, and West and Lucena were located there and running it now.

Lucena interjected, "At some point, we'd like to get together and talk about some stuff with you. Maybe over dinner?"

"Sounds good."

Apparently, I'm racking up dinner appointments with couples.

Grant then said to all four, "Let's get going. I'll direct you to the hotel, and introduce everyone there."

As they moved through the building toward where CDM's SUV was parked, Grant asked, "So, where are Sean, Chase, Brooke and Kent?" He was referring to the rest of the CDM group – Sean McEnany, Chase Axelrod, Brooke Semmler and Kent Holtwick.

Driessen answered, "Sean is where you'd expect, at home with his basement office and his van."

Caldwell commented, "Geez, Charlie, we have the best person on the planet in terms of getting information, and he has the most cutting-edge systems, but you make him sound like a creepy guy in his basement with a van."

Driessen laughed. "Yeah, I know."

Caldwell rolled her eyes, and said to Grant, "Chase, Kent and Brooke are in D.C. juggling the rest of our clients."

Grant commented, "Well, it's nice to have so many clients that you have to juggle when a new one comes on board, I assume?"

"Absolutely," answered Caldwell.

A few minutes later, the five were in a silver SUV moving through the streets of Rome.

Chapter 30

Cardinal Winston Treadwell was lying in bed reading when the doorbell rang. He looked over at the clock on his end table, saw the time, made a sound of exasperation, and then said out loud, "Who could this possibly be?"

He closed the book, got out of bed, and slipped a thick, terrycloth robe on over his pajamas, and put on his slippers. He went down the stairs of his townhouse, flipped on the switch for the outside light, below which leaned his cane, and peeked out the slim window pane running adjacent to the front door. At seeing who it was, Treadwell said, "What the...?"

He opened the door, and did nothing more than stare.

Cardinal Renaldo Bessetti smiled, and said, "Good evening, Cardinal Treadwell, I hope I did not wake you."

Treadwell looked beyond Bessetti into the darkness.

Bessetti said, "I am alone Cardinal Treadwell. Are you going to invite me in?"

Treadwell made no move. He replied, "What do you want, Renaldo?"

"Come, come now, Winston, I bring good news for you and for the Church."

Treadwell grudgingly stepped to the side, and said, "Come in."

Bessetti stepped inside with some enthusiasm, while saying, "Thank you."

Treadwell led Bessetti into a small kitchen. He sat down at the round table, and silently indicated that Bessetti should take a seat as well.

After Bessetti positioned himself directly across the table, Treadwell said, "So, Renaldo, what do you have that's good news for the Church and for me?" His voice dripped with sarcasm.

Bessetti glanced over his shoulder and said, "First, I have to ask a question that I have been wondering about: That cane of yours, why is there a frog at the top?"

"I don't see why this is any of your business, but it is seen by many as a symbol of transformation."

"Interesting and perhaps fitting," replied Bessetti.

Treadwell asked, "What does that mean?"

Bessetti said, "Regarding my visit, I have taken care of a major problem."

"And that would be?"

Bessetti unzipped a thin, leather pouch he had brought, reached inside, and pulled out a manilla folder. He took a picture out and slid it across the table.

Treadwell looked down at the photo. His mouth fell open at the sight of a woman with her throat slit. "What the hell is this?"

Bessetti slid another photo across the table.

Seeing a young boy also with his throat cut, Treadwell whispered, "My God, what is this?" He pulled his eyes away from the horrors captured in the photos. "What are you doing, Renaldo?"

"What am I doing? I told you, I have helped you, and by doing so, the Lord's Church."

"What are you talking about? Have you gone mad? Did you do this?"

"I had this done, Winston. And this as well." He took out the photo of Noah Lucas' body, and slid it across the table.

Upon seeing this last photo, Treadwell's entire body sagged. His hands shook as he reached out and picked up the last photo. He squinted and moved the picture closer to his face. But his hands continued to shake. So, he dropped the photo back onto the table, and moved his eyes closer to it.

Bessetti sat silently, and watched his fellow cardinal.

A tear formed and dropped from Treadwell's eye and onto the photo. "What have you done?" His voice was barely audible.

Bessetti responded, "What have I done? It's what you did, Winston. Isn't it? Noah was so young, and you had earned the trust of his family. How horrible. Your actions were the actions of a predator."

Treadwell pushed himself away from the photo and the entire table. He said, "You murdered him?"

"Because of what you did, something had to be done. This poor man had a difficult time, but he apparently found some solace thanks to his wife and child."

"Then why?"

"The Church has been through so much on this front. You know that, Winston. It cannot suffer any longer. Think about the reaction if it came out that one of the pope's closest aides turned out to be a sexual predator."

Treadwell winced at those last two words. "I am not a predator."

Bessetti actually chuckled. "Winston, I think what you did here, and who knows where else, neatly fits the definition of a sexual predator."

Treadwell raised his voice, "It never happened again."

"Somehow I doubt that. It does not fit the pattern."

"It is the truth. I have never done anything like that ever again. It was such a horrible mistake. When I think about it, it's like I am seeing someone else. It doesn't seem like it's me."

"Whatever you need to tell yourself, Winston, to get by each day is your business. But you did this, and the situation had to be dealt with, and for the sake of Christ's Church, I took action. You should be pleased. It must be a huge relief. After all, if what you say is true, then nothing now can come back and haunt you or the Church."

"Nothing can...? You murdered three innocent people. You're mad. You have to be turned in. Justice requires it."

"You have the nerve to speak of justice? That is laughable. However, if you choose to accuse me, there will be absolutely nothing to back up your claim. But there will be plenty of evidence about what you did, Winston. And then there will be talk about who had motive to see that Noah Lucas was dead, not to mention his wife and son."

"What?" Treadwell's eyes focused once again on the photos laying on the table.

Bessetti added, "And what about Pope Paul VII? I presume that you care about the Holy Father and his papacy. What will happen when what you, one of his closest aides – dare I say, a close friend? – did? The Holy Father would never recover from such a blow. Indeed, what about the papacy and the Church? Could they survive such a blow? You would be responsible for historic damage to the Roman Catholic Church, Winston. Are you prepared for that?"

Treadwell sat immobilized.

Bessetti continued, "So, it seems to me that you have three options, but only one protects the pope and the Church, as well as you. The first option would be to follow your initial reaction, and then everything comes toppling down, again, not just on you, but on the Holy Father and the Church. The second option, which I hope you are not considering, but some might. And that would be suicide. But that coward's way out would only make matters worse for Pope Paul and the Church, not to mention, placing your eternal soul in peril. No, Winston, my friend, the only option that makes sense for everyone is for you to accept that what I had done here is the best for the Holy Father, for the papacy, for the Church, and yes, for you, in the end."

Treadwell sat in silence for several minutes. He finally whispered, "What is it that you want from me?"

Bessetti smiled, "Ah, I knew you would see things clearly. I just need you to help me save the Holy Father, the papacy and the Church from another threat. This one comes from Pope Paul VII himself, and all you need to do is be my eyes and ears. All I need from you, Winston, is information."

Chapter 31

Haley finished telling Conrad what had transpired with the project over breakfast at their Rome apartment.

Conrad was in his typical three-piece suit, ready to head to his office. Haley was scheduled to lecture at the university today, and wore an off-white button-down shirt and brown pants, with a tan tweed sports jacket waiting by the front door with her laptop case.

Conrad's aide, Albro Dawson, was set to take her to the university, and serve as a personal bodyguard. He also had prepared breakfast for his employers.

Haley commented, "I know we have the apartment here, and no one can question Albro's ability to keep us safe."

As he entered the dining room to offer refills on tea and coffee, Dawson merely said, "Thank you, Mrs. Whittacker."

Haley smiled somewhat nervously in response. "I know we've been down this road before, Albro, but I really wish you'd call me 'Haley.'"

Dawson smiled, "I appreciate that, but I would not feel right about that."

Dawson exited the room, and Haley shook her head slightly.

Conrad said, "I know that you would like Albro to be a bit more informal, my dear, but that is not how he functions."

"Yes, I know." She took a sip of tea. "Anyway, what I started to say was that perhaps I should stay at the Trevisani with the group."

Conrad asked, "Why?"

"I don't like the idea of pulling Albro away from you while this is going on."

Conrad smiled, and said, "While I appreciate that, you mustn't be worried, Haley. I will be fine."

She took a deep breath, and said, "No, I don't like this. This group that's coming in to handle security supposedly ranks among the best in the world, at least according to Pastor Grant."

"He's an interesting fellow, to say the least, in terms of his experiences."

Haley replied, "What? Yes, I'm sure he is. But we will be well protected at the hotel, and I would feel better if Albro was at your side."

Conrad put down his cup, and looked at his wife. "Are you that worried, Haley?"

She nodded.

"Well, then, so be it. Albro will be at my side, and you will be well guarded by some of the best security people on the planet."

"Do you mean it?"

"Of course."

"Thank you, Conrad."

"You are thanking me. I thank you, Haley. I do love you."

Haley's smile lit up. "And I love you, too, Conrad. I'll make sure that I have everything I need, and after class, I'll stop back here, pick up my suitcase, and Albro can then drop me at the hotel."

He added, "Of course, you're not a world away, and this is not a prison. Anything you might need, I can bring over, or if you need to just get out and come home, well, it's all right here."

Chapter 32

While Conrad and Haley Whittacker were conversing over breakfast, Paige Caldwell was doing the same with her fiancé, who happened to also be the most powerful man on the planet.

However, while Paige was in her hotel room drinking black coffee and eating a protein bar, President Adam Links had just gotten into bed, with it being six hours earlier in Washington, D.C., compared to Rome.

Links said, "Apparently, I need to talk to my ambassador to the Vatican. I wouldn't know that any of this was going on if not for your now being on the pope's payroll."

"Hmmm. When you're done with your current job, I'll have to think about hiring you for CDM or not. After all, you'd think that you would be on top of this," taunted Caldwell.

"Thanks. That's funny."

Links and Caldwell had worked together at the CIA years earlier, and had a relationship. That was rekindled recently, to the point that the two were secretly engaged, with an eye toward getting married after Links left office.

Caldwell continued, "But in defense of whoever the ambassador happens to be, the pope has done a surprisingly good job at keeping this project under wraps."

"Except for the fact that two people involved might have been murdered."

"Well, yes, there's that."

Links asked, "What do you think of Pope Paul VII? We met a few years ago, and it was hard to get a read on him.

He was very careful, and there was a good deal of criticism swirling around him. People apparently were calling him the 'Do Nothing Pope.' Although it had to be hard to succeed Pope Augustine, given all that had occurred."

"My general impression is that he certainly is carrying more weight on his shoulders than when I first saw him as Augustine's aide. But at the same time, he seemed to be bearing it well. Stephen had said that it took time for him to gain his footing, but he's been growing into the office."

"Ah, the Lutheran pastor's assessment of the pope."

"For what it's worth. But his view was backed up by Father Ron McDermott, a Catholic priest who is here with Stephen, and has been drafted by the pope for another endeavor."

"What's that about?"

"Father McDermott is helping Madison Tanquerey undertake an investigation of some Vatican finances."

"Another undertaking that I know nothing about. What the hell?"

"You're welcome."

"Unbelievable."

"Hey, don't get mad at me."

"I'm not. You're the only person telling me anything, it seems. Well, at least about the Vatican."

"As a Catholic, you have no clue as to what the Vatican is doing. From what I understand, that's not surprising. However, you also happen to be the president of the United States."

"Paige." There was a shift in tone by Links, indicating that Caldwell's teasing had crossed a line.

"Just kidding, Adam. You need to get some sleep and I need to get to work. Love you."

"You, too."

The call ended, and Paige looked at the phone and smiled.

Chapter 33

Pastor Rusty Spuel's final blog entry on the church's website turned out to be the straw that broke the camel's back. It would be his last blog entry as the parish's pastor.

During a church council meeting at which Spuel was confronted by members who were displeased over just about everything, he stewed in silence and unmistakable anger. At each point during the meeting, when asked if he would like to respond or say anything, Spuel remained quiet. The meeting ended with a vote to form a subcommittee to start investigating the possibility of the church closing or joining with another nearby Lutheran congregation. The vote was unanimous.

Everyone around the long table looked at Spuel, who remained silent, with eyes looking down at the table. When asked to say a closing prayer for the meeting, Spuel merely got up from his chair, and left the room.

He entered his office, closed and locked the door, and sat down at his computer. A screed against this congregation, against his district president, against the president of the entire church body, and finally, against the entire Lutheran Church-Missouri Synod seemed to flow from a long pent-up rage and out through fingers banging at the keys. He tore others down, while raising himself up as the defender of the true faith. He posted the piece without even re-reading it once.

By breakfast the next day, his broad, scattershot, disturbing attack on seemingly everyone provided more than enough cause for the congregation to discharge him from his duties.

Pastor Rusty Spuel's tumultuous time at this particular Lutheran church came to an end via a tumultuous crash. And his anger was now unconstrained.

As he packed up his office, Spuel mumbled about people in the Church working with Satan. He took down a picture of his seminary class from the wall. He fell back into the desk chair, and pulled the photo out of its frame. Spuel picked up a marker and his stare moved from face to face in the photo. After ten minutes, he had circled four faces, folded the photo several times, and shoved it in his pocket.

Chapter 34

Paige Caldwell, Charlie Driessen, Jessica West and Phil Lucena wound up claiming the conference room in the hotel. The meeting was meant to finalize protection details and review the investigation, such as it was so far. The gathering had started over lunch, and continued on after food was finished and cleared away.

Pastor Stephen Grant was part of the gathering, as was Sean McEnany, being piped in on one of the laptop screens from his base of operations in his Long Island basement.

Caldwell looked up from her laptop. "Okay, then we're good on assignments. Phil covering Father Kohli; Jessica with Haley Whittacker; Charlie handing Killian Dvorak; and I'm with Pastor Leonard."

From the other operating laptop positioned on a counter of a small kitchenette area, McEnany said, "That's fine. But what about Madison Tanquerey and Father McDermott. They're not directly part of this, but given the situation, they need to be covered as well. Do you want me to come over?"

Caldwell replied, "That depends."

"On what?"

"On Stephen."

"Me?" replied Grant.

Caldwell continued, "Hey, the pope wants you to be in on this. You might as well earn your pay."

"That's fine. I have no problem with that. However, I'm pretty sure that I'm the only one in the room not getting paid." He smiled.

Driessen said, "Do you want a consulting contract, Grant?"

"No. I'm good. Thanks for asking, though, Charlie."

Driessen grunted in response.

Caldwell observed, "Good. That leaves you, Sean, to focus exclusively on who might be behind this. As for both Father McDermott and Madison, we'll probably have to do some juggling, depending on what the others are up to at the time."

Driessen said, "It would be a hell of a lot easier if our scholars just stayed put here until this is over."

West chimed in, "It would, Charlie. I agree."

Caldwell sat back in her chair. "We're all in agreement on that. And we will limit their movements as much as we can. But they also are teaching and lecturing, and we're trying to keep this under wraps as much as possible. Plus, Madison and Father McDermott are doing their own thing for the pope, and they'll be circulating as a result."

Lucena interjected, "Yes, I do think that this is the best we can do, given the circumstances."

West smirked at him, and he smiled ever so slightly.

Driessen said, "Yeah, great. Now, listen, the pope's guy, Vincent Mazzoni, has worked some bureaucratic miracle and we're all cleared to carry. So, stop by my room after this meeting, and I'll hand out weapons."

Grant asked, "Does that include me?"

Driessen nodded, and said, "Yeah, and I even have a Glock 20 for you. I know how much you love that gun."

"Great. Thanks."

Caldwell asked, "Sean, do you have anything new?"

"Not yet, but I should soon. I'm supposed to talk with some law enforcement people who can give me more on the deaths of Professor Fuchs and Pastor Fletcher. You know, is this person writing to the pope telling the truth or just a nut, or most likely, of course, both? I've also started the process of doing deep security reviews on Vatican staff."

West commented, "That's a monster undertaking." She had firsthand knowledge of such operations from her days with the FBI.

"Yeah, I know. But I've got help. Chase, Brooke and Kent are pitching in as they can. But this needs to be done. I know I'm a bit over the top with this, given what we do, but the Vatican's background checks are worth shit."

Driessen commented, "Gee, I'm just shocked to hear that."

Grant added, "Yes, well, churches don't really default toward doing deep background checks on their people – and apparently that includes the largest church in the world with the biggest bureaucracy."

Driessen said, "They should be going deep."

Grant replied, "I'm not disagreeing with you. I'm just telling you what the deal is."

McEnany said, "Anyway, as concerns pop up from these checks, I'll get them to you guys, and then we can figure out how to proceed with each. Given that our concerns focus inside the Vatican, the direct approach probably will make the most sense. I get the information to you guys, and you track the person down and have a conversation."

Driessen said, "I like it."

West added, "So do I."

The conversation proceeded, covering a variety of details. And then Paige said, "I've got two more items to cover, and then we can deal with anything each of you need to go over. First, after we're done here, we'll talk with the people we've been asked to protect to make sure this works for them. I think this will be a pretty easy group to work with since they're academics who like staying inside doing research, and they're intelligent individuals who understand what this is about. Plus, they obviously cared about Fuchs and Fletcher. However, keep in mind, they're not under house arrest. They ultimately can do as they please. But so can we. If someone gets antsy to leave on their own, push in the opposite direction. But if they insist on it, let them go, and then, of course, follow them closely."

That's very CIA of you, Paige.

Driessen chuckled, and said, "I like that, too."

Caldwell actually smiled, and then said, "As for the last item on my list, I hand the floor over to Stephen."

"Excuse me?" responded Grant.

"We need a quick summary as to what this is all about. What are these scholars and the pope doing? To get specific, I guess the questions we need you to answer are: What did Martin Luther and Jan Hus do? What happened? And why are these people dealing with this some 500 or 600 years later? Who would be made happy by it, and who would get pissed off? You know, to sum up for those of us who aren't theologians, what's the big deal?"

Grant looked at Paige, and then around at the others in the room. His eyes returned to Paige, and he said, "You realize that you're protecting the people who are the experts on this? They can answer any question you could possibly have. Why not have them give you a rundown?"

"Because we don't need to become experts. And I don't want to waste time listening to academics drone on about their fields of study, quite frankly. We just need the basics to help us understand possible motivations. If any of us want or need a deeper dive, then we'll go to one or more of our scholars. For now, we need a summary from someone who understands what we do and understands what the issues are." Paige smiled. "And you're the perfect person to do that. Heck, you might be the only person who can do that."

Lucky me. Thanks.

Grant said, "Well, thanks for giving me a heads-up in advance."

Caldwell merely responded, "No problem." She continued to smile.

"So, the *Cliff Notes* version of great moments in Christian history? Alright, here goes. Starting with Hus, he's far less famous than Martin Luther, but he was a key figure in what some have called the 'First Reformation.' He was born around 1373 in ..."

Driessen interrupted, "Did you say '1373'?"

"I did."

"We're not going to cover some 600 years right now, are we?"

"No. I'm going to give you what you need, like Paige asked. Again, the *Cliff Notes* for investigative purposes." Grant waited for more from Driessen, but got nothing more than a grunt. So, Grant continued. "He was born in Bohemia, which basically is the Czech Republic today. He studied, taught and actually became the rector at the University of Prague, or Charles University."

Lucena interrupted this time, but in his unfailingly polite way. "I'm sorry, but excuse me, Stephen."

"Yes, Phil?"

"That is the same university where Killian Dvorak teaches today, correct?"

"Yes, that's right."

"Thank you."

"You're welcome." Grant turned back to addressing the entire group. "Hus was ordained a priest in 1400. As for his role as a reformer, he offered some major complaints about the Catholic Church in his time. And keep in mind, there already was a Czech reform movement occurring, and this entire period that we're talking about was highly charged politically."

Driessen commented, "Oh, gee, something different."

Grant smiled, and said, "Yeah, I get your point, but this was very different in terms of focus and degree. First, Hus was highly critical about immorality and abuses among the clergy."

Driessen again interjected, "You did say 'very different,' right?"

Grant replied, "Touché. As for abuses at the time, Hus spoke out against the selling of church offices and indulgences, priests being guilty of breaking their vows in an assortment of ways, including having girlfriends and selling access to the sacraments, such as money for forgiveness, as well as pilgrimages to view relics. Given this emphasis on priests and, for that matter, popes behaving badly, there was a good deal of focus on following the Ten Commandments and living a devout life. However, he also understood the sinfulness of man, and wrote of the need for Christ to draw us to him, and without this drawing, we couldn't follow Him. By the way, Hus gained attention when he was appointed preacher at Bethlehem Chapel, which was a church established, again, by reform-minded Czechs, with the preaching provided in the common language, rather than in Latin. That was another controversy."

Grant paused, and took a sip of an iced tea that he had been drinking. He continued, "Hus's sermons on abuses and immorality within the Church gained attention and a strong following among the people in Prague. All of this naturally made him an assortment of enemies in the Church, with officials sending spies to report back on his sermons. Interestingly, on two of the biggest issues of the day – one being controversies over Communion" – *not getting into transubstantiation here* – "and the other a papal schism, with at one point three people simultaneously claiming to be the pope, Hus held the traditional Catholic view on the first, and didn't weigh in on the second. He did venture into other areas of controversy, including regarding the role of the pope. Hus emphasized that the pope and others in the Church should be obeyed only so long as their teachings jibe or align with Holy Scripture. As long as leaders in the Church subscribed to what Scripture said and taught, Hus had no qualms. But he reminded friends that, as he put it, 'We ought to obey God rather than men.' He hammered away on the truth that Christ, not the pope, was the head of the Church. And Hus went so far as to question the status of leaders within the Church when they betrayed the Gospel. This didn't sit well with the pope and other officials. Moreover, Hus would emphasize that the Church wasn't an enterprise run by popes and councils, but instead was the gathering of believers on earth and in heaven."

Grant paused, looked around the room.

They're still listening.

Grant resumed, "Getting back to Communion for a moment, Hus did stake out some controversial ground at the time. He was against the practice of withholding the chalice from the laity. So, someone going to church then would receive the bread, but not the wine. Hus thought this was wrong, a mistake that ignored, again as he put it, 'Christ's example and truth.' And when he defended himself against charges of being a heretic, Hus cited Scripture to defend his positions, which oddly, wasn't all that common at the time for theologians. In the end, I've read some articles here and there that have pointed out that the reason for Hus's strong criticisms of clergy immorality is that such behavior can serve as an obstacle between Christ and individuals."

He looked at Charlie, and said, "Yes, another point of relevance for today." Grant continued, "But some of these and other points relating to Hus, to varying degrees, persist as points of debate and division within the Church."

Now completely immersed in a role he loved, that is, talking and teaching history, particularly church history, Grant smiled and observed, "Make no mistake, Hus was not exactly a shrinking violet. He was fully in on the hot, confrontational manner of these so-called churchly debates of the era. For example, I read that Bethlehem Chapel was decorated with posters, in pairs, making clear assorted points. So, one pair had the pope on horseback, adorned richly, contrasted with Christ in poverty carrying the cross. And another two contrasted a kingly pope with his feet being kissed versus Christ kneeling and washing the feet of disciples." Grant chuckled at that.

Charlie said, "I think I like Hus."

Grant noted, "And the other side played just as hard, if not more so. At one point, I think it was King Vaclav who threatened Hus by declaring, 'If those whose concern it is will not take care of you, I myself will burn you.'" He paused his talk, and was about to ask if anyone had questions.

Caldwell asked, "Are you sure this is the *Cliff Notes* version?"

Grant nodded, and said, "I get it. Fair enough."

This is not a class at St. Mary's. It's a briefing for what these people need to know.

Grant plowed ahead. "Now, as for Martin Luther, there's a heck of a lot more to wrestle with in terms of his theology, his sparking the Reformation, seemingly countless church debates that he weighed in on, and the fact that, unlike Hus, Luther is far more well known today, and far more likely to generate heated debate even nearly 500 years after his death. But I'll hit the highlights."

Caldwell commented, "Thanks. That's appreciated."

Grant explained, "Luther was born in 1483, and was supposed to become a lawyer. But he had doubts about such a career, and during a storm, with lightning striking nearby, he allegedly called out, 'Help me, St. Anne! I will become a monk!' And after further reflection, he did become a monk."

West asked, "Who is St. Anne?"

"The mother of Mary."

West nodded.

Grant continued, "Luther became a priest in 1507, took his doctorate in 1512, and became a professor at Wittenberg University. From that position, he continued with a deeper exploration of Scripture, and his teachings, his protests, reactions to him within the Church and his responses, negotiations, threats, and more played out over years. For our purposes, on October 31, 1517, Luther supposedly posted his *95 Theses* on the church door in Wittenberg."

West asked, "Supposedly?"

"Debate exists among scholars if the act of nailing them to the church door is reality or myth. But whatever the means, Luther issued this challenge to the sale of indulgences, and invited academic debate."

Lucena interrupted this time. "Excuse me, what are indulgences?"

Grant answered, "These were documents from the church that a person could buy for himself or on behalf of someone else, including someone already deceased, that would reduce one's time in purgatory."

Lucena replied, "Well, interesting."

Grant continued, "Indulgences actually are still around in the Catholic Church, but they differ in certain ways from those available during the Medieval Church. Anyway, Luther challenged the sale of indulgences, and this didn't sit well with a pope – at the time Leo X – who was an extravagant spender. He had to pay for rebuilding St. Peter's Basilica and an assortment of other endeavors, such as the costs of war and assorted celebrations. So, selling church offices was a big thing, and indulgences were an income stream. As my wife, the economist, will tell you, hit the revenue stream of any institution, and it's not going to go well. And that was the case for Luther. In fact, I know some theologians who claim that if it hadn't been for the money, the Catholic Church probably would have ignored Luther. There's a point there, but in the end, I don't agree. There was much more there that eventually would have required responses. The floodgates were giving way. Luther's challenge to indulgences brought in a host of underlying theological issues, such as the question of authority. Much like Hus a century earlier, Luther argued that popes, councils, and tradition were all subservient to God's Word in Scripture. To drive home his point, Luther would say that 'a simple layman armed with Scripture' was superior to popes and councils without Scripture."

Driessen commented, "So, it wasn't just money but power as well. That's double jeopardy."

Grant nodded. "Right, and then toss politics into the mix, which were even more volatile during Luther's time than Hus's. Before I get further carried away by the enthusiasms of both a pastor and lover of history, as a way to sum up Luther's theology, if you will, I'll explain the 'solas' that emerge as the foundations of Luther's Reformation."

"'Solas'?" asked West.

"'Sola' is Latin for alone." Grant went on, "Luther's theology grew out of his anguish over being unable to find or see a gracious God. But then he came to understand that the 'righteousness of God' wasn't about God demanding that we do things, like acts of penance, but instead, it was about, as St. Paul wrote, 'The righteous shall live by faith.' This was liberating for Luther, and it gave him true comfort. This justification by faith was much more than an intellectual acknowledgment or assent, but instead, understanding of our reliance upon Christ. This basically is Luther's 'Sola Fide' or faith alone. And then there is 'Sola Gratia,' or grace alone. Here, Luther banished any chance for being human-centered. God's grace comes from completely outside ourselves. It is in no way our own act, but instead, it is a free gift from God. And even the faith needed to accept and hold on to such grace is given to us via God's grace. Luther found certainty in that we do not depend upon our own strength or works, which inevitably falter, but on the unshakable promise and truth of God."

Time to wrap this up, Grant.

He added, "As for 'Sola Scriptura' or Scripture alone, I already explained that, with Luther's emphasis on Scripture standing above popes, councils and tradition. His point ultimately was that popes, councils and tradition didn't judge Scripture, but it was the other way around. And finally, for Luther, everything came back Jesus Christ alone, or 'Solo Christo.' For Luther, all of Scripture points to Christ, and grace only comes through the cross, through Christ's wounds, through his resurrection, through his redeeming all of humankind. If one word were capable of summing up Luther's theology, it would be 'Christocentric.'"

Grant took a slug of his iced tea. "Now, it must be understood that to this very day, while there is more agreement than 500 years ago, serious disagreements and arguments persist on many of these points among theologians. There also are points of debate with Luther on the understanding of Communion, the role of clergy, allowing clergy to get married, the papacy, and more."

Caldwell commented, "So, there's still plenty of disagreements among Christians that some people might get really pissed off if a pope might be considering accepting or even honoring the likes of Hus and Luther?"

Before Grant could respond, Driessen asked, "What exactly happened to these two guys?"

Grant said, "Hus was invited to a church council, the Council of Constance, presumably to defend himself. Though he was promised safe passage, he wound up being arrested. Only days after arriving, he was tossed into a prison cell in a Dominican monastery on an island in Lake Constance, and almost died there due to the conditions. By the way, that place has been turned into a luxury hotel, for whatever that's worth." Grant shook his head, and continued, "He was declared guilty of heresy, and sentenced to death. Hus would not recant, and he actually prayed for his judges and accusers. He eventually was bound to a stake, wood piled to his chin, and while the fires raged, he sang, 'Jesus, son of the living God, have mercy on me.'"

The room was silent.

Grant then said, "Luther fared better. At the Diet of Worms in 1521, he, too, was called on to recant. He also was worried about being killed, but famously declared, 'It is neither safe nor honest to act against conscience. Here I stand, I cannot do otherwise. God help me. Amen.' He also would note, 'My conscience is captive to the word of God.' After failed negotiations, he was condemned but granted safe passage back to Wittenberg. Along the way home, he was kidnapped by armed horsemen, who turned out to be sent by Frederick the Wise, Luther's prince. They took him to Frederick's Wartburg Castle for his own protection. He eventually returned to the fray, however; scandalized many by marrying Katharina von Bora, a former nun; and eventually died in his bed in 1546."

Caldwell observed, "So, these are the kinds of wounds, I assume on both sides, that tend to persist for hundreds of years?"

"Yes, for many, they do. Back in the early eighties, in an article marking the 500th anniversary of Luther's birth, one historian noted that the Roman Catholic Church excommunicated Luther in 1521, and then spent the subsequent centuries 'excoriating his memory.' But the writer also noted that things had started to change, with some in Catholicism treating Luther 'more as an alumnus than an apostate.' For good measure, many view the Second Vatican Council, which met in the 1960s, as accepting some fundamental parts of Luther's Reformation. It's also worth noting that neither Hus nor Luther sought to start a new church. And Luther explicitly declared that he didn't want a church to carry his name, and yet, here I stand before you as a Lutheran pastor. They both considered themselves to be faithful to Christ's Church."

No one responded, so Grant decided to make one more point. "Here's a weird factoid that many see as prophetic. Facing the fires, Hus supposedly warned, and I think I have this quote right, it's kind of stuck with me, 'Today you will roast a lean goose, but a hundred years from now you will hear a swan sing, whom you will leave unroasted, and no trap or net will catch him for you.' 'Hus' meant 'goose,' and Luther would post his *95 Theses* 102 years later."

Driessen chimed in, "As for the lack of desire to start new churches, I guess being the guy viewed as splitting the Catholic Church apart, while another person is burned at the stake raises questions about intentions."

"Yeah. To stay with the animal analogies, in a 1520 papal bull condemning Luther's works and threatening excommunication, Pope Leo X called Luther 'a wild boar' who had invaded 'the Lord's vineyard.'"

West commented, "Now some are opposed to Pope Paul VII letting the wild boar back in, and by doing so, saying that the Church and past popes were wrong. And they're willing to take deadly actions to protect pope and Church. Others see Luther as something wonderful, a swan." There was no question in her tone. West simply offered this as a declaration.

Driessen added, "The more things change, the more they stay the same, right, Grant?"

"Apparently, Charlie."

Caldwell said, "Thanks for the history lesson, Stephen. Anything else?"

Grant smiled, and said, "Well, the last treatise that Luther wrote was titled *Against the Papacy at Rome, an Institution of the Devil.*"

Caldwell actually laughed, and said, "How diplomatic."

Grant replied, "Luther was many things, including, I would argue, a great theologian, but a diplomat? Not so much."

Caldwell said, "Okay, well, all of this does in fact provide things to chew on regarding possible motives."

Additional topics were covered, and the meeting ended nearly a half-hour later. While everyone else scattered, Grant lingered, as did Caldwell.

She said, "I got a better appreciation for you as a pastor while you were providing that history lesson."

Grant was taken off guard, and replied, "Well, thanks. Twenty years as a pastor actually isn't that far off, so hopefully I'm getting the hang of this."

"Twenty years. Holy shit. How did that happen?"

Grant replied, "I'm not sure if it feels like it's gone fast, or if our time together at the CIA seems like a long time ago. Depends on the day, I think."

After he said it, the phrase "our time together at the CIA" seemed to hang in the air for Grant.

Caldwell looked him directly in the eyes, and said, "The last time we were in Rome seems like a hell of a long time ago."

"I agree. It does."

Where is this going?

Caldwell said, "You should know that I do forgive you."

"I'm sorry. Forgive me? For what?"

"How you ended things, you know, not exactly smoothly or, quite frankly, properly done. And I know how much you appreciate or desire that things be done properly."

"Paige, are you kidding me? The way *I* handled us breaking up?"

Caldwell continued, "Stephen, you really need to get over this. It happened a long time ago. You're a married pastor, now. And I'm, well, you know. The time has long passed to move on."

"Paige, come on..."

Caldwell giggled. She got up, walked over to Grant, leaned down, and kissed him on the cheek. She whispered, "Why are you so easy to tease?"

Grant looked up, and Paige was still leaning down. Her face was just a couple of feet from his. He said, "I honestly don't know."

Her smile broadened, and Caldwell said, "I also have to wonder why it's easy to tease you when it comes to our past?"

"And I have to wonder why you keep teasing me."

"Why? Because it's just so damn much fun." She stood up straight, and said, "You need to call your wife."

Grant watched as she left the room.

Paige Caldwell knows how to push my buttons like no one else ever has.

Grant returned to his room, and took Paige's advice. He called Jennifer. Stephen gave her a full rundown on everything that had happened during the day, including the meeting with the CDM group.

He finished by saying, "It was the fastest lesson on Jan Hus and Martin Luther I certainly ever gave."

Jennifer said, "And let me guess: You loved every second of it, and wanted to tell them more?"

"You know me too well."

"I do. Anything else of interest?"

The conversation with Paige briefly passed through Grant's thoughts, but he pushed it to the side. He replied, "Not really. But I might have more to tell later. I'm going to have dinner with Richard and Madison in a couple of hours. They vaguely mentioned wanting to talk about getting married, but I don't have anything more than that."

"You better call me after that dinner with the details."

"I certainly will."

"Good. I unfortunately have to get back to work now. I love you."

"Love you, too."

Chapter 35

It was just after seven, and Pastor Stephen Grant was finishing dinner with Pastor Richard Leonard and Madison Tanquerey.

They had ventured to a small restaurant just around the block from the Trevisani hotel. Grant wound up adopting a split role that had become all too familiar in recent years.

On the one hand, Grant had a Glock 20 holstered under his sports jacket. He kept a close watch on the surroundings during the short walk to the establishment, and then made sure that they had a table in the back of the dining room. He sat with his back against the wall, thereby being able to see everyone who entered, exited and moved about the restaurant.

On the other hand, his conversation with Leonard and Tanquerey largely focused on their work regarding the Lutheran Response to Christian Persecution, and how that was being influenced by their time in Rome. Being in a public place, they put aside any conversation about the investigations and related concerns.

At one point, Richard said, "Even under the best of circumstances, the work that Madison and I are doing related to the Vatican will put us on hold regarding LRCP for at least several months. How much of a problem is that?"

Stephen reassured them both that it would be fine. Referring to Rachel McEnany, whom they were working with on the effort, he explained, "Besides, Rachel and I have more than enough information and material for presentations around the U.S. Given that we're both doing this part-time, we've still managed to get a lot done, with the website, some mailings, assorted video presentations and a few in-person talks."

"The website looks great," noted Madison.

"Thanks. That's all been Rachel. She's been the leader on this." Stephen took a sip of his espresso. "Pope Paul also has put me together with his aide, Father Concepcion, to get serious about working with the Vatican on the persecution issue. Given our other priorities at the moment, we haven't gotten together yet to talk, but I hope to make that happen soon. Plus, I was supposed to meet some people elsewhere in Europe after staying at the monastery, but those meetings wound up being cancelled given what happened."

Richard and Madison nodded.

Stephen decided to shift gears, "So, what's happening with the wedding? You wanted to talk with me about something, right?"

"We did," said Richard. He and Madison glanced at each other.

Madison then asked, "Richard and I would be honored if you would officiate at the wedding?"

Grant smiled broadly, and said, "Of course! I'd love to do it. Thanks for asking me."

Richard said, "Stephen, you've been so important in my life since Dad died. You've been a mentor, a guide and a friend." He paused, and then added, "You've been a friend to both of us."

Tanquerey added, "You have, and I appreciate it so much."

"Well, I feel the same way, of course. You're both dear to me and to Jennifer."

Richard said, "Now, before you officially say 'yes,' we're going a bit unconventional."

"Really. Just how unconventional will a pastor in the Lutheran Church-Missouri Synod get with his wedding?"

Richard said, "Well, actually, it's the location. For an assortment of reasons generally beyond our control, we've been putting off a date. So, we decided not to wait much longer. We're going to do the wedding here in Rome."

"That sounds great. And I like the idea of my Lutheran pastor friend getting married in Rome."

Richard smirked, "Yes, I thought you'd appreciate that, and what it might get some of our brother pastors speculating about."

"Guilty as charged."

Madison smiled at Stephen. "Well, we have a place and a date."

"Where?"

"Christ Church here in Rome. It's a beautiful Lutheran church. Have you ever been in it?"

"I haven't."

Richard added, "We basically can rent the church for the day, and do our own service. And it really is a spectacular church."

"Sounds like that will work. I'm looking forward to seeing the church, and to the wedding. We could use something positive."

"I agree," said Richard.

Madison added, "We're doing this all last minute, but we're going to invite a bunch of people, but make sure that they know that we understand that making a trip to Rome might not be in the cards."

"I'm sure people will understand."

"Jennifer better make it, though," added Madison.

"Madison, there is no possible way that you could keep her away."

Chapter 36

Pastor Stephen Grant was driving a navy blue SUV, with Madison Tanquerey next to him and Father Ron McDermott in the back seat.

"Are you sure you want me tagging along on this?" asked McDermott.

"Sure, Father, why not?" replied Tanquerey. "Are you in on this or not?"

"I'm definitely in. In fact, I'm finding all of this rather intriguing. However, I'm not sure if I'll help or just get in the way."

They were on their way to an unexpected meeting in a village about an hour south of Rome. Tanquerey had received a call in the early morning, suggesting a lunch meeting.

She said, "This man, Luca Moretti, said that he was only talking to us because Pope Paul VII asked him to do so. And he rather solemnly talked about it being past time to 'make amends' and that he needed to do penance. For all of those reasons, I thought it best that you be at my side when I talk to him."

"I get it."

"Besides, I think we're starting to make a good team."

McDermott said, "Well, thanks. And I agree."

Tanquerey looked over at Grant, and said, "I hope you don't mind waiting in the car? I think three of us, including two clergy members, would be a bit much. I don't want to put him on the defensive."

Grant replied, "I completely understand. I'm just here for security." He smiled.

"Right," said both Tanquerey and McDermott in unison.

About twenty minutes later, Tanquerey and McDermott entered a small building. There was only a tiny outer reception area, with a now empty desk and a door leading to an office.

The aroma of simmering meat and tomato sauce was thick in the air.

Tanquerey called out, "Hello," as McDermott shut the door to the street behind them.

A deep voice came from the office. "Come in. Come in."

The two visitors walked through the door and were greeted by a large man wearing a white apron over a white shirt and black tie. He stood at six feet five inches. His thick hair and eyebrows were a mix of black and gray. Luca Moretti's head and body were wide as well, as was his smile.

In contrast to the reception area, the office was large, including a desk with a computer and assorted papers spread across it, book cases and filing cabinets, a conference table, and a small kitchen area.

As Tanquerey and McDermott took in the scene, Moretti turned away from a stove, and started to say, "Welcome, Ms. Tanquerey, it is..." He then spotted McDermott and his eyes went to the priest's collar. "Oh, forgive me, Father." He looked a bit bewildered, and looked quizzically at Tanquerey.

She extended a handshake, and said, "Hello, Mr. Moretti, I am Madison Tanquerey, and this is Father Ronald McDermott. It is nice to meet you."

Moretti shook both of their hands, and seemed to bow just a bit when shaking McDermott's.

Tanquerey continued, "I'm sorry if we've taken you off guard. I had mentioned that the person working with me on this story would be coming, and that person is Father McDermott." She paused. Moretti still seemed a bit confused. Tanquerey added, "Father McDermott was invited by Pope Paul VII to work with me on this."

That last point apparently made a difference. Moretti's face was transformed, and he smiled broadly. He said to McDermott, "Father, it is an honor to have you here." He then looked back and forth at his guests. "Forgive me. Please take a seat at the table. I promised lunch, and we can talk and eat. I hope that linguini and my special family sauce is acceptable."

Tanquerey said, "It smells wonderful. I'm sure it will be delicious. Thank you."

Moretti dished out the meal, provided glasses of Barbera red wine, removed his apron, took a seat, and asked Father McDermott to pray. After the prayer and Moretti seemed satisfied that his guests were enjoying the food, he asked that his guests call him "Luca." After a few bites of food, his tone turned more serious. "I was surprised when the Holy Father contacted me directly. I had spoken to him here and there over the years, but to be contacted directly by the pope, and asked to do something." He shook his head as he took another fork full of linguini and sauce.

Tanquerey commented, "That is not something that happens every day."

"To say the least. Ah, but you two have an idea, right? After all, Pope Paul VII has asked you as well to do this work."

McDermott said, "I definitely understand the weight of the request."

"Of course you do, Father. Let me explain. I am an accountant. Now, I know that can seem funny to some, considering, for example, the Italian reputation for being less than consistent in paying taxes. But I have built a good business, and provided for my family." He stopped and took a deep drink of wine. "However, I have not always done everything the right way." His eyes went to McDermott and then back to Tanquerey. "I also have done other things." He put down his fork, wiped his mouth with a napkin, and pushed his chair back from the table a foot or so. "I have been thinking more about this. I look into the eyes of my young grandchildren, and I feel joy. But I also wonder what they would think of their grandfather..." He paused and then looked at McDermott. "And then the Holy Father called me directly, and he asked nothing more from me" – he turned to Tanquerey – "than to speak with you, Ms. Tanquerey, and to help however I could. This was much more than a coincidence. This was my chance to confess, to do penance, and to hopefully be forgiven. This was God, working as he does through the Holy Father, to give me a chance." He wiped a tear away that had formed in the corner of his eye.

Tanquerey and McDermott had stopped eating, and sat silently. Moretti stood up, and walked across the room to his desk. He picked up a thumb drive that was sitting next to his computer. He came back to the table, and sat down.

While holding the thumb drive, Moretti said, "When it comes to money, the Church is not all that different from dealing with government. I have found that no one really knows or cares what's happening with money except when it comes to making sure that there are funds there for them. This reality has made it far easier to slip things through unnoticed. I have done work at the request of the Vatican. But I also have done work through the Vatican at the request of others."

Moretti's eyes kept going back to McDermott. The large accountant refilled his glass, and offered to do so for the others. But both Tanquerey and McDermott declined.

Moretti took another swig of wine, and said, "I have done so for various entities, including one regional organization – a criminal entity – the Oldani mafia. The Oldani family is under the lead of Enzo Oldani. What might interest you is that Signore Oldani not only started giving to the Church about a dozen years ago, but that he also had me work with the Vatican to set up a special fund. He makes regular and irregular contributions to that fund. The best case for the Church is that it is unknowingly accepting funds generated from drugs, arms deals, extortion, and political corruption. But I often wonder about what that fund and those dollars are being used for. It could be the most worthy endeavor, or it could be something quite different. I, unfortunately, do not know. Everything that I do know that has anything to do with the Church is on this thumb drive."

He handed it over to Tanquerey, who said, "Thank you, Mr. Moretti."

Moretti said, "As you go through the material, if you have questions, just let me know. I will help as best I can."

Tanquerey replied, "Luca, aren't you worried?"

The large man chuckled and took another swig of wine. "Am I worried about Enzo Oldani finding out about this meeting, and what I am telling you? Eh, not terribly. You see, Enzo and I grew up together. We were like brothers. He will not suspect me of anything, other than complete trust in him."

"Then why are you doing this?" asked Tanquerey.

"I have already told you – for the Holy Father, for the Church, for God, for my family, and yes, for my own soul."

It was McDermott's turn to say, "Thank you."

"I do not deserve any kind of thank you. I merely hope and pray for forgiveness. Father, might I ask that before leaving today, you would hear my confession?"

"Of course, Luca."

"Bless you, Father," said Moretti.

Chapter 37

"Yes, I've reluctantly come to agree with the two of you," declared Pope Paul VII.

"Good. We only bring this up so that you are able to fulfill all of your responsibilities, as you yourself have identified them over the years, in the papal office, while also making sure that the Luther-Hus endeavor and the related investigation are able to proceed," said Father Mariano Concepcion.

"Yes, yes, I understand, Mariano, you have made good points. You no longer need to sell me on the basic idea." Throughout the conversation, the pope made clear that he was bothered by the underlying point of what Concepcion and Treadwell were saying – in effect, that he could not do all of this without some aspect of his papal responsibilities suffering – but also was annoyed by the logic of their points.

Cardinal Winston Treadwell added, "May I make a suggestion on what could work best?"

The pope waved his hand in acquiescence.

"Father Concepcion and I actually discussed this before we approached you on the matter. We were thinking that Father Concepcion could handle dealing with the more day-to-day needs of the group at the Trevisani, including their work with the university as well. Meanwhile, I could be a point man with the two investigations, both what Ms. Tanquerey is doing and the CDM group." As he was speaking, Treadwell spun the cane in his hand.

The pope sat silently behind the large desk in his behind-the-scenes office reserved for day-to-day work, rather than public ceremony. He finally said, "Mariano, yes, you will deal with our expanded group at the hotel in regard to the daily and university-related needs. You've been handling a good deal of that already, and it makes sense for you to do all of it. Of course, you will keep me up to date on key matters."

"Of course, Holy Father."

"Winston, it makes sense for you to deal with Ms. Tanquerey. After all, you know my thinking on this, and you have plenty of administrative and financial experience from your Australia work. I will remain, though, as the main contact person with the CDM group and Pastor Grant, and keep the two of you up to date or brought in on matters."

Treadwell began, "However..."

The pope cut him off. "There will be no 'howevers' on this. Let's move on to what is next on our agenda."

Chapter 38

After the meeting with the pope ended, Cardinal Treadwell was back in his own office and made a call to Madison Tanquerey.

After cordial greetings, Treadwell said, "I just wanted to let you know that the pope is trying to create enough time for everything that needs to be done. That can be quite a challenge, as I'm sure you understand."

Tanquerey replied, "I certainly do."

"Well, I wanted to let you know that the Holy Father has appointed me as a kind of point man for you. So, if you need anything on this end, you can contact me, and I will make sure the pope knows and we will make sure things happen for you."

"I appreciate that, Your Eminence."

"Believe me, I understand how cumbersome and slow the Vatican bureaucracy can be."

"Again, thank you."

"I know you're operating independently, as the pope assured you would be the case, but at the same time, feel free to contact me to pass on anything vital that you might think the Holy Father might need to know."

Tanquerey hesitated in her response, and then she finally said, "Actually, there is one thing that I was debating whether or not the pope should hear from me at this point."

"Yes?"

"We still have further research and investigating to do, and I don't want to create any unwarranted concerns until we're absolutely sure. You know, before we have our ducks in a row. But still, the pope should know that a source has raised the possibility that some organized crime money might be making its way into the Vatican."

Treadwell took in a deep breath. "Oh, dear Lord. Do you have anything firm that you can pass on to me at this point, you know, in terms of something that we need to be concerned about immediately? I, of course, will keep it in complete confidence. Only passing it on to the Holy Father."

"Your Eminence, to be perfectly honest, the journalist in me is not comfortable with aspects of this conversation, but I also understand the pope's concerns and what we're in the middle of here. And after all, if it weren't for his worries, I wouldn't be doing this investigation at all."

"I understand," said Treadwell. "And I know the pope would not want you to violate any journalistic principles."

"I feel comfortable telling you that I have my budget person combing through the information we received. At this point, I would think that the pope should at least get information on any monies that came in from anyone in the Oldani family."

"That was the Oldani family?"

"Yes, that's right."

"Thank you, Ms. Tanquerey. I will tell the pope, and as long as he approves it, I will let you know what we find, and what the pope might do accordingly."

"I appreciate it."

"Ms. Tanquerey, I know the pope appreciates what you are doing. He is unsure as to whom he can trust within the bureaucracy on this, but I know he respects you. Good night, Ms. Tanquerey."

After the call ended, Treadwell sat back in his chair, and stared at the cellphone now resting on his desk. Tears began to trickle down his red cheeks, and they soon became a steady stream. After several minutes, he opened one of the drawers in his desk, and pulled out a box of tissues. He proceeded to wipe his eyes and blow his nose. After several deep breaths, some degree of calmness seemed to descend upon him.

Treadwell whispered to himself, "What other choice do I have?"

He picked up the cellphone once more. The number he called was not in his contact list. He punched in the digits from memory.

Treadwell relayed what he had heard. But there were gaps in knowledge of which he was unaware. Madison Tanquerey had never mentioned to Treadwell that Stephen Grant had been fully informed on the meeting with Moretti.

Chapter 39

The vineyard rested in the hills southwest of Rome. It had produced white wines – a Frascati and a Pinot Grigio – for generations. Enzo Oldani had bought the property forty years ago. In fact, it was his first sizeable purchase once his power and profits had become substantial, and clear to both his friends and enemies. Oldani not only used the vineyard to make and sell world-class wine, but it served as his personal retreat.

Father Pietro Filoni drove a small, unassuming compact car. As he turned off the narrow road to the front gate, there was little hesitation on the part of the guards. Once seeing who was behind the wheel, they immediately started opening the heavy gate. A guard leaned down and said, "Welcome, Father. It is good to see you."

Filoni smiled thinly, and replied, "As it is to see you, Marco." Once the gate was fully open, Filoni said, "Thank you, and may God bless you."

The guard smiled broadly, and said, "Thank you, Father."

In recent years, Father Filoni had become a regular visitor, and instructions were made that he should be allowed to move about freely.

Fifteen minutes later, Filoni was standing in a spacious room off the back of the vineyard's villa. Windows on three sides, running from floor to ceiling, looked out onto the vines growing on the gentle hills.

From behind Filoni came the noises of shuffling and a cane clicking on the tan-colored tile floor. Enzo Oldani stopped next to Filoni, leaving a distance of a few feet between them. He looked out the window just as Filoni continued to do.

Oldani said, "We have completed the harvest."

"A good vintage, I trust."

"It appears so." Oldani turned, and said, "It is good to see you, son."

Filoni looked at a man in his seventies, with white hair and facial features similar to Filoni's own, namely, a thin face with narrow eyes. He replied, "Thank you."

The curtness of the reply visibly annoyed Oldani. While moving to a nearby leather chair, he said, "Thank God, this knee is improving, but not fast enough." He looked up at Filoni, and asked, "So, why the unexpected visit?"

The priest stared down at his father. He answered, "Perhaps it would be best if Jaco and Giorgio joined us."

"What? Is this actually about business, Pietro? You never took an interest in business until I started channeling donations to your efforts. I still say that you should never have become a priest. It is a waste of your talents. I had you taught and trained in what would be needed, both in terms of how to run this business and how to protect it and your family, and then you walked away." Oldani shook his head in disgust.

"It is not the time for this conversation, again."

Oldani raised his voice. "I will decide what is the best time for discussion on this or any other matter. You could have been at my side, and ready to take over when it was time for me to retire. But what am I left with instead? Your two sisters are not serious people."

"Half-sisters," interrupted Filoni.

"Ah, there it is once more. Your self-imposed inferiority. I have never called you or thought of you as being illegitimate. In fact, I have never treated you so. Your mother has been taken care of beyond her dreams, as were you. I have cared for both of you."

"When it was convenient, and in secret. This place certainly is not my home."

"What would you have had me do, *Father*, get divorced?"

That jabbing question went unanswered. Instead, Filoni said, "Are you aware what your dear friend, Luca Moretti, has done?"

Oldani's stare intensified. "What are you possibly talking about?"

"The person whom you trust the most has turned his back on you, on your family. He has handed over the Oldani books, if you will, to a reporter."

"That is ridiculous. How would you possibly think this? Who has misled you?"

"You are an old fool."

Oldani started to rise from his seat, leaning on the cane. "Who do you think you are addressing, you little bastard priest?"

Filoni swept the back of his hand across Oldani's face, and sent his father crashing down onto the tile floor. "You went from helping with your money, but now you have put everything at risk. You have put the Church at risk. That cannot be allowed." He reached inside his black sports jacket, and pulled out a tactical folding pocket knife, and began to unfold the blade.

Oldani looked up in fear. "Pietro, what are you doing? Have you lost your mind?" He called out, "Help! Help!"

Filoni crashed down on his father, who tried to fight off his son. But the priest was stronger and far more agile. Oldani froze when the point of the knife was positioned atop his chest.

Oldani pleaded, "Please, Pietro, don't."

Filoni started to slowly push the knife into Oldani's chest. As he did, Filoni whispered, "Each time that I have been forced to protect the papacy and the Church with deadly resolve, I truly prayed with and for the person's soul. That will not be the case with you, Father."

Oldani screamed, and Filoni plunged the knife in deeper, with the blade moving past ribs and into the heart. As life drained away from Enzo Oldani, his eyes never left his son's.

The door to the room burst open, and two men entered.

Giorgio Lupo sprinted forward, while Jacopo Bruno moved more slowly.

Lupo stopped just a few feet from the grisly scene, with his mouth wide open.

Filoni withdrew the knife, and stood up.

Lupo asked, "What the fuck have you done, Pietro?"

"I did what was necessary. Now, the question for you is…"

Lupo interrupted by yelling, "You little shit!" He sprang toward Filoni. But Giorgio Lupo had lived luxuriously as Enzo Oldani's number two in charge. Filoni quickly stepped to the side, and then drove the knife into Lupo's chest. After Lupo toppled to the floor next to his old boss, his face still exhibited anger. But then the reality of approaching death transformed anger into fear.

Filoni knelt next to Lupo, and said, "May the Lord who frees you from sin save you and raise you up."

After removing the knife and wiping it clean on Lupo's shirt, Filoni looked up at Bruno, who had stood motionless watching the entire scene. Filoni said, "You were right, Jaco. Apparently Giorgio was not interested in joining us." He looked down at Lupo, and commented, "I give him credit for his loyalty." He then looked at Bruno, and added, "Something quite worthy."

Bruno replied, "Most certainly."

Filoni said, "I am counting on you now, Jaco, to be my face, eyes and ears."

"I am more than happy – in fact, I am honored – to do so. You are the rightful head of the Oldani businesses, and the fact that you are putting them all, ultimately, to the highest purpose, in the service of the pope and the Church is most admirable."

Filoni slipped the knife back into his pocket, and then walked over to Bruno. Filoni placed a hand on the man's shoulder, and said, "You are now part of our mission. You are a critical member of the Shadow Servants of the Holy Father."

Jaco Bruno was a veteran of the mafia. He even seemed to look the part, with a black beard covering a scar and some of the pock-marks on his face, slicked back hair, and a slightly overweight but powerful body. But he took a deep breath, and uneasily said, "Thank you, Father."

Filoni said, "May God bless our work together."

*   *   *

The two priests sat waiting in a dark sedan. The door to the small building finally opened, and out stepped a short plump woman. She pulled her coat up a bit tighter in the early evening air.

She quickly walked to her car, started the vehicle and drove away.

Fathers Michael Russo and Lorenzo Conti waited a few minutes to make sure she didn't return. Russo started the vehicle, and then parked in front of the building.

When the two men walked through the front door, Luca Moretti called from the office, "Please, come in."

As Russo came into the office, Moretti looked surprised, and said, "Father, what can I...?" He cut himself short when seeing the second priest.

When each priest pulled a handgun out from beneath their jackets, Moretti sighed, and leaned back in his chair. The priests positioned themselves on opposite sides of the office, but remained silent.

Moretti said, "You two are with Pietro, correct?"

Neither man responded.

Moretti shook his head. "I was foolish to think that this could be done in secrecy. But if that is the case, what about Enzo? Does Enzo know that you were sent here?"

Finally, Russo answered, "Enzo Oldani is dead."

All Moretti could say was, "Shit." He added, "Did Pietro murder his own father?"

Russo ignored the question, and instead said, "We assumed that you would have some kind of weapon within reach at your desk. But you would never reach it in time, and if you somehow managed to get off a shot at one of us, the other would make sure you died."

Moretti sat immobilized, staring at his desktop.

Russo added, "The other point to consider, Mr. Moretti, is what your assistant will find in the morning. Or even worse, what if your wife or other family members were to come here during the night to see where you are, to see if you are alright? What would they find? It would not be something they would forget for the rest of their lives."

Moretti remained unmoving.

"Now, on the other hand," explained Russo, "this can be done in a civilized manner. You would join us for a ride. And when the time comes, we will pray, even give you Last Rites, and then you will feel nothing. One shot, in the back of the head. This is your choice, Mr. Moretti. I pray that you do not choose the selfish path."

Moretti chuckled. "Did you say, 'the selfish path'?"

Five minutes later, Father Russo got back behind the wheel, and now sitting next to him in the front passenger seat was Luca Moretti. Father Conti, in the back seat, held a gun trained on Moretti.

As the car pulled away from his office, Moretti stared blankly out the window. Tears gently rolled down his cheeks.

Chapter 40

At the start of the call from his hyper-secure, high-tech basement office in his Long Island home, Sean McEnany announced, "I know I shouldn't be, given how often it's happened, but I'm always surprised at how an investigation, or in our case investigations, can turn on a dime from being starved for information to suddenly being awash in it."

He went on to explain, and was just about to wrap up the first part of his briefing to CDM colleagues in Rome.

McEnany said, "So, while none of this would be enough to bring any indictments, it's certainly enough for me and our purposes. The timing of the murders of Professor Fuchs and his wife, Ruth, are, of course, just too perfect to be coincidence. And it's hard to argue with my contact in the local PD who didn't like that the case was closed, and written off as a robbery gone wrong or too far. The bodies were in the wrong place, and the wounds clearly pointed to execution over the theory that was settled upon – that this was one or more robbers who saw an opportunity for an easy score and they didn't care if this older couple was home or not. In fact, my contact has been so bothered by this that he's been doing his own investigation, on and off, to try to figure this all out. He's a good cop, smart, and the fact that he hasn't been able to uncover anything speaks to, in my mind, that this was a professional undertaking."

He paused, and looked into the camera atop one of the desktop computers. "Questions?"

Sitting in the hotel conference room with Charlie Driessen, Jessica West, and Phil Lucena, along with

Stephen Grant and Madison Tanquerey, Paige Caldwell looked around. She then turned to the laptop screen, and said, "None here. We're with you."

McEnany then proceeded to report on what was found regarding Pastor Fletcher. "First, it was very hard on Pastor Fletcher's wife, Ada, and their family, so if we can somehow thank them for allowing the exhuming of the body, let's make sure we do it."

Caldwell, Driessen and Grant all voiced their agreement.

McEnany continued, "I just received the report from my friends in Germany. You were right, Stephen, traces of a genetically-designed poison based on jellyfish venom were found in the heart and lungs. It never would have been found unless you were looking for it. This confirms that Pastor Fletcher was murdered." McEnany then asked, "Stephen, how the hell did you know to look for that?"

"It's a story from my CIA days. Ask me one night over a couple of beers, and I'll tell you the story." Grant glanced at Caldwell, and spotted the slightest of smiles.

McEnany continued, "Alright, we'll do that. Now, as for the Oldani family angle. Once more, thanks to Madison for sharing on this."

Tanquerey replied, "Of course."

"The breakdown on the accounts from your man in Washington was excellent." McEnany then went on to show some spreadsheet information on screen, as he went through the overarching points. "The bottom line here is that we can see Oldani money going into a variety of accounts at the Vatican – six in total. The crosschecking that Madison's guy did lines up with what I found. Namely, four are pretty standard undertakings, one for supporting local Catholic schools in Italy, another for maintaining of St. Peter's Basilica, one on supporting the Latin mass, and the other focuses on anti-poverty work in various spots around the globe. As for the other two, they have pretty generic names, but I can't track down any specifics beyond platitudes about supporting Catholicism and the Holy Father, and so on."

Tanquerey interjected, "That was the case with Roger as well." She looked around, adding, "Roger Neun is the finance expert I work with in D.C."

After providing some additional information, McEnany said, "This is progress, but there's more to get at, obviously."

Caldwell replied, "Right. So, why don't we go directly to the pope and see what he knows about these funds?"

Tanquerey agreed, adding, "It would be good to talk with Cardinal Treadwell, too. He's my contact for the pope."

Within an hour of McEnany's briefing coming to an end, he, Caldwell, and Tanquerey were on a call with Pope Paul VII. They updated him on everything that McEnany and Tanquerey had brought forward, and he confessed that he had no idea what those two accounts were. He promised to find out, and let them know.

*   *   *

Cardinal Treadwell approached the door to the pope's office. Father Concepcion was sitting at a nearby desk. Treadwell asked him, "Why has the Holy Father sent for me?"

Concepcion responded, "First, he wants you to look into something, and second, he is..." The priest paused, and then continued, "...displeased as to why certain information has not been reported to him."

Treadwell shifted uncomfortably standing in front of Concepcion's desk. He seemed to have difficulty in finding a spot to settle his cane. His voice shook ever so slightly. "Why? What is this about?"

"That's for the Holy Father to talk to you about. He said to send you in directly."

The pope was alone when Treadwell entered the office. And once the cardinal closed the door, and started to walk over to the desk where the pope was sitting, Paul VII, without looking up from what he was writing, said, "Winston, do you realize that I am trying to cut through the bureaucracy, limit its inefficiencies and root out wrongdoing, all in the name of being a good steward of the resources bestowed upon the Church to do His work?"

"Yes, of course, Holy Father."

"Good. Then why have you not informed me of the information that Ms. Tanquerey has passed on to you about the Oldani crime family?"

Treadwell swallowed hard, and said, "I was going to inform you, naturally, when it became clearer as to what is happening, when a fuller picture was available."

The pope put his pen down, and sat back. He sighed, and looked at Treadwell. "Yes. I knew you would say something like that. This is what I feared when we spoke about distributing some responsibilities."

"I meant no harm."

"Yes, yes, of course you didn't, Winston. I understand that, but we need to be much clearer on you keeping me up to date. After all, for all of your knowledge about the Church and the Vatican, there is a chance that I might have some additional insights that might clarify or help in certain situations." A sarcastic tone was not typical for Paul VII, but he did sometimes slip into it when frustrated, as was currently the case.

"Of course, Holy Father."

The pope went on to drive home his point, and then said, "However, unfortunately, I know nothing about two of these accounts where Oldani money has gone."

"Unfortunately, I do not either, Holy Father. In fact, that was my planned next step. I mean, I was going to get the information on those, and then present it to you."

The pope stared at his secretary, and then said, "Good. Please keep in mind what we spoke of here."

"Thank you, Holy Father, and I apologize for not getting this information to you earlier."

"I understand. Thank you, Winston."

Upon leaving, Treadwell stopped to speak with Concepcion. "All is well. I made the mistake of not getting information to the Holy Father as quickly as he desired. We've cleared that up now."

Concepcion seemed pleased to hear this.

After finishing the conversation, Treadwell was descending a wide, ornate circular staircase. He suddenly exhaled, and leaned more heavily on the cane. His body started to sweat. The pace of his walking down the steps slowed while he pulled a handkerchief from a pants pocket below his robe, and patted his face. The cloth, though, couldn't keep up with the excretions of his sweat glands.

Chapter 41

Treadwell's pace had reaccelerated by the time he reached the reception area outside of Cardinal Renaldo Bessetti's office.

When the assistant spotted the cardinal, she jumped to her feet. "Your Eminence, how can I...?"

He cut her off, and pointing his cane at the door, asked, "Is he in?"

"Yes."

"Is he alone?"

The assistant swallowed, and said, "Yes, yes, he is."

"Make sure no one disturbs us."

"Of course."

Treadwell opened the office door without knocking, and quickly shut it behind him.

As Treadwell walked quickly but somewhat unsteadily forward, his cane never touched the floor. Bessetti rose from a chair and came around his desk. "Cardinal Treadwell?"

Treadwell grabbed a chair, and fell into it. He said, "Renaldo, we're in trouble."

Bessetti lowered his voice, "What are you doing? Why are you here?"

Treadwell's eyes darted around the room, "We are alone, right? Your assistant said you were alone."

"Yes, but this is not the place."

"It has to be. I told the assistant to not disturb us."

Bessetti took the seat next to him, and asked, "What has happened, Winston?"

"They're getting close, far too close. You have to stop this."

Bessetti's voice became more soothing. "Alright, Winston, tell me exactly what is going on?"

In rambling fashion, Treadwell reported what the pope now knew. He concluded with a plea, "You need to stop this. Can't you see that? They're going to discover everything."

Bessetti cut him off. "Quiet." He got up and started pacing. "I am not concerned about what they find in the accounts. The money has been funneled through parishes with priests who have, let's just say, experiences similar to your own, or other problems, that they will do just about anything to keep private."

Treadwell shifted uncomfortably in the chair. He then commented, "You're laundering the funds through parishes?"

Bessetti ignored the observation and continued pacing. Finally, he stopped in front of Treadwell. He looked down and said, "I think you might be right, Winston."

"What do you mean?"

"This media person and these other investigators have raised certain risks."

"So, you're going to put a stop to all of this?"

Bessetti smiled. "I am sure that is what you would like to hear. But no, Winston, we will merely lay low for a period of time. Put things on hold, as they say. That is the smart thing to do. But our work in protecting the Church and the papacy never stops."

"But..."

Bessetti's voice grew stern. "There are no 'buts,' Winston. The work needs to be done, and it will not be halted. Your part is now even more important. You need to keep me up to date on everything that the pope is thinking and doing, as it might relate to this Hus-Luther nonsense, and the work of these assorted investigators. We will have to remain vigilant."

Bessetti walked over to Treadwell, and gently pulled on his arm, indicating that Treadwell should rise from his seat.

The pope's secretary got up, and then was guided toward the office door by Bessetti.

"I know that you keep foremost in mind how your sins of the past would affect the Church and the pope if they were to come out. Therefore, I know that you are as committed as I am in working to protect His Church and His representative on earth."

Treadwell seemed dazed.

"Excellent," said Bessetti, as he opened the door.

As he left, Treadwell leaned on his frog-topped cane.

Chapter 42

Killian Dvorak sat down next to Haley Whittacker at the long table in the hotel conference room.

He whispered, "I need a favor."

She looked up from her laptop and spotted the smile on Dvorak's face. "I don't think I'm going to like this."

"You are right, you probably will not."

"What is it?"

"Ivana is in town for a surprise visit."

"Oh, you mean, your student?"

"Ah, she no longer is my student, so therefore, we have no obstacles to our relationship."

"Are you married to her, Killian, and how old is she, again?"

"Oh, let's not get into that."

Haley sighed. "What do you possibly want from me?"

Dvorak replied, "I know what our security guards have said, that while they advise against it, we are free to come and go on our own. That this is not a prison, and so on."

"Yes, and?"

"Well, I also know that they'll never let us completely go off on our own. They will follow us."

"And?"

"I want you to help me to sneak out tonight without someone following."

An incredulous look came onto Whittacker's face. "What do you care if one of the CDM people follows you to your liaison? They're not going to take compromising photos or anything like that."

"Of course, I do not care. But I would not want word to get back to the pope."

It was Whittacker's turn to smile broadly. "What is this? Would you feel guilty if the pope discovered what you were doing? There is some interesting psychological and theological questions swirling around this, Killian."

Killian actually returned the smile, and said, "You know, Haley, I appreciate you."

"Thanks?"

"And I would not want to put you in a compromising position. Forget I asked."

"I will, Killian. And perhaps your conscience is telling you to forget about a tryst with Ivana." She turned back to her work on the laptop.

"Perhaps."

As she typed, Haley's cellphone rumbled. She picked it up and said, "Hello, Conrad. How are you?"

Dvorak left Haley alone to speak to her husband.

*   *   *

It was just after 10:30 that night, and Charlie Driessen was sitting in a car across from a small hotel on the edge of the city. He was on his cellphone speaking with Paige Caldwell. "Yeah, he just went into the hotel. There was a certain bounce in his step."

"I guess he hasn't seen Ivana in a while," replied Caldwell.

"I assume he's going to be here for most of the night. This guy is getting laid and I'm stuck in a car down on the street."

"Do you have enough coffee and something to piss in?"

"Thanks for your concern."

"Hey, I'm here for you."

"Yeah, talk to you later." Driessen ended the call.

Chapter 43

After knocking and the door opened, Killian Dvorak stepped into the hotel room, and closed the door behind him. He placed his hands on Ivana's waist, and said, "I am so delighted that you chose to surprise me." His eyes never left hers.

When he moved to kiss her, however, Ivana pushed back, and said, "No, wait. I didn't want to…"

"What is it?" Dvorak asked.

Ivana's hands shook. "I don't really know."

"I can tell you, Dr. Dvorak." The answer came from Father Pietro Filoni, as he entered from the suite's bedroom. He was dressed in clergy black, as were the two priests who followed him into the room.

Dvorak looked quizzically at the priests, then Ivana, and back to the priests. "I'm not really sure what is going on here. What is this about, Father?" Dvorak looked more closely, and some recognition dawned on his face. "I have seen you before. You are Cardinal Bessetti's aide, correct?"

Filoni smiled, and replied, "Yes, you are correct. I am privileged to serve His Eminence."

"Interesting," commented Dvorak. "I am still unclear, though, as to what is happening. Is there something that the cardinal or you seek from me?"

Filoni coldly said, "Repentance would be a good place to start."

"Excuse me?" responded Dvorak.

"Well, there's obviously your inappropriate involvement with this young woman."

"Pardon me?"

Filoni pressed on, "Alas, though, there is much more, such as the falsehoods about the heretic Hus that you perpetuate, and would now inflict upon the Catholic Church, if given the opportunity."

Dvorak stepped forward, and stopped just a couple of feet in front of Filoni. "What the hell are you doing here? And who are these other two gentlemen?"

"All three of us are the Shadow Servants for the Holy Father, and for our purposes, think of us as an arm of the Council of Constance reaching forward in time."

A look of surprise came upon Dvorak's face. He said, "You apparently have some problems to work through. I think you need help."

The three priests jumped forward. As Father Russo grabbed Ivana by the arm, Father Conti wrapped his arms around Dvorak, immobilizing him.

Filoni reached inside his sports jacket, and pulled out a small thin case. He snapped it open, revealing syringes. He took one out.

Fear took over Dvorak's voice. "What are you doing?"

Filoni roughly pulled up Dvorak's sleeve, and started to push down on the syringe. While doing so, he said, "Your heresy will end tonight, and it will not be allowed to infect the Church. And the world, Professor Dvorak, will know."

Dvorak's eyes rolled back in his head, and Conti allowed him to slip to the floor.

Ivana started to scream, but Russo covered her mouth. Filoni shoved another needle into her am, and she quickly passed out as well.

Filoni looked at Russo, and said, "Please make sure she is restrained securely, Father, and we will let you know when we are finished."

"Certainly, Father," answered Russo.

Filoni looked at Conti, and nodded. Father Conti entered the bedroom, and then re-emerged with a wheelchair. Dvorak was hoisted into it, and arranged to look comfortable, with a blanket draped over him. Filoni opened the door, and Conti rolled Dvorak into the hallway. Filoni followed.

As the threesome moved down the hallway, Filoni asked, "You have the service elevator key?"

"Yes. It was simple to lift."

"And the site?"

"It is set up to your specifications, and nothing is traceable."

"Excellent."

Conti inserted and turned the key in the panel next to the elevator door, and pushed the button. Thirty seconds later, the doors opened. Filoni stepped in, and Conti then rolled the unconscious Dvorak inside.

The elevator descended to the small basement garage.

Conti rolled Dvorak to a large black Mercedes sedan. He opened the trunk, withdrew a can, and placed it on the floor of the back seat. Filoni then assisted Conti in depositing both Dvorak and the folded wheelchair into the spacious trunk.

Conti took the driver's seat with Filoni next to him. Father Conti drove the vehicle up the short garage ramp, and turned onto the narrow street behind the hotel.

Watching the front of the hotel, Charlie Driessen never saw the Mercedes leave.

*　　*　　*

It was nearly one in the morning when Fathers Pietro Filoni and Lorenzo Conti carefully descended the large pile of cut wood, with Conti holding the can from the car.

Chapter 44

Killian Dvorak struggled to open his eyes. Once he managed to do that, he worked to focus his vision.

While undertaking that task, he felt like he was unable to move his body. His mind also was at work on trying to recall what had happened to him.

And then came the feeling of a cold breeze on his face. But that was coupled with an odd smell. His mind shifted trying to figure out what he was smelling.

Dvorak tried to move, but that resulted in sharp pains from various parts of his body. That pain finally woke him up fully.

The smell was gasoline.

His arms were tied behind him. He was strapped to some kind of post by what felt like chains. But his entire body was being pressed against by pieces of wood.

Panic struck. His heart rate quickened. There was wood piled up around him, up to his neck.

He yelled, "What's going on? Help me!"

His eyes then focused on two men standing below him, and a few yards away from the end of the woodpile.

Dvorak recognized them – two priests. And what had occurred at the hotel rushed back to him.

The priest standing next to Filoni was holding a lit torch in the air.

Dvorak called out, "Dear God, what are you doing?"

Filoni stepped closer to the wood, and said, "Killian Dvorak, do you repent of your sins and your heresies?"

Dvorak started to truly realize what was happening, and panic further consumed him. He tried to see beyond the two priests, looking for some kind of hope.

"Dear God, dear God, help me. Please, help me," Dvorak said, as his eyes were finding nothing but darkness beyond the two men and the burning torch.

Filoni repeated, "Killian Dvorak, do you repent of your sins and your heresies?"

Dvorak started to struggle against the chains and wood, but the pain increased, as his skin was pierced. He grunted in pain. He whispered, "Dear Lord, they are mad. Help, please."

He then realized that there was no one else around.

Filoni called out, "This is your last chance, Killian Dvorak. Do you repent of your sins and your heresies?"

Dvorak struggled to gain control of his thoughts. He replied, "Yes, yes, I repent of all my sins, and any heresies, too."

"Good, Dr. Dvorak. That is good." Filoni paused, and then said, "Of course, there are still consequences. You must pay for your sins."

Panic reclaimed Dvorak. He called out, "Please, no, no. I repent. I repent. You heard me, didn't you?"

"I heard, Killian Dvorak. And may God have heard you as well. But there are punishments that must be meted out, and no chances can be taken in protecting His Church and the Vicar of Christ. You will receive the same justice as did the subject of your work, Jan Hus." Filoni turned and nodded at Conti.

Father Conti stepped forward, lowered the torch and began lighting the petroleum-drenched firewood, moving around the pile.

As Conti moved to spot after spot, alighting the wood, Dvorak screamed out, "Please no! Don't do this!"

The two priests watched as the fire spread quickly, and moved ever higher.

Dvorak focused on the approaching flames and wept uncontrollably.

As the fire came ever closer to his face, Dvorak went quiet, and then began to pray. He repeated, "Jesus, forgive me, save me." His body struggled against the chains and wood, and blood flowed from wounds, even as he continued to pray.

Below, Father Filoni raised his right hand in the air, and as he made the sign of the cross, he proclaimed, "May the Lord who frees you from sin save you and raise you up."

As the excruciating pain was amplified and his skin began to burn away, Dvorak continued praying, until finally, prayer gave way to a few minutes of horrific screams.

The fire engulfed more of his body, and then death mercifully arrived for Killian Dvorak.

As Filoni and Conti turned, the raging flames behind them cast long shadows on the ground. They got into the car, and drove off into the darkness.

Chapter 45

Paige Caldwell's eyes popped open when her phone buzzed. She grabbed it off the nightstand. The screen told her two things. It was 3:12 AM, and Charlie was calling.

She answered, "Are you still sitting outside that hotel?"

"Yeah. This is bullshit. I'm going in to get this guy, and I don't care what he's in the middle of doing."

She replied, "Okay, why did you wake me up to tell me this?"

"Are you shitting me? I called to make sure that, given the spiel you gave those people about making their own decisions, that you weren't going to be pissed off if I did this."

"You're a big boy, Charlie. You can make these calls without me."

"Screw you, Paige."

Driessen hung up. Paige laughed, and went back to sleep.

Driessen grumbled all the way into the hotel, riding the elevator, and walking down the hallway toward the room. He stopped at the door, took a deep breath, and knocked. He waited, and after hearing nothing, knocked again. He repeated this two more times, and then cursed. Driessen pulled out his phone, and hit the number for Killian Dvorak. He could hear the phone going off inside the room, but he heard no movement. The phone continued ringing until it went to voicemail.

Driessen grunted, "Don't like this at all."

He tried the door, which was locked. Driessen pulled out his Glock, stepped back, and then kicked his foot at just the right spot. The door crashed open, and Driessen moved in, scanning the situation with his eyes and the gun. When he saw the woman tied to the chair, head hanging down, and shirt drenched in blood, Driessen said, "Oh, no."

After checking the rest of the suite, he called Caldwell back.

She answered, "What do you need now?"

Driessen reported, "The girl is dead and Killian is gone."

Chapter 46

It was Pope Paul VII's bodyguard who first got the news about a person being burned at the stake at a location about 40 minutes outside of Rome. As the news went to the pope and then to Dvorak's fellow scholars and friends, and those assigned to protect them, no verification was needed.

Killian Dvorak was one of the world's leading scholars on Jan Hus, and like Hus, Dvorak had just been burned at the stake.

While Stephen Grant and Paige Caldwell headed to the location of the burning, Jessica West and Phil Lucena stayed with the group at the Trevisani.

The sadness and devastation ran deep with each individual. But Haley Whittacker seemed almost broken by the news.

Whittacker sat on the couch in the group's community room, with Father John Kohli's arm around her shoulder. She swung between crying into Kohli's shoulder to saying, "It's my fault. I knew he was going to leave."

Jessica West tried to explain, "Haley, this isn't your fault. We knew that Killian left to meet this woman, Ivana. We even followed him. But whoever did this, they took Killian without us knowing, and they killed Ivana as well. None of this is your fault."

But Whittacker replied, "No, I should have stopped him. I could have."

It took the return of Charlie Driessen to the hotel for Whittacker to start, at least, to regain some of her bearings.

Upon Driessen's arrival on the reserved floor of hotel suites, Lucena first pulled Driessen into the conference room and closed the door. Phil asked, "Are you okay?"

"No. I'm pissed off. I'm depressed, and I..."

"Feel like it's your fault," finished Lucena.

"It sure as hell is."

"Explain how that is the case. Did you doze off, and they dragged Killian out the front door?"

"Of course not." He paused, and then sat in one of the chairs at the long table. "Yeah, yeah, I know what you're going to say: 'You did everything you were supposed to do, Charlie, blah, blah, blah.'"

"This sucks and is hard on everyone, and I get how you feel. But as long as you actually know that it's not your fault, well, that's good," noted Lucena. "Now, you might be the right person to talk to Haley."

"Why?"

"She also thinks this is her fault because she knew where Killian was going, and feels like she should have stopped him."

A few minutes later, Driessen was exchanging condolences with Pastor Richard Leonard, Madison Tanquerey, and Father John Kohli. Jessica West gave him a hug, and asked the same thing that Lucena had: "You okay?"

Driessen nodded. He then sat down next to Haley Whittacker.

She looked at him, and said, "I'm so sorry."

Driessen shook his head. "Don't do that to yourself, Haley. If anyone can take blame for what happened to Killian, it's not even close. I'm first in line. And in fact, I do feel like it's my fault. Phil just helped the process of getting things straight in my head. At the same time, this is the crappy part of this job. Because no matter whose fault it was, in the end, we were hired to protect you guys, and now Killian has been murdered. No matter how you look at this, the plain, undeniable fact is that we failed. Killian is dead." He looked over at Lucena who nodded ever so slightly.

Driessen's eyes returned to Haley, and he continued, "But this is in no way about you. You can think that you could have stopped Killian from meeting Ivana. But that's really not the case, is it? This was not new or unusual activity for Killian. That, of course, doesn't mean that he deserved anything like this. And when we find out who did this, I'll be first in line to put bullets in their heads. So, none of this is about you, Haley. Just do what you need to do, like mourning and praying for your friend, if that's your deal. Leave the guilt shit to us."

Tears were flowing from Whittacker's eyes, but there was slightly different body language now. She whispered, "Thank you," while giving Driessen a hug.

Several minutes later, West brought her cup over to Driessen who was pouring himself some coffee. She said, "That was really nice what you said to Haley."

Driessen merely shrugged.

West smiled, and added, "In fact, I never knew you could be that nice. How come you're never like that around the people you work with?"

Driessen replied, "Because none of you are very nice." A slight smile could be detected, if someone looked closely, as he poured the coffee for West.

*   *   *

Caldwell was at the wheel, with Grant in the passenger seat.

They had been driving in relative silence for more than 15 minutes, when Grant finally asked, "So, what are you thinking on this?"

She didn't reply immediately. Grant knew her well enough from years past that he could see the internal debate going on in Page Caldwell's head.

Caldwell eventually responded, "You want it all?"

"Of course."

"Depends on what you're talking about. To understate things, I'm obviously upset that Professor Dvorak has been murdered, and in such a sick, horrible way. I feel guilty and kind of lost that this happened on our watch, while we were supposed to be protecting him, along with the rest of this group. What the hell did we do wrong to let this happen? But at the same time, I'm actually pissed off at Dvorak for being so stupid and irresponsible that it got him killed. And finally, whoever did this has gone from quietly sending a message to the pope, to now doing it out in the open, to say the least. It's like we've gone from trying to track down a person or group that was evil in a stealthy, strategic kind of way to suddenly pursuing an exhibitionist evil."

Grant nodded, "Yeah, is it a shift in strategy or has somebody snapped?"

Caldwell didn't reply.

Grant added, "I understand what you said on this happening on our watch."

"Our"? It's easy for you to slip into the "our" stuff, isn't it, Pastor Grant?

He added, "But you did everything you could in terms of making it clear to Killian what was at risk, and Charlie wound up following him." Grant paused to think before uttering his next point. "Don't be too pissed off at the man, however. I can recall us doing some things a long time ago that were stupid and irresponsible."

"Yeah, but we survived it."

"And sometimes were lucky to do so."

"It wasn't luck."

"What was it then?"

"It was us knowing our abilities and limitations, and even though we did some shit we shouldn't have, it wasn't flagrantly stupid. We didn't go somewhere that we couldn't ultimately handle."

"Maybe, maybe not. But you're looking at this through the eyes of a veteran who's seen it all. Killian Dvorak was an academic with an overactive libido. Yeah, it was dumb, but I don't think he realized the true risks. Even when danger is close, it can seem less than real until it hits someone in the face."

Caldwell didn't reply, and they drove on in silence.

As they first turned onto the dirt road leading into the site, they were stopped by law enforcement officers, who, upon identification waved them through, per earlier orders by Inspector Mazzoni.

Caldwell drove the SUV along a bumpy trail where the patch of woods had been overgrowing for decades. The road led to a more open area. After parking by the police vehicles, Mazzoni walked up and greeted them. He said, "This was truly twisted. It was straight out of the fifteenth century, and the burning of Jan Hus. Even to the point of the wood being stacked up to the man's chin."

Grant took note of Mazzoni's apparent knowledge of how Hus had perished.

He continued, "Just try to follow me closely. We're obviously still scanning for clues. The fire and rescue people put out what remained of the flames, and pulled out the remains of Dr. Dvorak. There wasn't much, unfortunately."

A few of the police vehicles were shining spotlights on the scene, given that dawn was still about an hour away.

As they moved closer, Grant was struck by the still-powerful smell of the recently extinguished fire. Scarred, burned wood was now scattered. A blackened and somewhat bent metal poll stood at the center of the terrible scene. It looked like an old flag pole to Grant. He felt a shudder. Scanning the area, Grant was able to see what appeared to be the remnants of a foundation for an old, long-gone building. He asked Mazzoni, "Whose property is this? What used to be here?"

Mazzoni looked at Grant and shook his head in a kind of disgust. "There used to be a convent here, a very long time ago. The property actually is still owned by the Catholic Church."

Selected on purpose. To amplify the message?

Caldwell asked the next question before Grant could. "What about the media?"

Mazzoni said, "I can't be completely sure, of course, but this has not gotten out yet. We were fortunate, if that is the right word, that it was a local officer who spotted the flames and was able to get the right people here."

Grant said, "So, this being church property but still remote from the general public tells us what?"

"The message to the Holy Father is clear: The Hus-Luther project must stop now," answered Mazzoni.

Grant declared, "That might be the best possible spin on what's occurred."

"What does that mean?" asked Caldwell.

"We've suddenly gone from two people involved in this project being rather quietly murdered, and a letter demanding that this effort needs to stop or things will get worse. And now we suddenly jump to Killian Dvorak being burned at the stake, and on church property no less."

Caldwell and Mazzoni listened while staring out over the remains of the fire.

Grant added, "This reeks of a group that is focused on a Medieval idea of the Catholic Church, and it's willing to do anything to protect it. We're looking at a case of the burning of a leading expert on Jan Hus, who himself was burned at the stake as a heretic. And in case there are any doubts, this burning took place on property owned by the Catholic Church."

Grant joined Caldwell and Mazzoni in gazing out on the burnt remains.

"From deliberate to exhibitionist. So, what's next then?" asked Caldwell.

Grant said, "I don't know exactly. But when I look at what happened here tonight, I do know that we should assume that everyone involved in this Hus-Luther project is in peril, and that must include Pope Paul as well."

Chapter 47

Renaldo Bessetti opened his eyes when the phone rang on the table across the room. He looked at the clock on the nightstand, and saw that it wasn't yet 5:30 AM. He struggled to get out of bed quickly to answer the call.

"Hello?"

"This is what you mean when you told me you were going to 'lay low'?"

Bessetti wiped his eyes, and seemed to be struggling with getting his bearings after being awoken. "What? Cardinal Treadwell?"

"Yes. What the hell have you done?"

Bessetti cleared his throat, and asked, "What are you talking about? What are you so upset about?"

"Don't play these games with me, Renaldo."

"Damn it, Winston. Tell me why you are calling at this hour of the morning."

Treadwell growled in anger. "Dvorak, you fool!"

"What about him?"

"'What about him?' You murdered him, or you had him murdered."

"Winston, I have no idea what you mean."

Treadwell took a deep breath. "You're telling me that you had nothing to do with Killian Dvorak being burned to death – burned at the stake?"

"Dear God, what?" Bessetti stared at a print of Sandro Bottocelli's *Map of Hell* from Dante's *Divine Comedy* hanging on the wall directly in front of him. He felt around for a chair. His hand found the arm of the chair, and he sat down while not moving his stare from the drawing.

Treadwell asked, "Renaldo, are you there? Renaldo!"

Bessetti snapped back to the conversation, pulling his eyes away from the wall hanging. "I'm here."

"Can you explain what's happened? Are you telling me that you don't know? Do you...?"

Bessetti interrupted him. "Shut up, Winston. I will let you know shortly."

Bessetti ended the call. He looked back at the *Map of Hell*, and asked aloud, "What have you done?"

Chapter 48

Rusty Spuel had been back in his parents' home in Pine Bluff, Arkansas, for a few days. The loss of his pastoral position at the church in Illinois obviously meant he was kicked to the curb from the parsonage as well.

With no other options immediately at hand, Spuel made the drive to Pine Bluff. He swore to his parents that this stay in his old bedroom would be for a few months "at most," until he received another call.

It was in the middle of the night when his cellphone buzzed. He looked at the screen and answered, "Edgar, this better be good."

"Oh, it is."

Rusty said groggily, "Go ahead."

"You wanted to know if I heard anything more on Pastor Leonard in Rome?"

When his brother paused, Rusty prodded, "Yes, and?"

"There's a guy I follow online who says that the pope has brought together a bunch of Catholics and Protestant theologians who are in his pocket in a plot to take over all Christian churches around the world."

"That sounds pretty out there, Edgar."

"Yeah, that's what I thought, too. Then I was thinking about Leonard going over there, and I thought, well, maybe there's something to this. And then this guy gets online tonight with a special update. Get this, he says that he has a report from Europe that some prominent Protestant theologian or historian, was burned at the stake earlier today."

"What?"

"There's more. This guy says that this theologian got wind of what the pope and his cabal were up to, and was ready to blow the lid off it. Well, we know that there's a dark state that the pope leads, and we also know what happens to people who take on that state."

Rusty sat up in the small bed where he had slept during his childhood into late teens, and then swung his feet to the floor. He started to nod. "Of course, there are many, many skeletons in the pope's closet, that's true."

"Yeah, you're the one who taught me about all of the evil that popes have done – both public stuff and the things people don't know about or choose to ignore. He's the antichrist, right?"

"He is, so we shouldn't doubt what he is capable of doing. Did your internet reporter identify who was murdered?"

"No, not yet. He said that they have a pretty good idea, but that it wouldn't be right to make such an announcement without knowing one hundred percent."

Rusty seemed to be mulling all of this over, as he scratched his cheek.

"It's pretty obvious to me, Rusty, that this is why Leonard is over in Rome. It can't be a coincidence. And it's pretty clear whose side he is on."

"It is, Edgar, it is. Good work on this. It's incredibly valuable."

Chapter 49

It was just before midnight – roughly 22 hours since the Dvorak death by burning – and Cardinal Renaldo Bessetti was not sleeping well after a day of being frustrated by a lack of information. He suddenly bolted up in bed. In the doorway of his room stood Father Pietro Filoni.

Bessetti's anger was unmistakable. "How did you get in here?" He wiped his eyes, adding, "And what were you thinking with Dvorak? That was more than foolish; it was incredibly stupid. And where have you been? Why have you not responded to my calls?"

Filoni stared back at Bessetti for several seconds. He then said, "Come down to the kitchen." He turned, and walked away.

"What the hell are you doing?" called Bessetti as he got out of bed, and put on a robe and slippers. The cardinal grumbled while exiting the bedroom.

As he came down the stairs, the light shone in his kitchen. Bessetti came in and found Filoni sitting at the table. The cardinal stepped forward and placed his hands on the back of one of the chairs. He looked down at Filoni. "What were you possibly thinking? And what gave you the right to take such action? You are *my* aide."

Filoni persisted to stare in silence.

Bessetti continued, "Now I have to figure out how to make sure this doesn't come back on us. We're supposed to be making our points clearly but quietly, pushing the pope in the right direction. You are an idiot."

Filoni sprang up, knocking his chair to the floor.

As Filoni came at Bessetti, the much older man lacked the ability to do anything about it. He couldn't even raise his hands quickly enough in self-defense. Filoni backhanded Bessetti across the face. The cardinal fell to the floor.

Filoni calmly walked over, picked up his chair, and sat back down. He then pulled a handgun out from under his jacket.

Bessetti was groaning and still sprawled out on the floor.

Filoni commanded, "Get up, and put yourself in that chair, Your Eminence."

Bessetti worked to push himself up from the floor. As he did, the cardinal asked, "Have you lost your mind, Pietro? What do you think you are doing?" He was surprised to see the gun when he got back to his feet. Filoni pointed the weapon at Bessetti and then at the chair. Bessetti dutifully sat down.

Filoni then stood up, and pulled a zip tie out of a pants pocket. He started to move behind Bessetti.

The cardinal said, "Pietro, why is this necessary?"

Filoni forcefully pulled Bessetti's hands behind him, wrapped the zip tie around his wrists, and pulled tight.

"I am doing what is necessary; what you have been unwilling to do. This is not about quietly nudging this pope in the right direction. It is time for action, to stop this entire effort in its tracks. And in the name of the one true church of Christ and the papal office, whatever is required will be done, even if that includes eliminating the current pretender."

"Pretender? Eliminate? Are you talking about killing Pope Paul VII? I told you why that..."

"I am not interested in your view on this, Your Eminence."

Bessetti suddenly had a look of calm, even arrogance. He said, "Oh, really? Do you think that the people who fund our efforts will go along with this sudden shift? They are not interested in public murders. They do not want a public war with the pope, and what that would result in. They do not favor such madness. Trust me, Pietro, they will not go along with this."

Filoni laughed.

Bessetti rarely saw Filoni smile, never mind laugh. The calm that had just appeared left the cardinal's face, substituted with a clear nervousness.

"You actually are the fool, Your Eminence. You think that Enzo Oldani cares?"

"How do you know about Mr. Oldani?"

Filoni smiled this time. "Enzo Oldani was my father."

"What...? Your father?"

"Oldani was not funding this effort because of you, Your Eminence. He was doing it for me, at least in part. It was his attempt to be some kind of father. He also thought he was being a good Catholic, and probably thinking of contributing such money as a kind of penance, or perhaps gaining an indulgence."

Bessetti didn't reply.

"You have nothing to say, Your Eminence? But you always have something to say. You love hearing yourself talk."

"Well, I am sure that your father would not agree with what you have done, and what you would like to do."

"Actually, you are right about that. He would not have agreed. But that no longer matters, since he is dead."

Bessetti's mouth opened in shock. He finally said, "You killed your own father?"

"Why are you surprised by this, Your Eminence? After all, you rarely hesitated before when ordering the deaths of people to protect the Church."

Bessetti said nothing.

"You also might be interested in knowing that I am now running the Oldani family business."

"You?"

"That's right. And while that is good news for the Shadow Servants of the Holy Father, it will not be for you, I am sorry to say, Your Eminence."

"Pietro, what are you saying?"

"Well, Your Eminence, you have done the work that the Church needed in recent years. You largely kept the worst instincts of this pope in check. You also cleverly kept him off balance. However, it always was clear that at some point, Paul VII would seek to assert himself. That started when he moved you out as his secretary, and then when he started moving ahead with this ridiculous attempt to clean the slate for two of the most egregious heretics in the history of the Church. He also is moving ahead in encouraging this reporter to delve more deeply into Vatican finances. None of this can be allowed to continue."

"Of course it cannot, Pietro. I see that. What can be done?"

"What I have started, Your Eminence, must be continued and expanded."

Bessetti licked his lips. "What can I do, to be of service to the Church?"

"I appreciate your seeing this for what it is now."

The smoothness of Bessetti's voice returned. "Sometimes we can get stuck, thinking that what we are doing is all that needs to happen. But circumstances change, and we have to change with them."

"Let us start with all of the details regarding the money laundering system you set up for my family's donations."

"Yes, yes, of course. Can we take off these restraints?"

"That will depend upon how forthcoming you are, Your Eminence."

"Yes, of course, I understand."

"And after we cover the financing end of things, I want to review everything we have on Cardinal Treadwell."

Bessetti actually smiled, and said, "Good, good. Allow me to start with the parishes and the priests involved…"

Some forty minutes later, Filoni said, "Is there anything else? Anything that you might have left out, Your Eminence?"

"No, I don't think so. Of course, if something occurs to me, I will make sure you know."

Filoni put down the pen he was using to take notes, and rose to his feet. He walked over to an attaché case that he had brought into the cardinal's home. It rested behind Bessetti, who could not see it from his position. Filoni took a roll of duct tape and a pair of scissors. He quietly cut a piece of the tape, and approached Bessetti directly from behind. He reached around, and quickly taped the cardinal's mouth shut.

Bessetti's eyes widened, and he thrashed his head back and forth.

Filoni returned to the bag and pulled out a long thick rope. He manipulated it so that a small section, less than two feet, could be pulled tight by his two hands.

As Filoni once again came up behind, the priest quickly swung the rope around Bessetti's neck.

The cardinal started to struggle frantically. But there was nothing that he could do to change what was occurring. He continued to struggle.

Pietro Filoni, however, did not waver in what he was doing. He said, "Your Eminence, rest easy. You have served the Church well, but your usefulness has come to an end."

Bessetti's screams were stifled by the tape over his mouth. Liquid began streaming out of his eyes, while mucus emanated from his nose.

As the final struggle to cling to life took hold in Bessetti, Filoni said, "May the Lord who frees you from sin save you and raise you up."

Chapter 50

While Father Filoni was meeting with Cardinal Bessetti, another unexpected visit was occurring at the Trevisani, with the reserved floor now housing a dwindling group of scholars.

A group was quietly sitting in the main gathering room with a movie on the television. Conrad Whittacker had arrived for dinner with the group and to stay with Haley for the night. They were sitting together on the couch. Scattered around the rest of the room were two other couples – Phil Lucena and Jessica West, and Pastor Richard Leonard and Madison Tanquerey – as well as Father John Kohli.

There was little conversation. Each couple seemed to be valuing the quiet time together. Kohli sat with eyes closed. He wasn't asleep, but rather apparently lost in thought.

Conrad's cellphone vibrated inside his suit jacket. He pulled it out, and merely answered, "Yes?" He listened, and then replied, "Excellent. Thank you." He ended the call, turned to Haley and whispered, "Albro has returned."

Haley smiled with a trace of concern. "Thanks. Stay here, I'm sure Jessica and Phil will come with us."

"Alright," he replied.

Phil and Jessica's eyes had moved away from the movie and to Haley, who nodded at them.

Haley leaned down to Kohli, and said, "Excuse me, John."

His eyes opened, and he said, "I wasn't asleep."

Haley smiled and then said, "I didn't think you were. Can you come with Phil, Jessica and me for a few minutes, and not ask any questions about it?"

Kohli sat up straighter in the deep armchair. He looked over at Phil and Jessica, who looked ready to accompany them. He said, "Sure, I guess."

The three rode the elevator down in silence. When the doors opened, Jessica stepped out first, and scanned the lobby. She then stepped forward and to the side. Haley stepped out. She spotted Albro Dawson standing in a dark corner of the lobby.

Still in the elevator, Phil said, "After you, Father."

Kohli exited, and then followed Haley.

Dawson stepped aside and moved away.

Haley stopped, and Kohli did the same a couple of feet behind her. Haley turned, and said, "I called her to let her know what happened. She insisted on coming immediately."

Kohli's eyes moved away from Haley and to a person sitting in a high-backed chair facing in the opposite direction. He walked toward the chair, and then came around to see Sister Katharine Malone.

He whispered, "Kathy?"

She slowly rose from the chair. "John, I'm so sorry about Killian. I had to come. I couldn't do otherwise, and live with myself. I needed to be here for you. That was all that mattered. Is it okay?"

He half-chuckled. "'Is it okay?' Kathy, thank you for coming. Thank God you came."

They fell into each other's arms. And after a long embrace, they looked into each other's eyes, and gently kissed.

Kohli said, "Before we go upstairs, let's sit down and talk."

Chapter 51

While John Kohli and Kathy Malone sat down to talk in a corner of the hotel lobby, Jessica West, Phil Lucena, Haley Whittacker, and Albro Dawson moved away to allow some relative privacy.

Whittacker whispered to Dawson, "Thank you, once again, Albro, for picking up Katharine from the airport."

"My pleasure, Mrs. Whittacker."

"I know we've been through this many times, but you really should just call me 'Haley.'"

Dawson replied, "You know how I feel about that, given that I work for you and Mr. Whittacker."

She sighed, and said, "Yes, I understand." She switched gears, "Albro, since Conrad is staying the night, you should head home and get some rest."

"Very good, madam. Thank you. I will just check with my colleagues. Good evening."

"Good night, Albro."

Dawson came over to Lucena and West, and said, "I believe that my work is done here. I assume you have this covered?"

Lucena said, "Yes, we do," as West nodded in agreement.

Dawson shook hands with each, and then left the building.

After Dawson was gone, West whispered, "I wonder how he lost the eye?"

Lucena replied, "That's what you're wondering?"

West smiled, and said, "Sure, aren't you?"

"Maybe."

West glanced in the direction of Kohli and Malone, and then whispered to Lucena, "I hope it works out for them."

"I think it will."

"And why are you so sure?"

"I'm the optimist in our relationship."

West smiled, and replied, "Depends on the day."

"Fair enough," said Lucena, smiling as well, and brushing his hand against his fiancée's.

They remained silent for a few minutes, scanning the room to make sure all was still secure.

West eventually leaned in close to Lucena once again. She commented, "I'm excited about being invited to Richard and Madison's wedding."

"I like them, and I'm sure that you might be doing some scouting for ideas."

"I most definitely will."

"Stephen is doing their wedding."

"I know, and I'm leaning with you to ask if he would do ours as well. Just let me think about it a little longer."

"That's fine with me."

West added, "And it would help if we at least pegged down a month to do this, never mind an exact day."

"Well, you..."

She placed a finger over his mouth. "Yes, I know. You are waiting on me on that as well."

Lucena shrugged ever so slightly.

"Okay, Phil, at the very least, I promise that we will have settled on whether or not to ask Stephen to do the wedding."

"Deal," said Lucena.

Chapter 52

When Father John Kohli went back up to the reserved floor at the Trevisani, he introduced Sister Katharine Malone to everyone. Matters had changed considerably since her last visit. When she had headed back to the United States, it was still the case that Kohli had been working with Haley Whittacker and Killian Dvorak.

Two deaths – Pastor Gerhard Fletcher's and now Dvorak's – had affected her relationship with Kohli and with Rome itself.

As for what Katharine was doing here and her relationship with Kohli, those matters would be left for discussions, if needed, at another time. Instead, there was casual talk about her flight, as well as her offering condolences on Dvorak's death.

Eventually, Haley Whittacker stepped forward and said, "Kathy, if you're ready to get some sleep, there's a second bedroom in my suite. If that works, you're welcome to it."

Malone glanced at Kohli who nodded ever so slightly. She said to Whittacker, "Thanks, Haley. If you're sure that won't be a problem, I appreciate it."

"It's not a problem at all."

Malone turned to Paige Caldwell, and asked, "Actually, I'm being presumptive. Is it alright for me to stay here, Ms. Caldwell?"

"Of course, Sister, it's all been arranged."

"Thank you."

Malone followed Whittacker out of the community room, and eventually others wandered off to their rooms, with

Pastor Stephen Grant, Father Ron McDermott, Caldwell and Charlie Driessen remaining.

Grant asked, "Was I the only one who didn't know Sister Katharine was coming?"

While Caldwell and Driessen shrugged, McDermott said, "Not the only one."

Grant looked at his friend and asked, "What are you thinking on this, Ron?"

"Meaning?"

"This apparent relationship between Father Kohli and Sister Malone?"

"Stephen, I'm kind of surprised at you. I don't know the details, nor do you, I assume. So, it's not for me to say."

Grant felt a stab of guilt. "You're right. Sorry."

Driessen smiled and grunted.

I'm going to regret this.

Grant said, "Charlie?"

"Yeah, I can tell you what's going on, and I'll bet any of you fifty bucks that John and Katharine eventually won't be 'Father' and 'Sister.'"

Caldwell chimed in, "Careful, Charlie, people can surprise you when it comes to deciding to work for the Lord." She looked at Grant.

Driessen actually chuckled at that, and then said, "I believe I've got the overnight guard duty."

Caldwell said, "I'll relieve you in a few hours."

McDermott declared, "I'm going to bed."

And Grant added, "Yeah, me, too."

Chapter 53

Twenty minutes later, Paige Caldwell entered her suite, and sent off a text. She tossed her phone on the bed, undressed and stepped into a hot shower.

Several minutes later, she slipped into bed. Just as her eyes closed, the cellphone buzzed. She answered, "I'm so glad you were able to call."

"Are you okay?" asked President Adam Links.

"Yeah, mostly. You received the information I sent about Professor Dvorak?"

"That was horrible, and twisted."

"It was, and we were supposed to be protecting him."

"What happened?" asked Links. After Caldwell relayed the details of what occurred and the aftermath, he added, "Well, you can't blame yourself, nor should Charlie. The professor made a bad choice, with a terrible cost. This is about these killers, and tracking them down."

"I know..."

As Caldwell's voice trailed off, Links interjected, "But nothing I can say will really convince you. And I'm sure it was the same case when you tried to convince Charlie that it wasn't his fault, either."

"Pretty much. It's one of those things that I'm going to have to find a way to deal with, and the best way to do that is, like you said, to get the people behind these murders."

"What's the plan?"

"We're working this on all fronts with the Vatican Gendarme Corps."

"The Gendarme people whom I worked with on a couple of occasions back in the day at the Agency were top-notch."

"Vincent Mazzoni is excellent, and he's the pope's personal bodyguard."

"Is Sean over there, or working it from back here?"

"He's working his magic from his home base. I'm desperately hoping that he'll get a breakthrough on something soon."

"You know he will, and if you or he need our assistance, just let me know."

"Thanks, I appreciate it. On a different note, we've got two people with us now who face some pretty big challenges in terms of becoming a couple."

"Really? More so than us?"

"Well, one is a Catholic priest, Father Kohli, and the other is a nun, Sister Katherine Malone."

"Yes, they might actually face more formidable challenges than us."

"I'm not completely sure about that. After all, you are the president of the United States trying to keep a relationship quiet."

"Right, but people would understand that, I think, more so than a priest and a nun getting together."

"Do you really think so, or is that just what you were taught growing up? I mean, does it still hold that people would be scandalized by this?"

"You might be right about the average Catholic. Would they even care? I wonder. But as for their vows, and what taking such a step would mean to their faith lives, if you will, that would be a significant matter for each of them, I would think."

"Hmmm, well..." A loud knock came at her hotel room door, and it didn't stop. She said, "I hate to do this, but someone's at the door, Adam. I have to go."

He replied, "Stay safe. Love you."

"You, too." Caldwell grabbed a robe from a chair, and she slipped it on and tied it as she moved through to the door. The knocking continued.

Caldwell opened the door, and Driessen was standing there. She asked, "What the hell is going on, Charlie?"

"The body of Cardinal Bessetti was just found. Mazzoni says he hung himself, and left a letter taking responsibility for the deaths of Fuchs, Fletcher and Dvorak."

"Holy shit. Give me two minutes to get dressed."

"Yeah. Move it."

Chapter 54

Stephen Grant kneeled next to the bed, folded his hands, lowered his head, and prayed. He started with Martin Luther's Evening Prayer, blessing himself, and saying:

> In the name of the Father and of the Son and of the Holy Spirit. Amen.
>
> I thank You, my heavenly Father, through Jesus Christ, Your dear Son, that You have graciously kept me this day; and I pray that You would forgive me all my sins where I have done wrong, and graciously keep me this night. For into Your hands I commend myself, my body and soul, and all things. Let your holy angel be with me, that the evil foe may have no power over me.

Grant then went on to request that the Lord be with a list of individuals, including assorted members of the St. Mary's congregation, various friends and colleagues, each person involved with his current endeavors in Rome, and of course, Jennifer.

He concluded with an "Amen," and then propped himself up in bed with a small pile of pillows, and called Jennifer.

"Anything new happening?" asked Jennifer as she answered the call.

"Well, now that you mention it, yes, there is. First, how are you?"

"Everything here is okay. I just miss you."

"Same here."

"And the arm?

"Just about 100 percent now."

"So, what's the news?"

"Father John Kohli's guest has returned – Sister Katharine Malone. I was out of the loop, but apparently, Haley Whittacker contacted her about Killian Dvorak, and she made arrangements to come back here to be with Father Kohli."

"She wanted to be there for him, so she flew across the Atlantic, again."

"That seems to be the case."

"That's special."

"It is."

"I know there's a romantic beneath the pastor and former CIA exteriors. But what do you think about this as a pastor?"

"Well, you've heard me talk about this before. I've never been on board with clergy celibacy being a requirement. If that's a gift and you can be a better priest or pastor as a celibate, good for you, I suppose. But if marriage is a gift for you, whether a pastor or priest, that's just as wonderful. In this situation, the issue is their vows and their relationship with the Church. If they head down the path of getting married, the question will be: Where do they end up within Christianity?"

"Father Kohli could become a pastor, right?"

"He could. There would be a process, of course, depending on where he might end up. But I think we're getting ahead of ourselves."

"True. But when I hear a story like this, I just hope it works out for them, you know, like it has for us. Our road wasn't direct, to say the least."

"It wasn't, but we wound up in the right place."

"We have," replied Jen.

Stephen could tell that she left something unsaid. "What is it?"

"I know what you're going to say, but the fact that I can't have children makes me worry about you. I've known this, and dealt with it since college, but you're..."

"Jen, we've had this discussion before, including several times before we tied the knot. There were no surprises coming into our marriage. In fact, if anyone has been throwing curves, it would be me and my untypical career as a pastor. And I'm not cutting this off, but you don't need to worry about me. You should never think that there is even a trace of regret. Our getting married is the best thing that's ever happened to me. Period."

"Okay."

A knock at his hotel room door annoyed Stephen. He didn't want to be pulled away from this conversation.

"Jen, hold on a second. Someone is at the door."

"Sure."

Stephen opened the door to see Caldwell standing there. He noted that she was dressed to go out, with an overcoat over a dark red sweater and black jeans. He pulled the phone down from his ear, and asked, "What's going on?"

Caldwell glanced at the phone in Grant's hand, and then said, "Sorry to disturb you, but we just received word that Cardinal Bessetti is dead."

"Pope Paul VII's former secretary of state?"

Caldwell nodded, and said, "Mazzoni says he was found hanging from the ceiling, and there's a note from him confessing to murdering Dr. Fuchs and his wife, Pastor Fletcher and Killian Dvorak."

Grant responded, "Oh, my God."

Caldwell said, "Charlie and I are heading over to Bessetti's house at Mazzoni's request. He asked for you, too. Are you coming?"

Grant turned away from Caldwell, and raised the phone back to his ear. "Jen, I..."

"Stephen, I heard. Go and let me know when you can."

"Okay. I love you."

"You, too."

The call ended. He looked back at Caldwell, and said, "Give me a few minutes to change. I'll meet you at the elevator."

Chapter 55

As Paige Caldwell, Charlie Driessen and Pastor Stephen Grant walked up to Cardinal Renaldo Bessetti's home, exiting were two priests, who headed in the opposite direction.

Inspector Vincent Mazzoni gave Grant and company access to the scene, but for the fact that they were left examining photos of the body and the suicide note on a tablet.

While doing so, Grant asked, "Who were the two priests leaving just as we arrived?"

Mazzoni answered, "Two members of Bessetti's staff. His top aide, Father Pietro Filoni, and..." He looked at his notes, "And Father Lorenzo Conti."

The group examined the photos and the scene.

While looking at the photos, Grant asked Mazzoni, "What's your read on them, I mean, the two priests?"

Mazzoni raised an eyebrow, and answered, "They answered our questions in straightforward fashion. They expressed shock at Bessetti's note, as well as his taking his own life."

"'Expressed shock' or were they actually shocked?"

"That's hard to say, obviously, but I did not get the feeling that either man was suffering from true shock, nor did either express an acute sadness. However, I have been around clergy long enough to say that they seem to process death differently than the rest of us. It's just part of life."

"Yeah, I know," said Grant.

Mazzoni said, "Well, yes, you would know. As for the cardinal's confession about the murders, both seemed bewildered. Filoni kept repeating, 'I cannot believe this.'"

Grant persisted, "What do you know about both of them?"

"Father Filoni has been at Cardinal Bessetti's side for as long as I have been around. He's a very quiet person, just always seemed to be around to do whatever the cardinal needed."

Grant persisted, "And?"

Caldwell, Driessen and Mazzoni all paused, and looked at Grant.

Caldwell asked, "Do you have something? Why the detailed interest in that priest?"

Grant replied, "I'm not sure. Call it a feeling for now. But this letter is just a bit too comprehensive for my taste. It seems to answer almost every question we would have." He looked at Mazzoni, and asked, "The handwriting matches Bessetti's?"

"At this point, it looks good. But we have to take a closer look to be sure."

Grant nodded. "I'm obviously speculating, but everything needs to be considered at this point. So, if anyone is going to be able to do a near-perfect job of forging a suicide note, it would be a person's longtime righthand man."

He didn't garner much response from the other three people.

Nonetheless, Grant pressed forward. "Inspector, I'm sure your people will note this, but please make sure they take a close look at the cardinal's wrists."

Mazzoni responded, "Wrists?" as he moved next to Grant to look at the tablet screen.

"Yes," Grant pointed at one of the photos of Bessetti's body. "Look at this." He enlarged the part of the photo capturing one of Bessetti's hands and wrist. "Look at that. It's not bruised, but there is a clear indentation. I can't say for sure, but that looks like something a zip-tie would leave behind."

Mazzoni looked closely. "You might be right."

Grant added, "Also, take a look at his cheek." He flipped to another photo. "Again, it's kind of vague. But there is a redness there. It's worth a closer look, to see what the cause might be. Quite frankly, I wouldn't be surprised if that came from a blow, like a slap."

Mazzoni nodded, "I will make sure these get the necessary attention."

Grant continued, "Do you have anything more on Father Filoni?"

Mazzoni said, "Given your points, I certainly do not have as much as I would like. I know he was raised by his mother, with his father not in the picture." He paused, and then added, "Thanks for raising these questions to make sure we look into them. I'm not convinced, but everything needs to be explored."

"I'm not convinced either, far from it. But it's all about being thorough."

After another twenty minutes of discussion and investigation, Mazzoni reflected, "We can't keep this under wraps. News is going to break, most likely on this and Professor Dvorak's death."

Grant said, "You're right. But you do have an option in terms of the initial report being straightforward without unwarranted speculation."

Mazzoni said, "Ms. Tanquerey."

"Right."

Mazzoni said, "I will have to check with the Holy Father first."

"That's your call. I only offer the suggestion."

Mazzoni thanked Grant, Caldwell and Driessen for coming and for their help. They pledged to keep each other up to date on anything uncovered. Mazzoni then went to get on the phone with Pope Paul VII, while Grant, Caldwell and Driessen left.

As they walked toward their SUV, Caldwell said to Grant, "Nice job. You're handy to have around."

Driessen added, "Yeah, good eye, Grant."

Grant merely nodded in response.

Once inside the vehicle, Caldwell pulled out her phone and said, "I'll get Sean on this immediately."

Chapter 56

Pope Paul VII sat in an armchair, rubbing his forehead with his eyes closed. "Renaldo."

In the living room area with him sat Cardinal Winston Treadwell and Father Mariano Concepcion. The pope had just finished relaying to his two aides what Vincent Mazzoni had passed along.

Concepcion commented, "This is so surreal."

Treadwell asked, "What else did Vincent say?"

The pope continued to rub his head and keep his eyes shut while answering. He concluded, "None of this can be contained any longer, so I gave him the approval to let Ms. Tanquerey run with the story."

Concepcion asked, "Is that wise?"

"Are there other options, Mariano? If you have any, I would like to hear them."

Treadwell absentmindedly scratched his cheek with the frog on the top of his cane, and said, "I certainly do not, and I assume allowing Ms. Tanquerey to do the initial reporting will give us some degree of fairness."

Concepcion added, "I guess that does seem to make the most sense."

The three sat in silence for a couple of minutes, with Treadwell then asking, "And Renaldo confessed to all of this?"

The pope nodded. "Take a look at the letter yourself." He reached over to a small, adjacent table, picked up a tablet and handed it to Treadwell.

After reading it, the cardinal handed the device to Concepcion.

Several minutes later, the pope rose from his chair and said, "Well, gentlemen, this promises to be a long day. Let's get ready as best we can, and we will meet in my office at 7:30."

Both agreed, exited the room, and headed back to their own residences.

As usual, Treadwell walked the few blocks to his townhouse. He moved slowly, apparently in deep thought. And about halfway into his journey, a look of relief passed over his face. His pace quickened, and he twirled the cane in his right hand.

Chapter 57

After leaving behind Cardinal Bessetti, Fathers Pietro Filoni and Lorenzo Conti made the drive to the Oldani home and vineyard.

By the time lunch was finished hours later, Filoni had been brought up to speed by Jaco Bruno on key matters regarding the Oldani businesses.

Then it was time to turn to Father Michael Russo, who had two major assignments.

Russo said, "The information that Cardinal Bessetti provided regarding the parishes being used to channel funds through checked out fully. It will be invaluable in making matters clear to each priest that in terms of their own circumstances, things have not changed." He proceeded to provide a quick review of each case.

"Excellent," commented Filoni.

Russo continued, "As we discussed, we will make sure that the Oldani family funds going to the Church continue. If we receive some kind of official word from the Vatican in terms of shutting down funds that Bessetti controlled, we will comply accordingly. In the end, with you now controlling the family funds, there's no reason to channel dollars through the Vatican for our efforts. It can be done directly."

Filoni looked at Bruno, who responded, "That will make it all easier to control and conceal. I completely agree."

"Good," said Filoni.

"That leads to my report on the Shadow Servants of the Holy Father. After thorough investigations, I have three targets who have just entered the seminary, and given their backgrounds and views are ready for our training as well." He picked up three files and handed them to Filoni. "Here is a dossier on each. Please let me know what you think, Father, and I can make some initial outreach to test the waters, if you will, and when I am confident, we can approach each."

"This is crucial to our efforts, Father Russo," declared Filoni. "Rest assured, I will give it close attention and let you know my thoughts."

Russo nodded.

Filoni added, "In the meantime, we do have the manpower of the Oldani family businesses at our disposal. Properly allocated, that alone could make a big difference for our efforts, especially for the near term. As for the final matter on our agenda, I will be visiting Cardinal Treadwell to let him know that he is not free from the consequences of his actions."

An alert buzzed from Father Conti's phone. He looked at the device, and said, "Father Filoni, the news apparently is breaking, and as you predicted, it's coming from Madison Tanquerey."

"Good," replied Filoni. "A video?"

Still looking at his phone, Conti said, "Yes, it is."

Filoni got up from his chair, and said, "Let's go put it up on a bigger screen."

Chapter 58

Rachel McEnany spotted Jennifer Grant at one of the booths running along the wall on the opposite side from the bar in Buckley's.

Jennifer got up and said, "Hi, Rachel. Thanks for coming. I appreciate it."

"Well, thanks for asking. It felt good to get out of the house after dark. It doesn't happen that often these days. I was able to get a sitter. Sean is working on the Italy matters."

Jennifer nodded, and the two sat down.

A waitress quickly arrived. "What can I get you?"

Rachel looked at Jennifer, and asked, "What are you having?"

"Just a white wine."

Rachel looked up at the waitress, and said, "I'll have the same."

While waiting for her glass of wine to arrive, Rachel looked around and said, "I've only been here a few times."

"We come fairly often. It's good pub food."

Rachel thanked the waitress when her glass of wine arrived. She then said to Jennifer, "I like the idea of you and I going out for drinks. It's usually our husbands doing it."

After some family and church related small talk, a second glass of wine was brought to the table for each. Rachel then asked, "You said that you had something to talk to me about, that you were looking for some advice?"

There was ample music playing that no one else occupying distant tables could overhear the conversation.

Nonetheless, Jennifer leaned in closer to Rachel and lowered her voice. "I don't want this to come out wrong, but how do you handle Sean doing what he does?"

"Ah." Rachel smiled. "Well, you know that I come from that background as well?"

Jennifer nodded.

"So, it's easier for me. I know the business. But I get that you'd be wrestling with this since Stephen is a pastor, but this thing from years past keeps popping up."

"Yes, that's part of it."

Rachel said, "It's like marrying someone who's an accountant, and then suddenly he takes up the most dangerous hobby imaginable."

"Yes and no. I knew who Stephen was when we got married, and you know that our relationship got started in a unique way."

"I do. That was very badass for an economist, by the way."

Both smiled.

Rachel then continued, "But at the same time, you didn't expect to be something akin to a cop's wife, where you had to worry about your husband making it home alive. While it's not an everyday thing for you, it happens more often than you expected."

"Right." Jennifer took a sip of wine.

"At the same time, you know who your husband is, and you understand that when he gets tossed into these situations, it's not because he goes looking for it, but it's because others understand how he can help and make a difference."

"Exactly right."

"And you support him, and would never think of telling him not to help. In fact, you encourage him to help. You tell him that you're fine with it, but at the same time, you're dying inside and you can't tell him how really worried and scared you are."

Jennifer looked at Rachel with her mouth open. She finally said, "You just described it all perfectly."

Rachel took a large drink of wine. "Jennifer, it actually doesn't matter that I came from the business. I know what you're dealing with because that's been my life since Sean and I decided to have kids, and he stayed in that line of work and I left it."

Jennifer actually had a tone of relief in her voice. "So, what the hell do I do?"

"What do you do? You do what you've been doing? Or, you can leave him, or threaten to leave him unless he keeps his efforts focused exclusively on the pastor thing."

Jennifer said, "I could never do either of those. I love him, and I understand the good he has done."

"Yeah, me, too. So, you have your answer."

Jennifer finished the glass of wine, and looked at Rachel. "Another?"

"Sure, why not?"

Jennifer waved over the waitress, and asked for two more glasses. The two remained silent. The drinks arrived, and each took a sip.

Rachel said, "There's something else."

Jennifer looked at Rachel, and after a few seconds, responded, "You've been working with Stephen on the Lutheran Response to Christian Persecution, so you've gotten to know him better."

Rachel nodded.

Jennifer said, "I'm not sure how to talk about this without coming off as a jealous wife who doesn't trust her husband."

"I'm going to sound like your husband now, but whatever you tell me stays strictly between us. I will add that we're friends, and you should have complete trust that you can say anything – well, just about anything – to me." She smiled.

"Thanks. You know about the history that Stephen has with Paige."

Rachel merely replied, "I do."

"I completely trust my husband. I was married before, and I know what it's like to be with someone you cannot trust. The difference between my first husband and Stephen could not be more different. I know that Stephen would never do anything to hurt me, including cheating. In addition, I actually like Paige. We've kind of become friends, and we enjoy making Stephen feel uncomfortable when together."

"But."

"Not really a 'but.' It's more a 'why.' Why then do I occasionally feel annoyed or bothered when Stephen goes off to something that needs to be done, but does it with Paige?"

Rachel laughed. "Oh, I don't know, Jennifer, maybe it's because you're human. You're normal. It's okay to get a little pissed off now and then when your husband goes off to fight evildoers with his old girlfriend. It doesn't mean that he's going to jump into bed with her, and it doesn't make you a bad person. It's just human nature."

Jennifer smiled. "I feel like an idiot for bringing it up."

"Don't. We all need to talk to someone about stuff like this. It helps. By the way, I think it's kind of nice."

"What's nice?"

"You trust your husband, but there's also enough passion there that you get a little jealous once in a while. That's healthy."

"I like your take on this."

They both took sips from their drinks.

"And by the way, I'm glad to hear that you trust Stephen to the extent that you do. He's a good man. He's been there for us, for Sean, and he has a confidence in knowing what the right thing is without even a trace of arrogance. He doesn't lecture. He guides. He knows when it's time for prayer and when it's time for action. In the end, he's a caring man who helps others as a pastor, and in these other ways."

Jennifer said, "He is. He's those things. Thanks. And from everything Stephen has told me, and from all that I've seen, Sean is much the same."

"He is, but in different ways. But, yeah, he is." Rachel added, "And thank God the two of them aren't around right now to hear any of this."

Jennifer laughed. "Agreed. You're right, Stephen isn't arrogant, but he does think a bit highly of himself from time to time, and this conversation would only feed that."

"Sean's the same way. It's something about men."

Jennifer smiled, and said, "Thanks for this. It's helped get my thinking straight."

"Sure. Okay, let's make a deal."

"Alright."

"Given who we're each married to, one night a month, we go out, do whatever we want, talk about what we want, and yes, bitch about husbands."

Jennifer said, "I'm in," and then clinked glasses.

Chapter 59

"Did you see the report?" asked Edgar Spuel.

On the other end of the call, his brother, Pastor Rusty Spuel, said, "I did. It confirms much of what your guy said."

"I know. Of course, this reporter ... what's her name?"

"It's Madison Tanquerey."

"Right. I assume she's either a lefty or part of the mainstream media. Like there's a difference." Edgar paused to laugh. "Anyway, she's not going to give the full story, but it's enough."

"You don't know who she is?"

"No. Should I?"

It was Rusty's turn to laugh – which happened only on the rarest of occasions.

Edgar pressed, "What is it? Who is she?"

"Madison Tanquerey is engaged to Pastor Richard Leonard."

"Holy shit. You're kidding? How did I not know that?"

Rusty replied, "I don't know. You should have."

"Well, why didn't you tell me?"

"Never mind that for now. I'm betting that this dead cardinal and this professor were working together to expose what the pope was doing, and they paid the price."

"No doubt."

"And the more I think about this, given that Leonard is over there and is engaged to this Tanquerey, you know that her report can't be trusted."

"Well, sure. What are you thinking?"

"It's obvious. The pope is controlling what is being released and when to suit his purposes."

"Right, but why would he release anything?"

Rusty said, "Because he's trying to shut down any further inquiries. He wants to throw people off the trail, and get the entire operation back underground."

There was a pause, and Edgar asked, "So, what next?"

"It's just become clear to me why God has put me in this spot; why he moved me out of that horrid call. I'm in a position now, without a congregation, to do something about this."

"What do you mean?"

"I know Leonard. I have the access to information. And I have the time and enough resources to do this."

"To do what, Rusty?"

"I can go to Rome, and play a role in stopping this Satanic undertaking."

Edgar responded, "Yes! Can I come with you?"

"No. I not only need you to stay on top of the real information on this, but you might have to run some interference for me here if anyone gets inquisitive."

"Okay," said Edgar with disappointment in his voice.

"Hey, Edgar, I need you to do this. I need your help. Can I count on you?"

Edgar's voice quickly regained a tone of enthusiasm. "Of course you can, Rusty."

Chapter 60

"Okay, I dislike this Father Filoni," announced Sean McEnany. He was speaking on a secure video connection from the basement facility in his Long Island home to Paige Caldwell, Charlie Driessen, Jessica West, Phil Lucena and Stephen Grant in their hotel conference room.

The group waited for McEnany to build upon his opening declaration.

He continued, "Namely, I don't like anyone in the vicinity of a series of murders who seems to have a blank slate background."

"What the hell does that mean?" asked Driessen.

"It means, Charlie, give me something, anything. This priest's background is so mundane and simple that my suspicious mind thinks that it has to be scrubbed. Raised by his single mother. He did well in school, kept to himself, few friends. His time at university was marked by excellent grades, and nothing else. And the same seems to go for his seminary career. He served a small parish north of Rome, and eventually wound up as Bessetti's aide. His mother died while he was at school. No one else in his life. None of my contacts have anything on this guy."

Caldwell observed, "Well, considering the extent of your network, I would think that should make us feel better about Father Filoni. Right?"

"Maybe. And the same basically goes for the others working for Bessetti. Again, two other priests – Father Michael Russo and Father Lorenzo Conti – have amazingly clean and boring backgrounds."

Driessen commented, "Well, they are priests." He glanced at Grant, and added, "It's not like most guys with collars have backgrounds as colorful as Stephen's."

"Thanks, Charlie," replied Grant with a smirk.

Driessen chuckled.

Caldwell looked around the table, and no one indicated that they had anything to add or ask. She said to McEnany, "Sean, I'll always trust your instincts, so keep digging as you see fit. But let's make sure we cast a wide net. The Bessetti letter doesn't mention anyone else, but obviously, if the letter is legit, the cardinal didn't pull all of this off without help. Either way, we're looking for others."

"Right. Thanks."

After that video conference ended, a call was made to Vincent Mazzoni, who had nothing of significant value to add into the mix. The letter was written on paper the cardinal used, and with his pen. And it appeared to be in Cardinal Bessetti's handwriting, but Mazzoni cautioned that such analysis was not one hundred percent. In addition, the coroners had nothing conclusive to offer regarding the wrist markings and cheek for Bessetti.

Caldwell and Grant then spoke directly to Pope Paul VII, and all they could offer were reminders that no matter how the details turned out regarding Bessetti, others were involved, and the pope and his aides needed to be aware of that and on guard.

Pope Paul VII concluded the conversation by saying, "Thank you, once again, for all that you are doing. God bless you."

After that call came to a close, Caldwell observed, "He's being generous. He's frustrated."

Grant agreed, "We all are."

After the meeting wrapped up, Lucena and West asked Grant if he had a few minutes.

"Sure, what's up?" he replied.

Caldwell and Driessen left the three alone.

Lucena started, "Given what's happened, I'm not sure that this is the right time to broach the subject."

Grant could see that this was important to the two of them. "Whatever you want to talk about is fine. The three of us understand what's going on, but at the same time, we also know that life keeps, well, going. That doesn't mean we hurt any less over what's happened, nor does it mean that we're disrespecting Killian, or being crass. It's simply that we still need to deal with many things."

West said, "Thanks for that." She glanced over at Lucena, and he smiled and nodded. West looked at Grant, and asked, "We very much would like you to perform our wedding. Would you be willing to do so?"

Grant smiled broadly. "Would I be willing? Of course. I'd be honored." He got up from his seat, and walked over to West and Lucena. They, too, stood up, and Grant hugged each one.

Grant commented, "There is still joy to be found even in the darkest moments."

The conversation went on, with Lucena and West confessing that they still hadn't settled on a time and place as yet.

Grant said, "You let me know the time and place, and I'll be there."

West said, "And I know that you'll want to talk with us beforehand about the wedding and our faith. We understand that, and I don't think you'll have any problems with that. I mentioned to you before that you've had a very real effect on both us."

Lucena added, "You really have, Stephen."

"Well, that's not about me. That's the Holy Spirit, and it's wonderful to hear."

West said, "I promise that we'll get back to you soon with more on what we're thinking on when and where."

"Great. It's interesting that when coming to Rome, the seat of the Catholic Church, this Lutheran pastor is filling up his wedding schedule."

West smiled, and said, "We're excited about Richard and Madison's wedding."

Grant replied, "Me, too."

Chapter 61

After going to his room for the night, Stephen showered, put on shorts and a Cincinnati Reds t-shirt, said his prayers, and called his wife.

While finishing up the call, Jennifer said, "You really are racking up the weddings."

"They're appreciated lights amidst all of this darkness."

"Why don't you kick back and watch a movie to get your mind off things?"

"Good idea. Maybe I'll watch an Irene Dunne movie, and it'll also remind me of you."

"I've said it before. I can't complain when my husband compares me to a Hollywood starlet, but sometimes it's a little weird."

"Haven't you gotten used to the weirdness of being married to me yet?"

"I'm working on it. Watch your movie. I love you."

"I love you, and thanks for putting up with all of the weirdness."

After the call concluded, Grant opened his laptop.

But his decision on which movie to watch was cut short thanks to a knock at the door. He hopped off the bed. When he opened the door, Grant was surprised to see Father John Kohli standing in the hall. He said, "John, is everything okay?"

"Stephen, do you have a few minutes?"

"Sure. Please, come in."

As he entered the room, Kohli asked, "Are you sure I'm not intruding?" The priest also appeared to be dressed for bed or late night relaxation, with a Triumph Bonneville motorcycle long-sleeve shirt and sweat pants.

"Not at all." Grant tried to read a man that he didn't really know, and with whom he had only chatted with in passing since meeting. "How about a beer?"

Grant saw Kohli exhale and appear to be a bit more at ease.

Kohli answered, "Yes, I could use a beer right now."

Grant pulled two cold bottled beers out of the suite's small refrigerator, and handed one to Kohli. They grabbed seats in the suite's living room area, and both took a drink. Grant could see that Kohli wasn't comfortable. Grant decided that easing into the ultimate point of the visit was in order. He asked, "I've heard you talk about riding, and I have to ask about the shirt: Do you have a Triumph?"

"Not my own. Back home, I have a Kawasaki Ninja ZX-6R. But Pope Paul VII graciously supplied a bike to use during my work here in Rome. And it's a Triumph Bonneville Speed Twin. He apparently talked to someone because I always wanted a Triumph."

"Well, the Kawasaki or the Triumph, both are nice rides, from what I understand."

"Do you ride, Stephen?"

"Not in recent years. It's actually been some time, but I did have the opportunity a few times, going back a number of years."

"While you were with the CIA?"

Grant replied, "Actually, yes."

Both took swigs of beer.

"I bet you've had some varied experiences."

"It's definitely been interesting. And given your writing and being here, involved in this project at the invitation of the pope, the same can be said of you, I assume?"

Kohli nodded, and commented, "It's definitely getting more interesting by the day, it seems, and more complicated."

As Kohli took another drink, Grant asked, "Is that what you wanted to talk about?"

"It is. I've been at a loss as to whom to talk to, and then I thought that perhaps you wouldn't mind, since you're a pastor." He paused, and added, "A fellow member of the clergy."

"Whatever you tell me is, of course, in complete confidence, and if I can somehow help, I'm more than happy to do so."

"Thanks." He sat back in his chair and smiled. "What I'm thinking about oddly fits in with why I'm here and working on this project, given that one of the things Martin Luther did that was so shocking at the time was marrying a former nun."

"You and Sister Katharine?"

Kohli nodded. "If you would have told me ten years ago that I'd be in this position, I would have told you, 'Not me. No way.'"

"Yeah, life is funny that way."

"Before I came here, Kathy and I worked together for several years. She's the principal at St. Michael's High School in Florida. Well, she was."

Was?

Kohli said, "And I was the head of the religion department, the basketball coach and school chaplain. She and I developed a friendship. We both played basketball in high school and college. She rides as well. And of course, there is our faith."

"I understand."

"We developed a friendship. But looking back, there was clearly something more underlying that friendship. We spoke about it once briefly, and awkwardly agreed to keep our relationship as friends, maintaining our vows. And we did do that. Life being what it is, we allowed our deeper feelings to emerge as Kathy dropped me off at the airport to come here."

"It was a moment when you could do so but without subsequent consequences since you literally were getting on a plane to fly across the Atlantic Ocean."

Kohli swallowed the last of his beer, and said, "Apparently, you're right."

Grant got up, took the empty bottles to the counter, and grabbed two more beers from the refrigerator.

As Grant did so, Kohli continued, "I think the fact that I was no longer at St. Michael's allowed us to subconsciously do things that we otherwise wouldn't have. Kathy came to visit for a vacation. We were planning an extensive ride around Italy. And then Gerhard died. That affected us in unexpected ways. I was so grateful that Kathy was here, and she was, too. After the funeral, we did actually get away for a day, and rode down the coast. And well..." Kohli took a big drink from the bottle.

Grant said, "I get it."

Kohli looked at the beer bottle as he turned it nervously in his hands.

Grant asked, "What happened?"

Kohli cleared his throat. "There was a morning after effect. Kathy was thrown. She slipped out in the very early morning, left me a note that, without getting into the details, amounted to saying that she loved me, was confused, and needed to think about what had happened. And while I was knocked off kilter by her leaving alone, her letter reflected everything I was thinking and feeling as well."

"And now she's back."

"Yes, she is. Haley took it upon herself to contact Kathy with what happened to Killian." He took another sip of beer, and took a deep breath.

Grant waited and then said, "And?"

"I wasn't fully prepared for what she did. Kathy knew that she simply couldn't leave the school to fly back to Rome to be with me during all of this, without, well, causing concerns, questions and accusations around the school. So, she quit."

Grant actually said, "Wow."

"Yeah, wow is right. The questions and accusations will still swirl back at Cape Canaveral, but St. Michael's will be able to truthfully respond that they had no knowledge of ... whatever is happening between their former principal and chaplain."

Grant could see how the last point caused Kohli some pain to say.

Kohli continued, "So, let's just say that Kathy's days as a nun are numbered."

"And where are you on this?"

Kohli looked down at the beer bottle again. And then he looked back up at Grant, and answered, "I love her, without reservation. She's sacrificed everything, flew across the Atlantic, to be with me because she knew I would be hurting. That's love."

"Yeah, I'd say so." Each man took a drink. Grant asked, "So, what's next and how can I help?"

"Actually, you've already helped by letting me just say these things out loud to an understanding ear other than Kathy's."

Grant smiled, and said, "Well, that was easy. Glad I could help."

Kohli laughed and said, "Right. This is all so simple. What am I getting all worried about?"

"Seriously, what is next?"

"Actually, Stephen, I know my days as a priest are numbered as well." He paused, and then added, "This is the pain for Kathy and me. I love being a priest, and I honestly believe that I have made a contribution to the Church. And Kathy feels the same way, especially as the principal at St. Michael's. We're both bewildered as to what's next, quite frankly, and praying that where we're headed doesn't undo some of the positive things each of us contributed to over the years."

"My guess, John, only based on this being our first real conversation, is that if the two of you want to continue to make contributions to the Church, you'll find ways to do so. I had a friend, who long before I briefly knew him, actually had to wrestle with the question you are wrestling with right now. He was a Lutheran pastor who wound up leaving the life of a pastor behind for a career in the CIA."

Kohli commented, "Bizarro Stephen Grant?"

Grant laughed and said, "In a sense, I guess. But he offered some advice that helped me, and it might do the same for you. It was straightforward but important. He basically said to be honest with God, with others and with yourself, and that includes being honest about how you can serve the Lord and others well. Make the best decision you can. Some people will accept it, and others won't. All you can do in response is to pray and be compassionate."

Kohli nodded and said, "All true."

Grant continued, "As you try to figure this out, I am completely serious in saying that you can always find an ear willing to listen with me."

"Thanks, Stephen. I appreciate that."

"I have another thought, and consider that it's coming from a Lutheran pastor."

"Okay."

"Well, you have direct access to the head of the entire Catholic Church. I know Pope Paul VII a bit, and I can confidently say that he'd manage to carve out some time to speak with you and Kathy about what you're doing and what that might mean in the long run."

Kohli looked Grant in the eyes, and said, "That would be direct, to say the least."

"I tend to be the direct type."

Kohli chuckled. "Yeah, I can see that. And maybe Pope Paul VII will react a bit more positively than Church leaders did when Luther married Katharina von Bora."

"I have two reactions to what you just said. First, you are already using the word 'marriage.'" He paused and when he didn't get a response from Kohli, Grant continued, "Second, I think this pope will be more gracious." Grant held up his bottle, adding, "One other thought: You have a head start on Luther."

"What does that mean?"

"Luther and his Kathy, or Katie, as he called her, had to grow into a deep love. You and your Kathy apparently already are there. But you know all of this. Heck, you wrote the book."

"Thanks, Stephen."

After John left, Grant went to pick up his phone to text Jennifer. But he stopped himself.

That was under the pastoral cone of silence. Maybe I'll be able to tell Jen more at some point down the line. But not now.

He looked at the clock. It said 1:12 AM.

Too late for a movie? Ah, let's give it a shot.

He pulled up *The Awful Truth* on a streaming service.

Maybe Cary Grant and Irene Dunne working on keeping a marriage together works for tonight.

Stephen propped up some pillows on the bed, and hit "play."

Chapter 62

"Mama, that dinner was wonderful, as usual," declared Father Pietro Filoni.

Father Lorenzo Conti added, "Thank you, so much, Ms. Carbonali." Father Michael Russo echoed Conti's compliment.

"Ah, you boys. It makes me so happy to hear you say that you enjoyed dinner. I don't think they feed you right over at the Vatican." She paused, and as she blessed herself, said, "Lord, forgive me. I, of course, meant no disrespect."

"Yes, Mama, we know," commented Pietro.

The three priests pitched in cleaning the table, and washing and drying dishes. Angelina Carbonali insisted that the dishwashing machine never got dishes and pots "fully clean," and "It leaves terrible spots on the glasses."

Afterwards, Conti and Russo left Pietro alone to talk with his mother.

Into the conversation, Angel asked, "Are you sure these men will be necessary?"

"I'm just being cautious, Mama. I want to make sure you are safe. There are people trying to hurt the Holy Father and the Church who would like to use me."

"I am so sorry I brought this on you, Pietro."

"Mama, none of this is your fault. We know whose fault it is."

"Yes, I know, I know. But at least he has provided for us, including this house and your schooling."

Pietro Filoni sighed ever so slightly, as he did every time his mother said anything nice about Enzo Oldani. "Well, we're taking care of all of this now. Mr. Oldani is out of the picture."

"But how?"

"Mama don't worry about that. There are good people, good Catholics, who care deeply and have stepped forward."

"God bless them."

"Yes." Pietro paused, and then added, "You know, Mama, the only reason that Enzo provided you this home and for my education was to keep you quiet."

It was Angelina's turn to sigh. Also, the perpetual pleasantness that had been on display throughout her son's visit vanished. A mask suddenly seemed to be lifted. She said, "Yes, Pietro, I know why Enzo gave me this house on some secluded acres. I know why he paid for your education. I know why he gave dollars to the Vatican." She provided an answer to that last point, "Because the funds were tied to your work. Much of this was done to ease his guilt. But that wasn't all of it. I also understand that the guards he provided over the years were here for two reasons – to protect us and to protect him. Now, why don't you tell me how is it that we suddenly can be cut off from Enzo Oldani's support?"

Pietro looked into his mother's eyes. "Enzo is dead."

Angelina appeared surprised, but not saddened. "Dead? How is it that I have not heard about this?"

"Few people are aware. It is not generally known."

She nodded and waited.

Pietro said, "So, there obviously will be no more regular visits by Enzo."

Angelina simply responded, "Apparently."

"As you know, his two daughters do not care about the family business. Jaco Bruno has taken over running things."

"Jaco? What about Giorgio?"

"Giorgio is dead, and so is Luca."

"Well, it appears that Jaco has tidied things up for himself. I did not see him having those skills."

Pietro merely said, "He doesn't, Mama."

Mother and son looked at each other in silence for nearly a minute.

Angelina finally stood up from the table, and walked around to her son. She leaned down and took his face in her hands. "Do you know what you are doing, Father Filoni?"

"I do, Mama."

She kissed his forehead, and then rested her head on the top of his. Pietro put his arms around his mother. They remained in that position for a few minutes.

Angelina finally whispered, "Everything you are doing is for the Church?"

"Of course, Mama."

"Good. I pray that you will succeed in the Lord's work."

"Thank you, Mama."

She stepped back from her son, and the mask of pleasantness returned. "Now, what can I send you, Lorenzo, and Michael home with tonight?"

"Michael will be staying here for a while, with the additional guards."

"Good. I like Michael. It will give me a chance to try out some new recipes on him." Angelina turned and started walking to the kitchen. She said over her shoulder, "Come, Pietro, tell me what I am sending home with you."

Chapter 63

"Can I get you something to drink?" asked the flight attendant.

Rusty Spuel looked up from a book, and said, "Yes. I'll have a Sprite."

The attendant looked to the person seated next to Spuel. "How about you, ma'am?"

"A Coke would be nice. Thanks."

The attendant filled two small cups with ice, and pulled out two cans of soda.

The attendant went to hand a cup and the Coke to the heavy-set woman sitting in the window seat. With his attention back on his book, the attendant had to say, "Excuse me, sir."

He looked up, and seemed annoyed that it wasn't his drink. Spuel leaned back as the cup and can were passed in front of him.

The woman said, "Thank you."

The attendant then handed a cup and soda to Spuel, who mumbled, "Thanks."

As Spuel poured the carbonated beverage into the ice-filled cup, the woman next to him took note of his book. "Oh, you're reading a history of the popes."

He said, "What? Oh, yes, I am."

"I'm reading about St. Peter's Basilica."

"That's nice."

"Have you ever been to Rome before?"

He took a sip of soda, and then said, "No, I have not."

The woman smiled, and enthusiastically said, "This is my first time, too. I'm really looking forward to seeing everything."

Spuel put his cup down on the tray and picked up his book. "This is more of a work thing for me."

"Oh, what do you do?"

"I'm a pastor."

The woman brightened again. "That's interesting. What kind of pastor are you?"

"Lutheran."

"Are you involved in some kind of ecumenical meeting, or something like that?"

Spuel turned for the first time to look at the woman. He said, "I have no interest in that kind of thing. In my view, the pope is the antichrist."

Spuel turned back to his book, while the woman looked completely taken aback. She managed to say, "Well, I'm sorry to take you away from your book."

Spuel said nothing in response.

Chapter 64

The leftovers from Angelina Carbonali's dinner, wrapped in aluminum foil, rested in a bag on the back seat of the car. Father Lorenzo Conti was driving, with Father Pietro Filoni in the front passenger seat.

Conti asked, "Do you think that Cardinal Treadwell really believes that he is free and clear with the death of Cardinal Bessetti?"

"At the very least, he is tempted to believe it. After all, it offers him hope that he has escaped the consequences of his abhorrent actions in this life."

Conti merely nodded in response.

Filoni said, "The required personnel from the Oldani family will be there?"

"It's all been arranged by Mr. Bruno."

"Good. Cardinal Bessetti was too fond of thinking that he could manipulate and control people. He assumed that they did things for the same reasons he did, or at least that he fully understood their motivations. The problem with someone like Cardinal Treadwell, though, is that he could be one moment of feeling guilty away from confessing, and undermining our entire efforts. It's not like he is committed to protecting the Church the way we are."

"That most certainly is true."

"Given his history, he is able to push off guilt for a very long time. However, the years and pressure can reach a breaking point. It's time to make sure that point is not reached."

Conti parked the sedan around the street from Treadwell's home. Filoni pulled the hood up on his oversized coat. His face was lost in shadow. He got out of the car, and walked to the rear of the residence. He knocked on the backdoor.

Three dark figures moved toward the house from another direction.

It took Treadwell a few minutes to flip on the back light and open the door. He squinted at the figure standing on his back steps. Only Filoni's chin could be seen in the light.

Treadwell said, "Yes?"

Filoni asked, "Your Eminence, may I come in?"

Treadwell's eyes widened, and he took a step back.

Filoni stepped into the house. Treadwell continued to back away ever so slowly. Filoni closed the door behind him, and then removed his hood.

The three dark figures moved into a corner of the yard devoid of light.

Treadwell stammered, "F-F-Father Filoni."

"Yes, Your Eminence. You didn't think that this ended with the death of Cardinal Bessetti?"

Treadwell stopped backtracking any deeper into the kitchen, and suddenly stood a little straighter. "You murdered Bessetti?"

"I did. I have killed to protect the Church and the Holy Father."

"You're mad."

"Am I, Your Eminence? I also have killed for you."

Treadwell lashed out, "No! No. You did not do that for me."

"Well, technically, you might be right. However, protecting you protected the Holy Father and, therefore, the Bride of Christ."

Treadwell replied, "I have my sins. And they are horrific – perhaps unforgiveable. Do not try to shift yours onto me, however."

Treadwell then lunged for one of the knives in a block sitting on a counter. He managed to grab one of the handles, but Filoni moved with too much speed. While lunging toward Treadwell, the priest slipped a tactical knife from its sheath attached to his belt. He drew the blade across Treadwell's right arm. The cardinal screamed in pain, and immediately dropped his kitchen knife.

Filoni now stood against Treadwell. With his left hand, Filoni was partially holding up the older, fatter man. His right hand held the knife that now was positioned against Treadwell's neck. The two men were frozen, Treadwell in fear and Filoni apparently in thought. The priest stared into the cardinal's bulging eyes.

Suddenly a look of serenity came upon Filoni's face. He then started to thrust the knife into and across Cardinal Treadwell's neck. While doing so, Filoni said, "May the Lord who frees you from sin save you and raise you up."

Filoni let the dying Treadwell slip to the kitchen floor. He dropped the knife next to the cardinal. Filoni then put his hood up, turned and exited the back door. The three men emerged from the darkness. As they approached, Filoni held up his hand. The three froze. Filoni ordered, "Everything must be clean."

One of the men replied, "Of course. Yes, sir."

Filoni lowered his hand. As the men passed him by, the priest said, "May the Lord guide your work."

Filoni disappeared into the night, and the three Oldani family men entered the house.

As they started their work, one said, "He just said that the Lord should guide our work. That's pretty fucked up."

One of the others said, "You got a problem with your job?"

"Me? No. But I don't expect a priest to be okay with it, never mind a priest actually running one of the families. Come on, that's pretty fucked up."

"What is it with you and your mouth? I've told you before: Shut up. And you especially need to shut up when it comes to Filoni. We're not supposed to know that he is calling the shots. Get to work. You screw this up, and I am guessing you're going to have a lot more to do to make up for it than saying a bunch of Hail Marys."

"Okay, okay. Take it easy."

Chapter 65

"Thanks for setting up this call," said Sean McEnany.

Supervisory Special Agent Rich Noack replied, "Given the circumstances and who's involved, I'm glad that the FBI is able to help out."

Noack and McEnany had worked together several times in recent years. However, more often than not, Noack was left puzzled and somewhat annoyed that McEnany usually had better information than did the entire FBI.

Noack added, "And anytime I have some asset or information that you don't have, it makes me feel a little better about what we're doing at the Bureau."

McEnany replied, "I understand, Rich. Of course, you understand how my network works, and you've simply become another source in that network, right?"

Noack sighed, and said, "Yeah, yeah, I get it." He paused, and then said, "By the way, these two guys are more than willing to help. They can't believe that they're moving up to better accommodations within the federal prison system for what they're being asked to share."

"Hopefully, a federal prison can still make their stays less than pleasant."

"I'll have the warden work on that. In the meantime, I'm patching them through now."

"Thanks, again."

There was a click, and McEnany said, "Hello."

"Yeah, we're here."

"And who am I talking to exactly?"

One deep, scratchy voice said, "What, you don't fucking know? I thought you asked for this."

A second higher voice joined in as the two men laughed.

McEnany interrupted, "Okay, enough of that shit. If you answer the questions to my liking, I'll pass that along. If you don't, well, then screw both of you."

The scratchy voice said, "Geez, okay. Don't be so touchy. Just havin' a little fun. I'm Artie Barbaro."

The other man said, "Yeah, I'm Joey Fregosi."

"Alright, Mr. Barbaro and Mr. Fregosi, I'm short on time, not to mention patience. So, I'll cut to the chase. What do you know about Enzo Oldani's extramarital affairs?"

Fregosi answered, "Yeah, this is about Enzo. Interesting. Anyway, he was pretty faithful to his wife while she was alive. And what I mean by 'faithful' is that, you know, he didn't flaunt his affair. He kept it pretty quiet."

Barbaro added, "Yeah, and I heard there was only the one. You gotta respect that."

McEnany said, "Your sense of morality and discretion are so noble. Whom did he have this affair with?"

"Her name was..." started Barbaro.

Fregosi interrupted, "Was? She's still around, right, Artie?"

"Yeah, you're right, Joey. As far as I know. Anyways, her name is Angelina Carbonali. I heard she's pretty smart. You know, she acted all sweet, but she actually knew the business."

"Enzo obviously had it for her big time. He set her up with a nice place, and they kept their thing going. In fact, it turned out that after his wife died, Enzo was with Angelina longer than he actually was married."

McEnany asked, "I know Enzo had two girls with his wife. Did he and Angelina have any children?"

Barbaro laughed. "Right, you don't know," he said, while Fregosi laughed as well.

"Yes, that's right, I don't know. That's why I'm talking to you two."

Barbaro replied, "Okay, okay. This is more mysterious, but the rumor has long been that Enzo Oldani and Angelina Carbonali had a kid who – now get this – who became a freakin' priest."

Fregosi jumped in, "Yeah, and not just some ordinary priest. But some kind of badass priest in like a secret society. Crazy, right?"

Barbaro said, "But there's more. Tell him the latest, Joey."

"Alright, alright, I'm gettin' there."

"What is it?" asked McEnany.

"Now take this from where it's comin'. Obviously, it's freakin' hard to verify information in here, if you know what I mean? But anyway, this is the wildest shit yet. Supposedly, this badass priest offed his father – that's right, murdered his own dad, Enzo Oldani – and is secretly running the entire Oldani family. Wild, right?"

The two prisoners were laughing riotously. Sean McEnany wasn't.

Chapter 66

It was early afternoon in Rome, and early morning on Long Island, when Paige Caldwell looked at her phone, and saw that Sean McEnany was calling.

She answered, "What do you have?"

"I've got it all. That's what I've got. Are Charlie, Jessica and Phil around?"

Caldwell was sitting with the three at the long table in their hotel conference room. "They're all right here. Should I get Stephen?"

"Yes."

Caldwell came back to the room in less than a minute with Grant in tow. She put her phone down on the table with the speaker on. "Okay, Sean, we're all here."

"This entire thing began to break last night," started McEnany. "I've been working with some good people to put this together since."

Grant knew that McEnany rarely signaled that he was excited, except when he put all of the pieces together on something like this.

This is as close to animated that Sean's voice ever gets.

McEnany explained, "I was provided three videos from the same day at Sydney Airport. And guess which unholy trio appears in them?" He didn't wait for any guesses. "There were our Fathers Filoni, Conti and Russo. Your response? Big deal, Sean. Who cares that they went to Australia? Well, the day before these three get on a plane to leave, three deaths were reported. A family – husband, wife and child, Noah Lucas, Melanie and their young son,

Sebastian – died in a suspicious fire. Police had nothing, no suspects, no motives. But it turns out that there were rumors – well, more than rumors if you get to the right people – that Mr. Lucas suffered abuse as a teen at the hands of a local priest. That priest was Winston Treadwell."

Grant uttered, "Holy shit."

McEnany said, "Yeah, you can say that again. Coincidence that these three happened to be in town when Mr. Lucas and his family die in a suspicious fire, and he apparently was abused by Cardinal Treadwell decades earlier? No way. Sorry, I'm not buying it."

There was an uneasy silence in the room. Caldwell quietly said, "That's good work on your part, Sean."

"Wait, there's more," McEnany declared. "I have my own contacts inside the Vatican."

Driessen commented, "Of course you do."

McEnany continued, "So, this guy is working covertly on the inside to gather information on abuse and abusers in the Catholic Church. He's got two jobs, in effect. First, he is working to identify abusers, or suspected abusers, who are still operating in the Church, and secondly, until they are exposed and dealt with, he is trying to keep a close eye on them, trying to head off additional suffering."

West interjected, "Geez, that sounds like it could be a mighty undertaking. I hope he's got a lot of help."

McEnany merely replied, "Some, but not enough. But he did relay to me that one of the locals in Italy with a sordid past came to him with a confession and a strange story. This priest was being extorted by Cardinal Bessetti. In exchange for not going public with this priest's, let's say, indiscretions, he agreed to use the local church as a conduit for resources. His parish would accept money from a Vatican account, and then turn those funds over to an account apparently controlled by the cardinal."

Lucena said, "Cardinal Bessetti was laundering funds through this local church."

"That's right. I haven't been able to check out all of the churches where funds were distributed to from these accounts, but I'm guessing that we'll find that these places have priests with sordid backgrounds."

"Shit, Sean, what else do you have?" asked Driessen.

"This priest said that he got a visit from a couple of threatening gentlemen who are part of the Oldani crime family. They visited to let the priest know that he shouldn't get his hopes up because Bessetti died. They assured him that his sins were known to others, and that he should continue to do as told. I guess this priest discovered a bit of a moral backbone even when confronted by these mob thugs, and after he challenged these two guys, one leaned in and said, and this supposedly is a quote: 'Bessetti was just a tool. You don't want to cross Father Filoni.'"

Caldwell interrupted, "He named Filoni?"

"He did. So, after getting this news, it was time for an even deeper dive on Filoni. Sure enough, it turns out that Father Pietro Filoni's story was scrubbed clean of certain things. The woman widely identified as his mother, Angelina Filoni, was not his mother in reality. I spoke to a relative, and it turns out that she never had any children. Once I was able to directly tie in the Oldani family, it turns out that Rich Noack at the FBI had a couple of mob residents of the federal prison system who were willing to chat about their knowledge of relationships in the old country. Now, what they told me sounds insane until you plug it into everything we're seeing."

McEnany went on to relay what Artie Barbaro and Joey Fregosi told him.

When McEnany was finished, Caldwell and the group at the hotel called Vincent Mazzoni to relay what they had heard. He took the information, asked a few questions, and said that he would get back to them.

After hanging up with Mazzoni, there was agreement that sitting around and waiting was not an option.

Driessen asked, "So, who wants to visit Father Filoni's mom to ask her some questions?"

Caldwell replied, "Exactly what I was thinking."

West was annoyed at Caldwell for deciding that she would be staying behind with the scholars at the hotel, while the CDM team, including Grant, would head to the home provided to Angelina Carbonali by Enzo Oldani. Fortunately, Artie Barbaro and Joey Fregosi knew where it was, and passed that information along as well.

Caldwell said, "Okay, let's all change into tactical gear, collect what we need, and meet back here in five."

As people started moving, Grant stopped Caldwell, and said, "I think I'll wear the collar."

"What? Why?"

Chapter 67

Stephen Grant was behind the wheel of the large SUV. Paige Caldwell was in the front passenger seat holding a tablet. She was turned to more easily talk to Charlie Driessen and Phil Lucena, who were in the second row of seats.

Driessen commented, "Nothing ever goes wrong when you're making plans on the run, and getting ready to step into the unknown world of a mobster's mother. Oh, yeah, the mobster is an insane priest and we're letting the Lutheran pastor just walk up to the front door and knock."

Caldwell looked up from the screen displaying a satellite view of the property where Angelina Carbonali resided. "So, what? We should wait?"

"Well, how about a pause, so we can..."

The ring from Caldwell's phone cut him off. She looked at the screen, and answered, "Inspector Mazzoni, what do you have?"

"Cardinal Treadwell is gone."

"You just can't find him, or something more than that?"

"He wasn't home or at work. I assumed we just needed to track him down, but then I spoke to Father Concepcion. He reminded me that Cardinal Treadwell never left his home or office without his frog cane."

"His what?"

Grant nodded, and whispered, "Yeah, I saw it."

Mazzoni said, "Never mind the details of the cane. The point is that he is never without it. Never. But it is standing by the front door of his home."

"Any evidence of foul play?"

"We're going over it right now. I would be shocked if we found anything. At the same time, I would be surprised if he was okay. Even if this were him fleeing in some kind of panic because he found out about what we discovered, that cane would not be where it is. Father Concepcion hammered that home with me."

Caldwell looked at Driessen, and then at Lucena and finally Grant. The three could hear the conversation. Driessen finally said, "Yeah, okay."

Grant and Lucena then nodded.

Caldwell said, "Inspector, I'm going to send you an address."

"An address?"

"Yeah, we could use some back up."

"Back up? Where are you, Ms. Caldwell?"

"Very shortly, we're going to visit Angelina Carbonali."

Mazzoni didn't respond immediately. He eventually asked, "Do you think that is wise?"

"Inspector, things are moving way too fast, and people are dying. We've got a crazy-ass priest on the loose who apparently has control over the foot soldiers of a crime family. I think we need to catch up, quickly."

Grant added, "Everything tells me that Bessetti was the check. Without him, Filoni is fully engaged in waging a holy war. He's capable of anything."

Caldwell said into the phone, "Did you hear that?"

Mazzoni answered, "I did." He paused. "If Pastor Grant is correct, my first responsibility is to secure the Vatican."

Caldwell looked at Grant. He heard Mazzoni's comment, and nodded in agreement. She said to Mazzoni, "I understand. Send whomever you can."

"I will."

The call ended, and Driessen said, "Okay, forget everything I said before. Let's review the latest version of our flying-by-the-seat-of-our-pants plan."

Lucena asked, "Shall I?"

Caldwell responded, "Sure." She handed him the tablet.

"We have the necessary communications equipment to stay in contact, and the benefit of surprise. The plot of land is not all that big – about six acres. It's wooded, which actually works to our advantage as opposed to those guarding Carbonali. There also are roads running on the north and south sides of the land. Gives us easier access and entry." He looked at his watch, and continued, "By the time we're ready, it'll start to get dark. Another point in our favor. In terms of weapons besides our Glocks, we're far from being fully stocked. We have two Beretta rifles, two H&K submachine guns, and a dozen grenades. Oh yes, and we have a half-dozen vests."

Grant commented, "Okay. If that's not fully stocked, I want to know what is."

You slip into this so easily.

Grant took over the review. "Once I'm in, you guys will be able to get close without being spotted. You hear from me, and you either move in or retreat. You don't hear from me within 45 minutes, as we discussed, and you move in."

Driessen said, "You're dropping us in the spots we settled on before, and then you're just going to pull up, tell them who you are, and that you're working for the pope? And the assumption is that the combination of your collar and being direct will get you in the door to see Angelina Carbonali, or perhaps even Filoni himself, if he happens to be there?"

Grant merely responded, "Yes."

Driessen looked at Caldwell, and asked, "And this makes sense to you, too?"

"'Makes sense' might be a stretch, but it is our best chance at avoiding a blood bath."

Driessen grunted, and added, "Let's hope so. Quite frankly, I'd rather just have Grant as part of a surprise assault from four different directions."

"Yeah, I know, Charlie," said Grant. "But I'm not comfortable just going in guns blazing when there's a chance that we can get things done in a different way."

"That different way might get you killed, Grant. Father Filoni isn't one of your typical clergy buddies."

"True," replied Grant. "And as you like to point out on occasion, I'm not a typical pastor either. And if it turns ugly, you guys will arrive from three different directions, and I'll be on the inside."

Driessen persisted, "On the inside without a weapon."

"I'll improvise."

After dropping Lucena and Driessen in different places, it was Caldwell's turn. She got out of the SUV with her gear, and said, "Charlie better not be right. Be careful."

Grant said, "You, too."

Caldwell's look lingered, and then she slammed the door shut.

Five minutes later, Grant pulled the SUV onto the long driveway cutting through some woods and eventually leading to the large home. Two men with rifles hanging over their shoulders emerged from the trees and took up position in the middle of the thin road.

It would have been easy to pick these two off. Geez, Grant, what the hell is wrong with you? Less CIA, more pastor.

Grant stopped the vehicle and lowered the two front windows. The men approached on both sides. The man on the driver's side was tall, thin and had a thick, dark, unruly beard. The person on the other side was a shade smaller, but his body was thick and his head was bald.

The bearded guard asked, "Father, what can we do for you?" He spoke Italian.

Grant simply asked, "English?"

In a heavy accent, the bald man replied, "Why is an American priest here?"

Grant directly replied, "I've been working for Pope Paul VII, and I've come to speak with Ms. Carbonali."

The man smiled, and said, "Ah, you are working with the Holy Father?"

"I am."

"You are coming to speak to Ms. Carbonali on behalf of the Holy Father?"

Grant thought about his answer. He replied, "Yes, I am."

That's technically true, in a sense.

The bald man seemed impressed. When he translated, however, the tall bearded man was far less impressed. They proceeded to argue in Italian.

The bald man said, "Forgive me, Father...?"

Grant replied, "Stephen."

"Forgive me, Father Stephen, but my co-worker is a heathen. However, he is right. Security is very tight here. If you do not mind, we have to search you and your vehicle, and then we need to call in that you are here and get clearance for your visit."

Grant said, "I completely understand."

Five minutes later, Grant had been cleared to proceed, and was driving the SUV toward the house. The item missed by the guards was a tiny, two-way communicator inside Grant's ear. Unless trained to look for it, the earpiece was designed to be missed.

In his ear, Grant heard Caldwell say, "Well, that was easy."

Driessen's voice then warned, "Never say that."

Grant commented, "I agree with Charlie in this case."

Grant parked the vehicle, and as he exited the SUV, the front door of the Tuscany-style home opened, and out stepped two more men with rifles. Grant noted that they had the same kind of casualness that the two men who stopped the vehicle had. Behind them came a priest with a shaved head and a large nose. Grant noted that he was on the young side, probably mid-30s, and he was built like a fire plug.

The priest extended a hand, and as Grant shook it, Father Michael Russo said, "This was an unexpected visit, Father Stephen? Do many Lutheran pastors use the title of 'Father'?"

"Ah, no, very few."

"I did not think so, Pastor Grant."

"And you are?"

"Father Michael Russo." Russo turned and started to walk slowly. With Grant at his side, they entered the building and the two armed guards followed. "So, you're interested in talking with Ms. Carbonali. Do you mind if I ask why?"

"Of course not. I was going to ask her about her son, Father Pietro Filoni. Father Filoni isn't here as well, is he?'"

Russo stopped walking. He continued to stare ahead, and said, "You are direct, Pastor Grant. Arrogant, in fact."

"Well, I don't intend to be – arrogant, that is. I'm just looking for answers to some disturbing things going on, including assorted murders. Perhaps if I could speak with Ms. Carbonali..."

Grant stopped talking when a woman in her late sixties emerged from a doorway just a few feet away. She had dark hair, narrow eyes, and a thin nose. She also wore a look of anger. Angelina Carbonali said, "Pastor Grant, Father Russo here has told me a good deal about you. You're a very dangerous man, in several respects."

"Well, I don't know about that."

Carbonali interrupted him, "I do. Again, thanks to Father Russo."

"And your son?" Grant pressed.

Carbonali slapped Grant's face. She said, "You probably came here thinking that you could tell me things about Father Pietro Filoni that would somehow turn me against him. Or, that I would at least give you some information that would help you stop him in doing what must be done. You're only going to discover that I am completely dedicated to Pietro Filoni, and that he is doing God's work in eliminating enemies of the one true Church of Christ and enemies of the Vicar of Christ, no matter who those enemies might be."

In his ear, Grant heard Caldwell give the order. "We're moving in."

Carbonali continued, "You are among those enemies, not simply because you are a follower of that heretical monk, Martin Luther, but also because you are in league with this pretender in the papal office. Your insolence in coming here will be rewarded with your death."

She looked at Father Russo, who nodded ever so slightly.

Carbonali added, "My son hates Lutherans most of all, and I can see why that is the case."

*   *   *

The two men guarding the driveway entrance stood with their backs to the woods. There was little chance that they heard Phil Lucena approaching in the woods behind them. That wasn't only due to Lucena's stealthy abilities, but because the two men were arguing with each other.

As the bearded man threw up his hands, and called the other "superstitious," Lucena sprang from the darkening tree line. He had an Ontario MK III tactical knife in each hand. He drove the point of a blade into each guard's back. As the men called out in pain, and started to fall to the ground, Lucena held onto each knife. And once the weapons were withdrawn from the bodies, he leaned down, and finished the job by drawing a knife across each man's throat.

Lucena slipped the knives back into the holders strapped to each of his legs. He then swung the submachine gun off his back and into his hands, and began moving quickly in the direction of the house, while scanning the area with each stride.

*   *   *

While Grant was being slapped and lectured, and Lucena was moving on his targets, Paige Caldwell stopped in a patch of trees on the northeast side of the house. She quickly spotted a target.

One of the guards was strolling around on a deck wrapped around the home's second floor.

Caldwell took the rifle off of her back, and leaned her left side against one of the trees. She positioned the rifle in just the right spot, looking through the scope with her right eye.

Behind the guard were large windows. The inside lights created a clear silhouette of the guard.

Caldwell trained her gun sight, adjusting for a rather steady wind of about 10 to 15 miles per hour.

She watched and waited.

The guard's habits quickly became apparent. At each end of the deck, he would stop at the railing to look around a bit.

As he approached one end, Caldwell took in a breath and held it. When the man stopped, she gently exhaled and pulled the trigger.

The guard violently fell backwards and down to the wood decking.

*   *   *

As Angelina Carbonali turned away, Grant took in his surroundings and options.

Three against one. Four if you count Angie. Tight hallway helps. Need to shift their focus for just a second or two. Sorry about this, Angie, but you're not exactly a lady, are you?

Grant lifted his right foot, and shoved Carbonali forward. She yelled in surprise, and fell forward with her hands spread out trying to cushion the fall.

At the same time, Grant drove an elbow into the jaw of the guard standing to his left.

Russo and the other guard were to Grant's immediate right, and they initially reacted the way he had hoped. Their attention went to Carbonali falling forward.

Grant turned and drove his fist into the exposed throat of the man he had just elbowed. He knew the sound and feel. The man would suffocate to death shortly. However, the strap on the guard's AK-47 was still under an arm, and Grant didn't have the time to untangle things.

So, he turned and hurled himself at both Russo and the second guard as the two were returning their attention to him. Thankfully, the guard only had the AK-47, which would be difficult to position in the mayhem of close combat – or at least that was Grant's hope.

At the same time, Grant saw that Russo was more appropriately armed, with a handgun and a knife under his sports coat, just waiting to be unleashed.

The guard managed to drive an elbow into the side of Grant's head. In return, Grant shoved a foot into the man's knee, and the guard's leg gave way.

But as the guard was falling to the floor, Russo swung his left arm around Grant's neck, and positioned his right to pull tightly. The priest was a muscular individual, and Grant knew he wouldn't last long in this position.

Grant had to force himself not to reach up in a futile attempt to pull Russo's arms away. Instead, with seconds left before he passed out and then, no doubt, died, Grant was positioned to drive his left fist into the genitals of Father Russo. The force of the blow resulted in a loosening of the priest's grip. Grant was able to push himself in a different position. He got his hand on Russo's holstered handgun.

As Grant started to pull the weapon out, Russo managed to reimpose his vicelike stranglehold and the second guard began moving toward Grant and Russo. Grant pulled the gun up and pointed at the face of fury coming at him, and pulled the trigger. The guard's face exploded in blood and bone matter.

Russo pulled his right hand away from the grip on Grant's neck. He grabbed Grant's right wrist and started to pull it in a direction it wasn't supposed to go in order to force Grant to drop the weapon.

While Russo succeeded in doing so, Grant was able to reach up with his left hand, and find Russo's left eye. Grant summoned all of his strength, and drove two of his fingers into the priest's eye. That was too much for Russo, who released his grip on Grant's neck in order to pull the fingers away from his eyes. Grant offered minimal resistance, as he now concentrated on pulling out Russo's other concealed weapon.

Only able to see out of one eye now, Russo reached out for Grant's neck once again. But Grant slid his body slightly off of Russo's. The knife was free, and in Grant's right hand. He drove into Russo's chest, and waited as he felt life drain from the man.

Grant rolled onto the floor, only to look up to see Angelina Carbonali standing several feet away. She had watched the death struggle play out in front of her while sitting on the floor after Grant had kicked her. When she saw Russo dying, Carbonali stood up and picked up Russo's gun, which had slid toward her. She was pointing the gun at Grant, and said, "I will not let you hurt Pietro."

This is how it ends? Jesus, please be with me.

Grant didn't close his eyes, so he was shocked when the sound of the gunshot essentially coincided with blood emerging from Angelina Carbonali's chest, and her staggering backward and tumbling to the floor.

Grant whipped his head around to see Charlie Driessen standing behind him with his gun still pointing in the direction of Carbonali.

Driessen said, "That bitch was Filoni's mother. What a shock that her son is such a piece of shit."

Grant laid his head back on the floor, and said, "Charlie, thank you."

"You're welcome, Grant. I've done this a few times over the years, it seems. It's like I'm your fucking guardian angel."

That made Grant laugh. "Well, that's one possibility."

Caldwell and Lucena arrived, and actually paused when seeing the blood soaked hallway.

Lucena whispered, "Oh, my God."

Caldwell asked, "Charlie, how did you get here so fast?"

While looking at Caldwell and Lucena, Charlie responded, "I heard what you two were dealing with, and obviously what was going on in here. There was no one on my side of this place. So, I basically strolled in, and bam, blew Father Filoni's mommy from hell back to hell."

He looked down at Grant, adding, "Just before she had the chance to send you to heaven – I assume."

Chapter 68

Jacopo Bruno welcomed Inspector Vincent Mazzoni, one of the inspector's men from the Vatican police force's corps, Paige Caldwell, Charlie Driessen and Stephen Grant.

Introductions were made, with Mazzoni, in English, presenting Caldwell, Driessen and Grant as special advisors to Pope Paul VII.

Bruno said, "Please sit down." They were in a large sitting room just inside the front door to the Oldani home. As people found seats, Bruno continued, "You said that this was an important matter that could involve the Oldani family somehow. How can I help?"

Mazzoni said, "Thank you, Mr. Bruno. Where is Enzo Oldani himself? I would like to speak to him."

"I apologize, but Mr. Oldani is out of the country, along with Mr. Lupo, and they are not reachable. Rest assured, though, that I have the ability to make necessary decisions for the Oldani family's various enterprises."

Mazzoni commented, "We are here to talk about a series of egregious crimes, including murder."

Bruno leaned forward in his chair, "My God, how can I help? What has happened?"

Grant watched Bruno as Mazzoni presented what had occurred, and who was involved, including Angelina Carbonali, Father Michael Russo, and the names of the assorted guards who had died this very night. Grant noted that Bruno's responses, while a touch stilted, were otherwise flawless. He communicated surprise, shock and ignorance quite adeptly – as expected.

Mazzoni eventually asked, "I assume that you are aware that Mr. Oldani had a son with Ms. Carbonali, and that son is Father Pietro Filoni."

Bruno replied, "Inspector, are you sure about this?"

"Yes, quite sure."

"Father Filoni? He has been a priest to this family, a friend of this family, for some time. I know that quite well. I have seen Father Filoni pray with and guide this family firsthand on many occasions. I have never gotten even a whiff of what you claim. This sniffs of some kind of set up, even a bizarre conspiracy. I will not accept your assertions until I hear differently from Mr. Oldani himself."

"I think you might have to wait some time. We have reason to believe that Mr. Oldani is deceased."

Bruno laughed robustly. "I can assure you, Inspector, Mr. Oldani is quite well."

"Well, why not let us chat with him? He can answer some questions, and clear all of this up?"

"There is nothing to clear up, Inspector, and I have very specific instructions." Bruno rose from his chair, signaling that the meeting was over. "Now, I am very sorry to hear about these horrible killings, and if some people that are loosely linked to the Oldani businesses were somehow involved, I assure you they were operating on their own. I also trust and pray that they will be dealt with severely by the justice system."

Mazzoni said, "One last question, Mr. Bruno. Do you know where Father Filoni is, or how I can get in touch with him?"

Bruno smiled, and replied, "Inspector Mazzoni, how would I possibly know that? I believe that would be a question for the people you work for at the Vatican. Again, thank you for coming, and please let me know if we can be of service if you choose to deal with the reality from our perspective."

Once Mazzoni and his group had left the grounds altogether, Bruno picked up his encrypted phone and dialed a number.

Father Pietro Filoni answered, "Yes."

Bruno reported, "They know what you thought they would, and apparently not much more. I believe they left appropriately dissatisfied."

"Good. Are you set with what I need for the next action?"

"Of course. Just give me the green light, and things will move on this end."

"Excellent." Filoni ended the call.

Bruno put the phone down, and walked over to a small bar in the corner of the room. As he poured himself a glass of Scotch, he said out loud, "So smart, but such a foolish man."

Chapter 69

Pastor Stephen Grant had not really slept. Instead, he spent most of the morning repeatedly going over in his mind what had happened the night before – the fight, his actions, and the results.

Grant had killed three men. And even though no real choice existed in the heat of the action, Grant allowed himself to consider his initial choice in terms of putting himself in that situation.

He came to the same answer that Jennifer had given him during their phone conversation in the middle of the night. "How could you not do what was needed? You had a responsibility." She was right.

Grant also noted that he rarely had second thoughts about what he had to do in the line of duty, lacking a better phrase, when he was a SEAL or with the CIA. That was different in recent years when he was pulled back into action.

Yeah, because you're a pastor now.

But it all felt so raw this time, coupled with a more intense feeling of separation considering how long he had been away from Jennifer and home. In the past, Jennifer, their home and St. Mary's allowed him to get his feet back underneath him.

This is a waste.

Grant looked at his watch. It was almost eleven o-clock, and he decided that it was time for a change of scenery. He needed to not only get out of the room, but out of the hotel as well.

Time to get grounded in who you are.

Grant changed into his clericals, and then paused looking down at the Glock 20 sitting on the table.

You have a responsibility, Grant.

He slipped the holster and gun into the small of his back, and put on his black sports jacket.

Grant knocked, and was told to come in. He found Madison Tanquerey and Pastor Richard Leonard in the room that had become the working headquarters for Tanquerey and Father Ron McDermott.

After quick greetings, Grant asked, "Where's Ron?"

Tanquerey answered, "He's in his room, I believe, getting ready for a call from St. Luke's – something about hiring a new teacher."

Grant paused, and then said, "Hey, I need a change of scenery. If you guys do as well, I was thinking that I could finally get a look at Christ Church – you know, before the wedding."

Tanquerey said, "Great! Let's do it."

Leonard smiled and agreed.

With Grant serving as security, it took the trio twenty minutes to pull up and find a place to park the SUV in the narrow streets around Christ Church. As they walked toward the building, Grant was struck by the white stone; each of the church's three towers topped by terracotta roofing and a cross; the large arch over the front entrance; and above that arch, three statues, with Jesus in the middle and St. Peter and St. Paul on each side.

But as impressed as he was with the exterior, the inside of Christ Church nearly took his breath away.

There was no one else around as they stepped into the nave.

Tanquerey said, "It's beautiful, isn't it?"

"It is," agreed Grant.

The interior had a Byzantine feel to Grant, especially with the gold, ornate arched ceilings. Jesus the Teacher loomed above the altar, which was marble, along with the stairs, railing and pulpit. A crucifix hung behind and above the altar. Along the sides of the nave were marble arches, with an aisle and windows just beyond on each side. Another walkway rested on top of the arches as well, with large arched windows. Those upper walkways led around to the choir loft and organ in the back of the space. Three large chandeliers also hung down from the ceiling – one on each side and the third in the back.

Grant pulled his eyes away from his surroundings to look at Leonard and Tanquerey. "Well, for throwing together a wedding in rather last-minute fashion, at least by today's standards, you certainly landed a marvelous church. I promise not to be overwhelmed by the venue when I officiate."

"Well, thanks," said Leonard, "that's good news."

As they slowly started to move up the center aisle, discussing certain aspects of the architecture, a person came through one of the doors in the back. The three didn't take notice initially as their conversation echoed while the person moved quietly.

But then a voice unevenly called out, "Richard Leonard, you are an apostate."

The three turned and saw a man standing at the back of the center aisle. He was wearing a long, dark brown coat.

The man continued, "You will pay for conspiring with the antichrist." He then pulled a shotgun out from underneath the coat.

Grant immediately moved in front of Leonard and Tanquerey, and he reached for the Glock holstered under his jacket.

But Leonard grabbed Grant's shoulder, and whispered, "Stephen, don't."

Grant replied, "What?"

"Just wait a second. I know him."

"What does that...?"

"Hold on. Trust me." Leonard stepped out from behind Grant, and held his hands out in front of him. "Rusty. Rusty, what are you doing?"

Rusty Spuel said, "Ah, I'm, I'm so glad you remembered me, Richard. I haven't forgotten you. And I see that you're in the middle of the conspiracy here. Someone has to stop it."

Leonard took a slow step forward. "What are you talking about, Rusty?"

Grant slowly withdrew the Glock from its holster, and held it low at his side. Tanquerey moved directly behind Grant, and whispered in his ear, "Please, don't let anything happen to him."

Right. He's not exactly making that easy. Dear Lord, help us.

In response to Tanquerey, Grant merely nodded ever so slightly.

"You're part of this entire conspiracy, and I'm here to stop you and hopefully, God willing, the entire thing."

Leonard continued to slowly advance, as he and Spuel spoke. "Rusty, I'm not sure what you're talking about, but I can tell you as a fellow pastor and a brother seminarian that I'm not part of any conspiracy."

"Of course, you're, you're going to say that."

"Rusty, you and I had our disagreements at sem. But we were all there trying to do the same thing, right? Trying to learn God's Word, to become His disciples, to go out and spread the Good News, and tend to whatever flocks wherever we were assigned."

"But there are people who work against us, who stand with Satan."

Leonard nodded. "And there always will be until the Second Coming. In the meantime, we have our jobs to do. We have to be the salt and light. I would not go against that, and I don't think you would either. But if you do this, you will not be doing His work."

"No! I will be."

Grant readied himself to act.

Leonard continued, "I don't think you truly believe that." Leonard slowly turned his body, and pointed to the mural of Jesus above the altar. "Look at Him. There is Jesus the

Teacher. Through his life, death and resurrection, He has taught the world about true love, forgiveness, redemption and salvation. What you are thinking about doing, that's not His way. It's not our way as pastors."

Tears started to roll down Rusty Spuel's cheeks. "You, you don't understand. This is the only way for me. I have to be able to help. I've... I've failed so miserably. I don't know how. I... I killed a church, Richard. It was my fault. Maybe I can save *the* Church from this horrible papist plot. Don't you see? I have to do something..."

"Rusty, there is no conspiracy. Yes, we've all done things that we wish we could take back. And as pastors, you and I, we have done things that have hurt the faithful and the Church. I feel that pain, too. But we all come up short without His help, without Him."

"I know, but the pope..."

Leonard added, "You're also not going to get any argument from me that there have been some popes throughout history that have done horrid things. After all, there are reasons why I'm a Lutheran pastor and not a Catholic priest. But right now, there's an effort under way with a major objective to have the Catholic Church recognize at least some of the wrongs they did when it came to Jan Hus and Martin Luther. That's what I've been working on as a Lutheran. Whether it works out or not, we should be able to agree that the effort is worthwhile. Right, Rusty?"

"That's what you're doing?"

"It is."

"I don't understand. Why can't I help? Why can't I get people to understand what I'm trying to do?"

Leonard now stood just a few feet in front of Spuel.

Grant watched spellbound, but with the Glock at the ready.

"Richard, I failed. I killed a church."

"Rusty, we all come up short. We've all sinned. But with Him there is forgiveness, and love."

Spuel fell to his knees, and dropped the weapon. The crash of the metal echoed throughout the church.

Leonard kneeled down in front of Spuel, reached out, and placed his hands on the man's shoulders.

Spuel fell into his former classmate, and Leonard in turn dropped back against the side of a pew. With his back against the pew, Leonard had his arms around Spuel, who was convulsing as he cried.

Grant walked slowly forward. He slipped his Glock back into its holster, and picked up the shotgun. He looked down at Leonard and Spuel through moist eyes.

As Madison Tanquerey approached, she was unable to remove her eyes from her fiancé, who was now holding a man who clearly had come to kill him just minutes earlier. She also did nothing to stop the tears flowing down her face.

Chapter 70

Hours later, Stephen Grant was on the phone with Jennifer. He just finished relaying to her what had occurred at Christ Church. She listened in raptured silence.

Jennifer simply said, "Wow. I don't understand this twisted pastor, but thank God you were both there."

"Well, thank God Richard was there."

"What does that mean?"

"Richard stepped forward … as a pastor. I was ready to pull out the Glock."

"And thank God, Stephen, that you were there ready to do that. If this pastor was just a bit more far gone, you would have been ready to protect both Madison and Richard, not to mention yourself."

"I understand, but my reaction was…"

"Was what? Were you just going to shoot the man, or would you, too, have tried to talk some sense into him?"

Would I?

Stephen said, "I hope so."

Jennifer declared, "I know so."

"Do you?"

"Stephen, you have had two days that most people on this earth can't possibly imagine. Even though I'm married to you, I can't fully grasp it because I have no reference point. Richard's a fellow pastor, and even given who his father was, he also is unable to fully get it. And you know what, Paige and Charlie don't get it fully either because, even though they can grasp what actions were necessary, they have no idea what it means for a pastor to take such actions.

There are very few people on this planet who can relate. Perhaps the only person you know who could understand this kind of thing would have been that man you had mentioned to me a couple of times. The one who actually went from being a pastor to the OSS."

"Scott Sheridan."

I wish I could talk to him today.

Jennifer confirmed, "That was his name. Right."

Stephen sighed, and simply said, "I really wish I was home right now."

"I wish you were, too. You will be soon."

"How are you so confident in this flawed, sinful man you married?"

"I've heard enough of your sermons to know that we're all flawed and sinful. But someone reminded me recently that you're a good man."

"Well, that's appreciated. Who was that?"

"Never mind who, but this person gave me a little refresher that you were a unique person who knows when it is time for prayer and time for action, and that you exude a certain confidence in knowing what the right thing is. Oh, yes, and that you're a caring pastor. Keep that in mind, but don't let it go to your head."

"Thanks, Jen."

Chapter 71

"Holy Father, are you sure this is a good time?" asked Father John Kohli, with Sister Katharine Malone standing next to him.

Pope Paul VII said, "Let us take the time we have here and now to talk. After all, I should be a pastor to both of you."

Kohli and Malone both said, "Thank you."

The pope said, "Please, sit down and tell me what is happening with the two of you."

The pope, Kohli and Malone each took an armchair in this sitting room just a few doors down a narrow hallway from his personal office in the Papal Apartments.

The pope held up a hand, and said, "First, I have to ask: Are you enjoying the motorcycle?"

Kohli seemed taken off guard, but answered, "Yes, very much, thank you."

The pope smiled, and said, "Good. Don't tell anyone because a pope cannot get into the endorsement business, but I have always favored Triumph. They produce the best bikes."

"Do you ride, Holy Father?"

Pope Paul VII sighed. "Yes. Well, I used to ride. I have not since I arrived at the Vatican, working with Pope Augustine. I think everyone in this building and a few adjacent ones would try to stop me from riding now."

Kohli nodded, and then added, "Sister Malone rides as well."

"Yes," said the pope, "I heard."

Malone said, "My father started me working on and riding motorcycles."

"Your preference?"

Malone said, "Triumph bikes are excellent, but I'm partial to Honda."

The pope nodded.

Malone added, "Holy Father, please don't forget that one of your predecessors was a skier. There were more than a few in the Vatican who weren't too keen on him skiing, but he was the pope, so he told them he was going skiing and that was that."

Pope Paul VII smiled, and said, "True, Sister. Now, let us get to why you are both here."

Forty-five minutes later, Kohli and Malone were walking side by side across Saint Peter's Square. They strolled slowly, with heads down, and a couple of feet apart.

Malone said, "I'm not really sure what else we could have expected."

"I know," replied Kohli.

"Actually, it turned out better than what some might have expected."

"I appreciated that he said he sympathized with what we were going through, and that he would respect our decision."

"He was very kind, and pastoral. It's not like he condemned us to hell if we do this." She smiled, and Kohli did as well. But each smile carried a sadness.

She asked, "So, what's next?"

Kohli looked around at the many people moving about the expansive area. And then he turned to Malone, and said, "We need to start thinking about a lot of things."

"Well, yes, we do." She paused, and added, "What exactly do you mean by that?"

"For one, we're going to need new jobs. Secondly, I believe I have to go shopping for a ring. What size is your finger, again?"

Malone's smile was broad and bright. At the same time, a deep breath was uneven and revealed her nervousness. "We're doing this?"

"Aren't we?"

"Is this some kind of weird proposal?"

"I'll do it properly later. I promise."

"I don't think I can kiss you in St. Peter's Square," said Sister Katharine Malone.

"Probably not a good idea."

Chapter 72

Conrad Whittacker returned from lunch to his company office in Rome. He tugged on his vest, and just as he sat down at his desk, the cellphone in his suit jacket pocket rumbled. He pulled the phone out, and saw that it was a blocked number.

Whittacker paused, and then answered, "Hello?"

"Conrad, we have to talk."

When he heard the voice of Jacopo Bruno, Whittacker's erect posture dissolved into a distinct slouch. "Yes, well, of course. Let me just close my office door."

As he closed the door, Whittacker said to his assistant who sat just outside the office, "Please, no interruptions."

The woman replied, "Yes, sir."

Whittacker returned to his own desk, sat down, and said, "I have some excellent news on new orders for the windmill division."

"Yes, that's good news, but another time. I have a few quick questions on our other partnership."

Whittacker didn't respond.

"Did you hear me, Conrad?"

"Yes, Mr. Bruno, I heard. I was hoping that I had provided you with more than enough information on that front, especially considering what happened to ... to Pastor Fletcher and Professor Dvorak."

"What exactly happened to those two gentleman, Conrad?"

"What? Oh, um, I have no idea."

"That's right, Conrad, you have no idea what happened in those two unfortunate cases. Neither do I."

Whittacker again didn't reply.

"Let me review our deal, Conrad. You came to us seeking funds to save your company, the company that your family built, but was on the brink of going under. Is that correct?"

"Yes."

"We provided you with the cash flow needed to not only stay afloat, but to make the investments needed for success."

"Of course. I greatly appreciate that."

"I know you do, Conrad. I also know that we agreed to be silent partners in the transformation from a coal business into the windmill and vehicle battery industries."

"I appreciate that."

"I hope you do. In fact, I hope you appreciate our full agreement. Considering that we're not asking you to do very much."

Whittacker protested, "Not very much...!"

"No, Conrad. Not very much. In fact, it represented very little investment from you."

"Very little? I used my wife to hand over information to you about the project she is working on, and ..." His voice broke. Whittacker recovered, and continued, "And what Pastor Fletcher and Professor Dvorak were doing. As a result, those two men are dead."

Bruno sighed. "I am detecting ungratefulness, Conrad. Do you know what happens to people who are ungrateful for the investments we make in them and in their businesses?"

"Pardon me?"

"It is a simple question, Conrad. Do you understand what happens to people we do business with who turn out to be ungrateful? It does not turn out well for them, or for the people they love."

"Wait. What? You can't..."

"Conrad, do you understand who you are doing business with? Did you do your due diligence before accepting our investment? If not, shame on you. That's just sloppy business."

"Yes. Well, I am not sure... I mean..." He was struggling to talk. Whittacker finally said, "Yes, I appreciate everything you have done." He took a deep breath. "How can I be of assistance?"

"Are you sure about this, Conrad?"

Whittacker cleared his throat, and tried to sit up a bit straighter in his chair. "Yes, yes, of course, I am."

"I am very glad to hear that. I need two simple things from you. First, you have been to the hotel where your wife is working with her colleagues several times?"

"Yes."

"I need you to provide me with every detail about how the rooms are being used. Second, I am going to call you back later, and give you a time by which you need to have your wife removed from the hotel."

"I'm sorry. What is going on?"

"Conrad, I am simply gathering information. You are providing information. That's all that is going on here. As for your wife, I just want to make sure that she is ... safe."

Whittacker swallowed hard.

"The safety of both you and your lovely wife, Haley, are in my hands, Conrad."

"Yes, yes, thank you."

"You are welcome, Conrad. Now let's get to the details of what's happening at the Trevisani."

After the call ended with Jaco Bruno, Whittacker sprinted to the door of the executive washroom that was several feet from his desk. He fell to his knees and reached out for the toilet. Conrad Whittacker managed to raise the cover just in time, as he proceeded to throw up several times into the bowl.

Chapter 73

An ironic temptation to be just a tad less vigilant when it came to their own personal security existed for some in the business of providing security to others.

Inspector Vincent Mazzoni had been spending night after night at the Vatican. He kept a small room with a couch at the Gendarmerie Corps office, and there was a shower to use there. But Pope Paul VII finally banished him for a couple of days. Mazzoni reluctantly obeyed.

This was the first night at home in his own apartment in days.

His exhaustion was apparent when, after taking a hot shower, he fell onto his bed and quickly drifted off to sleep.

"Inspector Mazzoni."

The sound of a voice in his bedroom triggered a reaction from Mazzoni. His eyes shot open, and he reached for his weapon. Before his shower, Mazzoni had left it on the nightstand. It was no longer there.

In the darkness, Mazzoni could see two figures standing at the end of his bed. Only the white squares resting at the base of each man's neck, and the shine of two guns pointed at Mazzoni stood out. He pushed himself up on his elbows.

A voice instructed, "Please, do not move any further."

"Filoni."

"That's right, Inspector."

Mazzoni's eyes darted around the room.

Father Pietro Filoni said, "There is nowhere to go. There is nothing you can do."

A look of resignation came across Mazzoni's face. He said, "You are a sick man, and you defile the Church and the pope by what you do."

"From what I have seen, Inspector Mazzoni, you are a man of God. You only have been misled by this *faux* pope. For that, I am sorry."

Mazzoni retorted, "The minions of the Evil One often fail to grasp who pulls their strings. They rationalize evil, saying that they are serving a larger good."

Anger crept into Filoni's voice. "I serve the ultimate good, the Lord and His Church."

Mazzoni actually laughed. "You are not just evil, Filoni, but you are a fool. I almost feel pity for you. Almost."

Filoni stepped forward with the gun donning a suppressor still pointed at Mazzoni. Filoni started to say, "May the Lord who frees you..."

Mazzoni interrupted, "Shut up! Don't you dare. The last thing I need is a blessing from a piece of shit like you."

Filoni then squeezed off three shots – one in the face and the other two in the chest.

Blood seeped from the naked body of Vincent Mazzoni onto the white sheets.

Chapter 74

Being late was not an option for Albro Dawson. He was given a time by Conrad Whittacker to pick up Haley from the hotel.

But Dawson was now staring at a dented door on the Rolls-Royce Phantom. He was speaking to Haley on the phone.

After explaining in detail what had happened, with the other driver failing to pay attention, and ramming into Dawson, Haley Whittacker said, "Albro, don't worry about it. Whenever you get here will be fine."

"Mr. Whittacker was quite insistent, however."

"I'm sure he was. He's very antsy about me staying at the apartment tonight. That's fine. It'll be nice to stay there for a change, given everything that's happened. You should deal with the accident. You know, I could just take a taxi."

"Mrs. Whittacker, given the situation, that is not an option."

"Oh, right. Okay, well, I'm fine here obviously. Just come on over when you're finished."

"Thank you for being so understanding."

"Thank you for everything, Albro. I'm not sure what I'd do without you."

After the call ended, Albro Dawson had a slight smile on his face as he put his phone away.

*   *   *

The three Gendarmerie Corps officers positioned on the street outside the Trevisani hotel didn't have a chance. Two were in a parked car watching the front entrance of the hotel, and another was around back. Each received bullets to the head courtesy of suppressed guns in the hands of Oldani crime family soldiers.

Those mafia soldiers were operating under the leadership of and according to a plan drawn up by Father Pietro Filoni.

*   *   *

Four Oldani men easily slipped into the closed dress shop at the other end of the block from the Trevisani Luxury Suites. They quickly emerged onto the store's roof.

The buildings had all been built flush against each other, so it was just like moving across one large roof. The heavy boots each wore, with a combination of rubber and steel souls, made clicking noises.

They stopped atop the Trevisani.

*   *   *

Filoni entered the hotel lobby through the front door, followed by Father Lorenzo Conti, along with two other men. They all were dressed in black, including masks covering their heads.

Filoni pointed a gun at the two individuals behind the front desk. "Hands up." The man and woman complied with fear on their faces. Filoni added, "Now, do not move." He ordered two of his men, "Tie them up, blind folds, gags, and dump them in the back room. Do it quickly."

While that task was being undertaken, three more men entered from the back of the lobby, having come into the building via a back service entrance. One reported, "All is clear."

Filoni nodded.

With the hotel employees now secured, Filoni said, "You know your tasks. May the Lord bless our work."

Two men followed Father Conti toward the staircase, while the other three stood with Filoni waiting for the elevator doors to open.

*   *   *

Conti climbed the stairs quickly, but less than stealthily. The assault plan failed to account for a Vatican Gendarmerie officer sitting outside the door to the top floor. That knowledge had eluded Conrad Whittacker.

The officer waited with gun drawn. Once he spotted that the men climbing the stairs were masked, in tactical gear and carrying semi-automatic AK-47s, he chose not to issue any verbal warning. Instead, the guard met the intruders with a string of gunshots. One found a home in the skull of the Oldani man right behind Father Conti. The other Oldani soldier fired with a suppressor attached to the rifle – not that stealth mattered any longer. The guard's shots had announced the arrival of invaders.

Two shots hit the Gendarmerie officer, and he fell forward, dropping down the square, open staircase. His body bashed the railing twice before hitting the concrete floor below.

*   *   *

Jessica West was on watch in the seventh floor hallway. It was quiet. She sat in a folding chair, just to the right of the elevator and toward the end of the hallway away from the stairs.

West was flipping through a wedding magazine on her Kindle when the shots from the staircase rang out. She dropped the Kindle, jumped to her feet, and pulled out her Glock 21 that had been strapped to her right leg. She began moving in the direction of the shots when the staircase door partially opened, and tear gas cannisters started to get thrown into the hallway. She fired off shots at the opening, and pulled the collar of her black sweater up over her nose and mouth.

*   *   *

Paige Caldwell was wearing sweatpants and a t-shirt while sitting with her legs crossed on the bed in her suite. She had been talking to President Adam Links for nearly 15 minutes.

Links said, "Is Stephen handling all of this alright? I mean a bloodbath like that one night, and then that nut showing up the next day at the church."

Caldwell said, "Stephen's normally the last person that I'd get too worried about, even given this mess. But he seemed to be..."

Caldwell heard the shots in the distance from the staircase, and refocused her attention and language. "Fuck. Got to go."

"Paige, what...?"

She tossed the phone aside, and turned to move off the bed. But the sound of smashing glass was followed by shards of the broken window slamming into her back. That was followed by a masked man who had swung down from the roof. He used speed and steel-heeled boots to explode into the room. As he came through the window he released the rope, but had little control over his landing. The Oldani attacker wound up flying over Caldwell, barely catching her with a glancing blow from his foot on her left shoulder.

The intruder managed to stop his momentum after tumbling over twice. As he struggled to pull the AK-47 into a firing position, Caldwell was on her feet, pointing a Glock 21 at his head.

The man froze.

Caldwell said, "You stupid fuck. Maybe a little more practice was in order." She pulled the trigger, and part of the man's skull was sprayed against the hotel's formerly dull, beige wall.

Caldwell sprinted toward the suite's door.

*   *   *

Charlie Driessen also was sitting on his bed, wearing boxer shorts and a t-shirt. He had just finished cleaning and lubricating his Glock 23. The model was new to Driessen, and in recent months, he was singing the weapon's praises to anyone who would listen at CDM.

He was smiling at his handiwork when shots went off in the distance.

Driessen turned his head, and said out loud, "What the hell?"

He picked up a magazine laying before him on the bed, and slipped it into the gun.

A dark figure then came crashing through the window of his hotel room. This masked intruder apparently was more skilled than the opponent Caldwell was facing at the same moment. This invader landed rather adroitly on his feet.

But the bed was on the other side of the room, well away from the window. Driessen sat watching as the person landed. He then calmly raised the Glock, and Driessen squeezed off three shots that sent the Oldani soldier back out the window he had just crashed through.

Driessen grunted a bit as he moved to get off the bed, and then headed toward the door.

*   *   *

Stephen Grant knew that he would have a tough time sleeping, and his three fellow clergy members on the hotel floor seemed to understand that might be the case. So, the four men had been drinking beer and sitting in the living room area of Grant's suite for the past couple of hours.

Amidst all that had happened, they managed to share some laughs and stories.

Grant could feel himself moving in the direction of something closer to normal, until gunshots from afar interrupted that progress. He stood up and looked at his three hotel suite guests. All he could think to say was, "Stay here."

As he turned to go to the bedroom where he had stowed his weapon, Grant heard the window shattering.

Shit. Coming in via the windows.

He accelerated through the doorway.

The intruder was picking himself up off the floor, and gaining control of his rifle.

Grant hurled himself at the man, making contact with and wrapping arms around the midsection. He then drove the intruder backwards.

The Oldani soldier had the strength and balance to turn his body. He only needed to do so slightly to steal control from Grant.

Grant wound up bearing the brunt of the impact against the wall. He was unaware that Leonard and McDermott had followed him into the room. McDermott was first, and came upon the intruder after Grant hit the wall. But the Oldani soldier quickly turned and hit McDermott in the face with the butt of the AK-47. The priest fell to the carpet unconscious.

When Leonard entered the room, he turned in a different direction. He zeroed in on the nightstand, opened the drawer, and reached inside. He pulled the Glock out of the drawer, turned, and fired off two shots at the attacker.

One shot found the target, and was enough to drop the man.

Grant regained his breathing, jumped up, and grabbed the weapon from Leonard. Grant said, "Thanks. Please check on Ron."

He sprinted out of the bedroom and past an apparently frozen Father John Kohli.

*　　*　　*

When the fourth masked invader from the roof swung through the window of Kohli's room, he found no one. He was able to move through the room to the suite door.

The Oldani soldier opened it and stepped into the hallway, searching for a target.

The group's community room was next to Kohli's. As the intruder stepped into the hallway, the community door opened as well, and Haley Whittacker stepped out. She managed to see the intruder before he spotted her. Whittacker reacted by trying to grab the man's rifle. He pulled her hand away, and shoved her to the floor. Haley's glasses bounced off her face. She was face down and closed her eyes. The Oldani soldier pointed the gun down at her, and pulled the trigger.

Haley's eyes didn't open, and blood began emerging from the hole in her back.

The intruder turned to look inside the room. Madison Tanquerey and Katharine Malone stood staring beyond the attacker at Haley. And then their eyes moved to him. He was framed by the doorway, with tear gas swirling behind him. He began to raise his rifle in their direction. But then a blur of a man seemed to fly into the attacker. Knife in hand, Phil Lucena landed on the invader, shoved the blade into his neck, and pulled hard. He then withdrew the knife, rolled and sprang to his feet.

*　　*　　*

Jessica West had been trained to deal with tear gas, as well as advancing gunmen.

She looked to see where the tear gas was spreading. One suite door had a larger crack at the bottom, and air was leaking from the room into the hallway. That was creating a small area where the tear gas was diminishing.

She moved there, and waited for the staircase door to again open.

The door opened slowly, and the Oldani soldier stepped into the hallway first.

She waited unmoving.

Father Conti then started to step out right behind the Oldani man.

West quickly drew her weapon up, and steadied her aim, even as her eyes started to water. She squeezed off a shot, and then a second. The Oldani soldier fell when the projectile entered his chest, quickly followed by Father Lorenzo Conti as assorted carotid arteries were ripped apart in his neck by the second shot fired by West.

*   *   *

The elevator doors opened in front of Lucena just when he got to his feet.

The three Oldani men with Filoni were surprised by Lucena standing right in front of them. As a result, they hesitated for a half-second. That allowed Lucena to move back in the direction from which he came.

The shots being fired by West came next, and the three attackers stepped from the elevator not sure which direction to move and fire. That confusion cost them dearly.

As they stepped into the hallway, so did Paige Caldwell, Charlie Driessen and Stephen Grant. Shots came at the intruders from both sides. As their bodies were being riddled with bullets from the weapons of West, Caldwell, Driessen and Grant, Pietro Filoni took a step back and hit the elevator button that would close the door and take him back to the ground floor.

Grant had caught a glimpse of the masked individual inside the elevator.

Everyone then turned to see Katharine Malone trying to staunch the bleeding from Haley Whittacker's wound.

Grant knew there was nothing he could do for Haley.

That was Filoni.

He sprinted to the other end of the hallway, opened the door, and descended the staircase as fast as he could.

When he reached the bottom, Grant glanced at the fallen Gendarmerie officer. He prayed against what he saw that the man had somehow survived.

Lord, be with him.

Grant slammed through the door into the lobby, and he caught a glimpse of Filoni exiting the front door of the hotel.

Grant sprinted across the lobby, and out onto the street. He looked to his left, and saw Filoni running away.

Grant pursued, and started to gain ground. By the time Grant had entered the Piazza del Gesù, he was a mere 20 yards behind Filoni. Grant stopped and called out, "Filoni stop, or I will shoot you!"

The priest stopped, pulled his mask off, and turned to look at Grant.

They stared at each other in front of the Chiesa del Gesù, the mother church of the Jesuits.

Grant started to move toward the man, while pointing the Glock. He said, "You no doubt have at least one weapon on you. Slowly remove it and toss it away."

Filoni looked at Grant and then at the church looming over the two of them. "St. Ignatius was right, you know. He wanted to stomp out Martin Luther and his little followers. I love that statue of St. Ignatius in St. Peter's with his foot on Martin Luther, and Luther in agony with a serpent wrapped around him. The world, the Church, would have been better off if Ignatius and others had succeeded in destroying Luther and his ilk. And we will be better off today by continuing that work, including stopping this fake pope and his madness."

This asshole wants to debate theology?

Grant replied, "I don't give a shit what you think about Ignatius, Luther, Pope Paul, or anyone else. You're a sick, twisted, evil individual who will face the consequences of his actions."

"Yes, I am sure that you do not care. I also don't care, Stephen Grant."

"What is it that you don't care about?"

"Your life. My mother died at your hands."

"Well, that's not technically true. I killed Father Russo, and a colleague killed your mother."

Grant saw the rage mounting in Filoni.

The priest said, "You and the other heathens you associate with murdered her. I will kill you now, and them later."

"Really?"

Grant continued to have the Glock trained on Filoni.

Father Filoni pulled back his jacket to reveal a holstered handgun.

"Filoni, don't try. You would be committing suicide."

"Is that what you think? I do not. I have done the work of protecting His Church. He will not abandon me."

Phil Lucena and Jessica West were emerging from the darkened street into the square to witness what came next.

Filoni called out, "The Shadow Servants of the Holy Father will never fail!"

Filoni reached for the gun, but just as his hand touched the handle, it slowly fell away. He dropped to his knees, and looked at Grant with hatred burning in his eyes. Grant's shot had entered Filoni's chest, and even as blood streamed forth, the apostate priest tried to hang on. He hovered in that kneeling position. But finally, the hatred in his eyes gave way to lifelessness, and he fell face down on the stone ground.

West and Lucena ran up, and along with Grant, they stared down at the now-dead Father Filoni.

West said, "Nice shot, Stephen."

Lucena asked, "Who the hell are the Shadow Servants of the Holy Father?"

Grant replied, "I have no idea."

Chapter 75

Conrad Whittacker sat motionless at the dining room table in his and Haley's Rome apartment. When his phone rang, he jumped slightly, looked at the screen, and answered, "Albro, where the hell are you with Haley?"

"Sir, we are at the hospital."

"What?"

"There was an attack at the hotel..."

"You didn't get her out of there? She needed to be out of there."

Albro Dawson hesitated, and said, "Sir, I arrived at the hotel late due to an accident. I was able, with help, to get her to the hospital."

"What is it?"

"She has a gunshot wound. Sir, there was a good deal of bleeding. You should get here as quickly as possible."

"Damn it, Albro. You were supposed to get her home."

"I know, sir. I cannot tell you how sorry I am."

Whittacker took a deep breath. "Is she going to make it, Albro?"

"The staff would never say either way, sir, but I have seen things go either way in cases like this."

Whittacker's voice fell to barely above a whisper. "Albro?"

"To be honest, I have my doubts, sir. But I pray that I am wrong."

Whittacker said, "I will be there shortly."

"Please hurry, sir."

Whittacker ended the call, and dropped his head onto the table. He wept bitterly, wailing, "Haley, Haley, I'm so sorry. What have I done?"

When he arrived at the hospital, Conrad Whittacker listened to doctors and staff in a fog. Albro Dawson remained at his side, stoically, throughout.

After several hours, a doctor came into the room, and declared, "I believe we have it under control. Mrs. Whittacker has stabilized. We might have to go back in, but I believe she will pull through this."

Dawson smiled broadly.

Whittacker remained in his fog. He extended a hand in formal fashion, and said, "Thank you, Doctor. That is wonderful news."

Both Dawson and the doctor looked at Conrad quizzically.

The doctor said, "It will be some time, but we will let you know when you can go in to see your wife."

"Yes, of course. Again, thank you." Whittacker returned to his chair.

Dawson looked at the doctor. "Thank God for you and your staff, Doctor. Thank you for what you have done."

The doctor's expression of concern was transformed into a grateful smile when he turned to Dawson. "Thank you, Mr. ...?"

"I am Albro Dawson. I serve as an aide to Mr. Whittacker ... as well as to Mrs. Whittacker."

The doctor looked Dawson in the eyes, and asked, "Will you be staying with Mr. Whittacker while he waits?"

"I will."

By his nod, that was the answer the doctor was seeking. "Good. Nice to meet you, Mr. Dawson."

A couple of hours later, Conrad Whittacker was invited in to sit with his wife, who remained unconscious.

At the same time, Albro Dawson worked his way through the twist and turns of the hospital. And then he stepped out into the early morning sunlight and breeze. He pulled out his phone.

Paige Caldwell answered, "Yes."

"Ms. Caldwell, this is Albro Dawson."

"Oh, everyone here is so excited to hear about Haley."

"It is wonderful news, to say the least."

"Your actions in deciding to move her before an ambulance would arrive probably saved her life."

"She certainly would not have survived if your team were not there, and they had not known what they were doing." He cleared his throat. "Actually, I am calling for a different reason. It might be nothing, but right now, it is deeply troubling me."

Chapter 76

While Conrad Whittacker and Albro Dawson were in the hospital waiting to hear about the fate of Haley, Father Mariano Concepcion arrived to wake up the pope.

He banged on the pope's bedroom door.

Pope Paul called out, "Yes, what is it?"

Concepcion said, "I have news." He paused. "It's grim."

The pope said, "Please go in the kitchen. I will be right out."

While the two sat at a rectangular wooden table in the pope's personal kitchen just down a short hallway from his bedroom, Concepcion relayed the news of all that had gone on during the night.

Concepcion's apartment was in the Apostolic Palace as well, just a floor below the pope's far more expansive living area. They each still wore pajamas with bath robes tossed on as well.

They had just finished praying for all those who had suffered during this latest string of horrible events. They requested that Jesus be with Haley Whittacker and the medical staff trying to save her life. But the pope wept while praying for Vincent Mazzoni. In fact, he broke down twice while trying to pray for the man who had become his close friend.

Now they sat in silence at the table.

The pope looked smaller than usual. His shoulders slumped. His head hung down. He looked more than a decade older than he actually was. His voice was weaker.

The pope observed, "Mariano, I am not sure what to do with this."

"Sir?"

"With all of this. Cardinal Bessetti and his mad assistant, Father Filoni. Winston. The family in Australia. And dear God, three people I invited to be part of a project that I hoped would help in uniting Christians have been murdered, with a fourth precious life hanging in the balance. The Oldani crime family funding the Church. Officers from the Gendarmerie murdered, and ..." His voice broke again. The pope struggled to regain control. "And Vincent. And more. What have I done?"

Father Concepcion replied, "You have done what you thought was best for the Church, its people and the rest of the world. I have seen that up close. Please, Holy Father, do not doubt that. I know what you are going through right now. I am here going through it as well. However, I do not believe that any of this should be laid at your feet."

"That is kind, Mariano, but I fear that I have done great damage to the Church."

Concepcion leaned forward in his chair, and placed his hands down on the table. "This is a conversation for another time, Holy Father. But I think you should be completely transparent with the Church and the world about how all of this came about and unfolded. Ms. Tanquerey is here and already reporting. Let her tell the full story. Trust her to do her job properly; trust the people to understand; and in the end, put it in His hand and trust Him. It will get ugly at first, but trust Him."

Pope Paul VII took in a deep breath, and said, "Thank you, Mariano. You are a good man."

"As are you, Holy Father." Concepcion added, "There was one other thing. Before he was shot, according to Pastor Grant, Father Filoni said, 'The Shadow Servants of the Holy Father will never fail.'"

Pope Paul VII sat back in exasperation. "And who the hell are they?"

"I have no idea," responded Concepcion.

"Just what we need, more fodder for another conspiracy in the shadows of the Vatican. Can I task you with looking into this, and finding out if this goes in any way beyond Filoni and his fellow evildoers that already have been dealt with?"

"Of course, Holy Father."

Chapter 77

Dawson returned from making his call to Paige Caldwell, and sat down in the hospital waiting room.

In less than ten minutes, Conrad Whittacker came in.

Dawson asked, "Is everything alright?"

Whittacker still wore a foggy look. He nodded, and said, "She is doing better. Thank God. I am going to step out for a short time. I need you to stay here."

"Sir, but..."

Momentary clarity came upon Whittacker's expression. "Albro, you will need to stay here, and make sure that Haley is doing well."

Dawson replied, "Yes, of course, Mr. Whittacker."

"Good." He turned, and started walking to the door. He stopped, and said over his shoulder, "I will be back shortly."

Dawson continued staring at the doorway after Whittacker had disappeared.

*　　*　　*

It was an hour later when Jaco Bruno was having breakfast on the rooftop patio of the Oldani home. His top aide held a cellphone in his hand, and said, "The guard reports that Mr. Whittacker is looking to come in. He also reported that Whittacker was acting very nervous."

Bruno said, "I'm sure he is. Let him in."

Bruno shoveled a mixture of egg and sausage into his mouth. As he chewed, Bruno watched a Range Rover driving closer to the house. He swallowed and said to his aide, "Once he parks that vehicle, I want our men on him quickly. He is not here to talk about windmills and batteries."

The aide moved quickly. He entered the glass door that led to Bruno's bedroom, moved through that space, and descended the stairs. He barked out orders, and five men with submachine guns suddenly assembled behind him at the front door. The aide looked out a small window, and once the SUV came to a stop, he opened the door, and commanded, "Move, now!"

The men surrounded the vehicle, and Conrad Whittacker sat unmoving behind the wheel.

Two stories up, Bruno had returned to his food, with his back to what was developing below him on the circular driveway.

Bruno's aide stood on the front steps of the house, and called out, "Mr. Whittacker, please keep your hands where we can see them, and slowly get out of your vehicle."

Above, Bruno took another hearty forkful of eggs.

Whittacker's hands were on a shotgun sitting on his lap. He was rubbing the steel barrel, while his eyes darted around at the men who surrounded his SUV. He reached over to the controls, and lowered his window slightly. He yelled out, "Where is Jaco?"

Bruno chuckled at hearing that, and then took a deep drink of orange juice.

On the ground, Bruno's aide replied, "Mr. Bruno is eating breakfast. I am sure that he would like to have you join him, but we need to make sure that you're, well, not intent on doing something rash. That would be unfortunate."

Conrad Whittacker screamed for the first time in his life. "Breakfast! That bastard is eating?" He struggled to get the door open, and then to maneuver the shotgun into a firing position while getting out of the vehicle.

None of that mattered in the end. Once the door opened, and Whittacker started to get out of the SUV with the gun, the three Oldani men on that side unleashed automatic weapon fire. One burst of fire from each man's weapon put an end to Conrad Whittacker's prim, proper, British old-school life in the most brutal of ways.

On the patio above, Jaco Bruno shook his head, and finished his sausage.

Chapter 78

Conrad Whittacker's body didn't disappear. Instead, it was dropped and found in a garbage dumpster behind a row of restaurants in a seedy section of Rome.

Before the news went public, an inspector from the Gendarmerie Corps, knowing what had occurred, including the injuries to Haley Whittacker, contacted Paige Caldwell with the news.

Caldwell said, "Please give me some time to see if we're going to be able to let his wife know before it goes public."

The inspector replied, "I understand, but with everything that has already happened, the news buzzards are circling. I will hold them off as long as I can."

"Thanks."

Caldwell was sitting at the conference room table across from Driessen, who asked, "What the hell is going on now?"

"Conrad Whittacker is dead. They found his body in a dumpster, and his body was chewed up with GSWs."

"Shit. Well, apparently, Dawson was right to be concerned."

A knock came at the door, and Grant stuck his head in. "Hey, some good news. John just received a call. Haley is awake, and talking." Grant saw the look on their faces, and asked, "What's happened?"

*   *   *

Paige Caldwell hung well back in the hallway, while Pastor Stephen Grant, Father John Kohli and Sister Katharine Malone entered the ICU.

A few steps closer to the small room where Haley Whittacker was, and it was Grant's turn to wait.

When Whittacker saw Kohli and Malone in the doorway, she smiled weakly and said, "Hey, you guys. I'm so glad you're here. I honestly thought I'd never see you again."

Kohli managed a smile and replied, "Yeah, we were worried about the same thing." The smile didn't last on his face. He looked at Albro Dawson who was wedged into a chair in the corner, and asked, "Would you mind, Mr. Dawson?"

Dawson glanced at Haley, and they exchanged concerned looks. "Not at all," he said.

After Dawson left the room, Malone came in and Kohli shut the door.

Grant stepped forward, and said, "Mr. Dawson, we haven't officially met. I'm Pastor Stephen Grant." They shook hands, and Grant continued, "Can you come with me? Paige is waiting for us."

Dawson nodded, and then said, "This is about Mr. Whittacker."

They reached the hallway, and Caldwell came over. She said, "I'm sorry, Albro, but Conrad is dead."

*   *   *

Back in the ICU room, once the door was shut, Haley asked, "What's wrong?"

Kohli said, "Haley, considering what you've just been through, I'd normally hold off on this perhaps until you were a bit stronger."

Haley pushed the glasses up on her nose, and waited.

Kohli looked over to Malone, who gave him a slight nod. He continued, "Haley, I have bad news. Conrad has died."

A look of shock hung on Haley Whittacker's face. She opened her mouth, but nothing came out. She then looked back and forth at Kohli and Malone. Tears began to form and flow, and her hands began to shake. Kohli and Malone moved to each side of her bed, and as they each reached out, Haley grabbed their hands.

Whittacker again looked back and forth at this priest and this nun, two people who had become her friends. Haley asked, "Why? What happened?"

Kohli looked into Whittacker's eyes. He said, "Haley, the rest of this is going to be almost as hard to hear, perhaps worse."

"Worse? How could it be worse?" she protested.

Kohli persisted, "Are you sure you want to hear all of it now?"

Whittacker took in several quivering breaths. She didn't bother to wipe away tears that continued to slip from her eyes. "Please, John, tell me."

Kohli proceeded to tell Haley every gruesome fact, step by step, largely as it had been relayed to him before leaving the hotel. It was all based on what had been discovered by Sean McEnany and Madison Tanquerey, along with local law enforcement.

Even as Father John Kohli likely was still processing and wrestling with this information, he told Haley that her husband had turned to the mafia to keep his business afloat; and as a result, the Oldani crime family exerted pressure on him for information. After Haley questioned who the Oldani family was, Kohli explained that Father Pietro Filoni turned out to be an out-of-wedlock son to Enzo Oldani, and that Filoni apparently killed, or had his father killed, and took over the operation.

When Kohli paused, Haley managed to ask, "What information did Conrad provide?"

Kohli said, "He was using your position with the pope's project to get and pass along information."

Haley Whittacker whispered, "Oh, my God. He used me to..." She swallowed hard, and took another deep breath. She looked Kohli directly in the eyes. "Tell me the rest, John."

Kohli proceeded to relay, "The CDM team is investigating if Conrad provided information that led to..."

"To?" asked Haley, as she wiped away tears.

"That led to the deaths of Gerhard and Killian, and the attack in which you got injured."

"Lord," declared Haley. She looked at Kohli. "I told him everything. He was my husband." Tears resumed. "But... but he knew that they were going to attack us, including me?"

Kohli glanced at Malone, and then looked back to Haley. "Well, that last part isn't fully right. It all became clearer, according to what I've been told, when Mr. Dawson told Paige that Conrad had left strict instructions to pick you up from the hotel, and bring you back to your apartment."

Haley sat still and in silence for more than a minute. Then she said, "Yes, he was very insistent that I come home to the apartment for the night. Albro was late due to a car accident."

Kohli nodded.

Haley continued with emotion draining from her voice, and the tears ceasing. "It's also true. Conrad knew where Gerhard was staying on the night he was killed. He also was aware that Killian was going to meet... What's her name?"

"Ivana."

"Right," she looked directly at Kohli. "Her, too?"

Kohli nodded.

Haley had another look of pain come across her face. She said, "Albro told me that four police officers lost their lives during the attack at the hotel."

She squeezed the hands of Kohli and Malone tighter.

Haley stared at Kohli, as she seemed to be trying to process still more death linked to her husband. She looked at the far wall, beyond her two friends, and said, "So, my husband caused the deaths of at least seven people due to information that he got from me. And I almost died as a result as well."

Kohli managed to reply, "I'm so sorry, Haley."

Malone added, "None of this is your fault. You know that, right?"

Haley looked at Malone blankly. She turned back to Kohli, and asked, "You didn't say. Where was Conrad found? How did he die?"

Kohli again hesitated.

Haley said, "John, please, I need to know this."

"He had been shot many times, and his body was found in a ... dumpster. The police said it was something of a statement killing, likely by the mafia. But at this point, the investigation is proceeding."

While her face remained drenched in sadness, the tears had dried up. Haley said, "I appreciate that you two told me all of this. It had to be incredibly hard, but hearing it from you, John, and having you, Kathy, here as well has helped."

Kohli said, "We're here for you, no matter what you need."

"Thanks. Right now, I think I need to think about all of this. I assume someone is telling Albro about this, too. Can you ask him to come in when he's ready?"

"Yes, of course," answered Malone.

Kohli asked, "Would you like me to say a prayer before we slip out of the room?"

A sad smile returned to Haley's face. "Yes. I could use some prayer right now."

Chapter 79

Grant and Driessen were alone in the conference room at the hotel.

Driessen got up and walked over to a small refrigerator in the corner of the room. As he bent down and started to open the door, he asked, "Want a beer?"

"What time is it?"

"Does it matter?"

"No, it doesn't. Yeah, I'll have one."

The two men took sips in silence, and then Driessen pushed his chair back, and swung his feet up on the table. Holding the beer on his stomach, he said, "What a shithead."

Grant leaned back, and replied, "Which shithead?"

"Yeah, that's a point. But I was referring to Conrad Whittacker."

"Imagine what's going through Haley's head when she hears all of this."

"I can't. I don't want to. That's one of the things that you need to do as a pastor that I could never handle."

Grant actually smiled, and said, "Well, I'd be curious as to what parts of being a pastor you think you would be good at…"

Driessen interrupted, "Screw you, Pastor Grant. I still can't believe you're a fucking pastor."

"There are times, Charlie, when I can't believe it either. But I still want to hear about what specifically would suit a Pastor Charlie Driessen."

Driessen took a long drink from the bottle. "I could never deal with this kind of thing, you know, helping a person like

Haley Whittacker, such a nice person, get through something like this. I get that they'd need help and guidance, and all I'd be able to come up with is: Yeah, people generally suck. Don't be surprised when they make clear to you that they suck. And get over it."

"Well, I can see how that wouldn't be the part of being a pastor that you'd particularly excel at. But from what I understand, you did help Haley at one point."

Driessen shrugged, and took another drink.

Grant said, "I'm often amazed at what will motivate people to do evil."

"What do you mean?"

"Well, while my theology tells me about sinful human nature, it still kind of surprises me when evil is used to defend or advance a good cause."

"Are we being naïve, Grant?"

"Sure. But nonetheless, it's still there with me. I've always gotten doing evil within an evil system, like the Nazis, the Soviets, terrorists, and such. But it still takes me a bit off guard, at least at first, when I hear about the type of stuff we've seen in recent days."

"Such as?"

"My wife has taught me that free enterprise can be a moral good, with people serving others under a system that generates previously unachievable levels of wealth and reduction in poverty. Yet, at the same time, here is Conrad Whittacker doing evil, with people dying as a result, including his wife nearly being killed, in order to save his business. A fellow Lutheran pastor made a trip from the U.S. to Italy because he was easily seduced by conspiracies, had assorted personal problems, and was willing to kill a person he knew from seminary because they had past disagreements. And then there's Cardinal Treadwell, who reminds me, once again, that a variety of leaders within the Catholic Church covered up sexual abuse, including abusing children, for decades in the name of protecting the Church. And then there's the mind and actions of Father Pietro Filoni who apparently would do anything to protect the

Catholic Church and the papacy from any threats that he deemed serious."

Driessen replied, "Well, those are happy thoughts."

Grant smirked, took a deep drink, and finished his beer. He got up and asked, "Charlie, do you want another?"

"Sure. Thanks. Hey, Grant, are you okay?"

Grant handed a beer to Driessen, sat back down, and took another drink. He said, "Charlie, don't you know that people generally suck; we shouldn't be surprised by that; and eventually, we need to get over it?"

"Look at you, Grant, learning something valuable from me."

Grant smiled. "Thanks."

"You're welcome."

Chapter 80

Nearly ten days had passed since Father Pietro Filoni met his demise. Pastor Stephen Grant and Father Ron McDermott were just finishing an early morning breakfast with Pope Paul VII and Father Mariano Concepcion in the pope's personal kitchen.

The pope actually had prepared a breakfast specialty from his home country of the Dominican Republic. Los Tres Golpes features mangú, or mashed plantains with salt and butter, along with fried eggs, cheese and Dominican salami.

McDermott commented, "Once again, thank you, Holy Father, for this wonderful meal. I never thought I would be having breakfast prepared by the pope."

The pope smiled, and said, "You're welcome. I admit to having a longing for home in recent days. As a young priest, I used to enjoy making various meals. I've decided to get back to doing so. It feels, well, somewhat therapeutic."

Grant added, "It certainly was delicious."

The pope noted, "I am well aware that one cannot eat a breakfast like this every day. But once a week, why not? Again, I thank you" – he looked at both Grant and McDermott – "for what you have both done in these recent weeks."

They had discussed only what was necessary over the meal regarding all that happened. In fact, much of the discussion focused on how to deal with the fallout, for each person involved and for the larger Church. The pope was pleased that Haley was doing better, and out of the hospital. He also seemed glad to hear that McDermott continued to work with Madison Tanquerey on what she was turning into a multi-hour documentary on what had happened in recent weeks.

Grant asked, "So, Your Holiness, what is your thinking on next steps regarding the Hus and Luther project?"

"Father Concepcion and I have been discussing this, but I am not quite ready to announce or discuss anything. I have to speak with a couple of people."

"I understand."

The pope smiled, adding, "You and Father McDermott will be among the first to know."

McDermott seemed a bit surprised to be included in that comment.

The pope said, "However, you two gentleman will be the very first to hear that I am going to make Father Concepcion a cardinal and my secretary of state. But please keep that confidential."

Grant and McDermott congratulated Concepcion.

The pope continued, "That leaves me with another need. I like to have at least two close aides with whom I can discuss matters, and have complete trust." He paused and looked directly at McDermott. "Father McDermott, I am hoping that you would be interested in the position?"

McDermott replied, "Excuse me, Holy Father?"

Grant smiled broadly.

McDermott swallowed, and asked, "Are you asking me to work with ... for you ... here at the Vatican?"

Pope Paul VII replied, "Yes, Father McDermott. I would like you to become my personal aide."

McDermott stuttered, "I... I..."

The pope said, "I understand if you need some time to think this over."

Grant watched in sheer delight for his friend.

Come on, Ron. You know the answer.

McDermott recovered his usual composure. "Holy Father, there's no need for me to take any time. I would be deeply honored to be your aide. I only hope that I would truly be able to help you and the Church in such an important role."

There you go. That's the Ron I know.

Pope Paul VII smiled and stood. As he moved around the table, he said, "I've seen what you have done with Ms. Tanquerey. I know you performed ably with Pastor Grant on more than one occasion recently, and I've checked up on you, and it's rather amazing, but no one in your diocese has much to say that's bad about you."

Now would be the time to joke: Well, Your Holiness, you obviously haven't spoken to everyone. But I won't. If Tom were here, he would.

Grant was thinking about their mutual friend, Father Tom Stone, who loved needling Ron.

McDermott got up, said, "Thank you, Holy Father," and then he knelt and kissed the pope's ring.

The pope said, "Get up, Ron." McDermott seemed to pop into a standing position. "Is it alright when we're meeting informally to call you 'Ron'? I have heard that this is what you might prefer."

"Yes, Holy Father, 'Ron' is fine. Whatever you like, of course."

Now, now, Ron keep it under control.

As the pope turned to go back to his seat at the table, Father Concepcion stepped forward, and extended a hand to Ron. "Welcome, Father McDermott. I look forward to working together."

"As do I. Thank you, Father Concepcion."

Concepcion added, "We'll quickly get to 'Mariano' and 'Ron.'"

McDermott nodded and smiled.

Grant was so pleased to be at the table to listen to the subsequent conversation about what Ron would be doing, and that he would have whatever time was needed to go home and make sure all was set with St. Luke's before returning to the Vatican.

Grant was particularly glad when the pope said, "And since you know Pastor Grant so well, and given that the Vatican is forming a partnership with the Lutheran

Response to Christian Persecution, I will be looking for you to handle this important issue."

McDermott smiled, and said, "Of course, I would love to do that."

More good news!

The pope added, "Father Concepcion was going to handle that issue, but he not only will have new duties to perform, he also gets to play the bad guy when it comes to the fallout of the report forthcoming from Ms. Tanquerey, and well, you, Father McDermott, regarding the financing issues the Vatican faces. We will not just be cleaning house, but pointing things in a new and, God willing, improved direction under a reorganization called 'Missions That Matter.'"

At the end of the breakfast meeting, Concepcion left first with McDermott to get him some additional information.

The pope and Grant were alone.

The pontiff said, "Too bad you weren't a Catholic, Stephen."

Grant smiled, and responded, "Or, too bad you're not a Lutheran."

The pope laughed robustly at that. "Thank you. That's the first real laugh I've had in some time. By the way, I understand your wife, Jennifer, has arrived."

"She has."

"I look forward to meeting her on Saturday."

"You're coming then?"

"No one else knows that, including my new personal bodyguard, but yes, I will slip in. Shall we keep it a surprise?"

"Yes. That's wonderful."

"I am not sure why I find the need to tell you things, Pastor Grant."

"I have one of those faces."

"Perhaps. Nonetheless, I will need a complete pledge of confidentiality from you."

"You have it, Your Holiness."

"My fingerprints will not be found anywhere, but I believe that things might work out for Father Kohli and Sister Malone."

Grant's face brightened. "What does that possibly mean?"

The pope smiled, and said, "Well, I am sure that I have no idea. However, do not be surprised."

"Thank you, Your Holiness."

Grant was surprised when the pope didn't shake his hand, but instead, put his arms around Grant for a hug. They patted each other on the back, and then the pope stepped back and said, "God bless you, Stephen Grant, and thank you for all that you have done for the Church."

"And God bless you, Pope Paul."

Chapter 81

"This turns out to be a night of multiple celebrations," declared Pastor Richard Leonard. "And trust me, Madison and I are more than happy to share, so to speak, the limelight. Each person actually requested that Madison and I make the announcements, and lead the congratulations because we're getting married tomorrow, and I think each person felt guilty that they were going to look like they were stealing, well, part of the limelight."

There was laughter in the crowded gathering room on the top floor of the Trevisani Luxury Suites.

"First, I am exceedingly pleased that Haley" – he looked to Haley Whittacker who was sitting in the room's most comfortable chair – "has accepted an offer from Pope Paul VII to be a full professor at the Pontifical Lateran University, while also overseeing the remainder of the project focused on Jan Hus and Martin Luther."

Applause followed, and a line of friends formed to give her a hug, handshake or kiss on the cheek, or some combination of these.

When things quieted down a bit, Richard said, "Oh, and by the way, Madison and I will be staying in Rome for a while, as I assist Haley on the project and we work here as a kind of European base of operations in terms of our work in exposing and putting a stop to Christian persecution."

Leonard seemed to be taken off guard by the subsequent positive reaction, and he and Madison accepted best wishes from all in attendance.

Richard finally said, "Well, that was unexpected and appreciated. I now turn the next announcement over to my beautiful, soon-to-be wife, Madison."

Madison said, "I'm so excited about this. Father Ron McDermott and I started out, well, not as strangers, but we didn't know each other very well. We started working together in recent weeks, and not only do I have enormous respect for his ability to learn the journalism business, but more importantly, now I can claim this wonderful man as a dear friend."

Stephen Grant looked at McDermott, leaned down to Jennifer, and whispered in her ear, "Watch. You will not see an embarrassed Ron McDermott very often."

She hit his arm, and said, "Shhh."

Madison continued, "He, too, will be staying in Rome as – get ready for this – a personal aide to Pope Paul VII."

The room again erupted in response.

When Jennifer approached McDermott, she had tears in her eyes. She said, "I already knew this, and I'm crying. I'm going to miss you so much."

Grant watched as his wife hugged one of his closest friends on the planet, and he felt a lump in his throat.

McDermott said to Jennifer, "Well, I'll be around for a few months getting things set, and given your jet-setting economist life, I expect frequent visits."

"Count on it."

"Plus, Stephen and I will be working together on the efforts against Christian persecution."

"I know, and that makes it hurt a bit less."

When the room settled down once more, Richard Leonard said, "There is one more announcement. I was just told this. Many of us in this room have found new friends in Father John Kohli and Sister Katharine Malone. As I look around the faces here, there are no strangers. You all know the story, and it is a delicate one. And we have all been concerned, and..." Leonard stopped. He looked across the room at Kohli and Malone standing next to each other. "John, you have to do this."

John said, "Thanks, Richard, I think?" He smiled, and there was laughter in the room. "I just received today a gracious and unusual invitation from a bishop of a small Eastern Catholic Church headquartered in Texas. Actually, Kathy and I each received offers from the bishop." He glanced at Kathy and they both smiled. He continued, "This bishop wants to start a high school, and he needs a principal, and people to run the religion department as well as coaching whatever sports they can get started. Somehow he heard that we both would be leaving our current positions, and that we might be ideal fits. The bishop also mentioned that this church, being one of the Eastern bodies but aligned with the pope, allowed for married priests, including men from outside their traditional homeland." The room was now silent. "There are requirements, of course, including on the education front and also that the married men being considered be married for at least five years and that their wives be fully on board with the idea. So, all of you are invited to a wedding in Texas early next year."

The room now erupted with perhaps its greatest enthusiasm.

When John and Kathy made their way to her chair, Haley wore a big smile along with tears of joy.

As they hugged, Kathy said, "You will have to be torn away from your Vatican duties, of course, to be my maid of honor."

"Really?"

"There's no one else who I" – she paused and looked at John and then back to Haley – "who we would want."

Haley almost squealed, "Yes, yes. I am so happy for you guys."

From the side of the room, Jennifer said, "I guess that's what the pope was telling you to watch out for."

"It most definitely was."

She whispered, "Too bad you can't let everyone know about Paul's other surprise."

Stephen said, "I have no problem keeping that quiet. More happy surprises are a good thing."

"Does it feel weird officiating at your friend's wedding while having a pope in the audience?"

"Oddly, no. I'm just excited for Richard, and I can't help but think about how happy his father would be if he were here." He paused, and then added, "As for the pope? Nah, I'm a Lutheran."

"Funny."

He looked across the room at the CDM group of Paige, Charlie, Phil and Jessica gathered in a circle. Jennifer followed his gaze, and said, "And in this group, I assume you're not an option for John and Kathy's wedding, so Jessica and Phil would be up next. They haven't set a date yet, right?"

"Not yet."

Jennifer hesitated, and then asked, "What about the secret couple? Do you think they'd ask you?"

Officiating at Paige's wedding?

Stephen looked in his wife's eyes. "I hadn't thought about that. That would be weird. Would it be for you?"

She leaned in close to his ear, and said, "I think it might be fun to see how uncomfortable it would make you. In fact, I'm guessing that Paige and I would both enjoy that." And then she kissed him on the cheek.

Yeah, weird.

Chapter 82

Christ Church in Rome didn't require any extras for a wedding. It was an exquisite setting, beautiful in all respects.

As the organ played, the pews were less than twenty percent filled with the immediate friends and families of Pastor Richard Leonard and Madison Tanquerey. Not only was the wedding across the Atlantic from their homes, but they purposefully kept word of the event limited. The couple decided that they wanted the wedding to be small but special. The guests included Madison's new employees – Roger Neun and Sofia Chavez – and everyone from the top floor of the Trevisani hotel, given the bonds that had been formed over recent weeks. Those bonds, however, extended to one person who didn't stay in the hotel.

A side door to the nave opened, and in stepped a hooded individual. As he walked to the bride's side of the aisle, he removed the hood, and a murmur spread among the attendees as they recognized Pope Paul VII. He nodded at the bride's family, and moved into a vacant pew a few rows back.

At this point, Pastor Stephen Grant, Pastor Richard Leonard and his best man, another pastor who was a friend from seminary, stepped out from another door to the side of the sanctuary. As they took positions, Leonard and his best man's eyes went to the pope standing in a pew.

Grant ascended the four steps toward the altar, turned, and said, "Please rise."

His eyes and Jennifer's found each other, and he gave her a knowing look. She smiled.

As the music started to play, whatever eyes that were on the pope turned to the bride starting to come down the center aisle, escorted by her father.

Madison Tanquerey's eyes seemed larger than usual, and her skin glowed along with her smile. Her long brown hair, with blond highlights, was largely up in a stylish arrangement, with several curled groups of strands hanging down. The ends of those strands brushed back and forth on her chiffon covered shoulders. The white dress had a high neckline with pearls, from which the chiffon flowed down, finally coming to the main part of the gown made of charmeuse, and decorated with small pearls arranged in the shapes of flowers and leaves.

She happened to glance to her left, saw the pope, and actually whispered to her father, "Oh, Daddy. My God, the pope is here."

Paul VII smiled and nodded.

After her father kissed her and she stepped next to Richard, Madison whispered, "Did you know he was coming?"

Richard shrugged and replied, "I didn't."

The two then looked at Grant, who said, "I might have had an idea, but silence was requested."

Madison gave him a look that Stephen assumed was good natured.

Several minutes later, after the Scripture reading, Grant ascended the stairs into the pulpit of Christ Church. The marble around the outside of the pulpit featured assorted carvings, starting with Jesus, and then moving to John the Baptist, St. Paul, St. Stephen, and St. John the Gospel writer, with the eagle upon which the lectern rested representing the Gospel of St. John proclaiming Jesus as the Word of God. And below those carvings was written "God's Word with us in eternity."

Grant offered brief personal reflections on Madison and Richard, and then drew on the reading from Colossians 3 regarding forgiveness, love, and allowing Christ to rule in marriage. He concluded his homily this way:

> Finally, since we are here in Rome, with a special guest in our midst, I cannot resist offering three quotes from Martin Luther about marriage, which are favorites of mine. One is about how the married couple and others see a marriage; the second is about the kindness, forgiveness and love that is noted in our reading today; and the third is about Christ and marriage.
>
> First, Luther proclaimed, "There is no more lovely, friendly and charming relationship, communion or company than a good marriage."
>
> Second, he also said, "The Christian is supposed to love his neighbor, and since his wife is his nearest neighbor she should be his deepest love."
>
> Third, Martin Luther, taking his cue from St. Paul, noted marriage as a symbol of Christ and His Church, with Luther talking of marriage as "a sacred sign of something spiritual, holy, heavenly and eternal."
>
> May God bless your marriage, Madison and Richard, and may each of us be there to help your marriage in whatever needs you might have. Amen.

Twenty minutes later, with the ceremony coming to a close, the couple kissed, and they turned to the assembled. Stephen leaned in behind them, and said in a low voice, "I'm pretty sure that the pope is going to leave the way he came after you're down the aisle. So, if you want to say anything to him, you might want to make a quick stop while heading down the aisle."

The couple did, in fact, stop.

Madison said, "Thanks for coming, Your Holiness. This was a wonderful surprise."

Richard added, "Yes, thank you."

"I wanted to come, but I knew that if I let the news out, it would turn your wedding into a circus. So, my surprise was appropriate?"

Madison replied, "It was. Thank you for coming."

"May God bless your marriage. Now, go, and greet your guests as husband and wife."

As Madison and Richard continued down the aisle, the pope quickly greeted the close family of each. As he then went by Grant, he said, "Nice homily. I actually like those Luther quotes as well."

The two men shook hands, and the pope added, "Now that Father McDermott is going to be my aide and working with you, as well as the happily married couple, against Christian persecution, perhaps we will see more of each other, Pastor Stephen Grant."

"I truly hope that is the case, Your Holiness."

Pope Paul VII started to put his hood back up, but he paused to look around. "I love this church. It's Lutheran and Eastern all at the same time."

"I have come to love it as well."

The pope smiled, and again started to put his hood up. But Grant said, "Before you go, can I introduce you to my wife?"

The pope said, "Of course." He turned and Jennifer was standing just a few feet away. Stephen again reflected on how beautiful his wife was, noting that the dark green dress was made beautiful due to her, not the other way around. Pope Paul VII said, "Mrs. Grant. Oh, excuse me, Dr. Grant, it is a pleasure to meet you."

Jennifer offered the smile that Stephen knew so well, the one that made friends and made them feel warm and welcome. "The honor is all mine, Your Holiness."

"Your husband is a unique man, but I can see that his spouse, his lovely wife, very much is unique as well. Plus, there is your reputation as an economist. I enjoyed your book, and learned a great deal."

Jennifer's mouth fell open. She quickly recovered and said, "You've read my book? Thank you so much."

"I try to break free from the old saw that clergy, especially popes, do not know what they are talking about when they speak on the economy."

"I hope the book helped."

"It did. I trust that I will see you again soon. I have some other questions on the economy."

"That would be wonderful."

The hood finally went back up, and Pope Paul VII started to walk away.

Stephen was surprised when Jennifer called after him.

"Excuse me, Your Holiness, but might I request one thing?"

The pope turned, and said, "Yes. What can I do?"

"Please take care of Ron. He is very dear to us."

Pope Paul VII took his hood down once more, walked over to Jennifer, put his hands on her shoulders, and said, "You can count on it." He gently kissed Jennifer on the cheek, put his hood back up, and then proceeded out the door to a waiting dark vehicle and two casually dressed security guards.

He left Jennifer and Stephen standing still and watching the door where he'd departed.

Jennifer said, "That doesn't happen every day."

Stephen walked over, put his arm around his wife's shoulders, and said, "You bring out the best in people."

Chapter 83

Nearly four months later, Stephen Grant was the last person to arrive at the diner for morning devotions with Father Tom Stone, Pastor Zackary Charmichael, and Father Ron McDermott.

He sat in the booth next to Zack, directly across from Ron and diagonally from Tom.

As was typical with these four friends, they ordered breakfast and then read from the *For All the Saints* devotional.

The food arrived, but as they ate, it wasn't the group's typical banter or debate when they got together on three mornings each week.

The previous four months had been fairly typical, except for the fact that Ron was preparing step-by-step to leave St. Luke's for the Vatican. Now, Ron's exodus was upon them. He had shipped most of his personal items ahead to Rome, and had two suitcases in Stephen's Jeep Wrangler in the parking lot.

Their conversation focused on his new work, and how exciting it would be. But then their food was finished, and the waitress had taken everything away.

The four men sat quietly for a minute, and then Ron stood up. "Okay, let's not make this messy. After all, we'll be talking regularly, especially with Stephen and I working on persecution matters."

Grant watched as Tom followed Ron out of the booth. The two men were the closest of friends, even though their personalities often were so different.

Tom simply looked at Ron, and said, "Too late for that my friend. I am going to miss you dearly." Tom's eyes welled up with tears, as he reached out and hugged Ron.

Most people would have been surprised to see tears in Ron McDermott's eyes, but Grant understood. He wasn't closer to anyone else in the world, other than Jennifer, than these three friends, and he knew that they felt the same way.

Leave it to Tom to get this started.

Suddenly, four clergy were standing in a diner, crying and hugging.

Zack started to break it up by saying, "Hey, old guys, don't forget about technology. We'll be talking via video calls."

Ron said, "We will."

Zack hugged him again. And with tears back in his eyes, he said, "Ron, see if you can do some good in the Vatican. God bless." And he left first.

Ron looked at Tom, and said, "I knew you would make this hardest."

"I am who I am. But Maggie informed me that our summer vacation this year will be in Rome. So, you're only going to be free of me for a few more months."

Ron said, "Good."

Tom hugged him again, kissed his friend on the cheek, and left the diner.

Ron looked at Stephen, and said, "Holy crap, this is not easy."

Stephen nodded, and said, "Come on. We'll save our pathetic scene for the airport."

Ron laughed.

An hour later, Stephen removed the second suitcase from the Jeep, and placed it on the ground next to the other. He looked at Ron, and said, "I am going to miss your sage advice, my friend."

"What are you talking about? We're going to be working together on a somewhat frequent basis."

"Yeah, I know. But there's still that ocean and not seeing you face-to-face several times a week."

"Yeah, I know." The two men embraced, and Ron said, "You've taught me a lot, Stephen, and as a result, made me a better priest."

"You've done the same for me – more than you know."

"Talk to you soon."

"Sounds good. And hey, remember all of the times that you claimed that I had better contacts in the Catholic Church than you?"

"Yes, I do."

"Well, you're not going to be able to say that anymore."

"God bless, Stephen."

"You as well, Ron."

Ron grabbed his suitcases and rolled them into the terminal. The doors slid closed behind him.

Grant got into his Jeep. He pulled away from the curb and into the crazy traffic of JFK Airport.

Chapter 84

"Well, if the Italians aren't going to do anything about it," commented Albro Dawson.

Paige Caldwell replied, "Hey, we agree. We're here with you."

Everyone in the Sikorsky Black Hawk helicopter was wearing two-way communication devices in their ears.

Dawson said, "With me? You've graciously taken the lead. My God, this is even your helicopter. I am along for the ride. But I greatly appreciate it."

"You're the one who got the thumbs-up from your government. I'm kind of amazed."

"I still have friends in the military and at MI6. And they want him for more than the Conrad crap."

Jessica West said, "Some of us have friends in the right places in government." She glanced at Caldwell, who smirked in response.

From the cockpit, Charlie Driessen said, "But technically, this isn't our helicopter. It's being lent to us by a ... different friend."

Caldwell commented, "However, I would love for CDM to have our own." She looked around in admiration. "The Black Hawk has never failed us, and I'm tired of borrowing others."

While patting the M3M .50 Caliber Gun she was manning in the door, West added, "I agree. I love this gun."

Driessen replied, "Yeah, well, when we have our own aircraft carrier to move it around the world, I'll think about it."

"You're such a buzz kill, Charlie," said Caldwell.

Dawson said, "You're an interesting group to work with."

"You don't know the half of it," commented Chase Axelrod, who was sitting next to Caldwell and across from Dawson.

Phil Lucena added, "It's always fascinating."

"You can say that again," came confirmation from Kent Holtwick in the cockpit, next to Driessen.

Caldwell, Dawson, Lucena, and Axelrod would be making the descent, with submachine guns or Glocks in hand. West was at the gun door, and the two pilots were ready if more firepower were needed. But the Brits had specifically requested to keep the collateral damage to a strict minimum. They wanted a quick extraction with minimal fallout.

The reports would put the target in one of two places at this time of the morning: either at his rooftop patio table eating breakfast or in the bedroom on the inside of the glass doors off that patio. If he turned out to be elsewhere in the building, adjustments would be made.

Driessen announced, "We're on approach."

Holtwick asked, "Shall I take it, Charlie?"

"Yeah. I'm good on weapons."

Holtwick turned the Black Hawk and brought it in low. The helicopter came in over a set of hills to the east of the Oldani home and winery. Holtwick flew in steadily, seeming to skim the grape vines, with the sunrise behind him.

Driessen announced, "He's apparently eating breakfast."

"Good," commented Albro Dawson.

Jaco Bruno had just taken a large bite of poached egg sitting atop toast. He turned toward the sound in the air. He chewed, squinted into the sun, and then picked up a napkin to wipe away the yoke dripping down to his chin. What was occurring suddenly seemed to dawn on him. But by the time he finished wiping his face and rose from his chair, the Black Hawk was sweeping in close.

As the helicopter came to a stop to hover a mere 75 feet above the patio, the propeller winds tossed aside the breakfast table's umbrella, followed by the food on the table, and then the table itself.

Bruno held a hand up in the air, seemingly in an attempt to block the wind and to gain some sound footing.

Four ropes dropped from the two side doors of the aircraft, and down the relatively short distance slid four figures in black.

One person with a pistol in hand made the mistake of being the first to step out through the glass sliding door from Bruno's bedroom.

West pointed the .50 caliber gun and fired. The man fell, and then she shattered the glass door and wall of the bedroom.

Once their feet touched down on the patio, each person moved according to plan. Axelrod went to one side of the patio and Lucena to the other. Their job was to discourage interest by anyone on the ground in what was occurring on the rooftop patio, as well as working along with West to stop opponents coming from the bedroom.

Meanwhile, Caldwell and Dawson moved toward Bruno with Glocks in hand.

Dawson called out, "Mr. Bruno, the British government would like you to come with us."

Bruno looked defiantly at the approaching figures.

Additional Oldani family soldiers tried to enter the fray via the bedroom, but Axelrod and West were ending such efforts, while Lucena dealt with a couple of men who decided to move into the open on the ground in order to fire at the helicopter. They never got the chance.

Bruno replied to Dawson, "The fucking Brits? Are you kidding me?" He started to reach inside his coat where a handgun rested.

Dawson warned, "Really, Jaco? Please, try it. That would make me feel so much better."

Bruno didn't even hesitate. As he started to pull the gun out, Dawson fired off one shot that dropped the latest leader of the Oldani crime family to the stone of the rooftop patio. Dawson walked over, and looked down. While Bruno was bleeding from the stomach, his face was still contorted in anger.

Dawson pointed the gun at Bruno's face, and said, "Thank you. My day did get better." He pulled the trigger.

Caldwell was standing next to Dawson, and commented, "Well, you did ask him to try it."

"I did," replied Dawson.

The two turned and looked around. Axelrod and Lucena had stopped firing, apparently having run out of targets.

Caldwell took a deep breath, and said, "I think our work is done here."

Dawson said, "I agree."

As they walked back toward the ropes hanging down from the helicopter, Caldwell asked, "Was that all for Conrad Whittacker?"

Dawson stopped and turned to look at Caldwell. "None of this was for that piece of garbage. It was all for Haley."

Caldwell smiled, and said, "Good. That's why we're here, too."

There was no way that Paige Caldwell could know that Albro Dawson was now calling Haley Whittacker by her first name, and what that meant.

Chapter 85

The phone on his nightstand rumbled. Stephen Grant opened his eyes, and reached out. He looked at the glowing screen.

A text from Paige in the middle of the night. What's this about?

Caldwell had texted, "It was great seeing you and Jennifer at John and Kathy's wedding last week. Riding off on their motorcycles was a nice touch."

Grant sighed. He replied, "Right. But why are you texting me this now?"

"Well, we just finished up a little excursion back into Italy."

Hmmm.

"What does that mean?"

Caldwell answered, "Jaco Bruno was supposed to be sitting across from me right now, wrapped up in a bow for the Brits. They gave us the greenlight to extract him."

"Supposed to be?"

"Not a bright guy. He tried to take us all on with his little pistol."

I know what that means. Can't say that I regret hearing this.

Grant typed, "Everyone safe?"

"All good. Too bad you missed the fun."

Grant looked over at Jennifer. He returned to his cellphone, and texted, "I'm good where I am."

"LOL. You'll get another chance, I'm sure."

"Godspeed, Paige."

"Thanks, Stephen."

He put the cellphone down, and placed his head back down on the pillow.

Jennifer said, "Whom were you texting?"

"Paige texted me to let me know that the Brits had sent them to get Jaco Bruno."

She said, "They were successful, I assume?"

"Yes, let's just say that Jaco Bruno is no longer the head of the Oldani crime family."

"Some additional justice for Haley and the others."

"I think so."

"Do you regret not being there?"

"Absolutely not. I am where I want to be – at home with you."

"But it's still worth celebrating, I'd say."

"Celebrating?"

"Sure, I'm awake now, and so are you."

"What do you have in mind?"

Jennifer slipped on top of her husband, and she showed him what she meant by celebrating.

Chapter 86

Another three weeks passed, and Pastor Stephen Grant, Rachel McEnany, Pastor Richard Leonard, Madison Leonard and Father Ron McDermott were finishing up their first conference call regarding a joint effort to expose and counter Christian persecution at its worst in various parts of the world.

The key tasks coming away from the meeting were to decide upon which of the hotspots they had discussed would serve as a starting point, choosing which strategy would be the best way to start making a difference there, and coming up with a list of other Christian church bodies that should be contacted for participation in this undertaking.

Richard and Madison jumped off the video conference call first, as they both had lunch meetings to attend.

Rachel was next. "Time for my other job as a pre-school teacher. Good seeing you, Ron."

"You too, Rachel."

Grant said, "Look how much you've grown and loosened up."

"What does that mean?" replied Ron.

"So many more people call you 'Ron' than used to be the case, and you seem to be embracing it?"

"Well, when the pope tells you that he's calling you 'Ron' in private, you learn to roll with it."

"On another matter, Richard said that the Hus-Luther work continues, and that Haley is doing great leading the project."

"That's what I've heard."

"What else have you heard, you know, from Pope Paul on this?"

"I've become a source of information for Stephen Grant. I'm moving up in the world."

Grant laughed, and said, "Okay, I get it. You can't say anything."

"Actually, the Holy Father told me to pass some bit of news to you, if you pledged to keep it private."

"Cone of silence, Ron."

"Well, the pope wasn't sure if he had said this to you or not, but he has this dream that if this Hus-Luther project turns out the way he'd like, statues of both Hus and Luther would be added to the collection in St. Peter's Basilica."

"That would be noteworthy."

"It would. Only Cardinal Concepcion and myself are aware of this, and now it will be you as well: The Holy Father has hired two sculptors to begin work on each statue."

"That's exciting."

"The pope figures that worst case scenario, if things don't turn out exactly the way he would like, they would still make magnificent gifts from the Catholic Church to two of our fellow Christian Church bodies."

"Smart."

McDermott then chuckled.

Grant asked, "What?"

"After the Holy Father told me to pass this on to you, he also said to ask you, and I quote: 'Why do I find the need to tell you things, Pastor Grant?'"

Grant laughed, and replied, "Please tell the pope that I just have one of those faces."

McDermott shrugged, and said, "Will do. Talk to you soon, Stephen."

"Take care, Ron."

Acknowledgments

Thank you to the members of the Pastor Stephen Grant Fellowship for their support:

Bronze Readers
Tyrel Bramwell
Gregory Brown
Mark Friis-Hansen
Sue Kreft
Gary Wright

Readers
Sue Lutz
Terry Merrill
Robert Rosenberg

Beth keeps me going in many ways, including with her love and support, as well as her edits. I also continue to be very proud of my two sons, David and Jonathan, and I think my daughter-in-law, Mikayla, is pretty darn cool as well.

The Reverend Tyrel Bramwell again has used his talents and his generosity in creating the cover for this book. Please check out Ty's books, videos, and photographs as well.

Any and all shortcomings in my books are all about me, and no one else.

I continue to gain great encouragement from the fact that readers find enjoyment in my books. And as long as someone keeps reading, I'll keep writing. God bless.

Ray Keating
November 2020

About the Author

This is Ray Keating's thirteenth entry in the Pastor Stephen Grant series. The first 10 novels are *Warrior Monk*, followed by *Root of All Evil?*, *An Advent for Religious Liberty*, *The River*, *Murderer's Row*, *Wine Into Water*, *Lionhearts*, *Reagan Country*, *Deep Rough* and *The Traitor*, along with the short stories *Heroes and Villains* and *Shifting Sands*. A second edition of *Warrior Monk*, with a new Author Introduction and a new Epilogue, was published in early 2019; and a second edition of *Root of All Evil?*, with a new Author Introduction, was published in early 2020.

Keating also is an author of various nonfiction books, an economist, and a podcaster. Among his most recent nonfiction books are *Behind Enemy Lines: Conservative Communiques from Left-Wing New York* and *Free Trade Rocks! 10 Points on International Trade Everyone Should Know*. In addition, he is the editor/publisher/columnist for DisneyBizJournal.com and KeatingFiles.com. Keating was a columnist with RealClearMarkets.com, and a former weekly columnist for *Newsday*, *Long Island Business News*, and the *New York City Tribune*. His work has appeared in a wide range of additional periodicals, including *The New York Times*, *The Wall Street Journal*, *The Washington Post*, *New York Post*, Los Angeles *Daily News*, *The Boston Globe*, *National Review*, *The Washington Times*, *Investor's Business Daily*, New York *Daily News*, *Detroit Free Press*, *Chicago Tribune*, *Providence Journal Bulletin*, *TheHill.com*, *Touchstone* magazine, *Townhall.com*, *Newsmax*, and *Cincinnati Enquirer*.

Enjoy All of the Pastor Stephen Grant Adventures!

Paperbacks and Kindle versions at Amazon.com

Signed books at raykeatingonline.com

• *The Traitor: A Pastor Stephen Grant Novel* by **Ray Keating**

Stephen Grant – former Navy SEAL, onetime CIA operative and current pastor – looks forward to a time of prayer and reflection during a retreat at a monastery in Europe. But when he stumbles upon an infamous CIA traitor in a small village, Grant's plans change dramatically. While a debate rages over government secrets and the intelligence community, a deadly race for survival is underway. From a pro-democracy demonstration in Hong Kong to the CIA's headquarters in Langley to a monastery in France, the action and intrigue never let up.

• *Deep Rough: A Pastor Stephen Grant Novel* by **Ray Keating**

One man faces challenges as a pastor in China. His son has become a breakout phenom in the world of professional golf.

The Chinese government is displeased with both, and their lives are in danger. Stephen Grant – a onetime Navy SEAL, former CIA operative and current pastor – has a history with the communist Chinese, while also claiming a pretty solid golf game. His unique experience and skills unexpectedly put him alongside old friends; at some of golf's biggest tournaments as a caddy and bodyguard; and in the middle of an international struggle over Christian persecution, a mission of revenge, and a battle between good and evil.

• *Shifting Sands: A Pastor Stephen Grant Short Story* by **Ray Keating**

Beach volleyball is about fun, sun and sand. But when a big-time tournament arrives on a pier in New York City, danger and international intrigue are added to the mix. Stephen Grant, a former Navy SEAL, onetime CIA operative, and current pastor, is on the scene with his wife, friends and former CIA colleagues. While battles on the volleyball court play out, deadly struggles between good and evil are engaged on and off the sand.

• *Heroes and Villains: A Pastor Stephen Grant Short Story* by **Ray Keating**

As a onetime Navy SEAL, a former CIA operative and a pastor, many people call Stephen Grant a hero. At various times defending the Christian Church and the United States over the years, he has journeyed across the nation and around the world. But now Grant finds himself in an entirely unfamiliar setting – a comic book, science fiction and fantasy convention. But he still joins forces with a unique set of heroes in an attempt to foil a villainous plot against one of the all-time great comic book writers and artists.

• *Reagan Country: A Pastor Stephen Grant Novel* by Ray Keating

Could President Ronald Reagan's influence reach into the former "evil empire"? The media refers to a businessman on the rise as "Russia's Reagan." Unfortunately, others seek a return to the old ways, longing for Russia's former "greatness." The dispute becomes deadly. Conflict stretches from the Reagan Presidential Library in California to the White House to a Russian Orthodox monastery to the Kremlin. Stephen Grant, pastor at St. Mary's Lutheran Church on Long Island, a former Navy SEAL and onetime CIA operative, stands at the center of the tumult.

• *Lionhearts: A Pastor Stephen Grant Novel* by Ray Keating

War has arrived on American soil, with Islamic terrorists using new tactics. Few are safe, including Christians, politicians, and the media. Pastor Stephen Grant taps into his past with the Navy SEALS and the CIA to help wage a war of flesh and blood, ideas, history, and beliefs. This is about defending both the U.S. and Christianity.

• *Wine Into Water: A Pastor Stephen Grant Novel* by Ray Keating

Blood, wine, sin, justice and forgiveness... Who knew the wine business could be so sordid and violent? That's what happens when it's infiltrated by counterfeiters. A pastor, once a Navy SEAL and CIA operative, is pulled into action to help unravel a mystery involving fake wine, murder and revenge. Stephen Grant is called to take on evil, while staying rooted in his life as a pastor.

• *Murderer's Row: A Pastor Stephen Grant Novel* by
Ray Keating

How do rescuing a Christian family from the clutches of
Islamic terrorists, minor league baseball in New York, a
string of grisly murders, sordid politics, and a pastor, who
once was a Navy SEAL and CIA operative, tie together?
Murderer's Row is the fifth Pastor Stephen Grant novel, and
Keating serves up fascinating characters, gripping
adventure, and a tangled murder mystery, along with faith,
politics, humor, and, yes, baseball.

• *The River: A Pastor Stephen Grant Novel* by **Ray
Keating**

Some refer to Las Vegas as Sin City. But the sins being
committed in *The River* are not what one might typically
expect. Rather, it's about murder. Stephen Grant once used
lethal skills for the Navy SEALs and the CIA. Now, years
later, he's a pastor. How does this man of action and faith
react when his wife is kidnapped, a deep mystery must be
untangled, and both allies and suspects from his CIA days
arrive on the scene? How far can Grant go – or will he go –
to save the woman he loves? Will he seek justice or revenge,
and can he tell the difference any longer?

• *An Advent for Religious Liberty: A Pastor Stephen
Grant Novel* by **Ray Keating**

Advent and Christmas approach. It's supposed to be a
special season for Christians. But it's different this time in
New York City. Religious liberty is under assault. The
Catholic Church has been called a "hate group." And it's the
newly elected mayor of New York City who has set off this
religious and political firestorm. Some people react with
prayer – others with violence and murder. Stephen Grant,

former CIA operative turned pastor, faces deadly challenges during what becomes known as "An Advent for Religious Liberty." Grant works with the cardinal who leads the Archdiocese of New York, the FBI, current friends, and former CIA colleagues to fight for religious liberty, and against dangers both spiritual and physical.

• *Root of All Evil? A Pastor Stephen Grant Novel* by Ray Keating

Do God, politics and money mix? In *Root of All Evil?*, the combination can turn out quite deadly. Keating introduced readers to Stephen Grant, a former CIA operative and current parish pastor, in the fun and highly praised *Warrior Monk*. Now, Grant is back in *Root of All Evil?* It's a breathtaking thriller involving drug traffickers, politicians, the CIA and FBI, a shadowy foreign regime, the Church, and money. Charity, envy and greed are on display. Throughout, action runs high.

• *Warrior Monk: A Pastor Stephen Grant Novel* by Ray Keating

Warrior Monk revolves around a former CIA assassin, Stephen Grant, who has lived a far different, relatively quiet life as a parish pastor in recent years. However, a shooting at his church, a historic papal proposal, and threats to the pope's life mean that Grant's former and current lives collide. Grant must tap the varied skills learned as a government agent, a theologian and a pastor not only to protect the pope, but also to feel his way through a minefield of personal challenges. The second edition of *Warrior Monk* includes a new Introduction by Ray Keating, as well as a new Epilogue that points to an upcoming Pastor Stephen Grant novel.

Join Ray Keating's Email List

If you join Ray Keating's Email List, you'll receive Pastor Stephen Grant stuff, including a regular newsletter, special savings, various updates, and assorted contests and giveaways!

Join now by quickly filling out the contact information at

http://www.pastorstephengrant.com/contact.html

Join the Pastor Stephen Grant Fellowship!

Visit
www.patreon.com/pastorstephengrantfellowship

Consider joining the Pastor Stephen Grant Fellowship to enjoy more of Pastor Stephen Grant and related thrillers and mysteries.

Ray Keating declares, "I've always said that I'll keep writing as long as someone wants to read what I write. Thanks to reader support from this Patreon effort, I will be able to pen more Pastor Stephen Grant and related novels, while also generating short stories, reader guides, and other fun material. At various levels of support, you can become an essential part of making this happen, while getting to read everything that is written before the rest of the world, and earning other exclusive benefits – some that are pretty darn cool!"

Readers can join at various levels…

Bronze Reader ($4.99 per month)

You receive all new novels and short stories FREE and earlier than the rest of the world. In addition, your name included in a special "Thank You" section in forthcoming novels, and access to the private Pastor Stephen Grant Fellowship Facebook page, which includes daily journal entries from Pastor Stephen Grant, insights from other characters, regular recipes from Grillin' with the Monks, periodic videos and Q&A's with Ray Keating, and more!

Silver Reader ($9.99 per month)

All the benefits from the above level, plus you receive two special gift boxes throughout the year with fun and exclusive Pastor Stephen Grant merchandise.

Book of the Month Club ($19.99 per month)

This arguably is the best value...

1) Receive a FREE book EVERY MONTH written and signed by Ray Keating. Included are Pastor Stephen Grant thrillers and mysteries (new books in the month of release), other fiction books, and Ray's nonfiction books. If you request, Ray will personalize his signing to a person of your choosing.

2) Two special gift boxes throughout the year with fun and exclusive Pastor Stephen Grant merchandise.

3) Your name included in a special "Thank You" section in forthcoming novels.

4) Access to the private Pastor Stephen Grant Fellowship Facebook page, which includes daily journal entries from Pastor Stephen Grant, insights from other characters, regular recipes from Grillin' with the Monks, periodic videos and Q&A's with Ray Keating, and more!

Gold Reader (39.99 per month)

All the benefits of the Book of the Month Club level, plus your name or the name of someone you choose to be used for a character in <u>one</u> upcoming novel.

Ultimate Reader (49.99 per month)

All the benefits from the Book of the Month and above Gold Reader level, plus your name or the name of someone you choose (in addition to the one named under the Gold level!) to be used for a <u>major recurring character</u> in upcoming novels.

Check it out!
www.patreon.com/pastorstephengrantfellowship

Free Trade Rocks! 10 Points on International Trade Everyone Should Know

by Ray Keating

Paperback and for the Kindle at Amazon.com

Signed books at raykeatingonline.com

While free trade has come under attack, Ray Keating lays out in clear, simple fashion the benefits of free trade and the ills of protectionism in *Free Trade Rocks! 10 Points on International Trade Everyone Should Know.*

Tapping into his experiences as an economist, policy analyst, newspaper and online columnist, entrepreneur, and college professor, who taught MBA courses on international business and entrepreneurship, Keating explores and explains in straightforward fashion 10 key points or areas that everyone - from entrepreneurs and executives to students and employees to politicians and taxpayers - needs to understand about how trade works and how free trade generates benefits for people throughout the nation, around the world, and across income levels.

The 10 points or areas covered in *Free Trade Rocks!* are...

Point 1: Do People "Get It" on Free Trade?
Point 2: Economics 101 on Trade
Point 3: Debunking Trade Myths
Point 4: Trade and the U.S. Economy
Point 5: Trading Partners
Point 6: Trade and Small Business
Point 7: Ills of Protectionism
Point 8: Brief History of Free Trade Deals
Point 9: The Morality of Free Trade
Point 10: The Future of Trade

Keating makes clear that nations don't trade. Instead, businesses and individuals trade, and free trade is simply about expanding the freedom to trade by reducing or eliminating governmental costs and restrictions.

Regarding *Free Trade Rocks!*, Dan Mitchell, Chairman of the Center for Freedom and Prosperity, declares, "A common-sense explanation of why politicians and bureaucrats shouldn't throw sand in the gears of global trade."

And Self-Publishing Review gives *Free Trade Rocks!* four stars, and says: "International trade policy has come to the forefront of global politics, making *Free Trade Rocks! 10 Points on International Trade Everyone Should Know* by Ray Keating a timely and fascinating read for a suddenly curious demographic. Keating manages to bring this seemingly dull subject to accessible life with real-world examples often torn straight from recent headlines, along with a comprehensive and (mostly) impartial view on the topic. As the exclamatory title suggests, Keating is a fan of free trade, but his deep expertise spanning a wide range of subjects and career paths makes this book an engaging, informative, and essential read for those who want to weigh in on this hot-button issue."

Also, George Leef, the Director of Research at the James G. Martin Center for Academic Renewal, observes, "Ever since Donald Trump started talking about foreign trade, I have thought that what the country needs is a clear, easily understood book that explains why the government should not mess with free trade. Lo and behold, Ray Keating has written exactly that book. *Free Trade Rocks!* clears away the myths and misconceptions that trade interventionists count on."

Behind Enemy Lines: Conservative Communiques from Left-Wing New York

by Ray Keating

Paperback and for the Kindle at Amazon.com

Signed books at raykeatingonline.com

Enjoy this wide-ranging collection of columns and essays from Ray Keating covering faith, economics, politics, history, trade, New York, foreign affairs, immigration, pop culture, business, sports, books, and more. Keating is a longtime newspaper and online columnist, economist, policy analyst, and novelist. In these often confusing and contradictory times, Keating describes his brand of conservatism as traditional, American and Reagan-esque, firmly rooted in Judeo-Christian values, Western Civilization, the Declaration of Independence, the U.S. Constitution, and essential ideas and institutions such as the Christian Church, the intrinsic value of each individual, the role of the family, freedom and individual responsibility, limited government, and free enterprise and free markets. There's a great deal to enjoy, learn from, agree with, get annoyed by, appreciate, reflect on, roll your eyes over, and argue with in this book that offers perspectives on where we are today, where we've been, and where we might be headed.

Visit DisneyBizJournal.com

News, Analysis and Reviews of the
Disney Entertainment Business!

DisneyBizJournal.com is a media site providing news, information and analysis for anyone who has an interest in the Walt Disney Company, and its assorted ventures, operations, and history. Fans (Disney, Pixar, Marvel, Star Wars, Indiana Jones, and more), investors, entrepreneurs, executives, teachers, professors and students will find valuable information, analysis, and commentary in its pages.

DisneyBizJournal.com is run by Ray Keating, who has experience as a newspaper and online columnist, economist, business teacher and speaker, novelist, movie and book reviewer, podcaster, and more.

"Chuck" vs. the Business World: Business Tips on TV

by Ray Keating

Paperbacks and for the Kindle at Amazon.com

Signed books at raykeatingonline.com

Among Ray Keating's nonfiction books is *"Chuck" vs. the Business World: Business Tips on TV*. In this book, Keating finds career advice, and lessons on managing or owning a business in a fun, fascinating and unexpected place, that is, in the television show *Chuck*.

Keating shows that TV spies and nerds can provide insights and guidelines on managing workers, customer relations, leadership, technology, hiring and firing people, and balancing work and personal life. Larry Kudlow of CNBC says, "Ray Keating has taken the very funny television series *Chuck*, and derived some valuable lessons and insights for your career and business."

If you love *Chuck*, you'll love this book. And even if you never watched *Chuck*, the book lays out clear examples and quick lessons from which you can reap rewards.

Made in the USA
Middletown, DE
31 August 2021

47299662R00224